Oratorio in Ursa Major

Also by David Dalton
Fugue in Ursa Major

Oratorio in Ursa Major is a continuation of the
story that begins with *Fugue in Ursa Major.* However,
Oratorio is complete in itself and can be read first,
with *Fugue* read later as a prequel.

DAVID DALTON

ORATORIO IN URSA MAJOR

Acorn Abbey

Published 2016 by Acorn Abbey Books
Madison, North Carolina

ISBN 978-0-9916132-3-6

Acorn Abbey Books
Madison, North Carolina
acornabbey.com

PRCS0320160429

Cover illustration by Duncan Long

*For all for whom
the arc of justice
has bent too slowly*

*We are not to simply bandage the wounds
of victims beneath the wheels of injustice,
we are to drive a spoke into the wheel itself.*

Dietrich Bonhoeffer, 1906-1945

CHAPTER 1

For the third time, Mark tapped lightly on Jake's bedroom door. The boards of the old farmhouse floor squeaked under Mark's sock feet. The door was as resonant as an old fiddle, having been handmade from mountain pine a hundred years ago and finished generously with shellac the color of honey. This time, instead of silence, Jake muttered something sleepy and goofy.

"You'd better get up and come down," Mark called softly through the door. "He's being brave, but he's got flowers on the table."

Mark was pretty sure that Jake's response was, "Oh, no."

Downstairs, the table that previously had sat beside the kitchen window – the table on which Phaedrus had eaten so many meals, alone, for so many years – was too small for three and too shabby for a family. So the old table had been reassigned upstairs, where it now held the formidable stack of books that Phaedrus had sent upstairs as part of Mark's high-school home schooling. In its place now was a table twice as big. The new table was square, and it did not wobble like the old one. It wasn't shabby. In fact it was rather proud and ecclesiastical, heavily made of solid cherry. The window claimed one side of the table. That left one side each for Phaedrus, Jake, and Mark.

Sometimes, often for no reason that Jake or Mark could discern, Phaedrus would cover the table with a bright red tablecloth, and there would be flowers. On this bright morning in mid-October, a very unecclesiastical Erlenmeyer flask sat on the table, overflowing with the last of the season's yellow flowers. The fire was running hot in the kitchen's wood cook stove. There were biscuits in the oven. The aromas of a country breakfast filled the house. The window beside the kitchen table was open a few inches to vent the excess heat. The tablecloth fluttered lightly near the open window.

This morning, the reason for the tablecloth and flowers was clear. Jake was leaving tomorrow night, and he would be gone for a year. Jake was twenty-seven. A year was a long time.

Phaedrus had been up since dawn. Mark, with his teenager's appetite, had been drawn downstairs by the smell of coffee and biscuits. At last Jake padded quietly into the kitchen, looking sleepy, dark hair uncombed.

Who could blame him if he'd had trouble sleeping and had lain awake until 3 a.m.?

Jake took notice of the flowers and the red tablecloth. He gave Mark a quick glance. But neither of them said anything, because Phaedrus, as he stood over the stove scrambling eggs in an iron skillet, had that thoughtful look on his face that meant that he would soon say something important.

Good mornings were said, chairs were scraped against the floor, and Jake and Mark sat down and waited.

The matching red napkins were out this morning too, though the napkins were more faded than the tablecloth – more washings. Jake picked up his fork so that he could fidget. Mark, whose body language often echoed Jake's without Mark's being aware of it, picked up his fork and fidgeted, too.

Phaedrus was always matter-of-fact when he had news. He never played it for drama. He'd just deliver the news with a commendable economy of words and then go silent. Phaedrus always wanted to know what others were thinking. Jake had long ago figured out that Phaedrus' silences weren't necessarily a matter of etiquette, though his silences certainly were polite. Rather, it was more like a kind of nosiness, because Phaedrus really did want to know what was going on inside your head, and he left an empty space for you to say it, so that a vacuum sort of sucked it out of you, even if you were trying to hold it back. Phaedrus had all sorts of tactics for pulling out your thoughts.

The kitchen was silent now except for the sizzling

sounds from the stove and a wren outside the window. The suddenness of the quiet reminded Jake of concerts at Carnegie Hall, where his parents used to take him. The conductor would tap-tap-tap on his podium, and the hall would fall silent and wait.

"Jake," said Phaedrus, facing the stove and raking hash browns into a bowl, "I heard from Henry this morning. Your security clearance has finally been approved."

That was it. Then Phaedrus stopped talking and took the potato pan to the sink.

Getting the rest of the news this morning clearly would require some questions. Living here in the remote Appalachian mountains these past six months, after the world got blown up (there really was no nicer way to put it), Jake had figured out a great many of Phaedrus' Socratic methods. Questions were more than just questions. Questions exposed the thoughts of the questioner. Questions betrayed hidden feelings. The quality of your questions revealed whether you had been paying attention. Mark had learned a lot, too, in those six months. Mark knew that, according to the unspoken house etiquette, the first question this morning was Jake's question to ask, though Mark's curiosity was killing him. Mark looked at Jake and waited.

Jake just wrinkled his nose, masking his feelings.

"Great," Jake said. "One day before I have to leave."

Mark waited a moment longer to see if that was all Jake was going to do with the privilege of the first question. Jake was looking vaguely out the window now, officially passing the conversational ball to Mark. Mark pounced.

"Does this mean," said Mark, eyes on Phaedrus, "that we can talk about aliens now?"

"Yes," said Phaedrus. "That means that we can talk about aliens now."

Mark cast a quick look toward Jake and saw that Jake was grinning, though he was still looking out the window.

"Will it ruin our breakfast?" said Mark.

"I doubt it," said Phaedrus, "knowing how partial to breakfast you are."

Then Jake and Mark started to ask a question at once, but Jake stopped and pointed his fork at Mark.

"You go," said Jake. "This has been eating you alive for months."

"What do they look like?" asked Mark.

"Who said anything about *your* security clearance?" said Phaedrus.

The look on Mark's face instantly changed from excitement to panic to embarrassment. Phaedrus, whose teasing was always as soft as the paw of an old mother cat, spoke quickly to relieve Mark's embarrassment.

"Not to worry," said Phaedrus. "Henry said that you're in on it too."

Jake, who had gone tense in empathy with Mark, exhaled when he saw Mark's relief. Letting Mark in on state secrets, no doubt, was a consequence of Phaedrus' thoughtfulness, not Henry's, though Henry was nice enough. Phaedrus probably had cornered Henry on their secure and encrypted communications line and pressed Henry until Henry had agreed to whatever was necessary to not exclude Mark from important household business. Phaedrus had let Mark endure a moment's embarrassment as a kind of compliment, to emphasize Mark's being included in state secrets.

Phaedrus pulled a pan of biscuits from the oven, turned them out onto a board, and reached for the skillet of gravy that had been left to simmer on the hob, leaving Jake and Mark to simmer in suspense.

"Oh, no," said Mark. "It's complicated. We're not going to get a short answer." Mark was still blushing from his presumptuousness in matters of state secrets, so he had retaliated with a mild and measured kitten's-paw tease.

Jake suppressed a chuckle. It had taken months for Mark to develop the confidence to tease Phaedrus, but lately Mark was showing an ability to do a pretty good job of it. Phaedrus tried to keep a straight face and not reveal his amusement and pride in Mark's growing sassiness. Phaedrus liked sass. It meant that young people were thinking for themselves.

"Right you are," said Phaedrus. "It's complicated. So, then. There are different sorts of aliens. Shall I start with the aliens I met back in the 1970s, or with the ambassador who has been in earth orbit for the past six months? Or with the aliens that abduct cheeky teenagers to work in their copper mines?"

"The 1970s," said Mark, "since they would be the ugliest."

"The aliens I met in the 1970s actually are a lot like us," said Phaedrus, "except that they are to squirrels as we are to monkeys. You know what I mean – not earth squirrels, of course, but something like earth squirrels. Their home planet is heavily forested. I understand that they like to have their houses in trees, even now. They no longer have tails, the same as we lost our monkey tails. Their bodies are a good bit more springy than ours, and they're furry – though, yes, Mark, they wear clothes. They have very beautiful black eyes with bushy eyebrows. They're at least as clever with their hands as we humans are. They have large incisors, but they keep them filed down for aesthetic and social reasons, the same way we trim our claws. There's something cuddly about them, and it's said that they still like to sleep in family groups of six or more. But that may be just a slander that some of the old military guys made up."

"Can they speak our language?" asked Mark.

"Oh yes," said Phaedrus. "They speak our languages very well, though their S's whistle through their incisors. They're a very old civilization. They've had advanced technologies for thousands of years. I'm pretty sure that they've done some genetic tweaking on themselves, and maybe used other sorts of biological enhancements, to perfect their abilities with language. They are, as you would imagine, very smart."

"But this ambassador," said Jake, "he's a different species?"

"I have never met the ambassador," said Phaedrus, "and most of my knowledge of aliens is out of date. But Henry says that the ambassador looks totally human."

"How can that be?" asked Mark.

"Henry is not sure," said Phaedrus. "No doubt the

ambassador is from a different planet than the squirrel people. There are many planets and many species in this galactic union that soon will include earth. But Henry seems to think that the ambassador's people have been borrowing human genes for a long time. The galactic union has been sending probes to earth for thousands of years. Usually those are automated robotic probes with no one on board, but sometimes alien people make the trip. In any case, they've had plenty of time to borrow human genes – or to borrow ideas from human genes – and to work them into their own genome. Most visitations since prehistory have been the robotic surveillance drones. But there's an official galactic ambassador up there now, not just a reconnaissance ship. That's a big deal. What's happening right now is a very big deal in the history of the earth, though it's probably fairly routine in the galaxy as a whole. The three of us are very privileged to be in on the secret."

Phaedrus had sat down while he was talking. Mark's spoon made a tinkling sound as he stirred his coffee.

"So," said Mark. "No hives, no giant insects, no acid drool?"

"Not that I've ever heard of," said Phaedrus. "But Jake is now free to ask Henry – or the ambassador for that matter, when he meets him – any questions that he wants to ask."

Phaedrus and Mark both looked at Jake. Jake shrugged. He knew that his nervousness and his early-onset homesickness were showing. There was no way to hide it from these two. Jake was studying his eggs and clearly wasn't going to say anything, so another question popped out of Mark into the vacuum.

"So, who's picking Jake up tomorrow night? Henry's helicopter? Or will an alien ship abduct him? Wait. Let me guess. Since it's happening in the middle of the night, it's going to be an alien ship. Am I right?"

A cold burst of October air came through the window, ruffling the curtains. Jake shivered. Phaedrus pretended not to notice. Mark noticed too, but he knew that this was not a morning for teasing Jake too hard. Mark was increasingly attuned to the subtlety that Jake and Phaedrus were capable of. Less and less went over Mark's head now, and Jake rarely had to give Mark those furtive dirty looks anymore, or to explain something to Mark after the two of them were alone.

Mark waited for an answer, but Phaedrus' mind seemed to have shifted to something else. To Mark, sometimes Jake and Phaedrus were enigmas, but sometimes their thoughts were deafening. Months ago, when Mark had first come here, their introverted silences had confused him and frightened him. But now he was learning to decrypt the silences and not take them personally. Jake was afraid and homesick. Jake felt under-qualified and overwhelmed. Who could blame him? Still, Mark didn't know enough about Henry's big plan to size up how much real danger might be involved in this trip. As for Phaedrus, he felt afraid for Jake and very sad. It would be a hardship for Phaedrus, emotionally and otherwise, for Jake to be away for so long. The two of them were completely different, yet they were like peas in a pod. Mark couldn't imagine one of them without the other. They were like biscuits and gravy, a pair of shoes, like soap and water, or pencil and paper – things that always come in twos. At first, Mark, who enjoyed playing the brat to Phaedrus' old-fashioned reserve and Jake's effortless coolness, wondered if the scariness of an alien pickup cut too close to the quick this morning, so close to the quick that it foreclosed on Jake's options for a cool response. Mark hero-worshiped Jake's coolness. Given more time to study how it's done, Mark might be as cool as Jake someday. But Jake's coolness was missing in action this morning.

"Jake," said Phaedrus, "later today you'll get a long document from Henry spelling out some details of the mission. Henry says that you'll have twenty-four hours to decide whether to sign it. You can still decide not to go, you know. You already know most of the essentials. But Mark, this is all new to you, of course. The galactic union has put their time-travel technology at Earth's disposal. Jake and the four other members of the expedition team will travel on a long-haul cruiser belonging to the galactic union to the nearest jump station. That trip will take six months. I understand that those cruisers are pretty comfortable – easy traveling. When they arrive at the jump station, they'll be jumped back almost 2,000 years to 48 B.C. The cruiser will then return them to old earth, which will take another six months. The mission on old earth may take as long as a year. Then they'll go back to the jump station, jump back to the present, and fly back to here-and-now earth."

Mark managed to swallow his eggs and biscuit, but his mouth was gaping. He hadn't shaved for several days. The beard on his chin was short and soft. Mark was 17. He glanced at Jake, then turned toward Phaedrus.

"You're not just making this up, are you? Time travel? That's even possible?"

"This is for real," said Phaedrus. "Time travel is indeed possible, but it's very expensive. The galactic union has strict protocols for permitting time travel. It requires a jump station the size of a small planet. I was going to say that time travel is rarely used, but in a place as big as the galaxy, the protocols are invoked only too often, I understand. When the protocols are invoked, it's usually because something bad, something catastrophic, has happened to some planet. It means that something critical to the survival of a promising civilization has been destroyed. Earth is the latest planet to screw up and risk returning to its Stone Age, even though we knew better. Well, some earthlings knew better. Those who don't know better tend to get all the power. Then a catastrophe happens. Recovery from catastrophe may be possible with the right knowledge, but that knowledge tends to get lost – both in the catastrophe itself and in the ugly sort of histories that precede catastrophes. To the galactic union, the past is a kind of seed bank. The galactic union has determined that earth has much better chances for a decent future if some lost seeds are recovered from earth's past."

"Swallow, Mark!" said Jake. "You're forgetting to swallow!"

Mark swallowed.

"Jake is going to do that?" said Mark, with something like stars in his eye. "Our Jake? The Jake who is sitting across from me right now with holes in his socks? He's going to time travel?"

"Our Jake," said Phaedrus.

Jake looked down at his plate because he was afraid his face was turning red.

"Don't look at me," said Jake. "I have no idea why I should be doing this. It must have something to do with who I know – meaning our Phaedrus – or who Phaedrus knows, meaning Henry."

"Let's trust the ambassador," said Phaedrus. "The ambassador worked with Henry to choose the team. Clearly Jake meets the requirements of the protocol."

"But they never even interviewed me," said Jake. "Oh, Henry is friendly and makes good conversation, but there was never anything like an interview. It's probably just because I'm a good mule and can type fast. I'll be a beast of burden to carry notebooks for the scholars, and I'll be a secretary to help them type up their notes after we get home."

"Why 48 B.C.?" said Mark. "What's so special about 48 B.C.?"

"It's complicated, very complicated," said Phaedrus. "If you study hard in the year that Jake is away, you should have a good feel for the historical and cultural background. We'll work on that, but let's set it aside for now. Jake already knows most of the basics. That's all any of us know, really – the basics. The galactic union's experience, and therefore their protocols, are way beyond us primitive folk. Probably only the ambassador, who knows the protocols and who also knows a lot about Earth, can really see the big picture. But remember, Mark. You can't talk about this to anyone but Jake and me."

"Do I ever talk with anyone but Jake and you?" said Mark. "How long will you be gone, Jake? I got lost there."

"From your perspective," said Jake, "only a year. From my perspective, as long as three years."

"I don't quite get it," said Mark.

"It's time travel weirdness," said Jake. "From your and Phaedrus' perspective, it will be only a year, because the jump station will return us from the past to the present just an instant after we left. That will cancel the time in 48 B.C. plus one of the round trips between earth and the jump station. But from my perspective, it will be three years – two round trips to the jump station, each of which takes a year, plus the time on earth in 48 B.C."

"You'll be three years older when you get back, even though you've been gone for a year?"

"That's right," said Jake. "Weird, huh?"

Mark looked out the kitchen window, rather sadly now, as he processed this. Mark's sudden look of sadness reminded Jake of the day Mark had first come here, a bewildered teenager orphaned by what they now euphemistically called "the event." Phaedrus and Jake waited for Mark's attention to rejoin them in the kitchen. The three of them were always respectful of each other's feelings. They'd been through a lot.

At last Mark looked toward Phaedrus and said, "So Jake will be pushing thirty when he gets back. But you never answered my question. Helicopter or alien ship tomorrow?"

"Alien ship," said Phaedrus. "A small one. We used to call them gnats. They're small automated shuttles, just big enough to carry two passengers up to the cruiser, which is very big and stays in high earth orbit. There are no pilots on the gnats. They're robotic, controlled from the cruiser."

Now Mark looked at Jake. "Will we hear from you? Can we still have our family quarrels? You know, on video or something?"

"I'm not exactly sure," said Jake. "How does that work, Phaedrus?"

"From my and Mark's perspective, we'll be in communication with you for the entire year," said Phaedrus. "However, the jump station is 371 billion miles from earth. A radio signal requires 23 days to cover that distance. So communication will be delayed, depending on how far away Jake is as they travel out to the jump station. And yes, I think there will be enough bandwidth for video for the slow typists in the family."

Jake noticed that Mark had again used the word "family," and that Phaedrus had echoed it. Mark finally felt included here. He even felt pride. That had taken some time.

"And that means," said Jake, "that from my perspective, I'll be out of communication with you for two of the three years I'm away. Mark, do you want this biscuit? I don't feel very hungry." It was a feeble attempt to make light of everything, but Mark took the biscuit all the same. Then they heard the sound of a car horn through the open window.

"That would be the sheriff," said Phaedrus. "Mark, remember: not a word about any of this. It's classified. If you slip, Henry will send a helicopter and a couple of troops to carry you off and sell you by the pound to work in the copper mines."

"I won't say a word," said Mark. "But if they pay by the pound, then I see why you're always trying to fatten me up."

Soon the sheriff was in a chair near the stove, a cup of real coffee in his hands. There wasn't much real coffee left.

The sheriff had pretty much run this mountain community after "the event" six months ago. The sheriff and Phaedrus were in regular communication by radio. The sheriff always consulted Phaedrus on important decisions, and he was a regular visitor.

"So, Jake," said the sheriff. "I hear you're leaving us soon."

"I'm afraid so," said Jake. "Only for a year ... or so."

"To some outpost of the helicopter people in Scotland?"

"That's right," said Jake.

"You're a sharp young man, Jake. I'm not surprised that the helicopter people saw the possibilities in you, special training and all that. But now, you come back when they've trained you. We need you here."

"That's the idea," said Phaedrus. "Sharp people with special training stationed around the provinces, helping people put things back together. Sheriff, how are things looking at the storehouse? Will we have enough flour for the winter?"

"Everybody wants to hoard stuff at home," said the sheriff. "Enjoy the coffee while it lasts. But if nobody wastes any biscuits, we might just make it through the winter. It's the livestock that I'm mostly worried about. We're going to have to cut things close and keep just the best breeding stock. It's a shame. We don't have that much cattle, but it's more than we can winter over. Pray for an early spring, with lots of grass to make milk for the calves. Let your chickens scratch in the woods to save on corn and beans, but don't let any varmints carry them off."

"We'll go back to making coffee from roasted soybeans and chicory," said Phaedrus. "And the chickens can eat the coffee grounds. How is Susie Bowman doing?"

"Not so good," said the sheriff. "It's the grief and hard times that's killing her, same as the others we've lost since the spring. She's lost her will to live, dwells on the people who're gone instead of the people who're living. She has a few good days, but mostly bad. It'll be a slow thing, I reckon. She'll be fortunate to last the winter. It was a good summer, though, better than I expected. You know, there are less than a third as many of us as there used to be around here, before 'the event,' as you call it. That's not as many to feed, but it's also not as many to work. But we're tough, the ones who're still here. And a year from now we'll be tougher still. We're starting to get used to it. People really pulled together, worked hard, looked out for each other. It's a good little place we've got here, boys. A good little place."

Mark noticed how the sheriff had addressed his last statement to the boys. That meant that the sheriff was afraid of losing Jake, that Jake with his "special training" might not want to remain in the boonies. Ah. So that is why Phaedrus is so sad. It's not just about losing Jake for a year. He's also worried about losing Jake for good, even if he comes back from space safe and sound.

"Most of the credit for our good little place goes to you, sheriff," said Phaedrus. "You kept us all in harness, and you cracked the whip."

"Divvying up the work is the only way," said the sheriff. "Everybody saw that quick enough. And besides, there's something kind of special about this place. It takes more than just pasture land and turnip seed. It's not every little county that's got brains going for it like the brains in this house. And not just brains, but connections to the outside. It takes hard work to hold a place together. That's for sure. But it also takes brains, and connections." The sheriff's eyes settled on Jake, who was looking out the window again.

"Phaedrus," said Mark, serious now, "is there a biscuit left? Does anybody want the rest of those grits?"

And then, right on queue after the sheriff's remark about connections to the outside world, the sound of a distant helicopter came through the kitchen window, carried on the cool October air. No one seemed to notice, as they strained to look out the window, that Phaedrus' strong old hand was trembling as he handed Mark the last biscuit. Though Phaedrus could still handle the fifty-pound sacks of corn and soybeans, and though he could still hold the mule-drawn plow in a straight row, increasingly Phaedrus left the heavy work to Jake and Mark. But Phaedrus' hands were strong. Somehow his hands looked younger than the rest of him. There weren't even any age spots on the backs of Phaedrus' hands, though there were a few on his temples, where his temples met his white hair. Jake had never known anyone who could type as fast as Phaedrus. Phaedrus' hands could shuck corn or crack and clean walnuts faster than Jake and Mark could. Phaedrus had been a musician, and probably a good one, though there was no longer any electricity to drive the enormous organ out in the studio building.

The sound of the helicopter grew louder, though it couldn't be seen from the kitchen window.

"Sounds like you have company," said the sheriff. "Important company. Company above my pay grade – though nobody pays me anymore. I guess I'd better get going."

"No, no. Please stay," said Phaedrus. "There's someone on the helicopter whom you ought to meet."

The sheriff looked thrilled.

"Where does it land?" asked the sheriff.

"Up at the edge of the woods," said Phaedrus, "beside the road to the upper fields. Why don't you go out and watch it land? The rest of us will be out in a second."

"That thing probably burns more fuel in ten minutes," said the sheriff, "than my fuel ration for the entire next year. I'll see you guys outside. I've never seen one of the big military choppers on the ground and up close."

The sheriff picked up his jacket and hurried out. Jake and Mark waited at the table to hear what Phaedrus wanted to say.

"Remember," said Phaedrus, "that the sheriff doesn't have a security clearance like you guys. Don't say anything about you-know-what. Just follow Henry's lead. The sheriff's a good guy and has an open mind. Maybe at some point he can know more. But that's not our decision. OK, Mark? We'll talk more later about the rules that go with having a security clearance."

"OK," said Mark. "Not a word. I don't know a thing."

"Jake, are you OK?" said Phaedrus. "You look a little frazzled."

"To be honest," said Jake, "I always dread seeing Henry. I mean, he's a nice guy and all that. But, no matter what he asks for, the next time he parachutes in he asks for something more. What's he got against peace and quiet, and giving folks some time to plow and plant the winter wheat? How'd I ever get into his job jar?"

"Don't feel pressured, Jake," said Phaedrus. "Henry always descends on us with overwhelming force. But only you can decide whether to go along with what he wants."

Soon everyone was at the edge of the woods, and the helicopter was on the ground in the clearing fifty yards away, its blades spinning down. A door slid open, and Henry Snow, who obviously was a pretty important man in the planet's new leadership, emerged with his military wing man behind him. Henry waved from the helicopter steps. They all waved back and waited for the visitors to approach. A third person emerged from the helicopter, several modest steps behind Henry. The sheriff was waiting, standing tall, hat in hand, as though Henry was a head of state. For Jake and Mark, this was the fourth time they'd seen Henry fly in like this.

They all took their cues from Phaedrus. They'd never been instructed in VIP protocol, and they weren't exactly sure what Henry's status was. But Phaedrus always seemed casual and informal during these helicopter visits. Clearly Phaedrus and Henry had known each other for a long time. If Henry even had a title or a job description in the new government, Jake didn't know what it was. Still, the helicopter and the military wing man made a statement. There were handshakes all around, followed by a few minutes of polite small talk, mostly about the harvest. The military wing man, who had been introduced as Lieutenant Boyles, stood aside and seemed to be admiring the color of the trees. Apparently, deferring to Henry was part of his military protocol. That was a good thing, because it meant that civilians, not the military, were in control. The pilots stayed aboard the helicopter.

Henry introduced the third person as Tory Chan, a communications technician.

"It's a good morning for flying," said Henry. "I had

not been up in weeks. So I thought I'd drop in for a visit, take care of a little business, and see if I could interest anyone in a little field trip. And with your permission, Phaedrus, Tory will install a satellite transceiver in your communications shack."

"A new satellite transceiver?" said Phaedrus. "I'm honored, though radio has been working well enough most of the time."

"It will be a low bandwidth system," said Henry, "but it will be secure. Think of it as a Teletype terminal like we used in the old days. I enjoy these helicopter rides to visit you guys, but a satellite line is quicker and doesn't burn fuel. As long as those satellites are still up there flying, we should use them."

"I'm grateful for the satellite equipment," said Phaedrus, "as long as it doesn't want too much power out of our old solar panels and as long as it's got the bandwidth for low-resolution video. You mentioned a field trip?"

"Yes," said Henry. "A field trip for all of you – you, too, Sheriff, if you have time. A couple of you will have to sit on the bench in the back, but there are good windows back there, too. What do you think?"

There were expressions of interest all around. The sheriff looked thrilled, though he was fidgeting with his cap, which he still held in his hands. Mark looked like a pre-teen who was queueing up for the wildest ride at the fair. Mark, Jake, and the sheriff admiringly circled the helicopter while Phaedrus took Tory to the radio room to point out a place for the satellite hardware. Tory would stay behind and do his job while the others had their field trip.

With the polite assistance of the lieutenant, soon everyone was on board and strapped in. The sheriff's cap was back on his head. Henry and Phaedrus were talking quietly. Jake and Mark sat on the bench in the rear. Lieutenant Boyles, who was young, efficient, and rather formal, handed everyone a headset with a microphone. Henry thumped his microphone a couple of times, and then his voice came through the headphones.

"Everybody ready?"

They all nodded.

After a minute of silent suspense, the helicopter's engine started with a powerful shudder. Then the engine idled for another minute, while the pilots went through their preflight check list. Suddenly the big blades spun up, and the helicopter lifted straight up. When it was well above the treetops, it tilted forward and accelerated. Everyone was glued to a window. Down below, there was smoke from the kitchen chimney. Phaedrus had closed the dampers in the cook stove before they left the house, and the fire was smoldering now. Tory, who was in the yard unboxing a satellite dish, waved. The October hay fields were lush and green. On the hillsides, many of the trees were turning yellow and red. Their precious livestock – two cows and the two mules in the upper pasture – seemed unconcerned about the roar overhead and went on eating grass. Slow-moving clouds hung over the mountain ridges. A flock of crows fled from the path of the helicopter.

Jake could feel the heaviness of this impressive military machine. He wondered if its frame contained armor plating. Its engine sounded massive. As the sheriff had observed, it must require an indecent amount of fuel to keep it aloft. Probably, thought Jake, that was part of the reason for its feeling of heaviness – the weight of the fuel in its big tanks. The helicopter's course was southward. It didn't fly in a straight line, though. It flew with a kind of graceful lilt in spite of its weight, partly from the wind and partly because the pilots seemed to be enjoying themselves and playing with the air currents. The pilots were steering around the higher mountains, flying from gap to gap, to keep their altitude lower. For a while they followed a river. The lilting feeling reminded Jake of skiing down a slalom course, or playing a video game, or riding a motorcycle. They were winding and banking with the river's curves. Down below, there were few signs of life. Jake saw two men with a small rowboat beside the river, but no motor vehicles moved. There was no gasoline to be had anymore down there, though the sheriff got a small ration from somewhere. Even Jake's beloved Jeep was occasionally put to use on county business. Lucky are the people who had kept a horse before the event, thought Jake. Horses and mules were now worth almost their weight in silver. The sheriff had brought them their two cows and two mules. Like Mark, the livestock had been orphaned and needed a new family after the event.

The helicopter left the river and headed over dense forest. Ridges, some with outcroppings of bare rock, alternated with small streams meandering through still-green valleys. Jake saw a herd of deer scattering down a slope, fleeing deeper into the forest at the sound of the helicopter.

"Can everybody hear?" said Henry into his microphone. Everyone nodded.

"We'll soon be about a hundred miles south of your place," Henry said, "roughly in the direction of Asheville. I want to show you a little place we're fixing up. It's a campus, no longer in use, of course. It's tucked up inside this national forest that we're flying over. It's a quaint little campus. It's small, it's remote, and it's pretty. We think it's the perfect site for one of our new education centers. Because it's close to you – less than an hour by helicopter or six or seven days by mule – I thought you guys might want to be involved in the place."

Henry had winked at Jake when he said the word "mule." Jake had winced when he heard the words "six or seven days."

"Phaedrus," Henry continued, "you'd be perfect for teaching some of the classes. Jake, you too – after you've returned from your training. Mark, learn all you can from Phaedrus and Jake, and by the time you're twenty we'll put you to work, too. Sheriff, I imagine you have your hands full at home, but this place will be a resource for you."

"Education?" said the sheriff. "What kind of education matters anymore other than how to grow beans and how to set broken bones? And surely you wouldn't take these guys away from us. I need them."

"Sheriff, you'll never lose them for more than half a year. Phaedrus will make me promise that," said Henry. "You'll gain more than you lose – I promise you. As for this particular place, it won't exactly be the practical arts. This place is small and isn't really equipped for that. This place will be more concerned with, shall we say, the cultural arts. To get the lights back on, we can't neglect any kind of learning. Elsewhere, we're also bringing some of the agricultural and technological universities back on line, including the university at Blacksburg to the east of your county. We're also getting a couple of medical schools going again. But this place will be different. It will be concerned with more monkish arts, kind of a think tank. The plan calls for places like it scattered here and there around the provinces, like the monasteries during the Dark Ages. They'll be networked. They'll be accessible and as open as possible. The people inside them will work with the people outside and help keep people on the same page."

The sheriff, a practical man, frowned and looked doubtful. Henry continued.

"The people who survived the event are traumatized, Sheriff. They're confused, cut off. We can't abandon them and let them drift in isolation for too long. Restoring order – and restoring hope and meaning for the survivors – that's not something that can be left to chance. Your county is well in hand. But other places aren't doing so well. Lots of places have no leadership, or, worse, predatory types are taking over. They'll try to set themselves up as lords. We can't let people fragment, or risk having demagogues claw their way up and make serfs out of people. We'll soon return to a kind of feudalism if there isn't some centralization. We need a culture that everyone shares. People need to have things in common, a public life. They have to think of themselves as one people."

"Not that having a vote ever did them any damned good," said the sheriff. Henry chuckled.

"Is that a cynical comment about voters? Or about government?" asked Henry.

"Both," said the sheriff. "The voters were idiots, and the government was a puppet show. But I never could figure out who was pulling the strings."

"You're a smart man, Sheriff," said Henry.

"So who was pulling the strings?" asked the sheriff. "Something tells me you must know."

"Does it matter?" said Henry. "They're not pulling the strings anymore."

"I guess not," said the sheriff. "I just hope that whoever is pulling the strings now are a better sort of people."

"I hope so, too," said Henry. "But the rebuilding won't be just a repeat of the old order. It will be something new."

"Fiddlesticks," said the sheriff. "There's only one form of government – peons at the bottom and lords at the top. Are we talking about a new order? Or just new lords?"

"You're not the only person who feels that way," said Henry. "And I don't entirely disagree. What if we called it a new contract between the peons and the lords? There aren't many peons anymore. That means that the value of peons is much higher than it used to be. There used to be far too many of us. The value of people fell too low. Most people's value even became negative. Some of the lords, as you call them, used to refer to the excess peons as useless eaters. But now the people are truly needed, and the old lords are dead. The people deserve more than bread and circuses and pie in the sky. They need a common culture."

"They need bread and they need pie," said the sheriff. "But screw the circuses, and screw the sky."

"There's no more television," said Henry. "The circuses are gone. But people still need ways of getting news. People need stories. They need books. People need places they can look to for some justice and for moral support getting organized again. After Rome fell apart, it was the church and the petty kings that provided that service all through the Dark Ages. But it won't be the church this time. And it can't be petty kings, with one county at war with another. We need local organization — local but coordinated. We're not going to try to be Rome. We're not going to set up a command and control system of taxes and troops. We're going to try something else. Organization and justice, but no Rome. Comfort for the afflicted, but no church. I hope I'm not offending anyone." Henry glanced at the sheriff.

"The sheriff was never much of a churchgoer," said Phaedrus.

"Church never did much for me," said the sheriff. "It married me, and it buried my mom and dad, but that's about it. Still, how do you get people to forget the church? What do you put in its place? We've still got our little old church buildings in our little old county, you know. The mice and the squirrels are taking them over. The raccoons have moved into a couple of them. There'll be no way to heat them this winter. I'd store hay in them if we had the hay. I don't think we've got even a single preacher left in our end of the county, and I can't say I'm sorry about that. But people still go to those little churches, you know. Some walk for miles, just to sit in them. I think they see it as a proper place to worry, or grieve, or pray."

"We have to remember that need," said Henry. "Obviously the first things people need are food, medicine, and some security. But after that they need some hope, and some meaning. If we don't help them with that, then the worst kind of people will step into the vacuum selling snake oil and salvation."

"I can see how that would be," said the sheriff. "There'll soon enough be men who'll say they've been called to preach. They'll preach their own little minds, same as always, with one hand reaching for your wallet and the other hand up your daughter's skirt. But, like I said, what do you put in the place of it?"

Henry glanced at Phaedrus to see if Phaedrus wanted to say something. But Henry saw that Phaedrus' thoughts were closer to home today. Jake, too, seemed to be in a reverie, looking out his window. The helicopter was flying through a low cloud at the moment. There was not much out there for Jake to see.

"Let's just say," said Henry, "that some of the best minds on the planet are working on that – finding hopes better than snake oil, and a substitute for the circus."

The sheriff laughed.

"Phaedrus," said the sheriff, "I always thought that you were an atheist, like me."

"I always get myself out of conversational jams like this," said Phaedrus, "with two words – 'existential predicament.' Atheist? Who knows? Too many things are beyond our knowing. It's part of the human predicament. But people do have a religious instinct. There's no denying that. They need some kind of structure that gives them meaning and hope – and hopefully something that doesn't turn them against each other. American religion, in its last miserable days, became more about us against them than anything else."

"Surely you're not saying that it was a religious calamity that we just had," said the sheriff. "With all due respect, Phaedrus and Henry, it wasn't the church that wiped out six billion people last spring."

"No," said Phaedrus. "Tell you what, Sheriff. Come Christmas Eve, let's build a fire in the stove in one of those little churches, put up a tree, light some candles, and just let people come in and talk. You and I won't say a word. Let's just listen. By the time the candles have burned down, I think you'll agree with me. The natural goodness of people who actually need their neighbors again will warm the room. Doctrine and dogma, not so much. I don't think you'll hear much about us against them. The church called it 'the still, small voice.' Kant called it moral cognitions *a priori.* Same thing. Things work pretty well when people need each other and when everybody gets a fair piece of the pie."

"I get your point, Phaedrus," the sheriff said. "And now that you mention it, we really ought to do something about Christmas. But, like I said, all this is above my pay grade. I'm glad smart guys like you are thinking about these things. I like poking fun at you, but I'm just a country sheriff. I never thought I'd get to ride on one of these helicopters, though."

"Phaedrus," said Henry, "your friend is awfully senatorial for a country sheriff."

"I've also never known him to lose at a game of poker or to turn down a glass of wine," said Phaedrus.

"Wine," said the sheriff. "I miss that."

Jake listened to all this in his headphones. Existential matters, Jake had realized, are not really Henry's passion. Organization was Henry's passion. Clearly, though, Henry saw the existential needs of the people as critical to the future, and that's why he looked to Phaedrus. Why else would they be on this helicopter, rapidly burning off the remaining stocks of fossil fuel, to visit some kind of abbey in the middle of a forest? Why else would Earth be getting assistance from extraterrestrials – extraterrestrials! – to diagnose and fix what Phaedrus called earth's "cultural failure." Mark was looking out the window, fidgeting with the zipper of his jacket, and seemed not to be listening. But Jake knew that Mark was listening, was learning fast, and was honoring Phaedrus' orders that he not talk about secrets.

The clouds thinned and lifted. The helicopter had cleared the highest mountains of their flight and was now slowly reducing its altitude along with the terrain. The deep forests of the western North Carolina mountains became less evergreen and more deciduous. The small streams had merged into a narrow, quick-moving river in a wilderness valley. On the ridges, the trees were a bright mixture of fall colors, lit by the slanting yellow light of the October morning. There were faint lines through the forests – forestry and fire roads, no doubt. The helicopter, despite its mass, was being thrown around a bit by the mountain winds, but somehow Jake felt perfectly secure. Every gust of wind that hit the chopper blades would make the chopping louder and deeper. After each bump from the wind, the helicopter would quickly return to straight ahead and level. The pilots probably had flown in the oil wars in the Middle East. They knew their business, and they knew their aircraft. This was a cushy gig by comparison with the oil wars – flying VIPs and their clients over scenic mountains, on cultural missions.

Jake did not want to leave these mountains. It was safe here. Destruction and turmoil seemed far away. It was beautiful here. It was home now. It was not possible to imagine what it would be like flying in space, on an alien craft that he could scarcely imagine, 371 billion miles from Earth. It would be years before he would see these forests again. Being away from Phaedrus would be hard. Only Phaedrus seemed to have any way of making sense of everything that had happened. Only

Phaedrus seemed to have a vision of a livable future. Even tough old men like the sheriff and Henry Snow needed Phaedrus as an anchor. Because of Phaedrus, and Phaedrus' resources, Jake had felt remarkably far from danger during everything that had happened. For those who had no such anchor and no mountain refuge, it must have been unimaginably awful.

How has this happened to me? thought Jake. I'm a nobody, an underachieving architect from Charlottesville. Why am I not among the dead? On my own, I would never have met anyone like Phaedrus. But my parents knew him.

Jake's father and mother had known Phaedrus at Oxford. Henry, too, was from the Oxford set. If the capital before the previous Dark Age had been Rome, and if the capitals before the event were financial and political centers like New York, London, Tokyo, and Washington, then the capital during this new Dark Age, thought Jake, was surely Oxford. Jake was pretty sure that the other end of Phaedrus' new satellite circuit would be in Oxford. The smart people had come up with a radical master plan intended to save the earth. The smart people had displaced – murdered, really – the rich and powerful, who could never imagine that the rich would not forever remain in control. To the smart people, the super-rich were the most useless eaters of all.

New York was a ghost city now, as were London and Tokyo. The old financial centers no longer mattered. The cities were now dark and dead, except for bands of scavengers. A few people had stayed alive in the suburbs, but most of the survivors were hardy rural people who still had the old-fashioned skills and infrastructure to subsist.

Jake had not really witnessed the destruction. He had gotten out of Washington as the destruction started, and he had gotten to Phaedrus' remote place in the mountains just in time. He had seen very little with his own eyes, really, other than the desperate efforts to escape Washington, and then the distant flashes from the radiation bombs. It all was so abstract from a safe distance – the death of billions. Sometimes, back during the summer, many weeks after it was over, he had thought about the rotting corpses in the summer heat, in the cities, far away. The cleanup had mostly been left to nature.

Phaedrus had called the new order an intellocracy. The smart people were running the world now. The new elite were geniuses like Henry. Though it was the rich who had killed billions, and the intellocracy had killed only the rich, it still was ghastly what the intellocracy had done. And yet it must be true, as the new intellocracy claimed, that it was the only way to save the planet and that the old powers and the old cultural templates could not be trusted to rebuild the world. A controlled calamity and a new kind of order, the intellocracy said, gave humanity much better chances for a future than an uncontrolled calamity and the same old elites rebuilding on the same rotten foundations.

But it doesn't matter what I think, thought Jake. Even what Henry thinks is secondary. It's what the extraterrestrials think that really matters. So the galactic union has a protocol for such calamities, and Earth is now being stepped through that protocol. An alien ambassador is in orbit above the earth. If Jake signed Henry's papers today, then Jake would meet that ambassador soon. They have awfully good rides, these important people, thought Jake. I'll graduate from earth's helicopters, running on the dregs of our fossil fuels, to a long-range space liner of the galactic union, running on who knows what. Then I'll come home to mules.

Here on earth, when the remaining stocks of fuel are gone and these helicopters are beyond repair, there will be no more fuel and no more helicopters. These machines are useful while they last. They are being used to accelerate the process of rebuilding. But the age of fossil fuel will not truly and finally be over until the existing stocks of fuel are gone. Henry had not been joking about traveling by mule. Back at their little farm, they were getting to know their new mules. They were learning to train them and take care of them. Cattle, once again, were a measure of wealth. If I see these forests again, thought Jake, I'll probably be down below, leading a mule, making my way along a path in the forest from one Iron Age outpost to another. These fancy rides are a temporary thing.

Henry broke the silence as the helicopter began to descend toward a landing.

"What are you thinking, Jake?" asked Henry.

"Iron Age," said Jake. "I was thinking that it's the Iron Age again down there. I was thinking that we could slip farther back, into the Stone Age, if we don't hold on to some of our basic technologies. You know – Eighteenth Century technologies. Things like forges, water mills, wagon works, efficient ways of weaving. I'd feel guilty sitting in an abbey scriptorium and illuminating volumes of Kant unless I was sure that somebody knows how to make more paper."

"I assure you that paper and wagon wheels are on the radar screen," said Henry, "insofar as we still have radar. Monks and scholars need not feel guilty. They always earn their keep."

The sheriff looked as though he was about to say something, but the helicopter stopped moving and hovered.

A clearing in the forest lay beneath them. It couldn't have been more than a few acres. The clearing was in a narrow valley beside a small river in a rocky bed. The helicopter continued to hover while Henry spoke with the pilots. Henry's conversation with the pilots didn't come through the passengers' headphones, but Jake caught a few words. The pilots were asking Henry whether he'd like to land in a soccer field or in a grassy, tree-lined quad at the center of the tiny campus. Henry chose the quad.

The pilots centered the helicopter above the quad, then they slowly brought it straight down for a soft landing in the unmowed grass. The grass sworled and flattened from the helicopter's wind. After a season or two of abandonment, the grounds were looking weedy and overgrown. Through the trees that lined the quad, red brick buildings could be seen, solidly built but of modest size, with slate roofs and even a bit of ivy. The architecture, thought Jake, was a peculiar blend of Greek and Gothic, the sort of architecture that was at its best when overgrown with ivy and vines, after it had gotten a little shabby. The largest of the buildings, clearly a chapel, boasted columns. All the windows were framed by heavy shutters, painted green, some closed, some hooked open and drooping. There was a large fountain with a dragon meant for spewing water, but the dragon wasn't spewing. The water in its basin was green with algae. Everything looked worn and fraying at the edges, as though the campus had been maintained for a long time on a small budget before it was abandoned.

As they stepped out of the helicopter onto the grass, Phaedrus began to glow.

"I never knew this place was here," he said. "It has a charm. There's something severe about it, but it has a charm. It's as though someone chipped a piece off of Eton or Oxford and lost it in the woods."

"It was a prep school," said Henry. "Boys only. It was mostly rich boys, but not the brightest and best, if you know what I mean. The isolated location was to keep the boys from getting into more trouble, because getting into trouble was what got you here in the first place. It was not exactly the sort of place that looked good on a résumé. But the rich had a need for such places. They paid their faculty well – they had to, to get them to live out here. I'd like to save the chapel for last. Other than that, where would you like to start?"

There was a classroom building, an administration building, a small library, a dormitory, and a few small buildings whose use wasn't obvious. Phaedrus' eyes lit up when they entered the library. It was stuffed with solid furniture, and light poured through large windows – enough natural light to read by. There was a huge fireplace, which appeared to be in working order. There was art on the high walls in heavy frames, mostly portraits of great writers and philosophers. Lieutenant Boyles lent Phaedrus a flashlight, and Phaedrus went to explore the modest stacks. The place smelled strongly of old books and faintly of boys. One table was lined with computers. Mark joked to Jake that the computers were hopelessly old and not useful for gaming. The library was bright with light from the windows, filtered through trees. The electrical grid had been down since the event, and it would not be coming back. The sheriff spent some time inspecting the fireplace and said he had rarely seen one so big and fine.

"I like this architect very much," said Jake. "This is a reading room. A reading room ought to have good light, and this one does. This was an architect who loved books and wanted boys to love them."

Phaedrus returned from the stacks, and the visitors clustered near the fireplace, ready for Henry to lead them to the next part of the tour.

"Well, guys," said Henry. "You haven't seen the chapel yet, but what does the place need?"

"More books," said Phaedrus.

"We'll get you more books," said Henry, "even if I

have to steal them and fly them in from New Haven."

"Electricity?" said Mark.

"Strictly twelve volts," said Henry.

"A barn," said Jake. "It needs a barn, and some stables. It needs plows, tools, wagons, and a chicken house. There has to be a way to get some water into the plumbing – a small water tower, maybe. That quad should be a garden. I'm from Charlottesville. Think of what Monticello had. This place needs everything that Monticello had. Except for slaves, of course."

"Ha!" said Mark. "Boys are the new slaves."

"I like the way you think, Jake," said Henry, "though we'll have to do without a Jefferson until we can grow some new ones. We'll need some time to work on that. There was a lot to be said for classical educations. It was a mistake to let that get out of fashion."

"Six or seven days by mule?" said the sheriff to Henry. "That's a long way from my county. I need these guys at home."

"I know you do, Sheriff," said Henry. "This will be more a winter place. We'll find you some fast mules, I promise. And we'll make sure that you've got a good track through that forest, with way stations to stop for the night. But I'm just making an offer today. Everyone can decide for himself."

"What's the offer?" asked Jake. "Is there something that Phaedrus hasn't been telling us?"

"Phaedrus isn't covering up anything," said Henry. "There hasn't been any offer. Not until now. I've only hinted. I wanted everyone to see this place first. But here's the offer. I want Phaedrus to run this place. Jake and Mark, I want you to help him. Sheriff, I'm sorry. But you'll never lose them completely, I promise. We'll work with the agricultural calendar, just the way people used to do – staying home for the planting and harvest, with winters away for culture and the public's business. It will be like going down to London for the season."

Everyone looked toward Phaedrus, who looked thoughtful, and sad, always sad. But no one spoke for a moment.

"How many people do you foresee here?" asked Jake.

"It depends on the infrastructure," said Henry. "As you pointed out, the place needs to be largely self-sufficient. There's a pretty strong surviving settlement about fifteen miles from here where you could do some trading. We can subsidize you for a while. I'd say no more than twenty people to start, and no more than sixty or eighty at full capacity. The focus would be on doing agriculture and independent study during the spring and summer, with fewer people in residence, and then an academic season, a faculty, and a full house in the fall and winter."

"Not all guys, I hope," said Mark.

"Fully co-educational," said Henry.

"Excellent," said Mark. "Girl slaves."

"An abbey," said Jake.

"An abbey," said Henry. "It would be an administrative center, partly, coordinating the educational work for this part of the country. We'd give you good communications systems, a good faculty, and, like I said, good mules."

"How could you possibly find a faculty?" asked Phaedrus.

"We have a plan," said Henry.

"Could we hear it?" asked Phaedrus.

"It's classified, and complicated," said Henry.

"I'll deal with you later," said Phaedrus.

"Why so remote?" asked Jake.

"For security, mostly," said Henry. "Things are going to be tough out there for a long time to come. It's the Iron Age again, as you said. The medieval system had knights and soldiers to help keep order. We have to follow the same model. We'll put a small military unit in that settlement I told you about, fifteen miles away. They'll watch the road in and out. When there's a need to travel, they'll help get people where they need to go. When you have visitors, they'll help get them here. There are some things we'll have, though, that people didn't have during the Iron Age – radio and satellites and some solar power. You'll be in the loop here. You'll have data pipes to other centers, access to libraries, and as much of the old Internet as we were able to preserve – and that was a lot. We turned lots of tables, you know. People thought that those big data storage installations were about snooping. They were, to start. But in the end they were about preservation. We won't have the electrical power to keep those archives running all the time. But we'll find ways to sift all that data and make it available. You'll have access to all that."

A bigger picture was starting to form in Jake's mind. Clearly the intellocracy had been thinking and planning for years. They had used a kind of jui-jitsu against the old order, tricking the old order into investing in the secret plan that would double-cross and doom the old order and reboot civilization. The intellocrats had revealed their plan only to those few who needed to know, and not until they needed to know it. All along, Phaedrus had known more about the big picture than he could say, bound by his security clearance. In many ways, the power of this new intellocracy was frightening. What the rich had done to the useless eaters, before the rich themselves had been wiped out by the intellocracy, was unspeakable. And yet the intellocracy had a plan. The plan contained hope – maybe the only hope – for re-building a workable human order and letting the planet recover from what humans had done to it. An extrater-restrial union had offered to help. It was overwhelming. It made Jake feel obscure. And yet here he was, good rides and all.

"So what do you think?" asked Henry. Henry was looking at Jake.

"I think," said Jake, "that if those communications lines you spoke of led to Washington, or London, or Rome, I'd hide in the woods and plant beans and wheat. I'd block the roads and blow up the bridges, and I'd hoard guns. But since I'm guessing that those communications lines lead to Oxford, then I suppose I'm in."

Everyone laughed, including the sheriff and Lieutenant Boyles. Henry looked pleased. That meant that Jake had decided to sign.

"Let's check out the chapel," said Henry. "And after

that we'd better get going. Jake, thank you. You've made a good decision."

"It was the dragon that sold me," said Jake, "and the outré architect."

"What kind of architect did you say?" asked Mark.

"There's a dictionary over there," said Jake.

"How do you spell it?" said Mark.

The chapel had a modest elegance and was not as battered as the other buildings. Wide steps led up to the front doors, and behind the doors was a vaulted marble vestibule. Another set of heavy oak doors led to the nave of the chapel. They all soon saw why Henry had saved the chapel for last. There was one more piece of bait for Phaedrus – an organ. It was not a large one, but Phaedrus pronounced it magnificent. It was a baroque instrument, with a mechanical tracker action that needed no electricity. All it needed to be played was wind.

"Wait a minute," said Phaedrus. "This is a Flentrop. It has two sixteen-foot reed stops in the pedal organ. This is like finding a Bentley in a barn in West Virginia. Who built this place?"

"Old money," said Henry.

"Old money wasn't all bad, was it?" said Phaedrus.

"Old money was always more generous than new money," said Henry.

"And just listen to the acoustics in here," said Phaedrus. "Whoever the new inmates are in this place, some of them have to be musicians. With a choir. This room should be filled with people who know how to sing."

"Is somebody regressing?" said the sheriff.

"Even farther than you think," said Phaedrus.

Henry had stepped aside and spoken quietly to the sheriff and Lieutenant Boyles, who had nodded and left the chapel.

"One more thing," Henry said to Phaedrus, Jake and Mark as they clustered near the organ console. "The ambassador sent a little gift. Boyles and the sheriff have gone to the chopper to retrieve it. The ambassador asked me to tell the three of you that he knows how much is being asked of you, and that he knows that it isn't easy for any of you. He is particularly apologetic about Jake being away for so long. He wants you to know that he will accompany Jake for the entire trip, all the way out and all the way back. He wants you to know that everything possible will be done to ensure the success of the mission and the safety of the travelers. He wants you to know that history will remember this mission. He wants you to know that personal sacrifice for the benefit of one's world is the highest calling. His gift is a small thing, he says. But he says that it's small things, ordinary things, common things, that most enrich our lives. He says that he is grateful for your sacrifice and that he has very positive intuitions about the mission's outcome."

Once again, Henry was looking at Jake. Jake stammered.

"Wow," said Jake. "That doesn't sound very alien. It's very thoughtful. It's ambassadorial. I …"

Jake never finished his sentence, and they all fell silent for a while.

The sheriff and Lieutenant Boyles came through the

front doors and made their way down the aisle. The sheriff was carrying a box, which was open at the top. The sheriff was looking down into the box, grinning. He set the box down on the organ bench, and they all leaned over to look.

It was a kitten.

Its coat was black yet faintly luminous, like the night sky. Its eyes were unusually large and were a surreal blue. Its head, too, was unusually large, and its mouth was strangely wide and expressive, as though it could smile like a Cheshire cat. The kitten looked up out of its box, blinked, and made such a charming little trilling sound that they all broke out laughing. The trill had sounded like a question. The kitten fixed its eyes on Phaedrus. Phaedrus took that as an invitation and expertly picked up the kitten.

"Such eyes," said Phaedrus. "Have you ever seen such eyes on a cat? It has been a long time since I held a kitten."

The kitten opened its wide mouth again, but this time there was only a silent meow as it settled into Phaedrus' arms and held on with its kitten claws lightly extended.

"Boy or girl?" asked Mark.

"Girl," said Henry. "The ambassador says her name is Brigid. He says that Brigid's mother sends her greetings and expects visiting rights in perpetuity."

Back on board the helicopter, Phaedrus held Brigid in his lap as the helicopter lifted off and headed north. All were pensive. No one spoke. Jake had signed Henry's papers. Phaedrus had watched him sign, looking brave

– even looking proud – but sad, always, always sad.

As the helicopter climbed over a ridge north of the river valley, a simple melody like a child's nursery rhyme broke the silence inside the cabin. At first Jake thought it was an electronic chime from some system or other on the helicopter until he saw the look of wonder on Phaedrus' face. Brigid was cuddled in Phaedrus' lap, and she was singing.

—▸ ◂—

A band of moonlight through Jake's bedroom window was slowly moving across the foot of Jake's bed. In the past, that had always felt poetic, like an old folk song. But not tonight. The moonlight was a cold intruder tonight, as though it had come from space to fetch Jake away from earth too soon.

Jake had two basic positions for sleepless nights. The first position was for ordinary sleeplessness. Jake would lie on his side facing the window, so that he could see the sky. The constellations, spinning east to west, were like a clock to him. He always knew from the sky what time of night it was and how much sleep he was losing. The second position was for times of existential trepidation. Jake would fold up with his knees close to his chest, head under the covers.

He turned away from the window to duck under the covers and resume the trepidation position. As he turned, his hand raked the night stand and knocked off a book. The book hit the floor with a thud. Jake whispered a curse.

The trepidation position was particularly comforting in cold weather, under heavy quilts. This October night was a cold one. The heating fires were always allowed to die down at night. There would be frost tonight. It was long past midnight. Sleep seemed 371 billion miles away.

To look out the bedroom window at the stars, which was usually so comforting to Jake, was the opposite of comforting tonight. It was unnerving. The bottomless depth of space was just too much to contemplate. In space there was no up or down. If you imagined that you were going up into space, it was not so bad. But if you imagined that you were going down into a bottomless black depth, it could be terrifying. Jake had to imagine that he would be going up from earth, or sideways from earth.

To the stars, 371 billion miles was nothing. But for an earthling it was incomprehensible. Jake and his four fellow travelers would be the first earthlings to ever travel so far. Or would they be? How could I know? thought Jake. If probes and visitors from the galactic union have been coming to earth for aeons, then anything could have happened, long ago, unrecorded by history and leaving no trace.

Jake didn't know which frightened him more – the distance or the time that he would be away. A proper man, thought Jake, a fearless man with adventure propelling his body and curiosity burning his mind, wouldn't be hiding under the covers and cowering from the stars.

Jake put his head back on the pillow and rolled back toward the window. At the moment, clouds were partly obscuring the constellations. The limbs of the trees in the backyard were tossing in the night wind. Jake could hear the wind and the beating of his heart.

From downstairs he heard clanking from the kitchen stove. Was Phaedrus putting wood on the kitchen fire in the middle of the night? Jake got up, got dressed, and went downstairs.

He found Phaedrus in the kitchen, sitting near the stove. Brigid was in his lap. The room was dimly lit by a single oil lamp on the kitchen table. Jake's sock feet swished softly on the floor.

"I heard you drop a book," said Phaedrus. "It sounded like a heavy book, too. Are you still working on Roger Penrose and the laws of the universe?"

Phaedrus spoke softly, to avoid disturbing the kitten. As for Mark, who was asleep upstairs, nothing could disturb him at night.

"I was awake," said Jake. "But I wasn't reading. I was just tossing and turning and knocked poor Penrose off the table. How's Brigid?"

"I think she misses her mother," said Phaedrus. "She ate a little and drank a bit, but she squirms and won't stay asleep for long. I'm sure she's used to sleeping with her mother. She eats pretty well, though. It was nice of the ambassador to send such a generous stock of food. I don't know where we'd have gotten any cat food right now. Imagine that. The ambassador travels with a stock of excellent cat food. Where do you suppose it came from? There was no branding on the cat food, just those nice glass jars with the interesting lids. It looks so good that I thought we might have some of it with breakfast."

"Any more singing?" asked Jake.

"Not really. Her little trills are musical, but no singing. Maybe she'll be in a better mood in the morning. She seems to miss her mother less in the daylight."

"I miss my mother less in the daylight, too," said Jake. "I can't stop thinking about going so far and being away for so long. Then again, it's not really about my mother. She's safe where she is. I just dread leaving. It's something I never imagined saying, but I'm not sure that I'm ready to leave Earth, though I've imagined it a million times. It's hard to get my head around that."

Phaedrus was looking at him thoughtfully. Jake tried to manage a laugh. "I think I'd rather be home to see little Brigid grow up," he said.

"Jake, why don't you pull up a chair," said Phaedrus.

Jake pulled up a chair.

"Are your feet cold?" asked Phaedrus.

"Not if I point them at the stove," said Jake.

"How about some tea," said Phaedrus. "Something soporific?"

"That sounds good. You and Brigid stay where you are. I'll put the kettle on," said Jake.

"How about throwing in another couple of sticks while you're up," said Phaedrus. "And would you open the vent on the fire a little more? It's cold tonight. Winter is coming."

"Did Brigid really sing yesterday?" said Jake. "Did we imagine that? I've never heard anything like it. Cats can't sing. Can they?"

"I've been thinking some," said Phaedrus. "There are several things about Brigid that are unusual, like the size of her head and the shape of her little face. I'm wondering if cats have been going out into space for a long time. I'm also wondering if the ambassador's people have been doing some interesting breeding, or maybe modifying some genes. That little tune she sang yesterday, I recognized it. It's a nursery rhyme that all English children know. Someone surely taught her that."

"Who?" asked Jake.

"I don't know," said Phaedrus. "A chime in Henry's helicopter? The ambassador? Maybe even Brigid's mother, for all I know. But you'll be able to ask the ambassador when you meet him. We'll be in touch with you over Henry's Teletype. You'll be able to tell us what the ambassador says. And we'll be able to tell you how little Brigid is doing. Mark will want to shoot some video."

"You have to tell me how the winter wheat is growing," said Jake, "and how you and Mark are coming along training the mules. Don't forget to say how many eggs the chickens are laying, and how much milk the cows are giving. And I'll need to know how Mark's education is coming along."

Jake stopped, sighed, folded his arms around his chest, and suppressed a shiver. He had to buck up. He had to not make it any harder for Phaedrus than he knew it already was. They sat there for a while, listening to the fresh wood crackling on the fire.

"Phaedrus," said Jake at last. "I don't want to be just another person who leaves you."

Phaedrus was silent for moment. Brigid stirred in his lap. He stroked her, and she was quiet again.

"You want to be here," said Phaedrus. "That's what matters. It's very brave what you're doing. But you'll be back. It will be an adventure. Just think of what you'll learn. You'll have important work to do when you come home. And, when you're older, your memoir will be priceless."

"You always keep your perspective somehow," said Jake. "Things like a memoir would never occur to me."

"It's part of being older," said Phaedrus.

There was a pop from the fire, which was now burning strong, and the tea kettle was starting to emit simmering sounds.

"It's funny, isn't it," said Jake, "how we can't keep our minds from running loose on sleepless nights. My mind was a hundred billion miles away when I heard you putting wood on the fire. You know why I can't sleep. What's keeping you awake, Phaedrus?"

"Just existential chatter," said Phaedrus. "You know me. My mind is an existential chatter generator."

"I can't imagine that it's just chatter," said Jake. "There must be something to it."

"Who knows?" said Phaedrus. "Maybe sometimes. My chatter generator has lots of loops at its disposal."

"Do you have a favorite loop?" asked Jake.

"That's an interesting way to put it," said Phaedrus.

"Or how about a least favorite?" asked Jake. "Or what about the loop that plays most often?"

"Oh, that one," said Phaedrus.

"Seriously, what's the loop that plays most often?" asked Jake.

"I'd have to think about that," said Phaedrus.

"Come on, Phaedrus," said Jake. "It's so hard to get you to talk about yourself. You've owed me stories about yourself for ages. Maybe some of it is hard to talk about. But you've got a kitten in your lap. And I'm here. How about I pick a loop? All those years that you were here alone – what loop did that generate?"

"The loop of the lorn," said Phaedrus. "That's a Golden Oldie that's always in stock, isn't it? Everyone goes there from time to time."

"Not the same as you," said Jake. "You live on the fringes of a dozen bell curves. Ordinary people have a chance at matching up with half the population. But not you. Let's see. Two percent match your sexual orientation, and one in a thousand are as smart as you. So just those two fringes of the bell curve alone calculate out to one potential lover per fifty thousand, or .00002 percent."

"So that's why it was so hard and I always loved the wrong people," said Phaedrus.

"It really sucks," said Jake. "Not only did you have to deal with odds like that, but you also had to do it furtively and in the face of social hostility. It can't be what nature intended. I know you. You'd never settle for ordinary. So if you put rotten odds like that on one side of the equals sign, then on the other side of the equation you've got isolation, chronic rejection, sex once every seventeen years, either a dog or nine cats, and either a hermit or an alcoholic or a suicide case. When I met you, you had a dog and you were a hermit – some of the healthier options – and I'm not going to ask how long it's been since you've had sex. How did you handle it?"

"I suppose I tried to find some meaning in it," said Phaedrus. "Hence my existential chatter generator."

"That's some tough chatter to generate," said Jake. "I think I've known you long enough to hear your solitude loop. So did you find meaning?"

"I think I did," said Phaedrus, "when anger didn't get in the way. It was hard not to resent how others had each other, to resent the way that love came to them so easily, without their ever having to work for it, or having to wait years for it, or spending years trying to be good enough to deserve it, or trying to earn it, and still more years trying to get over it when it didn't happen. But eventually I realized that I was not alone. Sometimes I would lie awake in the middle of the night, and I would feel this immense flood of despair flowing in from the world. And it wasn't just the despair that was out there only at that moment. It would flood in from the past as well, as though it could never let itself be forgotten, as though some principle in the cosmos itself could not let it be forgotten."

Brigid stirred again, and again Phaedrus soothed her.

"And it wasn't even all from human beings. It was from all of creation. Think of all the animals born to be pets that instead spent their last days in cages, in terror, never being loved, without the least hope of anything or anyone to come to them and save them. Think of every orphan who ever lived, or every man who never came home from war, or every mother who ever watched her child die, or every parent who was taken too soon to see children grow up. Think of every child who never lived long enough for a first kiss, or every old person who died alone. All this would flow into my room at night, like a dark tide. I realized that if our own hardships don't connect us with that world of anguish out there, then we fall into a kind of narcissism. That connection to so much despair beyond ourselves is both unbearable and comforting at the same time – unbearable and narcissistic when we think it's only we ourselves who suffer, comforting somehow when it connects us with other living things.

"As for coveting the love that others have, love comes and love goes. Anyone can lose it at any time. Nothing lasts forever. But in that lies another paradox. Love dies. We die. Yet the intuition that love is eternal, that love lasts forever, is almost universal. Think how many songs have been written about that.

"And though our sheriff accuses me of being an atheist, I suspect, Jake, that the songs are right somehow – that, in some sense, love does go on forever. But, likewise, so does suffering. It's those two things that connect us more than anything else – love and suffering. They both seem to last forever. They want to never be forgotten. But that's the trick, I think. To let ourselves feel the way in which suffering connects us no less than the way that love connects us. All you have to do is look out your window at night, and the unloved and despairing will always be there with you. You're never alone.

"But there you have it. I'll trouble you with one more of my existential speculations, Jake. It's a hope that love and suffering somehow balance out. I am as much a fool for wanting to believe in the just world hypothesis as anyone else. It's a hope – an almost religious hope, I confess – that love and suffering are like matter and antimatter. The equations say that matter and antimatter had to have been created in symmetrical and precisely equal portions, and that when they meet they annihilate each other in perfect balance.

"I think – I hope – that love and suffering may be like that, at least on some cosmic scale. I hope that ultimately they balance each other out. I hope that they combine with each other and leave behind an afterglow of something like contentedness, or peace. There's often not much peace in love, you know, especially when love is not returned. I never found much peace in love. Maybe it takes practice to learn to turn love into peace. Maybe I never had enough practice to learn the knack of it.

"Love and suffering repel each other. They abhor each other. For those who have love, a reminder of suffering is a bore. It offends them. While those who despair repel the very thing they're most desperate for.

"But this balance between suffering and love, if it exists, can exist only on a timeless scale. In individual lives, there is never any balance that I can see. Love and suffering are distributed in grossly unfair proportions. Why should that be, in a universe in which all the other equations always balance? Why should God be exempt from his own moral law? I don't like it. It makes me angry. If I were ever allowed into the presence of God, I would beat him to death, if I could, for being so unfair. The angels would have to drag me off him. I'd gladly be flung into hell for a chance to remind God of his own principle of justice. It wouldn't be just for myself, you see. It also would be for all the other things that live in despair.

"I apologize for all this, Jake. I should keep it to myself. I try to. You're the last person in the world at whom I ought to vent my grievances. But you're also one of the few people in the world who understands or cares. All the same, I'm sorry."

"But I asked you," said Jake, looking out the kitchen window into the dark. "It's almost too much … too much to bear."

"There was music," said Phaedrus. "Sometimes I think that only those who have music survive. With the right music, somehow there is always a thread of hope and a strand of meaning."

"Yes," said Jake. "Jamie loved music, too. And what is the 'just world hypothesis'?"

"Roughly put, it's the idea – very prevalent – that people get what they deserve and deserve what they get, at least eventually. It's one reason why the rich have always thought so highly of themselves. It allowed the better-off to look down on the unfortunate, as though the unfortunate somehow brought their misfortune on themselves. The concept of *karma* is the most sophisti-cated codification of the just world hypothesis. The idea of karma posits a cosmos in which God can just stand back and watch, because the design of the universe automatically takes care of justice. The caste system in India is based on karma and the just world hypothesis."

"Do you believe the cosmos works that way?" asked Jake.

"No," said Phaedrus. "I don't. Not unless it operates on an impossibly long time line. How long has life on earth existed? Four billion years? It would take another four billion years to work back through all the suffering and injustice in that ocean of despair and make everything come out right."

"But nature made you, too, Phaedrus, the same way it made the most privileged, the same way it made all those who get more than they earn and more than they deserve. Did nature make you just so it could torment you?"

"No," said Phaedrus. "Of course not. Nature may have no sense of justice. Nature tolerates cruelty, but I don't think that nature is cruel out of a love of cruelty."

"Then why do things have to be so hard for some?" asked Jake. "Though of course I know the answer. I'm really just commiserating. I've thought about it a lot, because of – you know– Jamie. It's because of witless social arrangements that fence you off from love. Or social arrangements that, at best, require that you stick to your own kind. Hence the impossible odds, and always so much less for you than you deserve, less than your share."

"But in another four billion years," said Phaedrus, "who knows what might happen?"

"Maybe it won't take that long," said Jake. "Maybe the social arrangements are changing. Maybe our sense of justice is changing. Maybe it's a lie that we're not all the same kind. Maybe people are figuring that out. And I have another question. If you could have had one wish – other than a lover, of course – during all those years that you were a hermit, what would that wish have been?"

"Half a lover? Sharing someone else's lover?" said Phaedrus.

"No, no," said Jake. "That's too obvious. Some other wish."

"Then I would have wished for being allowed to live in the same moral universe as everybody else," said Phaedrus. "Rejection was never just a rejection, you know. It always came with a reminder that I belonged in another moral universe, separate and unequal. Anything other than rejection would have meant signing up for an inferior moral universe. Who in his right mind would want that? But maybe that's the same thing as what you just said. Take a deep enough core sample, and at some level or another we're all the same kind."

"I wish I'd always known that," said Jake. "It might have saved Jamie. But I had to figure it out. It took some time."

"It's not your fault," said Phaedrus. "That's what we're taught."

"Yes," said Jake. "And, when we learn better, we have a chance to make it up to someone. But Jamie's gone. You know, Phaedrus, I've never told this to anyone. And

I was the only person who knew. But Jamie died a virgin. He paid the price for living in an inferior moral universe. He paid the price every day, God knows. But he never got much for what he paid."

"Jake, I'm so sorry," said Phaedrus.

"But you're right," said Jake. "Nature has no sense of justice, and neither do a lot of people. It's up to us. And if it's going to take less than four billion years, then we have a lot of work to do."

"That's a loop worth keeping," said Phaedrus.

"Did I just generate an existential loop?" asked Jake.

"You did," said Phaedrus. "You said that if God and nature don't give a damn about justice, and that if the design of the cosmos doesn't arrange for justice automatically through karma, then it's up to us poor creatures."

"Speaking of creatures," said Jake, "I have a big favor to ask you."

"Yes?" said Phaedrus.

"You deserve that kitten more than I do. But since this is my last night on earth for a while and all, might I have her for the rest of the night?"

—◆—

It was more than an hour after sunrise when Jake carried Brigid into the warm kitchen. Phaedrus was stirring grits. He looked tired. Mark was sitting at the table, almost bouncing in his chair from excess energy.

"You've been hogging Brigid!" said Mark. "Look what I've got for her."

Mark had brought a couple of hard, still-green walnuts

from the yard for Brigid to use as balls. He had cut an old sock in half, had stuffed one half into the other, and had tied it up with string to make a mouse toy.

"Will she eat first, or play first, I wonder," said Phaedrus.

"Or pee first," said Mark. "I put a fresh sandbox on the porch."

"Ah," said Jake. "Cats pee, don't they."

As Jake opened the back door to set Brigid in the sandbox, Mark made a warbling sound that no doubt was meant to sound like a space ship.

"Phaedrus," said Jake, "Did you hear a space cadet? Somebody had too much sleep."

"That was just his stomach growling," said Phaedrus. "You've been holding up his breakfast. Sleeping is long and hungry work when you're seventeen."

"You should have started without me!" said Jake.

"No way!" said Mark. "You've even got the purple polka dot plate today, even if it's not your birthday."

"I'd rather have a birthday than a ticket to Alpha Centauri and the polka dot plate," said Jake.

"Phaedrus made his special grits," said Mark. "And I got up early to crack walnuts for the apple salad. Phaedrus made me crack and chop all morning. Phaedrus made mayonnaise! Phaedrus also has declared that today is a laundry day, because the weather's going to change. I've already started the fire in the wash house, and the water's heating. And that was after I milked the cow, I might add, since you and the cat slept late. But your turn's up with the cat. Hand her over."

Jake handed her over. Soon Brigid was knocking walnuts around the kitchen floor and swatting at the sock toy, which Mark dangled from a string.

"So she wants to play first," said Mark. "Then she can eat while we're eating."

"She's probably smart enough to beat you at video games," said Jake.

"If Phaedrus will spare me enough of his precious solar power," said Mark, "we'll see if she can. Of course, she probably trained on all the new games on some state-of-the-art space ship, instead of pathetic stuff that's ten years old like what we've got here. If she beats me, it's not my fault."

"Phaedrus, just don't let him sing in front of her," said Jake. "We wouldn't want Brigid picking up any Mark tunes."

"She'll never hear anything but Puccini," said Phaedrus.

"What's Puccini?" said Mark.

"Stuff you're too young for," said Jake. "Too much sex, violence, and offensive language."

"No danger of any of that around here," said Mark.

"I don't know about that," said Jake. "I kind of like the way your hair looks in the morning."

"Oh yeah?" said Mark. "Well, watch out, or I'll tell the sheriff. I'm under age, you know."

"By the time I get back, you'll have a favorite Puccini," said Jake. "And you won't be under age."

"What's a Puccini?" said Mark. "And the answer is still no, even after I'm eighteen."

Phaedrus started humming a Puccini aria as he set grits and eggs and biscuits on the table. Mark already had been sampling the Waldorf salad when no one was looking.

"Don't listen, Brigid!" said Mark. "Say Jake, Phaedrus has got news this morning."

"News?" said Jake.

"You tell him, Mark," said Phaedrus.

"It came in on the new Teletype during the night. Phaedrus let me read it. Here. I tore off the Telegram and brought it in."

"Mark has started calling them Telegrams," said Phaedrus. Mark handed Jake a piece of paper that had been lying on a cabinet. Jake read it.

"Henry's invited you both to Scotland!"

"Can you believe it?" said Mark. "Scotland!"

"But, can you both be away at once?" said Jake. "What about the cows and the mules? What about Brigid?"

"The sheriff's great-nephew is going to help us out some while you're away," said Phaedrus. "I think we can get him over here to look after things while we're gone. As for Brigid, why not take her with us? She seems to be used to traveling. And it'll be only three or four days. She can learn a Scottish strathspey."

"What's a strathspey?" said Mark.

"How will you get there?" asked Jake.

Mark made his space ship sound again.

"Seriously?" said Jake.

"I'd imagine so," said Phaedrus. "Scotland's not exactly in helicopter range. There are other aircraft, but

I don't think even Henry has fuel enough to put a long-range plane at our service, unless we were just additional baggage for a flight with other purposes. But I have a feeling that the ambassador is behind this, that the ambassador is being thoughtful. He must be very kind, and he must know a lot about handling humans. After all, he sent us a kitten. As for the problem of getting to Scotland, as far as I know, there's no real cost in operating the gnat shuttles, though I have no idea where the energy comes from."

"What's supposed to happen in Scotland anyway?" asked Mark.

"It's a month of training and getting ready for the expedition team," said Jake. "After that, we're off – 371 billion miles each way and almost two thousand years into the past. It still blows my mind. I'm sure a trip like that is something Henry wouldn't let a team undertake without some training and haranguing."

"Who's the team?" asked Mark.

"Five people including me," said Jake. "There will be a historian, I think, and a linguist. There will be a couple of military guys – Navy Seal types or the British equivalent – to keep us out of trouble. And me."

"What are you for?" asked Mark.

"I have no idea," said Jake.

"Seriously?" said Mark. "Who picked you? Henry?"

"I suppose so," said Jake.

"You look like a space cadet, I guess," said Mark. "But if you don't want to go, I will. And *you* can stay here and work your ass off."

Jake took a quick look at Mark. Mark had lowered his eyes, ashamed of letting his resentment show in front of Phaedrus. But Mark's lingering resentments were understandable. Teenagers wanted phones, malls, movies, and other teenagers. Mark had none of that now. Sometimes he took it almost personally.

"I'll suggest that to Henry, if you really want to trade places," said Jake. "But this means that we don't have to say goodbye tonight. I'll see you again in a month, all three of you, after I get my space cadet training."

"You have to keep the polka dot plate, though," said Mark.

The wash house was a narrow building between the barn and the orchard. It was made of concrete blocks, painted white. Its floor was of concrete, with a drain in the center. There was a stove for heating water, two big sinks, lots of buckets, and a washing machine that had been modified so that a hand-cranked wheel turned the dasher and wringer.

Mark had been cheery at breakfast, but now he was in one of those moods.

"I've already told you twice that I'm sorry," said Jake. "I got up late because I had trouble sleeping. And I'm sorry that I was ten minutes late getting to the wash house. You can take a long break or something to make up for it. I'm sorry, Mark. I'm really sorry. I know how hard you work."

"I'd better just get used to it," said Mark. "While

you're out riding around the universe with aliens, what will I be doing? I'll be doing the work of two slaves, that's what. It's milk the cows, chop the wood, start the fires, draw more water, crank the grinder, clean the chicken house, turn the compost, wash the solar panels, peel the potatoes, then milk the cows again. I think the sheriff sold me to the highest bidder. Sure, you and Phaedrus are rich, compared with the other folks around here. But rich just means that you've got more work to do."

"Mark, you know that's not how it is. You're here because ..."

"Because I'm stupid and needed a damned education?" said Mark. "Or just to make damned sure that I never have a minute left over for fun? What damned good is Greek, or math, to a slave who just milks cows and shovels chicken shit for the precious compost?"

"Mark, everybody works hard," said Jake. "You know things aren't like they used to be, for anyone. We all have to work hard. No matter who the sheriff sold you to, you'd still have to work hard. And you won't find a kinder slave driver than Phaedrus, or a nicer teacher. I thought you liked it here."

"I do like it here. You know I do. But when do I get a day off? When do *I* get to go anywhere? Do you know the last time I had a change of scenery? It was when I walked Mamie back from the Wilkinses, after they borrowed her when their mule died. A lot of fun that was, too. I was starving, and the Wilkinses were too damned stingy to even give me a sandwich for lunch."

"Mark, didn't you go for a helicopter ride not too many

hours ago? Didn't you get to see a new place where you can spend half a year each year, a place where there will be new people and lots more kinds of things to do?"

"OK," said Mark. "Yes. But for a whole damned year I've got to do the work of two slaves. No more rides, no new people. Just work and more work. Now he's got me churning butter, as if doing the damned laundry isn't demeaning enough. Churning butter! I thought that was women's work!"

"Do you like butter? Do you see any women?" said Jake.

"Ha! The last woman I saw was Betty Wilkins, and besides being a stingy old … "

"Do you think it's fair for Phaedrus to have to do all the women's work?" said Jake.

"No," said Mark. "He already does all the cooking, and thank goodness for that. I ate your cooking once or twice, and that was enough."

"Mark, do try to be glad for what we've got," said Jake. "It's not forever. Things will change. I'll come back to help you. Can't you be patient? I know a year seems like forever, but it's not. Phaedrus needs you. What would he do without you?"

"Shovel his *own* damned chicken shit and chop his *own* damned wood, I guess," said Mark. "Watch out! Don't crank the *damned* wringer so fast! If it mashed my *damned* fingers, then what good would I be? Who wants a slave with a hand mashed in a wringer?"

Jake stopped cranking the wringer and tried to hold it back, but he burst out laughing. Mark tried to look pissed, a wet T-shirt dripping in his hands, but he burst out laughing, too. Just then, the door scuffed open, and Phaedrus came in from the yard with a laundry basket.

"If that load is ready to go," said Phaedrus, "I'll get it on the line."

It was night now, and the kitchen was lit only by the oil lamp. A half-eaten chocolate cake with cherry icing was inside the cake pedestal on the table, under its glass lid. The chrysanthemums – dozens of them, with a few late roses – were in Phaedrus' best vase rather than the Erlenmeyer flask. There were walnuts on the floor and little bowls of cat food and water in the corner. The supper dishes had long ago been washed. The faucet dripped its usual drip. The hot stove pipe made little tapping sounds. The water kettle simmered. Mark was sitting at the table, fidgeting, and Phaedrus was standing near the stove.

"Where will it land?" said Mark.

"Same place as the helicopter," said Phaedrus.

"Is Jake coming down? Or has he chickened out?" said Mark.

"He's probably trying to get the zippers to close on his backpack," said Phaedrus. "Mark, I do believe you're fidgeting with that flashlight. Are you nervous?"

"I guess I am," said Mark. "In a month, we're going to have to ride on that thing, too."

They heard Jake's booted feet coming slowly down the steps, and then Jake came into the kitchen, wearing his pack. Brigid was curled up in a box beside the stove. Jake looked down at Brigid. He started to kneel, but the weight of his backpack made him reconsider.

"Should I wake her up to say goodbye?" said Jake.

"She just now went to sleep," said Mark. "She wore herself out knocking walnuts."

"I guess not, then," said Jake. "And besides, I'll see her soon. Well, the moon has set, five or ten minutes ago."

"What an obsolete way to tell time," said Mark. "Half an hour after moonset."

"I'm sure they don't think the way we do," said Jake. "From orbit, that's actually a pretty specific way of fixing a time. I'm also guessing that, if the gnat comes down in the dark after moonset, there's less a chance that anybody will see it."

"What kind of sound does it make?" asked Mark.

"No sound at all," said Phaedrus. "It's completely silent."

"How do they do that?" asked Mark. "Anti-gravity or something?"

"It has been almost forty years since I saw one," said Phaedrus. "We didn't know much about them then, and what little I know is forty years out of date. Our speculation back then was that they have gravity shields, but that their propulsion is based on something else. First they neutralize gravity with the gravity shields, and then they apply the propulsion. We didn't have a clue how their propulsion system works. This is just my own speculation, and I'm not a physicist. But, for what's it's worth, my guess is that their propulsion system somehow interacts with the Higgs field, which exists everywhere in the universe. Bending the Higgs field somehow causes the ship to go into free fall and fall in whatever direction they choose. Except that it's not exactly free fall, because they can control acceleration and deceleration. Gravity is neutralized, so there's no gravity on board the ship. Everything on board would just float around without gravity, except that they use the inertia of acceleration to create gravity on board the ship. There's no difference, you know. Both gravity and acceleration make you feel heavy. So, if you maintain a constant acceleration, you have inertia inside the ship that feels like perfectly normal gravity."

"Did you understand that, Jake?" asked Mark.

"I think I did," said Jake. "Though of course I have no idea how they do it."

"I did some calculations," said Phaedrus. "If my calculations are right, then the big deep-space cruiser that will take you out to the jump station will accelerate constantly for the entire trip. That constant acceleration will provide gravity on board the cruiser. The rate of acceleration required to maintain an earthlike gravity is well known. That's about 9.8 meters per second, squared. Or, to say the same thing slightly differently, that means gaining about twenty-two miles per hour in velocity every second."

"Wow!" said Jake. "If you keep accelerating like that for six months, you'd be going pretty fast."

"If my calculations were correct," said Phaedrus, "your maximum velocity, midway through the trip to the jump station, will be about one-fourth of the speed of light. Halfway there, they'll flip the ship and start to decelerate at the same rate it previously was accelerating. It's the deceleration that then provides the gravity on the ship. Just as you reach the jump station, your velocity will become zero. Pretty neat, yes?"

"Amazing," said Jake. "Did the math work out for the distance and the time it will take to get to the jump station?"

"It did," said Phaedrus. "If you travel for just under six months at a velocity that provides one-G acceleration followed by one-G deceleration, then the distance you've covered comes to about 371 billion miles, the number that Henry has been using."

"That's a long way," said Mark. "How many light years is that?"

"It's only a fraction of a light year," said Phaedrus. "It works out to about one-sixteenth of a light year."

"Did you understand that, Jake?" asked Mark.

"I did," said Jake.

"You guys are too smart for me," said Mark.

"Not so," said Phaedrus. "It's just that you're not done with your education. Besides, if one of your video games required that you figure out something like that, you'd do it in no time. But don't you worry. We're going to get lots of science into your curriculum. Which reminds me, Henry promised he'd get us more textbooks."

"From Oxford?" asked Mark.

"From Oxford," said Phaedrus.

"Scary," said Mark.

"One more question," said Jake. "Did you do the math on the trip to Scotland? Is that going to be a one-G thing, too?"

"I did do the math," said Phaedrus. "I had to make some assumptions. The distance from here to Scotland, if you were traveling on the surface of the earth, is about 3,700 miles. But of course you're not going to be traveling on the surface of the earth. Imagine that you cut a circle in half – an arc – and put one end where we are now, and one end on the destination in Scotland. The length of that half-circle would be almost 10,000 miles. To cover that distance with one-G acceleration followed by one-G deceleration would come to about 42 minutes."

"And that's exactly the number that Henry gave us," said Jake.

"There you have it," said Phaedrus. "If my assumptions are correct, then the gnat will appear to come almost straight down, from the center of the sky."

"I wonder why Henry never bothered to explain all this," said Jake.

"Probably because he knew Phaedrus would," said Mark.

"And remember," said Phaedrus, "the gnat is a drone, fully automated. There's no need for a pilot. You'll probably be traveling alone."

"We'd better go out," said Jake. "It's almost time. Let's don't wake up Brigid. She looks tuckered out."

They waited in the dark at the edge of the woods for only a few minutes. Then a disk-shaped object, no wider than Henry's helicopter, appeared straight over-head. At first it was descending at a frightening rate, as though it would crash into the earth, but soon they saw that it was rapidly decelerating. It came to a stop just above the level of the treetops. It slowly flipped, like a coin going from heads to tails. Then it came down slowly and settled down into the thick grass on three legs that extended from the disk just in time.

"Wow," said Phaedrus. "I don't have time to explain that flipping maneuver, but I think it may mean that there is someone on board."

"That was a gravity thing, wasn't it?" said Jake. "It was switching from deceleration gravity to earth gravity, and, if there's anybody on there, they flew in upside down."

"Exactly that," said Phaedrus.

On the ground, it looked like a saucer with a dome, sitting on its three spindly legs. A door silently slid open. Two or three steps extended. The interior was lit a warm yellow, but nothing much could be seen through the door.

"Well," said Jake. "I guess this is it. I'd better not keep it waiting. I'm so glad that this goodbye is only for a month."

Jake playfully seized Mark's head and rubbed his knuckles against Mark's scalp.

"There," said Jake. "Your hair looks better now. You work hard and study hard. By the time I get back, with Phaedrus as your teacher, you'll be a genius."

"I will," said Mark.

Jake was pretty sure he heard Mark sniffling in the

dark. Jake reached out to give Phaedrus a quick hug, but neither of them spoke. Then Jake disappeared through the open door, into the yellow light.

—▸ ◂—

Jake looked back through the doorway, hoping for a last glimpse of the house and a silhouette of Phaedrus and Mark standing in the knee-deep grass. The door politely remained open just long enough for a quick goodbye wave. Then there was an ethereal musical chime, and the door closed. The small interior of the gnat was warmly lit and cozy. The floor and lower part of the round wall was soft and carpeted. The domed ceiling glowed, candle-colored. There was nothing inside but two plushly upholstered chairs with padded arms. One of them was occupied.

"Pretty posh, wouldn't you say?" said a woman's voice. "When it's moving, you can't feel a thing."

"Hello there," said Jake. "I'm Jake."

"Hello there. I'm Aderyn."

A bin opened near the wall. Its purpose was apparent. Jake took off his pack and stowed it. The bin closed.

The empty chair rotated to face Jake, inviting him to sit. Jake sat. There was a thick belt with a buckle. Jake fastened it. The chairs rotated to face each other.

"Funny," said Aderyn. "It didn't say anything when you came in."

"The ship, you mean?" said Jake.

"That's right," said Aderyn. "It was chatty when I came on board ... told me where to stow my things, invited me to sit, explained the chairs and the windows. It had such an interesting accent. I was looking forward to hearing it again."

"What windows?" asked Jake.

"You'll see in a moment," said Aderyn.

"I wasn't expecting anyone," said Jake. "Would it be a breach of protocol to ask you …"

"I'm going to Scotland, too," she said. "I've been in America for the past week, to meet with Henry. He sent you a note. Here."

Aderyn handed Jake a folded piece of paper. Jake read it.

Make yourself comfortable and enjoy the ride. Aderyn is a member of your team. Her security status is the same as yours, so the two of you may talk about anything you like. I'll see you in a couple of days, in Scotland. – Henry

Jake looked up from the note. Aderyn had an informal but no-nonsense look about her. She appeared to be in her late thirties. She was wearing warm clothing that looked brand new, the sort of casual but efficient clothing that someone from New York might have worn to go skiing in Aspen. Jake felt shabby. Everything he owned was pretty worn now. He unconsciously stroked at his hair, which was longer and shaggier than it used to be, now that he cut it himself.

There had been no sensation of motion or of having left the ground, but the dome made a gradual transition from glowing yellow to transparent, and the cabin darkened. Their chairs rotated to face outward. Bright stars shone through the dome. Down below, dimly lit by starlight, was the earth, steadily receding as they gained altitude. If the dome had not been politely gradual in making the transition from opaque to transparent, Jake would have been startled by the altitude. Still, he gasped.

"Incredible, isn't it?" said Aderyn. It was dark inside the gnat now. There was only starlight.

Jake must have been gaping.

"But don't forget to breathe," said Aderyn.

In the starlight, Jake could see her smiling. A wave of homesickness had collided with a perception of celestial grandeur beyond anything Jake had ever seen from earth. His feeling of smallness had sucked the breath out of him. He just sat there. He could feel his heart pounding, aching for home but thrilled to be in a space ship.

Aderyn waited silently, revealing herself to be a fellow introvert who understood Jake's need to experience such awe in silence. Neither of them spoke for a while. Though the earth was lit only by starlight, Jake could make out the boundaries between land and sea. North America was receding. Their trajectory toward the northeast was apparent. The brightness of the stars pulled Jake's eyes upward.

"Try the button under your right hand," she said.

Jake toggled the button to the right, and his chair rotated. Through the transparent dome, the earth's horizon was visible. The earth was revealing itself to be a sphere. Over the North Atlantic, there were heavy clouds. The land was dark, beautifully dark. The era of perpetual electric lighting was over. The earth was just a dark sphere mottled by land and sea and cloud, receding into a starry sky.

"Pull back on the button," said Aderyn.

Jake pulled the toggle, and his chair silently tilted backward. He was facing upward toward a hemisphere of stars against the blackest blackness he had ever seen. Aderyn, too, had tilted her chair.

"I've never seen the Big Dipper look quite so big," said Aderyn. "But that's probably not what you call it, is it? Let's see…"

"Ursa Major," said Jake. "And if I had a pointer, I could show you Polaris, the North Star. To get to Scotland, steer with Ursa Major a little to your left."

"Then take a right at Alcor," said Aderyn, "and straight on till morning."

Jake laughed. "You know more about the stars than you let on," he said. "Not to mention English literature."

"Who can forget Peter Pan? As for Alcor, I don't know how I remembered that. Henry tells me that you're an astronomer."

"No," said Jake. "I'm an amateur. I'm just an amateur astronomer."

"Henry said you'd be modest."

"I have lots of reasons to be modest," said Jake.

"Now, now," said Aderyn. "If you know Henry, and if you're on the team, then you've got a curriculum vitae."

"Not really," said Jake. "I'm just an architect. And it's not that I know Henry. It's that I know people who know Henry."

Aderyn laughed. Her laugh was musical, with a kind of accent.

"Where are you from?" asked Jake.

"I'm Welsh," she said. "I grew up in the Glamorgan countryside and later lived in Cardiff. How about you?"

"I lived most of my life in Charlottesville," said Jake. "But since – you know – the event, I've been living on a little farm in the Appalachians, kind of in the middle of nowhere."

"Nowhere is the place you want to be these days," said Aderyn. "Nowhere is the new somewhere. But if you're from Charlottesville, then how did you get that Oxford cadence in your speech?"

"What?"

"It's very distinct," said Aderyn. "I seriously doubt that you picked up an Oxford cadence from American television."

"My parents were at Oxford," said Jake. "And I've been living with someone who was at Oxford."

"Ah," said Aderyn. "There's the Henry connection."

"So you're …"

"I'm the linguist," said Aderyn. "You've got English nailed. What other languages do you have?"

"Other languages? Well," said Jake, "none really, except a little Greek. I used to be really keen on Greek. And then, turning into a teenager or something got in the way."

"Greek?" said Aderyn. "Outstanding. Say something to me in Greek."

"Say something in Greek?" said Jake. "But it's been

so long. I don't think I can think of anything."

"Nonsense. You were keen on Greek, and you started before you were a teenager. So it's still there. What do you see outside these windows?"

Jake thought for a moment. Then he said, rather slowly:

"τὸν δ' ὃ γέρων Πρίαμος πρῶτος ἴδεν ὀφθαλμοῖσι
παμφαίνονθ' ὥς τ' ἀστέρ' ἐπεσσύμενον πεδίοιο,
ὅς ῥά τ' ὀπώρης εἶσιν, ἀρίζηλοι δέ οἱ αὐγαὶ
φαίνονται πολλοῖσι μετ' ἀστράσι νυκτὸς ἀμολγῷ,
ὅν τε κύν' Ὠρίωνος ἐπίκλησιν καλέουσι."

"Homer!" said Aderyn. "Generally I discourage translation into English, but it sounds beautiful in English, too. I was raised on Murray's translation from 1924. Do you remember it?" She recited:

"Him the old man Priam was first to behold with his eyes, as he sped all-gleaming over the plain, like to the star that cometh forth at harvest-time, and brightly do his rays shine amid the host of stars in the darkness of night, the star that men call by name the Dog of Orion. Brightest of all is he, yet withal is he a sign of evil, and bringeth much fever upon wretched mortals."

"That's it," said Jake. "My dad always insisted on lots of memorizing, and he was perfectly fine with my picking lines that were about the stars."

"Your dad knew Greek?"

"Yes," said Jake. "He taught the classics."

"And your mother?"

"She taught English," said Jake.

"Lucky you. You were born with an aptitude for languages. We'll have you speaking Celtic like a native in no time."

"Speaking Celtic?"

"Of course. How could we undertake such an expedition unless we all learn to speak Celtic? That's what I'm here for. English is my second language. I grew up speaking Welsh. We should be able to get comfortable with earlier forms of the language without too much trouble. But no more English. Speak to me now in Greek. Or, if you prefer, we can switch to a Celtic language, and I'll help you along. Which would you prefer?"

Jake stammered.

"Celtic," he said.

"*Da iawn*," said Aderyn. "*Yn gadael i fynd.*"

CHAPTER 2

Just before dawn, Jake and Aderyn stepped out of the gnat onto a Scottish upland lit by starlight. A military Land Rover was waiting for them. As the empty gnat silently fell upward and disappeared into the stars, a young military officer holding a flashlight approached. The flashlight emitted a dim, ruby light. The officer introduced himself as Second Lieutenant Randall Jones. He told them politely that in ten minutes he'd deliver them to a comfortable place where they could have some breakfast and get some sleep.

Jake and Aderyn were transfixed by the terrain. They were in a high place, lit by starlight, surrounded by rugged mountains. On the slopes of the mountains, stands of evergreen trees alternated with rock and rubble. Here on the upland, shallow soil supported patches of dense turf that held its own against the rock. If there were sheep, they were out of sight somewhere, safe in a fold. Everything was wet. Everything glistened in the cold light. It was not a comfortable place to be at such an hour, but Jones seemed to understand that they were in no hurry to get back inside another vehicle. He stood aside as they studied the horizon against the stars.

"Only the English," said Aderyn, "would think to call an upland a down. The English find irony irresistible. 'Oh, are you looking for Thomas?' she said, mimicking a rustic accent. 'He's up on the down.'"

Jake laughed.

"I would love to see this down in daylight," Jake said, "We don't have downs in the Appalachians. At least, we don't call them that."

"What do you call them?" asked Aderyn.

"The upper pasture?" said Jake.

"Not a bit of irony in that," said Aderyn.

Soon they were warm again inside the Land Rover. Jones was using only the blackout lights to see the way along a winding, one-lane road. Hairpin curve followed hairpin curve. The road was overhung with evergreen trees that mostly blocked a view of the sky, which was starting to lighten with the sunrise. Jake sat up front with Second Lieutenant Jones.

"I have some messages from Henry," said Jones. "Since you've been up all night and your body clocks are off by about five hours, Henry says that you should just rest up today and try to get some sleep and food and fresh air. Henry will be here tomorrow evening. One of your colleagues is here already. The other two will be arriving with Henry tomorrow. Henry says I should let you know, Jake, that the friends who saw you off will be notified of your safe arrival."

The road broke out of the overhanging evergreens. They were on another down. They passed through an open gate. This down had several buildings, a little too big to be houses.

"What's this place?" asked Aderyn.

"It's called Mount Grace, Ma'am," said Jones. "It was built as a convent in the 1920s. There was a small hospital then. The convent and hospital closed forty years ago. At some point after that the place came to be owned by the Home Office."

There was no exterior lighting. The buildings were dark except for dim lights in the lower windows of the second-largest building. Second Lieutenant Jones stopped the Land Rover at a side entrance to that building, near the lighted windows. As Jake and Aderyn emerged from the Land Rover, someone appeared from the building's side door, holding a flashlight. That flashlight, too, was dim red. In the morning twilight, they could see that it was a middle-aged woman. She was wearing a raincoat and a head scarf against the morning chill.

Aderyn declined an offer of help with her two bags, and Jones bade them all a polite good morning and drove away.

"Good morning to you both," said the woman. "My name is Rose, and you would be Aderyn and Jake. You must be very tired, so if you wish I will show you right up to your rooms and bring you a tray of breakfast. But no kipper for you, Jake, since you are an American."

"Actually, I like kippers," said Jake.

Rose winked at Jake and continued to make small talk as they made their way indoors, through a small sitting room with rustic furnishings, then up a flight of squeaky wooden stairs, which opened into a long hallway. The lighting everywhere was dim, as though the generators were turned off at night and only limited battery power was available.

"I'll have your breakfasts up here soon," said Rose. "And for lunch I'll have you some nice soup. It's already on the stove. I apologize for the modesty of our accommodations. We'll try to make it up to you with the kitchen, which is more generously supplied than most. Nothing here is *en suite*, I'm afraid. You'll find bathrooms down the hall. I've prepared your rooms on the south side of the building. It's always chilly here in the Highlands. Henry says that you're to be on your own for the first day. You'll usually find me in the kitchen, if you need me. If you can't find me, just leave a note on the table outside the kitchen door. Now, other than bringing you your breakfast trays in about ten minutes, is there anything I can do for you?"

They thanked her, and Rose retired down the corridor. Her steps could be heard descending the squeaky stairs.

Soon Jake was in an austere little bedroom that clearly had once been a nun's cell. There was a narrow bed, a table, a bookcase, a chair, a dim lamp, a small reading light over the bed, and a small window with its curtains closed. After a breakfast of kipper, fried egg, tea, and toast, Jake went to bed. The sheets were flannel. The quilts were generous. The pillow was soft. Jake wanted to think. There was so much to think about. But if he had been counting sheep, he would not have got past twenty.

— ◆ ◆ —

Rose was in the kitchen. Everything was old-fashioned in the kitchen, including Rose. She wore a dark wool dress and a linen apron. Her gray hair was done up in a bun. There were two big stoves, one fired by wood and the other by gas. Only the wood stove was operating this morning. At least six old pots – some of iron, some of copper – were boiling or simmering. There was an enormous tea kettle, steam curling from its spout. From the oven came the scent of hot bread. Though there was a dining room adjoining the kitchen, it clearly was not in service at present. It was late morning. Rose, drying her hands on a snow-white towel, directed Jake to a table in a warm corner of the kitchen.

"Did you sleep well?" she asked, as she stooped to open the oven door.

"Oh yes, very well," said Jake. "Thank you. That smells delicious. Is it biscuits?"

"Scones," said Rose. "And you've come downstairs just in time to have them hot. I have scones, Scotch broth, and lots of jam and butter. Would that suit you this morning?"

"It sounds delicious," said Jake.

Jake was pretty sure that the soup was the best he had

ever had. He could see barley, peas, carrots and potato. It was savory with herbs. Knowing that this was sheep country, he was reluctant to ask what was in the broth.

"The soup and scones are incredible," said Jake. "The scones are a lot like our biscuits, but they're richer – more character, somehow."

"There's an egg in the dough," said Rose. "And sour cream. I never make scones without sour cream, though some folks make do with buttermilk. We didn't have sour cream for the longest time. It was a hardship, a serious hardship. But I can see that you young folks arriving half-starved in the middle of the night are important young folks. The orders went out to the village from the higher-ups, and I haven't had such a richly stocked kitchen and so many people to look after for the longest time. There are just four of you here now, but I'm warned to expect ten by tomorrow. You'll all eat well, I'll promise you that. More soup?"

Jake wanted to go up to the down and see in daylight what he had seen the night before in starlight. He figured that it was no more than an hour's walk. Rose had told him that Aderyn was up two hours before him and was out exploring with another woman who had arrived yesterday. Rose had described her as somewhat older than Aderyn but just as sharp. They'd be out somewhere on the hills, Rose supposed, and they'd be hungry when they returned.

The grounds and buildings looked every bit the convent that the place used to be. There was statuary in small, neglected gardens. The stone buildings were simple but solid, a rustic combination of charm and piety. There was a small chapel surrounded by camellias. One of the gardens had a sundial. Jake paused to study the sundial. The sun was shining, and the gnomon cast a clear shadow. It appeared that the time was just before local noon. The shadow was remarkably long, indicating a high northern latitude. Jake realized that he had been so focused on the scones and soup that he hadn't even thought to ask Rose about their location. Then again, it probably would be best to ask someone to point to the location on a map, since Edinburgh and Glasgow were the only two places in Scotland whose locations Jake knew clearly. Jake guessed that he was well north of Edinburgh in the Highlands.

A narrow circular drive with broken pavement led to an iron gate set in stone columns. The gate was open, and the Land Rover was parked just outside the gate. Jake could see Second Lieutenant Jones standing beside the Land Rover, a microphone in his hand. He seemed to be using the Land Rover's radio. Jake paused to re-tie his shoes and went to the gate. Jones had just leaned through the vehicle's open window and put the microphone back on its hook.

"Is it OK to go out for a walk?" Jake asked.

"Of course," said Jones. "Just be warned that, if you run into any locals and they ask nosy questions, all you need to tell them is that some scholars have come up to talk economics with the Home Office. If they complain about the helicopters, tell them there won't be many. They hate helicopters. They say they scare the sheep and that the cows won't milk. Are you heading down toward the village?"

"No," said Jake. "I thought it would be nice to have the view from that place where we came in last night."

"About three miles down," said Jones, "you'll see a gate on the left and a steep track that leads up to the landing pad. The gate's open. There's a spring by the gate. The water's safe to drink as long as you don't catch a newt in the dipper."

Jake's legs felt springy and restless in the mountain air. He was running a serious sleep deficit, and he thought he might take a nap in the sun once he'd reached the down. The woods were dense on both sides of the road. Birds flitted through the underbrush and searched for food in the mulchy soil. At one point he thought he saw an owl gliding through the trees. The roadway was mostly overhung with dark evergreens, but when there were gaps in the trees Jake could see gray-blue sky.

He thought of Phaedrus and how Phaedrus would love Rose's kitchen. Though Rose's kitchen was five times bigger, somehow it had the same old-fashioned feel as the kitchen back home. The smells were similar – wood smoke mixed with the scents of hot breads, savory things in simmering pots, a touch of onion, a hint of cinnamon, and a clear hint of old house. If the word "home" could be translated into a scent, that would be it.

Phaedrus was such an odd combination of qualities. He had the mind of a man – independent, analytical, taxonomic. And yet he enjoyed fussing over the stove and generously feeding the young folk just as much as

Rose did. Mark, despite his occasional episodes of self-pity masked by ranting, had come out of his shell and was developing fast with the benefit of Phaedrus' tutoring and nurturing. Most of Mark's sullenness was gone. His confidence had steadily grown. Mark had never experienced anything like Phaedrus' Socratic methods of engaging the minds of the young. Jake had heard Mark imitating Phaedrus' recordings of Puccini operas while Mark was taking a bath, and as far as Jake could tell Mark had gotten every note of it right, though he made up the Italian. The Puccini jokes were endless. Jake often thought that he could go on living that way for the rest of his life, if it weren't for the absence of young women.

Speaking of whom, Aderyn was pretty hot, though she must be at least ten years older. If she were younger, she'd be perfect – pretty, smart, funny, and surely an introvert. She must have never been married, thought Jake, and she must not have any children, else she wouldn't be going along on an expedition like this one.

Jake was so lost in his thoughts that, before he knew it, he'd arrived at the open gate. Above the gate, in an old-looking work of concrete and stone covered with mosses, he found the spring. A couple of dippers hung on hooks. There were two old buckets, both a little rusty.

Jake drank a dipper full of water and was wondering what the buckets were for when he heard a kind of low rumbling sound. It was coming from the roadway, down the hill. He stepped back into the road to look, and soon, coming up the hill and around a hairpin turn, he saw a wagon pulled by two mismatched old horses.

The wagon's iron-rimmed wheels rang like bells on the broken pavement and lose gravel. A man, far from young, dressed in old tweeds, and walking so as to reduce the load on the horses, was speaking softly to the horses and encouraging them up the hill. Jake waited, charmed, as the wagon approached the gate.

"Whoa, girls," said the man. The wagon and the rumbling sounds stopped. The horses looked relieved, because the hill was steep and the wagon was heavily loaded.

"Good day to you, young sir," said the man.

"Good day to you, too, sir," said Jake.

Now Jake saw what the buckets were for.

"Shall I bring some water for your horses?" asked Jake. Jake had learned very well how to water horses and mules.

"That would be kind, and I thank you," said the man. "And I'll go have a dipper full for myself. I don't think I've seen you before."

"Name's Jake. I'm … up at the convent, you know, for a little gathering. Nice place. I wasn't really needed today, so I'm out for a walk."

"I'm headed up to the convent myself," said the man, "with a big order of groceries for Rose. If I was a praying man, I'd say a prayer for the sisters that put this spring-house here so many years ago. The water is as sweet as springtime, and it's at just the right place for man or beast climbing this hill."

"It's a magical spot," said Jake. They sat down on the old stone bench that the sisters had thoughtfully provided.

"Indeed it is," said the man. "When I was a boy, the old folks always said there was a faery that lived in that spring. They said it was there long before the sisters had the rock laid. Talk of faeries and such used to rile the sisters, but I've seen them cross themselves when they stopped here, before they'd drink. Lots of folks used to make fun of the sisters. And they were a grumpy lot, for the most part. But their little hospital saved many a sick child and birthed many a healthy baby, including me. I was christened with water from this spring. The sisters never could make me go to church, though. The church brought me into the world, and it'll probably send me out. But in between I think I'd side with the faeries. It's their spells that keep this spring so sweet, I do believe."

"So you believe in faeries?" asked Jake.

"A man would be deceived not to believe in 'em," said the old man. "Oh, I was baptized and all. We all were. But I believe in what I see with my own eyes, not what we can't see, like the sisters."

"You've seen faeries?" asked Jake.

"I have, many times. I saw 'em often when I was a boy. Sometimes you'd see 'em in the evening, when you were out on the hills looking for a missing lamb. It's harder to see 'em now. Some people say there're not as many of 'em, that they've gone farther up into the hills, that they don't like all the noise, that there are too many people. But it's quieter now, and not as many people. Maybe they'll come down again. They'll curdle your milk if you vex 'em, but they're better neighbors than most, and they've been here longer."

"I'll be on the lookout," said Jake.

"You're not a military man, I see, with all that hair," said the man.

"No," said Jake, stammering a little and not wanting to invite questions. "I'm just a visitor. I'm not even sure why they invited me. I'm not much of an academic. But it's nice to be here. It's a beautiful place."

"It's a good thing, keeping up the old convent. It's a good living for Rose. I only wish we'd had orders like this years ago, when the provender would have been easier to spare. Still, this past summer was a good summer for the beasts and the fields, a surprising good summer, and we're glad for the trade. We've got apples and potatoes to spare, and soon we'll have more ale than any of us dared to hope for. Rose can use up more flour and butter than any woman I've ever known. They're good neighbors up there, and they're good trade. It's only the helicopters that we'd be glad to do without, and a few of the young military men are too fond of our pub and our ale."

"I'm told," said Jake, "that there won't be many helicopters."

"I'd be glad of that," said the man. "My name is Thomas, and I'm glad to have made your acquaintance. Perhaps we'll meet again on the road."

"And I'm Jake."

"Well, Jake, I'd best be getting on and carry these things to Rose. And then I'll be able to ride on the way down. My old knees aren't what they used to be. I used to be as fit as you, I did."

"Rose has soup and warm scones," said Jake. "I'd say

she owes you lunch for bringing all these groceries up the hill."

"Aye, she owes me lunch," said Thomas, "though she'd never let me get away without it even if she didn't owe me."

Jake walked with Thomas back to the wagon. Thomas' steps seemed a little tired, in spite of the rest and refreshment. When Thomas placed his hand on the neck of one of the horses and reached out to scratch the horse's ear, the horse shook her head and made a nervous whinny.

"What's the matter, Jenny?" said Thomas. "She sees things sometimes. She always has, and I've had her since she was a tiny thing. Jenny's as sweet as my wife's damson jam used to be, rest her soul. But Jenny sees things. Maybe the faeries are coming down again."

"Maybe so," said Jake.

"I'd almost take you for one of 'em," said Thomas, "if you weren't so tall and all. No offense, of course. There are good ones and bad ones, just like people. The good ones always have a kindness in their eyes, and they're quick to see when an old horse needs a drink and an old man needs someone to listen."

They shook hands, and Jake stood beside the road and watched the wagon rumble up the hill, increasingly glad that the days of horses and mules and wagons had returned to the earth. Jake wished he'd had time to study the harness – something his own mules needed.

The unpaved track leading up to the down from the gate and the spring was twice as steep as the main road.

The track formed a kind of tunnel through the under-brush of a wide copse. A clear stream splashed its way down from the upland, over the mossy rocks, parallel to the track. The stream's banks were overhung with ferns. Though it was chilly in the shade, Jake soon was sweating from the climb. He removed his jacket and tied it around his waist.

After a twenty-minute climb, the track broke out of the dense shade of the copse into the sun. Suddenly Jake could see around him. He was now on the down. Except where there was rock, there was lush grass. Craggy mountains with patches of trees surrounded him on all sides. There was snow on the higher mountains. A few white clouds hung over the peaks. In the distance, on the horizon of the down, Jake could see a cluster of sheep. At the crest of the down, standing on a stony upcropping, were two human figures. One of them, no doubt, was Aderyn. They saw Jake and waved. Jake still didn't have his thoughts together, but now it was too late to slip back into the woods to prolong his privacy and fugue time.

Just as the night before, Aderyn was perfectly dressed for an outing in Aspen. She was wearing a dark cash-mere turtleneck and a rainproof jacket. Her companion was a rather severe looking woman. She was fit, but she lacked Aderyn's elegance. Jake judged her to be in her mid-40s. Aderyn introduced her as Judith, the historian.

"I hadn't expected anyone so young," said Judith. "What's your field, Jake?" It was an Oxford accent.

Jake stammered. There was an edge of judgment in

her tone. But Aderyn gave Jake an encouraging look that caused him to rally and deflect the question.

"Field? Well, the usual. Hay, mostly. I look after livestock, plant corn, cut hay. You know, things like that. There wasn't much else to do but work the fields, where I came from."

"Good fields to be in, I'm sure," said Judith. She was blushing, clearly having thought that Jake, with the thin curriculum vitae that she probably already had read and argued about with Henry, would be easier to cow.

Jake also blushed. He hated irony, and it was strange to hear himself using it.

Aderyn spoke to him in Greek. It took Jake a second of fast thinking to work out the meaning. She had said, "Don't worry. You'll get used to her."

Jake answered Aderyn in Greek, hoping he'd gotten it right. What he wanted to say was, "I came up here to listen to the crickets and the cuckoos."

Aderyn laughed, and Judith turned bright red. Clearly Homeric Greek was not Judith's specialty. She turned away to hide her irritation, and Aderyn silently mouthed a word of French, "*Touché.*"

After allowing a minute for the air to clear, Aderyn changed the subject with small talk about Rose's kitchen. As a peace offering, Judith brought some ginger cookies out of her backpack. The cookies were neatly wrapped in waxed paper.

"Rose gave me these this morning," said Judith. "It was the last of them, Rose said. Let's share."

They each found a rock and sat down to eat the cookies.

"I'm sure she's making more cookies even now," said Aderyn.

"And I just passed a wagon load of groceries heading up the hill," said Jake. "I have no idea what we're going to be doing here, but we're going to eat well."

"Henry will be here late today or early tomorrow," said Judith. "The other two members of the team will be with him. Once we're all assembled and well fed, Henry will give us a long, long briefing on the details of the mission."

"Do we know who the other two are?" asked Aderyn.

"We do," said Judith. "They're both military guys, commandos or something. It will be their job to protect us."

"Are we going to need protecting?" said Jake.

"Let's hope not," said Judith. "And I doubt it. In spite of the ugly things the Romans said about them, I'm sure the Celts were very decent people, as long as they liked you. Rural people are almost always generous and easy-going if they trust you. I think it's likely that we'll find them to be as easy to get along with as the Highlanders are now, or the rural Welsh or Irish."

"Let's hope they like us," said Jake.

"I'm sure they'll like you, Jake, and the young ones will like you a lot," said Judith. "But they may be wary at first. The simpler folk will be skeptical of who we are and where we came from. That's why we have to start in a place where there are some educated elite. We'll be able to get through to the Druids. Once they know that we're telling them the truth and they understand why we're there, they'll help us. I'm sure of it. I suspect that the Romans were anti-intellectuals compared with the Druids, or with the classical Greeks for that matter. The Druids valued knowledge. The Romans mostly cared about status and wealth and power. Whereas the Druids will want to know everything we can tell them. They'll fit all the pieces together easily enough. I also think that the Druids – and all the Celts for that matter – won't think it's strange in the least that there should be other worlds out among the stars. We will learn so much about the Celts and the Druids. Extermination and assimilation took them right to the brink of being lost to history. I'm a lucky historian. When we get back, I'll have to spend the rest of my life writing books about it. What about you, Aderyn? You should have a huge amount of material when we get back."

Jake braced himself for another barb about his not being an academic. But Aderyn, whose kindness and diplomacy seemed to surpass that of anyone he'd ever met other than Phaedrus, changed the subject.

"What do we know about the aliens?" said Aderyn. "That's a terrible word, aliens. There must be something else we could call them."

"E.T.'s?" said Jake.

"That would do," said Aderyn. "What do we know about the E.T.'s?"

"We don't know a thing," said Judith. "Henry just tells me to be patient until we meet the ambassador."

"I heard a little," said Jake, "though it's out of date. It's a consortium. There are many planets and ..."

Jake was interrupted by the sound of an explosion that rumbled across the down and echoed off the mountainsides. They sat startled and silent for a moment as the reverberations faded.

"That …,," said Aderyn.

"Can't be good," said Judith.

Jake sprang up.

"It came from the convent," he said.

Then Aderyn and Judith were up, and they all started to run, shouting to each other as they ran.

"Don't wait for me!" Aderyn shouted at Jake, who already was ahead. "Be careful! If you don't see Jones, stay out of sight!"

Soon Jake was crashing down the slope through the copse. He came to the spring. He drank two dippers full of water, then started up the road. He tried to set a pace that he could sustain, but it was difficult not to sprint. After the first mile, he paused to breathe, then ran on. By the time he reached the gate, he was breathing hard and was wet with sweat. The Land Rover was still parked outside the gate, but there was no sign of Jones. Jake stopped, thought for a minute, and then crept forward slowly, constantly checking around him for any sign of movement. He went through the gate, keeping low. He saw the wagon and the horses, and as he crept closer he saw that Jones was hovering around the wagon with some sort of instrument. Jones saw Jake.

"Get back!" shouted Jones.

"What's going on?"

"It was a bomb. Stay where you are. I'm almost done."

It appeared that Jones was checking the wagon for another bomb. Jake had almost made up his oxygen debt when Jones waved him forward.

"What happened?" asked Jake.

"It was a bomb. It was a small one, and primitive, but it killed the man who brought the wagon. It was in a flour sack. He jostled the sack on the way to the kitchen door, and it detonated."

"Is Rose OK?"

"Rose is fine. She's hysterical, but she's fine. She knew the man, of course."

"Can I …," said Jake.

"No. Better not," said Jones. "It's a mess over there. The specialists are on the way."

"Can I talk to the horses?"

"Of course," said Jones. "Maybe you can calm them down. I have no idea how to handle them."

"How about I get them out of harness and put them up? There's an old barn."

"The barn is full of clutter," said Jones. "But I think you'll find a stable you can use, if you toss some junk. Sure. Take the horses to the barn, but unhitch them here, and let's leave the wagon where it is for now. There's no metal on here to speak of, but the specialists need to check it before any more of these groceries go inside."

Jake slowly approached the front of the wagon on Jenny's side. He stroked her neck, then her nose. Her eyes were nervous. Both horses were lashing their tails.

"Hi there, Jenny," Jake said softly. "What did you see, old girl? We should have listened to you. And you, my friend, what shall I call you? How about Speckles? You've got such nice speckles. How would you girls feel about me taking this harness off? What do you think?"

The horses stood patiently while Jake figured out how to remove their harnesses. The old leather was stiff, as though the harnesses had hung for years without being used. Speckles whickered with relief when Jake lifted off the harness. Soon the horses wore nothing but their bridles and headgear.

"There, Speckles. There, Jenny," said Jake. "Does that feel better? Want to go to the barn now? How about a drink of water?"

Jake tried to keep his eyes away from the walkway leading to the kitchen as he led the horses toward the barn. An old well house half covered with ivy stood beside the grassy, rarely used path leading to the barn. The well still had a windlass, a rope, and a bucket. The big barn door creaked as Jake unfastened the rusty latch and swung the door open. Inside the barn, the floor was cluttered with garden tools, empty buckets, wheel barrows, and empty apple crates. There were still a few odd bales of hay in the loft, though it was gray with age. Jake lifted the wooden latch and looked inside the first stable on the left. It was empty. He led Jenny and Speckles into the stable.

"Such good girls," said Jake. "Now let me see if I can find you some water."

He picked up one of the empty buckets and returned to the well. A wooden flap on leather hinges covered the opening to the well. Jake lifted the flap and leaned over to look down into the well. It was lined with stone. There were cobwebs, but about twenty feet down, in the dim light, Jake could see water. The rope and windlass looked serviceable. He lowered the bucket and heard its splash echoing on the stone when the bucket struck the water. The rope tightened as the bucket filled and sank. Jake cranked the windlass, and soon the bucket came up dripping. The water was clean and cold. Filling the bucket was such an old-fashioned comfort that Jake retrieved a second empty bucket from the barn and filled it, too. Soon both horses were eagerly sipping water from the buckets.

Jake got the job done just in time. He heard the helicopter approaching.

"I'll take you girls out for some grass when it's a little quieter," said Jake.

He closed the stable door and went out to see where the helicopter would land. Across the barnyard and down the drive he could see Judith talking to Jones, shouting to be heard over the thunder of the helicopter. Her gestures were angry. The helicopter, which was hovering, appeared to be headed toward a small, unkempt lawn just outside the main gate. To avoid Judith and Jones, Jake headed toward the gate by an indirect route through an overgrown garden.

— ◆ ◀ —

Judith was still angry. She had been angry yesterday when she straggled back to the convent from the down. She had been angry all evening. She had been angry when she went upstairs to bed. And now she was angry at breakfast. Rose was standing quietly over the stove, her handkerchief handy. Jake, Aderyn and Judith were at the kitchen table. Rose had brought them tea and toast and was now scrambling eggs.

"I can't get a word out of any of them," said Judith. "They all keep saying the same thing: Talk to Henry. But where's Henry? I'm starting to think that, even if he shows up today, he won't tell us anything, either. What are they covering up? Somebody's dead. They have to tell us what's going on."

Rose started sniffling again. Aderyn got up to comfort her.

Jake buttered his toast and said nothing. Only Aderyn seemed able to handle Judith's steady outpouring of vexation and contrary opinions. But Aderyn, who seemed as sweet as her lilting Welsh accent and as warm as her cheerful brown eyes, was occupied at the moment with Rose.

"Fed him his last meal, I did," said Rose. "His last meal."

The helicopter was still on the lawn where it had landed yesterday. The military personnel who had flown in on it – five men and a woman not counting the pilots – had quietly gone to work. Jones had driven two of the military men down to the village in the Land Rover. The others had inspected every square foot of the convent and cleaned up the aftermath of the explosion. They had set up a headquarters somewhere inside the hospital building. Jake, Aderyn and Judith had been ordered to stay inside. But, through the windows, they had watched the military personnel at work. They had bustled in and out of their headquarters, picked up little objects off the ground with gloved hands and put them into vials, talked into their radios, wielded instruments and detectors.

Aderyn returned to the table carrying a bowl of scrambled eggs. Rose set to chopping onions for a pot of soup, and, for the moment, she was no longer crying.

"Wherever Henry is," said Aderyn, "you can be sure that this is what he's working on. If it's some kind of conspiracy, Judith, as you say it is, then the other end of the conspiracy is not here in the middle of nowhere. The brains, the leaders, are somewhere else. I'm sure that Henry will be here today, and he'll tell us what he knows."

"Henry never tells us what he knows," said Judith. "He tells us what he thinks we need to know, and not until he thinks we need to know it."

"Yes," said Aderyn. "That's why he'll tell us. We need to know."

Aderyn tried to change the subject.

"Jake," she said, "have you remembered that other Appalachian backwoods word that you think I've never heard? So far only two of them have bumfuzzled me."

"I'm still trying to remember it," said Jake. "I'm afraid my head has been a little whomperjawed. But, as soon as I can think of it, I'll heist up my galluses and mosey over."

Judith frowned at their clumsy efforts to change

the subject. Then there was the sound of the front door closing, then booted steps coming down the hall. Second Lieutenant Jones came into the kitchen looking tired and rumpled, as though he had been up all night.

"Good morning, everyone," he said. "I have a message from Henry. He'll be arriving later this morning with the other members of your team. You'll all meet with Henry at one o'clock. Meanwhile, with my apologies, I have to ask you to remain in this building a little longer. I'll come back at one o'clock to take you to the meeting room."

Jones glanced at Rose, who was dabbing her eyes with her handkerchief now, either because the onions had got to her eyes or because of her grief. Jones looked like he was trying to think of something comforting to say, but he left the room before Judith could ask more questions.

The meeting room was in the basement of the hospital building. The room was not large, about twice the size of Rose's kitchen. The room had been sparingly furnished by the military as a conference room. Someone had put pens and pads of paper on the conference table. The chairs were gray steel. One corner of the room had a computer terminal and some communications equipment. Jake looked longingly at the computer terminal. He had not yet been able to send Phaedrus and Mark a Telegram. One of the walls had a whiteboard.

Jake, Aderyn and Judith had been seated for only a moment when Henry entered the room accompanied by two men in uniform. Henry shook hands all around and introduced everyone. The two men in uniform were the remaining two members of the expedition team. Henry introduced them only by their names with no mention of rank. Jake didn't know how to read their ranks from their shoulder stripes. They were Glyn Harris and Andrew McGlennon. Harris was African, and McGlennon was Welsh. Henry, who never made a fuss about his power, did not sit at the head of the table. Instead they sat three to a side. Henry had brought a plain manila folder and a pen. He wasted no time coming to the point.

"I'm embarrassed to say that this was a complete surprise," said Henry. "Well, not a complete surprise. We knew that there are some who aren't on board with the purpose of this mission. But we weren't expecting any violent resistance. In retrospect, too many people knew, because the idea behind this mission has been discussed in some circles for a long time. Obviously there were leaks. However, what happened yesterday was a crude operation. Had the bomb detonated inside the kitchen storeroom, which probably was what was intended, it would have done some damage and might have started a fire. It probably wouldn't have hurt anyone. It's a shame that Thomas dropped it, though it's fortunate that he dropped it outdoors. The bomb was meant to intimidate the five of you and to taunt the rest of us. This bomb in no way threatens the mission. It was a poorly planned psychological operation, that's all. There was a stranger in the village a couple of days ago claiming that he was from the government and that he was auditing for hoarding. The village people believed him because he was rude and had a car. He was last seen yesterday morning. We'll soon find him and figure out what his connections are."

"How do you know you'll find him?" said Judith.

"We'll find him," said Henry. "As I said, this was a crude and poorly planned operation. The man in the village worked like an amateur. It'll be easy to track him down."

"Maybe somebody professional hired him," said Judith.

"That may well be the case," said Henry. "But, as I said, this in no way threatens our mission. However, clearly the dangers are, for now, and until we flush this out, higher than we thought. For that reason, you each are entitled to reconsider whether you want to take part in this expedition. Three of you are civilians. You have no obligation to take on risks that you're not comfortable with. If you want to go home, then we'll get you home in a day or two. To ensure your safety, we'll provide you with security for a while, until we get to the bottom of this. There's a second reason for the security. For anyone who chooses to go home, the security would be a deterrent to any leaks about this mission before the team departs a month from now. All of you already know a lot about matters that are highly classified."

"Do you think our families are in danger?" asked Aderyn.

"No, I don't," said Henry. "But, if you're worried, we can work something out to keep an eye on them for you."

"We need to know the details of the mission," said

Judith, "so that we can make up our minds about the risks."

"I can't tell you more at the moment," said Henry. "You all know enough now to assess the risks. First we need your decisions. If you feel that you lack information, and if you choose to err on the side of caution, then I understand. But, if you decide to stay, then the next step will be to talk about the expedition, in detail. That's really why I'm here today."

"How long do we have to decide?" asked Judith.

"Half an hour," said Henry.

"Half an hour?" said Judith. "How can we decide in half an hour, not knowing the details of the mission or knowing about what happened here yesterday?"

"I'm sorry," said Henry. "It's the best I can do. This incident has forced us to make some changes. We have to leave this place and go to an alternate location. That will happen tonight, actually. Tonight we'll either start your trip home or take you to the alternate location. None of this changes our plan for the expedition. We thought this remote location in the Highlands would be both secure and a pleasant place for the five of you to spend a month. We were wrong about it being secure."

"You were right about the pleasant place," said Aderyn. "I'm already missing Rose's scones and broth."

The two military men so far had said nothing. No doubt the risk of danger was routine for them, just part of the job. One of the men, Harris, appeared to be in his mid-forties. The other, McGlennon, appeared to be in his mid-thirties. They looked like commandos –

hardened and confident. Jake would have thought that they looked dangerous, except that they were there to protect them. The two commandos sat on Henry's side of the table, flanking him, as though they already had been protecting Henry this morning.

"This resistance that you mentioned," said Judith. "What's the nature of it? What's their objection?"

"Religious," said Henry.

"Religious?" said Judith. "They blew a man up because of a religious objection?"

"No doubt they only intended to make some noise and set a fire," said Henry. "Nevertheless, people have been blowing each other up because of religion for a long time."

Suddenly the bomb made sense to Jake. Nor did Aderyn or Judith look surprised. They already knew enough about the mission to understand.

"So," said Henry, "I have a couple of things to see to. We'll all come back here in half an hour. It's safe out there. You're free to go out for some air, if you like."

Chairs scraped against the concrete floor. Henry left the room with Harris and McGlennon. Jake noticed that McGlennon, the younger of the two, looked back over his shoulder at Aderyn. Jake went to check on Jenny and Speckles. Aderyn and Judith went to check on Rose, though Jake saw them later as he was drawing water for the horses. They were sitting on a garden bench, talking quietly. Jake also saw two men who appeared to be from the village. They were somberly looking over the wagon, so Jake guessed that they had come to retrieve the horses. Jake went back into the barn to say goodbye to Jenny and Speckles.

What I'd give, thought Jake, to have an oracle. It could be the stars, or a spring, or a well, or second sight like Jenny's. Even a tiny hint of what the future holds would make such a difference. It sucks to have to wing it. It sucks to not be able to discuss things with Phaedrus.

"What should I do, Jenny? What do you see?" he said, stroking Jenny's nose. She just looked at him with her brown eyes. She didn't seem to be afraid today.

Soon they were back at the conference table, sitting in the same places.

"Judith?" said Henry.

"I'll stay," said Judith.

"Aderyn?"

"Stay," said Aderyn.

"Jake?"

"Stay," said Jake.

"Good," said Henry. "I thought you'd all stay. We've learned a little more in the last half hour. The man from the village has been found, shot dead in his car about forty miles away. That's not a particularly good sign, frankly. It means that he was working for somebody smarter than he was, just as Judith suggested, and the real perpetrators have scrubbed him. But of course we'd already assumed that. Now that you're all in, you're all in. We can be much more generous with information that relates to the mission. We'll keep you posted as we get to the bottom of this conspiracy. Are there any questions about security before we move on?"

No one spoke.

"Good," said Henry. "All of you are eager to get down to business. First, let's talk about your roles. Though this is a civilian mission and has no military purpose, you can't protect a mission without someone being in command. Harris is in command. He'll listen to your views and help you carry out your civilian objectives, but for your safety he has the last word on everything. His word will be law. Understood?"

They all nodded. Judith frowned as she nodded.

"Glyn, is there anything you'd like to say?" asked Henry.

Harris cleared his throat.

"Just that I'm honored," Harris said. "And that Henry warned me not to be a hard-ass. This is a civilian mission. McGlennon and I will watch your backs, that's all."

"McGlennon will be second in command," said Henry. "In Harris' absence, McGlennon's word is law. Understood?"

They all nodded. Judith frowned again. McGlennon's eyes rested on Jake for a moment. Jake didn't have time to try to read what was in his eyes.

"After that, when decisions must be made and you can't agree, it's according to seniority – Judith, then Aderyn, then Jake."

Jake blushed. Judith chuckled.

"Judith, you promised to be nice," said Henry, smiling. "It doesn't mean that you have to take orders from each other down the line. It means that, if you can't agree amongst yourselves, Harris has the last word. Harris makes the calls on anything that has to do with safety and security. In your own fields, you call the shots."

"What's Jake's field?" said Judith.

"Judith!" said Aderyn.

"We're about to get to that," said Henry. "I would remind you, Judith, that this is not just an academic undertaking sponsored by a university. Your work and your knowledge as a historian are critical, but this mission has many objectives, and all of you were carefully selected to meet those objectives."

"By whom?" said Judith.

"Judith, we've been over this before. If we were able to send a dozen people on this mission, then sure, we'd have more Ph.D.'s, some research assistants, and all that. But as I said, the objectives of this expedition are not all academic, and some of the decisions about this expedition were not ours to make. It was the consortium, our off-world friends, who set the limit of five. They're providing the transportation, after all. It also was the consortium that specified the need for someone in Jake's role. The ambassador has seen and has been impressed by all your résumés and references, I assure you."

McGlennon winked at Jake. Jake wasn't sure what it meant.

"All right, all right," said Judith. "I get it. I'll shut up, because it sounds like we're finally going to hear about this consortium and the ambassador. They truly are, aren't they?"

"Are what?" asked Henry.

"Extraterrestrials," said Judith.

"Yes," said Henry. "That's not a surprise to any of you. All of you were gradually given that information in one way or another, at first in a deniable way. There was no way to recruit you for an expedition like this without some explanation for how such an expedition might even be possible. And we had to make sure that you could handle it. Jake and Aderyn are a little ahead of you, Judith, on that one. They've already ridden on a consortium shuttle."

"I heard," said Judith. "I'm jealous. It sounded pretty posh."

"Actually," said Henry, "the shuttle is small and plain compared with the main vessel. The long-haul transport up in earth orbit is anything but plain. But shall we continue?"

"You've been on the space ship?" asked Judith.

"Only for meetings, and only while it was in orbit," said Henry.

Jake was watching Harris and McGlennon to see their reactions to this talk about extraterrestrials. Their faces were blank and expressed only military discipline. Clearly both of them were well briefed already.

"Good," said Henry. "I want to give you an overall outline of the plan. Then I'll try to answer your questions about areas in which you might want more detail. The extraterrestrial consortium was closely involved in developing this plan. They and their probes have been visiting earth for aeons. They know a lot about us. Aderyn, you'll be impressed by the ambassador's abilities as a linguist. Judith, you'll be impressed by his knowledge of earth history. I'm sure the ambassador was chosen for this assignment because he has a particular interest in earth history. He'll be eager to learn from all of you. You will learn some things from him. He's all alone on that big ship, you know."

"Alone?" said Aderyn. Everyone looked surprised, including Harris and McGlennon.

"That's right," said Henry. "The ship flies itself. Everything is automated. The ambassador talks to the ship, and the ship takes his orders. The ship is not entirely under the ambassador's control, however. It calls home. Or, rather, it's almost constantly in touch with home."

"Isn't there a delay?" asked Jake. "The speed of light?"

"Yes," said Henry. "They're just as constrained by the speed of light as we are. Time travel they can do, at least to the past. And they can jump across space by using their jump stations. The jump stations also serve as communications relays. Most parts of the galaxy – the interesting parts, at least – are networked through these jump stations, both for travel and for communications. But they can't beat the speed of light. It can take months for a signal to make the round trip to the consortium's control center. However, I'm sure the ship is pre-programmed for all sorts of contingencies. They've been using automated vessels since we were in the Stone Age. Shall we move on?"

They all nodded.

"We've allowed a month for training before you depart. We'll start your language training and your history classes as early as tomorrow. Harris and McGlennon, this includes you, of course. The language and history classes, by the way, will continue on the ship. The consortium have offered some pharmaceuticals that should greatly enhance your language-learning abilities. Please don't be concerned about that. Their pharmaceuticals are very advanced. They've understood the neurobiology of humans for a long time. I'm told that there are no side effects other than some insomnia but that you'll feel as though your IQ has doubled. Your training also will include fitness work, self-defense, and survival skills, taught by Harris and McGlennon."

"Are there pharmaceuticals for that?" asked Judith.

"Actually, yes," said Henry.

"Fantastic," said Judith. "I want to be buff like Aderyn and Jake."

Jake saw McGlennon smiling. He was looking at Aderyn again.

"During the next month, we'll make a visit to your 48 B.C. destination on the Scottish coast so that you can see what it looks like in the present. It's south of Ballantrae, near a small seaport. A lot of archeological work has been done there. We believe the place was a kind of medical school and intellectual center for the Druids. As for the dangers of 48 B.C., this place is far enough from the trouble in Gaul that you'll be safe there, but close enough, by ship, that the Druids will know what's happening to the south. On this visit down the coast, you'll become familiar with the terrain. In about a month, after your training is over, you'll start your trip on the consortium transport. It's a long haul. It will take you six months to get to the jump station. In a matter of seconds, the jump station will take you to 48 B.C. Then the transport will return you to earth – or should we say, old earth. OK so far?"

"This jump station," said Jake. "How does it work?"

"I have no idea," said Henry. "I'm not sure I'd understand it even if it was explained to me. But with your IQ boosted and plenty of time to talk with the ambassador, maybe you can explain it to me when you get back. They can use the jump stations either for time travel or for faster-than-light jumps from one jump station to another."

"But didn't you say that they were constrained by the speed of light?" said Jake.

"I'm afraid I misspoke, in a sense," said Henry. "What I should have said is that their transport vessels cannot exceed the speed of light. Their jump stations, however, stay in one place and somehow warp spacetime. As I mentioned, they have a network of these jump stations all over the galaxy. Your first destination after you leave earth will be the nearest jump station. The consortium manages interstellar travel by flying the transport vessel to the nearest jump station at speeds slower than light. The jump station squirts the entire transport vessel through a hole in spacetime to another jump station, whichever is closest to the final destination. Then they complete the trip – the last mile, so to speak – at speeds slower than light. Obviously there are reasons why physicists call it 'spacetime.' At some level, space and time are the same thing. If you can control the warping of spacetime, you can jump in either time or space. If your destination was a consortium planet, you'd use the jump station for distance jumping. For this expedition, you'll use it only for time jumping. This must be very confusing. It's more than I can explain. I'm not a physicist. Questions about how this works are best directed to the ambassador. OK?"

They all nodded, though clearly no one was as curious as Jake.

"You'll arrive at earth in the spring of 48 B.C. We picked 48 B.C. for historical reasons. We have good historical detail on that period, partly because of Julius Caesar's book *The Gallic War.* Judith is very familiar with this period. Caesar has subdued Gaul after several years of ugly war and has returned to Rome, where there will soon be civil war. Christianity, remember, is still a hundred years in the future. Because of what has happened in Gaul, Rome's intentions will be quite clear to the peoples of Western Europe. North of Gaul, the Druids and Celts in England and Scotland have very good ships. They will be well aware of what has happened in Gaul. Caesar tells us in *The Gallic War* that, every summer, the Druids held a big gathering in Gaul near what is now Chartres. The old name is Cenabum. You will be arriving in Scotland – south of Ballantrae, as I mentioned – and you will spend your first months there, doing your field work, learning as much as you can, getting familiar with the culture and language, and earning trust."

"That's going to take a lot of trust, to believe a story like ours," said Judith.

"Judith, have you ever seen more honest faces than Jake's and Aderyn's?" said Henry.

"No," said Judith. Everyone laughed. Jake blushed.

"You'll find, somehow, a Celtic ship to take you to Gaul," said Henry. "If you're lucky, they'll volunteer a ship because they want to help you. Otherwise, you'll have gold and silver, and you can hire a ship. You'll need Celtic guides to travel in Gaul. You'll make your way from what is now Brittany to Chartres – Cenabum – for the gathering of the Druids. You'll warn the Celts about what is going to happen and encourage them to prepare for it. But, most important, you'll learn as much as you can about the Celts while they're near the peak of their achievements and before their long decline begins. You'll study their culture, language, laws, religion, music, science, politics, everything. When you return, we will use that knowledge to help us, as an old friend of mine says, to write a new operating system for our own world and to reboot ourselves on that new operating system. The Romans and the church went to a great deal of trouble to erase what we intend to recover, so you see why we have resistance to this mission from those who would prefer that we reboot the world on the same operating system as before. Jake, you have a question?"

"Is there not some sort of time travel paradox here? Can we really warn the Celts about what's going to happen without violating some law of physics?"

"The consortium and the ambassador assure us that

that's not a problem. Somehow these paradoxes have a way of taking care of themselves, they say. I don't claim to understand their explanation any more than I understand their jump stations, and our physicists don't either. It seems to me to boil down to a tautology rather than physics – nature allows time travel, therefore nature doesn't care what you do if you go back in time. The consortium does have a rule against transporting anyone into their future. Nature, apparently, may not forbid someone to travel into the future. And, obviously, after you've time-traveled to the past, the consortium technology will return you to the present. But the consortium won't transport anyone into their own future, as a matter of policy rather than physics. I don't understand why, and, again, our physicists don't either. The consortium must have learned that it can lead to bad results somehow. In any case, that's their rule. If it weren't the case, then we'd be interested in getting some Celts from 48 B.C. to volunteer to come forward into our time. But the consortium won't allow that. We can retrieve only their knowledge."

"I'll fill a thousand notebooks," said Judith.

"As I said, the consortium has been probing and study-ing the galaxy for aeons," said Henry. "There's probably not much that's new to them. They've seen it all before, and so they have policies and protocols. Apparently this is one of the reasons why they maintain their network of jump stations all around the galaxy. It seems that young civilizations like ours get themselves into trouble all the time. The instincts that helped a species evolve into a highly intelligent species and create a civilization seem to become destructive instincts once civilization reaches a certain stage. There are ugly odds that a calamity will ensue. It's at the calamity stage that consortium protocols allow the consortium to intercede. The survivors of the calamity are chastened – not to mention weakened – and are willing to listen to a greater wisdom and to submit to a galactic authority. The E.T.'s frown on belief systems that insist that one particular planet is special, or believers who think they have a patent on truth. Such dogmatic systems always encounter competition and resistance, and dogmatists try to beat down the resistance and eliminate the competition. The ugliest system usually wins, and nobler systems are made extinct. The protocol is to retrieve one of those extinct systems, one that is open-minded enough to deal with the realities of the galaxy while also meeting the existential needs of the population."

"Earth is submitting to E.T. protocols?" asked Judith.

"Yes," said Henry. "Earth's autonomy and isolation in the galaxy are history. Our species' autonomy and isolation are history. Galactic laws and protocols have kicked in. Earth is now under the jurisdiction of galactic law. We'll even get a vote in the galactic capital in a decade or two if we don't screw up on our probation. Do you think that's a bad thing, for earth to lose its autonomy?"

"No," said Judith. "I suppose it had to happen. It makes me feel safer, in a way."

"I think I'm beginning to see why the old order and the old religion truly had to go," said Jake. "They were doomed anyway, just because reality is more than they could ever handle. They would never have been able to cooperate. Remember Ronald Reagan? He longed for an alien invasion and even said so at the United Nations. He imagined a glorious holy war in which the nations of the earth would put aside their differences and unite to fight the aliens."

"That is quite right," said Henry. "That was in 1987. Someone gave President Reagan a bit more classified information than Reagan could handle. We learned a great deal from that incident, actually. When the history of the past 75 years is written, it probably will record that it was Ronald Reagan who convinced us and our extraterrestrial friends that the top layers of earth's elites would have to be eliminated. Earth's elites saw war as the only option. Reagan wanted to build orbiting weapons systems armed with nukes and lasers. They called it the Strategic Defense Initiative. Ostensibly this system was to protect the United States from the Soviet Union. But that was only a cover story. The truth was that the system was intended for war with extraterrestrials.

"And so it was then that the Oxford group started the planning for the elimination of earth's ruling elites. The galactic consortium, at that point, stopped communicating with sovereign states. The cover story was that galactic interests were spooked by earth's clever defenses and had decided to withdraw from earth for a century or so. On earth, the sovereign states and the financial elites thought that they'd won a showdown with galactic interests and had driven them back into space. Elites returned their attention to their problems here on earth. As the population continued to grow and the consumption curve got steeper, elites focused on their long-range plan for disposing of useless eaters. At the same time, the Oxford mouses, as we often called ourselves, were still secretly working with the galactic consortium. We did what we had to do to bring earth into the galactic consortium and to keep the earth out of a catastrophic war with crude nuclear weapons in our atmosphere that could have destroyed life on earth. So Reagan was right, in a sense. The encounter with extra-terrestrials did bring unity on earth. But not in the way that Reagan imagined, because he and people like him could imagine only war. They truly would have thought it nobler to destroy the earth in a glorious war than to join with the galaxy and grow up as a species."

"Wow," said Judith. "Recent history is not my specialty, but clearly I have some rethinking to do."

"The whole story will come out in a few more years," said Henry. "The Oxford press already has people quietly working on it."

"You know how much I love the Celts," said Aderyn. "But why the Celts?"

"Because," said Henry, "the alternative is utopian thinking. Has that ever worked? We can't just create a culture out of thin air by imagining it according to some utopian ideal. Rather, the galactic powers that be have learned that you have to go back into the history of a planet's civilizations and find something that has previously worked. The computer guys compare it with rolling back and recovering a database that has become corrupt. You move backward through the database, undoing corrupt transactions, until you reach a stable state in the database. Then you restart the database. Where real history is concerned, you won't find anything perfect. But you may find something that can work. And so that's why we compare the consortium's time-travel system with a seed bank. You go back and get good seeds, organic seeds, heirloom seeds that have not been genetically modified, after you've burned the fields where the bad seeds grew."

"What a metaphor," said Judith. "And what a euphemism about burning the fields. But you still didn't answer Aderyn's question about why the Celts."

"Many reasons," said Henry. "Celtic culture is close to the root and branch of all the cultures that grew out of the Mediterranean and Western Europe, all the way back to the Caucasus. You could easily argue that the Celts, or at least the Druids, expressed classical Greek culture far better than the Romans did. Rome and its religion went in a whole new direction. Rome went off the rails. The Roman systems were driven by the worst in human nature, and we got it from them."

"Aren't we being Eurocentric?" asked Aderyn. "I thought we were talking about an operating system for the planet. Why should Asian cultures, or African cultures, or Jews, or any tribe or people who have lost their land – in short, any people who don't speak an Indo-European language – why should they care about the Celts?"

"Good for you for asking that question, Aderyn," said Henry. "This team is only one of six culture teams. Elsewhere on earth, other teams are doing the same work we're doing, whatever is appropriate for the cultures within their regions. We're coordinating our work with theirs. I can tell you, though, that the other regions are in much better shape than we are. Their cultures – Buddhist cultures, for example – are not nearly as dysfunctional as ours. Our Western culture is the only one that is so dangerous that it required such a complete housecleaning. It's the only culture that is so dysfunctional as to require the consortium's time travel protocol. There's nothing flattering about the fact that everyone in this room but Harris has white skin. All of us come from a Christian background. We are the nastiest and most predatory culture that this planet has ever produced. Shame is appropriate here. I don't want to get into it, because it's not my specialty. But the fatal combination, we and the consortium believe, was Rome and Christianity. You might as well have mixed nitric acid and glycerin and gotten dynamite. And Aderyn, as a linguist you'll appreciate that what largely defines these five culture groups is the major language family to which they belong. But I'm talking about ordinary people here, not the international elites. Elites had a bubble culture of their own with no borders. But they're history."

"The sad thing is," said Judith, "that it was clear all along where Western civilization would end up, if you read history."

"Many foresaw it," said Henry. "But there was no

power that could stop it other than the final calamity. When the end approached, all you could do was store some rice and beans and get out of the way. In a few weeks, actually, you'll all meet someone who nailed the diagnosis years ago and who has thought longer and harder about these matters than anyone I know. He is an adviser to this team."

Henry looked at Jake as he said this. Jake knew that Henry was talking about Phaedrus.

"We've pretty much completed the overview of our expedition," said Henry. "I'd anticipate your being in 48 B.C. for less than a year. After the meeting of the Celtic council at Cenabum, you'll return to the consortium transport. In six months you'll arrive back at the jump station. You'll jump back to the present an instant after the time you left. Then you'll start the trip back to earth, which will take another six months."

"The ambassador, then, will accompany us to 48 B.C.?" asked Aderyn.

"That's right. The ambassador and the E.T. transport will remain in earth orbit while you five are in Scotland and Gaul. You'll have a means of communicating with the ambassador if there is any emergency. To the degree possible from high orbit, he'll monitor what you're doing, and, if anything unexpected comes up for which you don't have a contingency plan, then the ambassador's authority of course trumps Harris. The ambassador's ship, though, will be thousands of miles up. There's not much he could do other than send a shuttle to pluck you out of a jam. Even so, the travel time could be up to two hours. The ambassador can't watch your backs. Harris and McGlennon will watch your backs."

"I'm confused about the time element," said Judith.

"From your perspective," said Henry, "you'll be away from earth for up to three years – one year out, plus the time you spend on old earth, plus another year to get back. From my perspective, you'll be gone for only a year, because the time jump will erase a year of travel and the time on old earth."

"What about communication with you, with earth?" asked Aderyn.

"The consortium transport will be equipped for written communication and maybe a little video," said Henry. "We'll see to it that your families and loved ones have what they need to exchange messages with you. There will be a delay, remember, the farther you are from earth. No doubt the ambassador will keep you updated on the length of the delay in communications caused by the speed of light. I believe that's about twenty-three days at its maximum. Now I think it's time for a break. Without pharmaceuticals, this is brain-frying work. Are there any questions that won't keep until after break?"

"Just one," said Judith. "Exactly what will we be doing when we get back?"

"I can't give you details on that just yet," said Henry. "That plan will still be in development while you're away. But certainly you'll be teaching, advising, consulting, writing, helping us get the bugs out of the new operating system. You'll all be doing things that come naturally to you. You'll be doing the things you love. We're setting up what some of us affectionately call the monastery network. You'll all be involved in that, probably in an itinerant sort of way. You'll probably be offered multiple positions. You'll be able to take your pick of locations."

"I like choices," said Judith.

"I know you do," said Henry. "Now let's take a thirty-minute break."

They filed out of the room. Jake went last. He noticed that McGlennon was lingering at the bottom of the steps, as though he was waiting to say something to Jake. Whatever it was that McGlennon wanted to say, Jake was sure that he wasn't in the mood for it.

"Say, Aderyn," Jake called out. "I remembered that word."

McGlennon's eyes narrowed, and they all continued up the squeaky wooden steps.

—→ ←—

If I live, thought Jake, I'll never get on a damned helicopter again.

A few hours ago, before Rose went off to bed still sniffling, she had hugged Aderyn, Jake, and even Judith goodbye and given them each a brown paper bag filled with snacks. Around 4 a.m., Henry had seen them strapped into a waiting helicopter. Henry had said nothing about their destination.

During the first part of the flight, Jake had been able to distinguish up from down and north from south by the starry sky and the moon through the helicopter window. But after almost an hour of flying north above dark terrain with a mountainous horizon, they had flown out over the sea.

The weather had suddenly changed. They were in a black churn of heavy clouds and fog. The helicopter wallowed and lurched in the North Sea turbulence. It was like being in a kayak without a paddle, like being washed down a mountain rapids in the dark. Everyone looked miserable except for Harris and McGlennon, who looked merely experienced and highly uncomfortable. Several times, Jake saw McGlennon glancing at him, as though McGlennon was amused by Jake's unmanly motion sickness. For half an hour, Jake fought his rising nausea, longing for a sight of the horizon, longing to lie down, longing to be invisible, longing to just crawl under something and die. Suddenly the helicopter dropped as though it had flown into a vacuum. It plummeted in free fall, leaning sideways, for several seconds. Then suddenly it rushed upward, tossed sideways in the opposite direction.

Jake puked into the barf bag and tasted Rose's ginger cookies.

When Jake finally opened his watery eyes, feeling a little better, McGlennon was watching him with a look of irritating amusement.

Jake closed his eyes again and concentrated on getting into the most intense state of dissociation that he could muster. Dissociation, Jake knew, is an introvert's last defense against unbearable stimuli such as too much noise, inescapable disgusting smells, or too many people. For months, in quiet pastoral places, overstimulation had not been a problem. Jake couldn't claim that he was adjusting very well to the overstimulation.

Jake wished he could sleep, but it was impossible. Periodically he stole a glance out the window, hoping for a change from the awful blackness. At last he saw a vague dawn, thinning fog, and a blue sea heavily speckled with whitecaps. The helicopter slowed and gradually began to descend, as though it was going to drop into the sea. Jake leaned toward the window and strained to look down.

It was an oil rig – enormous, industrial, decaying, ugly. White waves crashed against its underbelly. Cranes leaned over its side. A tower painted white and orange loomed over one corner. Lights blazed into the morning twilight on its helicopter pad. The lights grew gradually closer. At last the helicopter descended and came to rest. As the helicopter's blades spun down and the door opened, the sound of the engine was replaced by the roar of wind and sea. Jake could feel gravity again. But beneath him, below the flimsy metal frame of the drilling platform, there was no earth. Around him there was nothing that stood still. There was only a shifting range of perilous white-capped mountains rising and falling on all sides. It was the ugliest and most terrifying place that Jake had ever seen.

CHAPTER 3

Harris called off their morning run because of the ice. Jake returned to his cramped little coffin of a cabin and tried to take a nap under a blanket, but he realized that, between the coffee and the noise, he'd never sleep. He had spent most of the night staring into the dark and checking his watch, and he had no energy for running. All night long, the roar of the wind and the squeal of the platform as it flexed with the colossal North Sea waves had made a noise like a freight train. It was an excruciating, misery-inducing sound that could have been used for torture. Jake couldn't banish the awareness of being on a mere man-made platform on stilts planted in the bottom of the sea, miles from land. That platform probably was being stressed within sight of its design limits. Before now, on quieter nights, when Jake had the energy to feel instincts other than the survival instinct, he was tormented by loneliness and the utter absence of any prospect for sex. But last night, the constant freight-train roar and the terror of being surrounded by deep, violent water left no room for any feelings other than dread and misery.

Jake put on his heavy-weather gear and made his way to an upper deck. He had to push hard against the metal door to open it against the wind. Outside, everything was covered with ice. Icicles hung from eaves and railings. The deck was treacherous, covered with a coating of ice. The sky was clearing now. The storm had moved on, leaving only a surging sea half white with foam, a platform white with ice, and a brutal wind. According to the weather readouts in the crew lounge, the wind was slowly subsiding.

Jake tried to brush the ice off a steel bench with his gloved hand. That didn't work, so he sat down anyway. He soon felt the coldness through his clothing. The vanishing warmth of his buttocks turned the ice to ice water. He'd soon be shivering, but as his young body cranked up his metabolism to keep his lower parts warm, his brain came awake. It was a good morning for thinking rather than running, if he could keep the freight-train noises from dominating his mind.

It was always Harris who took them out for runs. Every morning for the three weeks they had been on the platform, running had been the start of their morning routine. Harris ran with them. He would lead them in circles and loops around the platform, up and down steps, through dim corridors with metal walls, and up and down the winding stairs of the tower, single file. Indoors or out, there was always the sound of wind and sea and the squeal of metal on metal. Last night was not the first night that the sound had kept Jake awake. Sometimes the platform would shudder and vibrate at a pitch so low and so unnerving that it seemed to come from the bottom of the sea.

When they were outdoors on the platform, they wore military gear to defend against the weather. Their boots had naval soles, but they still had to be careful not to slip on wet surfaces. Jake had slipped and fallen only once. Judith had fallen at least three times, but she was getting better at keeping up with the others. The humiliation of falling, Jake thought, had made Judith a little easier to get along with. She had laughed it off. She wasn't as prickly.

It was their twenty-second day on the platform. Jake was counting off the days in his journal, in which he wrote faithfully every night. His journal was his only outlet for his thoughts. His notebook was growing by many pages each day. The platform had satellite links. There were several dishes and antennas on the tower, though the dishes were covered with ice this morning and weren't working. Henry had sent a few brief Telegrams that were meant to be encouraging. But otherwise they were incommunicado because of the strict security. Jake longed to sit by a warm fire and talk with Phaedrus. He had realized that he would never be able to talk intimately with any of his four expedition mates. Introverts needed someone to confide in.

Aderyn might have become a good friend but for the fact that McGlennon was signaling in every way possible that he had dibs on her. Gradually, Aderyn was letting herself be won over by McGlennon's swagger. Maybe it was an age thing. Jake was almost ten years younger than Aderyn. She and McGlennon were about the same age. Sometimes Jake felt like a school boy, having his Welsh grammar corrected by an aloof but devoted teacher.

Each day on the platform, seven days a week, they kept up the same schedule. They rose at dawn. They ran. They had breakfast. They had half an hour of free time. They had a two-hour history class taught by Judith, followed by two hours of physical training and self-defense taught by Harris and McGlennon. They'd have lunch, followed by another half hour of personal time. Then they'd have a two-hour language class taught by Aderyn. At four o'clock, they'd have drinks. Aderyn insisted on their speaking Welsh during their cocktail hour, on the grounds that alcohol relaxes the tongue for languages. But, one by one, they'd slip back into English. Their dinners always seemed to be in English. McGlennon and Judith, with their ever-dominant personalities, did most of the talking.

Jake heard the door slammed shut by the wind and looked up from his bench. To his surprise, it was Judith, bundled tight against the weather. She took slow, cautious steps in Jake's direction, bracing herself against the wind and being careful not to slip on the icy deck.

"May I sit?" she asked.

"Of course," said Jake. They had to raise their voices to be heard against the wind.

"I've been wanting to tell you," said Judith, "what an excellent student you've been. I love your questions. You've turned out to be my star student."

"I wish I'd discovered Strabo sooner," said Jake. "Though of course I read Caesar when I was very young. My dad insisted on reading Caesar, and in Latin as much as possible. How could I ever have guessed that I'd have a practical reason for studying *The Gallic War*?"

"And how could I ever have guessed," said Judith, "that I'd have a chance to do field work in Gaul only a couple of years after Caesar went back to Rome. I still find it hard to believe. Maybe after I ride in a space ship and meet an alien I'll believe it."

"It's fascinating about Divitiacus," said Jake. "Clearly he was one of the most important Celts in Gaul, and he was probably a Druid. Do you think he was betraying his own people? Or was he smart enough to get away with playing the Romans? Even if he thought that Romanization was inevitable, it's hard to imagine someone like Divitiacus stabbing his own people in the back. And where did he go when he disappeared from the record?"

"Who knows? Maybe we'll find Divitiacus," said Judith, "Maybe we'll get to ask him all those questions. What we don't know about Divitiacus is parallel to what we still don't know about what happened in Gaul. If Harris and McGlennon are as clever as they are fast on their feet, then they'll get us to the summer gathering at Cenabum."

"I can't get used to it," said Jake. "What would a nobody like me say to an icon of history like Divitiacus?"

"That's easy," said Judith, "you'd ask him questions. And you'd take notes on his answers and make sure you tell me everything he says. Caesar was very self-serving, you know. The Romans well understood the technology of creating celebrity and social status. If you were a Roman, the quickest route to celebrity was to be a great general. Then of course you had to write about it and present it as a history. Though I don't doubt that Caesar cared deeply about the history of Rome, I'm sure that he cared more about the prospects for his own fame and his own hopes for power. To Caesar, Divitiacus would have been a symbol of Gaul subdued. It was as though Caesar wanted to say, 'See there. Not only did I subdue Gaul with my military prowess. I also won over their hearts and minds to our Roman ways.' Caesar knew how to flatter the Romans and claim glory for himself all at the same time. If we ever really do get a chance to ask questions of Divitiacus, I would not be at all surprised to learn that Divitiacus did not eat out of Caesar's hand the way Caesar would have us believe."

"Are you going to tell us more," asked Jake, "about the archeological work you oversaw at the place Henry has chosen for our landing place in old Scotland?"

"Oh yes," said Judith. "Though I'll save most of that for our field trip there."

"One more helicopter ride to look forward to," said Jake.

"Maybe the weather will be better next time," said

Judith, "and maybe we won't need barf bags."

"You're sure that the place was some sort of elite center?" asked Jake. "It wasn't just a fishing village or something?"

"That's right," said Judith. "We wanted a place far enough from the troubles in Gaul to be safe. But we also wanted a place that was in close communication with Gaul, a place where elites knew what was going on. This place is right on the Scottish coast and was only a few days' sail from Brittany. The Celts were highly competent seafarers. Their ships were good enough to give the Roman galleys a lot of grief. That sail between Ballantrae and Gaul took you right past the island of Anglesey. Anglesey was already an outpost of the Druids in 48 B.C. Later it would become one of the Druids' last refuges. So the people at Ballantrae were well connected."

"It was a medical school or something?" asked Jake.

"We think so. We found evidence that they actually did surgeries there, and that they manufactured medicines and physicians' implements. We think they exported those things as far as Marseilles and probably beyond. It made them pretty rich. There was something like a hospital inland from Ballantrae. Those who could afford it and could survive the trip almost certainly traveled there for advanced treatment from Druid physicians. There is a particularly fine example of a Celtic broch there. It's on a promontory overlooking the sea. The brochs were stone towers. You had to be well off to live in one. A mile or two north of the broch, also on a promontory, was another impressive stone dwelling, fit for a minor king. The village was inland a mile or so from the castle and broch, in a more sheltered little valley. Farther inland from the village there were farms and fields. Altogether, we think the place supported at least five hundred people. That was a rather large settlement for the Celts. The Celts were a pastoral people, you know, with no great love for cities. But there was safety in numbers, and, if you lived on the coast, safety was your first concern. And of course larger settlements made more specialization possible. Specialization helps generate wealth."

"So they weren't hicks, these first Celts we're going to meet?" asked Jake.

"Oh, no," said Judith. "I feel sure we'll meet our first Druids there. I think there also will be a regional king. Because of their thriving export business and the shipping traffic that their medicine business produced, they should have excellent lines of communication. If you bring all those factors together – the civil and military power of a king, the educated elite that were the Druids, good lines of communication, and considerable wealth – then you have a hub of power and politics. It was probably the most urbane place in all of Scotland at the time, but it was remote enough to be as safe as any place could be in 48 B.C. We stand to learn a great deal there. And until we learn a lot and make some friends, it would not be safe to undertake a trip to Gaul. Gaul will be in turmoil."

"That makes me appreciate Harris and McGlennon a

little more," said Jake. "They're not the best of company on an oil drilling platform in the middle of the North Sea. But when we get to Gaul, I'm sure I'll appreciate why Henry picked them and why we need them. They even know how to use swords. Swords!"

By cocktail hour, the wind had subsided to its usual monotonous gale. The sea was more like rolling blue hills than snow-capped mountains. The ice had been cleared from the satellite dish, bringing the delayed news that a helicopter would soon be arriving, bringing visitors.

Aderyn, wine glass in her hand and eyes on Jake, repeated the comment that she had made in Welsh. Jake caught only the word for "legs," but because Aderyn was trying to keep herself from laughing, Jake knew that he was being teased. Aderyn said it a third time, and suddenly Jake got it. She was complimenting Jake on how nice his legs looked in their calisthenics sessions.

Aderyn waited patiently, smiling her most endearing Welsh country-girl smile, while Jake tried to assemble a response.

"Blast it," Jake finally said, in English. "My mother was a dancer, you know, before she was an English teacher. What's the Welsh word for dancer? Anyway, my mother said that dancers always say that only God can give you calves. Every other muscle in the body can be developed, dancers say, but only God can give you calves. So I take no credit for it. I guess I got them from my mother, or from God. Same thing?"

"See, Andrew?" said Aderyn. "Those toe-raises by the bar are of no use to any of us but Jake. You'd do better to spend our time on more hand-to-hand combat instead. Still, it's fun to watch Jake doing toe-raises."

McGlennon did not look amused. Jake took another gulp of Scotch, emptying his glass. Usually he had ale at cocktail time, or wine. But today when Harris had offered him Scotch, Jake took it, straight. The uncapped bottle was on the bar. Jake poured himself another. Aderyn was on her second glass of wine. Judith and Andrew were drinking ale. Periodically, everyone went quiet and looked out the window that overlooked the helicopter pad below. They would hear the helicopter long before they saw it, of course. Everyone seemed a little nervous with happy anticipation – everyone but Jake, who was trying hard not to reveal his feelings. It would be more becoming to not envy their happiness at seeing their loved ones for the first time in weeks. Jake still didn't know when Phaedrus and Mark would arrive. But when they did arrive, Jake was pretty sure that it wouldn't be by helicopter.

Harris always drank Scotch.

"What's the Welsh for Scotch whiskey," Harris asked Aderyn.

"*Wisgi,*" said Aderyn. "That's not too hard, is it?"

"Even I can follow that," said Harris. "I'm not sure I understand why we're learning Welsh, though. Will they understand Welsh?"

"Almost certainly not," said Aderyn. "Linguists don't know enough about Gaulish, though we know much more than we used to. The Gaulish language died out frighteningly fast after Caesar subdued Gaul. As for Scottish Gaelic, that's a living language today, though of course it will have changed a great deal in so many centuries. However, all these languages have the same roots. Learning Welsh will give you a head start. We linguists have ways of working out the differences in cousin languages pretty quickly. After a few hours of asking them a bunch of questions that seem like a game, I'll have the basics. Then I'll coach the rest of you. You'll see. I think you'll be surprised how quickly you'll be able to make yourself understood."

"How do you say, 'Drop the sword and put your hands in the air'?" asked Harris.

"How do you say, 'Another ale, please?'" said McGlennon.

"How about 'Which way is the ladies' room?'" said Judith.

They all looked at Jake, startling him. Jake had not been paying attention. But they were by now accustomed to Jake's moments of introverted reverie and moved on. Aderyn put her wine glass down for a moment, put her hands over her head, and translated, "Drop the sword and put your hands in the air." Harris muddled it in repeating it back.

In a lull in the laughter, they caught the sound of the helicopter. Harris, McGlennon, Judith and Aderyn all rushed to the window. As the helicopter approached the platform and started to descend toward the landing pad, they went out into the gale, carrying their drinks – all except Jake. He stood by the window and watched the helicopter settle onto the landing pad and shut down its engine. In spite of the wind, it was a precise, dead-center landing onto the target painted on the deck.

Four eager people stood at the edge of the landing pad as the helicopter door opened and four visitors emerged. Jake remained in front of the window and watched, Scotch in his right hand, left hand in his pocket because his hands felt cold. That would be Harris' wife. That would be McGlennon's wife. That would be Judith's 15-year-old daughter. And that would be Aderyn's boyfriend.

This, thought Jake, is a soap opera, and I need to be somewhere else when these two wives and Aderyn's boyfriend do the math on what's going to happen during such a long separation. Jake was well aware of the role in the soap opera that the math cast him in – odd man out, staring smolderingly out of windows – if spacecraft even had windows – always laughing a little too late when everyone else started laughing, scolding himself for feeling resentment for comforts that others possessed, gritting his teeth unconsciously when he imagined what they – Aderyn, at least – were doing at night, always hanging on existential tenterhooks between sublimation and irritability. Not only that, but McGlennon would smirk at Jake's frustration. Why, Jake asked himself, do I feel so irritable? How has Phaedrus managed being a monk for so many years? Phaedrus had the sublimation part nailed. But why did he never seem irritable? Sad, for sure, always sad. But never irritable.

Jake shifted his Scotch to his left hand and put his right hand in his pocket, trying to warm his clammy hands one at a time. Down on the helicopter pad, he watched them hug, watched the wives wipe away tears, saw Judith charmingly play the role of mother, read the look on the face of Aderyn's horny boyfriend. Jake was about to down the last of his Scotch and go to his cabin when one of the pilots emerged from the helicopter and asked Harris a question. Harris pointed to the lounge window at which Jake was standing, and the pilot started walking toward the steps that led up to the deck the lounge was on.

The pilot came into the lounge, carrying an envelope.

"Jake Janaway?" asked the pilot.

"I'm Jake."

"I have a note for you from Henry," said the pilot.

"Thank you," said Jake, conscious of being way beyond the point of merely tipsy. "Oh. It's cocktail hour. Would you like something?"

"I wish I could, but I'm still on duty. In a little while, for sure." The pilot gave a casual salute and left.

Henry's thoughtfulness was almost equal to Phaedrus' thoughtfulness. Surely that was because they had known each other during their formative years, decades ago. The note said that Jake would see Phaedrus and Mark at Ballantrae, three days from now.

For now, Jake would have to get by on the love of monks – the sweet, now familiar, achingly austere love of monks. Then again, for Phaedrus it must not feel so austere. For Phaedrus, I'm an ideal, the ultimate desideratum. No, wait. That can't be. It must be much worse than mere austerity, because Phaedrus has to sublimate not only his need but also his having me around but not having me. Well, one thing is for sure. I'm going to have two years in deep space to learn how that feels.

Jake went to his cabin. He wanted to cry himself to sleep. But the Scotch and his exhaustion took him first.

— ◄

After Jake's misery in being imprisoned on an oil rig, the Scottish coast was like a happy dream after a month of nightmares. Here Jake stood on firm ground while a feral sea crashed eloquently against rocks rather than terrifyingly against spindly metal struts. Here the sea's roar spoke of something indestructible, eternal and majestic rather than something that always threatened to crumple underneath you and drag you to the bottom of the depths in the dark of night. Here on this green coast, no matter how violently the sea crashed, the earth stood its ground, and the voices of the gulls rose above the sound of the violence. Phaedrus, always quick with a musical metaphor, had called the crashing of the waves an ostinato, the gulls a chorus, the wind a continuo. He had said that it reminded him of the Mozart Requiem.

Jake didn't say anything. He only wanted Phaedrus to keep talking, because the sound of Phaedrus' voice was a part of it all. Phaedrus' voice, raised to be heard over the sound of wind and sea, was like a force of nature. It was like the baritone in the Requiem's tuba mirum section. When Jake was about eleven, he had asked his father about the Latin in the Mozart Requiem, and his father had handed him a book that contained the text. His father had explained that it was an old hymn dating to at least the 13th Century and that a number of composers including Mozart had used it. It was Jake's first exposure to Latin verse, and he had been greatly surprised to find how handily Latin lent itself to rhythm:

Mors stupebit et natura,
cum resurget creatura,
judicanti responsura.

Liber scriptus proferetur,
in quo totum continetur,
unde mundus judicetur.

Judex ergo cum sedebit,
quidquid latet, apparebit,
nil inultum remanebit.

Quid sum miser tunc dicturus?
Quem patronum rogaturus,
cum vix justus sit securus?

Then Jake's mother, who loved poetry, had explained to Jake that the Latin verse was written in trochaic rhythm, each line with four feet, with the rhyme scheme A-A-A, B-B-B, C-C-C, D-D-D. She had challenged Jake to produce an English translation that exactly reproduced the rhythm and the rhyme scheme. Jake had worked on it for several days, then gave up, declaring that it was impossible. His mother had then gone up to the attic and returned with an old Catholic prayer book and had opened it to this:

> *Death is struck, and nature quaking,*
> *All creation is awaking,*
> *To its Judge an answer making.*
>
> *Lo, the book exactly worded,*
> *Wherein all hath been recorded,*
> *Thence shall judgment be awarded.*
>
> *When the Judge His seat attaineth,*
> *And each hidden deed arraigneth,*
> *Nothing unavenged remaineth.*
>
> *What shall I, frail man, be pleading?*
> *Who for me be interceding*
> *When the just are mercy needing?*

The translation, his mother said, was done by an English clergyman named William Josiah Irons in 1849. With the English language, his mother had said, nothing is impossible. Be proud, she had said, that English is your mother tongue. Also be relieved, his mother said, that English is your mother tongue, because it is an exceedingly difficult language to master.

Often Jake, when listening to Phaedrus talk, would remember this. He had never known anyone who spoke

English quite as confidently and casually as Phaedrus did. Phaedrus' English was simple and modest. He preferred plain words, though you learned that his reserve vocabulary was bottomless after you got to know him. During the last month, Jake had realized that, when Phaedrus wasn't actually there, then he had imaginary conversations with Phaedrus in his head. Jake wasn't sure how to make sense of things otherwise, without Phaedrus as a touchstone. But, in a day or two, Jake would be leaving and would be faced with bewildering experiences in a completely unknown world. How would he then make sense of it, without Phaedrus? In his own head? Maybe he'd just have to store it all up, and then work it all out with Phaedrus after he got back.

➤ ◄

They had all arrived during the night. The expedition members and Henry had come by helicopter, and Phaedrus and Mark had been transported over the North Atlantic on a gnat. Now they all were clustered on a high place overlooking the sea, surrounded by an ancient and enormous human-made ruin of rocks. An early-morning rain had moved on toward the Highlands, leaving a vast sky over land and sea, half of it blue and the other half white, with rolling clouds rushing toward the northeast. The sea was rough and full of whitecaps. Around them the land was gray with rock and green with grass and sea holly. They had seen a pair of rabbits browsing warily among the tiny flowers in the ruins. Judith was describing the ruins, and they all gathered close around her the better to hear. They listened carefully, because, unbelievable as it seemed, they were going to go back in time and see this place come alive as it used to be.

"We think," Judith said, "that at its peak this massive stone building housed as many as sixty people. At least a third of them probably were soldiers. Another third would have been family members and members of the court of this minor king, whoever he was. Another third would have been servants, or even slaves. Not just anyone, remember, could build with rock. What you know about castles really doesn't apply to 48 B.C. The era of castles came a thousand years later, after the Normans. In 48 B.C., most dwellings and even fortified places were made of wood, which was still plentiful, and they were roofed with thatch. But Scotland, obviously, has plenty of rock, and in 48 B.C. they certainly knew how to build with stone and to roof with slate. But only the elite lived in stone dwellings. That may not have been as luxurious as you think. Stone homes were cold and damp. But they were safer, and they could be built much higher. And of course living in a stone dwelling communicated status. Do you have a question, Harris?"

"How do you know," asked Harris, "that a third of them were soldiers?"

"For expedience, let's call it a castle," said Judith. "The castle was divided into two sections. One section contained much more spartan accommodations. About half of these more modest accommodations were for soldiers and half of it for servants. There were several rooms where our digs found the remains of the usual Iron Age weaponry. We found a fairly large and sophisticated ironsmith area. There were stables, the rims of heavy wheels that probably were used for military vehicles, and even the iron and bronze remains of harnesses. As for the total number of occupants, that can be deduced from the overall size of the place, the size of the feasting hall, the capacity of the kitchen and storage areas, and so on. It's not difficult to estimate how many people would have been needed to staff the castle or how many men could be accommodated in the military areas."

"How big was the feasting hall?" asked Aderyn.

"Small and cozy, by the later Norman standards," said Judith. "Probably forty if the hall was packed. But that was probably only on special occasions. On a daily basis, there probably were no more than fifteen or twenty sitting for dinner. The soldiers, of course, had their own separate mess hall on the inland side."

"But what about the broch?" asked Aderyn.

"The broch is a fascinating place," said Judith. "And of course we'll be going there next. The broch tower housed no more than ten or twelve people, we think. They lived even better than the king. It was almost certainly the seat of an important Druid, we think. The broch did not have its own defenses. It's only a mile from the castle, so it would have been the king's job to defend the broch."

"Did the height of the broch mean that its occupants had higher status?" asked Aderyn.

"Almost certainly so," said Judith. "A stone tower implied the highest status of all."

"And so the village fed them all?" asked Aderyn.

"That's right," said Judith. "Most of the people lived in the village. In 48 B.C., there probably would have been four hundred or five hundred people there. It's a fascinating site, with sophisticated manufacturing – things such as medical implements. They also did sophisticated glass work. It's clear that they made and bottled medicines. They exported their medicines and medical devices as far as Marseilles. The farms and fields lie inland from the village. In 48 B.C., this would have been an urbane and well-connected place, even though it was so far north. It was urbane, at least, by Celtic standards, because the Celts were a pastoral people. This location is probably a compromise between the safety of Scottish remoteness and the accessibility of Gaul and points south by sea. Henry, do you have any comments about why we chose this location?"

"I believe we've talked about all this before," said Henry. "We want you to be safe from the turmoil in Gaul. But we also want you to have access to elites who are aware of what is happening to the south and who have the power and resources to help you. You need time to adjust to the language, time to orient yourselves, time to build trust, time to refine your plan. You need help. You need the knowledge of elites. You need military backing. You have to find a ship. We can't just set you down in a simple fishing village. Nor can we drop you into all the unknowns and uproar of Gaul without giving you time to prepare."

"All hard work," said Judith. "I just hope these people like us."

"My guess," said Henry, "is that you'll be surprised how well you're received after they get over their initial shock and come to understand your mission."

"Flowers in the streets?" said Judith.

Henry always ignored Judith's taunting.

"Remember," said Henry, "that the ambassador will be keeping an eye on you from above."

"Drone strikes?" said Judith.

Henry didn't flinch. He was like Phaedrus in that he seemed to welcome a little sass, because it meant that people felt free to express what they were thinking.

"We talked about most of these things before," Henry said, "before you actually saw this place. But as I've previously mentioned, the ambassador's abilities to intercede will be limited. But I think his advice will be invaluable. You can be sure that the consortium chose him very carefully for this mission and that his qualifications are, shall we say, superb, on a galactic scale. Your confidence in him, I think, will not be misplaced."

For a while there was only the sound of wind, sea, and gull as they all reflected on this. There would be real danger. Henry's eyes met Jake's. Jake's eyes met Phaedrus' eyes. Mark, a farm boy who had never before been far from home, looked starstruck. Harris and McGlennon looked a little more modest than usual. Judith and Aderyn, as always, looked very, very smart.

"Judith," said Henry, "do you have anything to add here before we walk over to the broch?"

"I think we're done here," said Judith, "unless there are any other questions."

There were no questions, so they started walking through the turf toward the broch. There was a hint of a path about thirty feet inland from a ledge on the seaward side. Beyond the ledge was a steep drop toward a rocky, narrow beach a hundred feet below. Mark and Henry had the subtlety and kindness to know that Jake would want every possible minute alone to talk with Phaedrus, but Judith did not know that. Judith slowed her pace to come alongside Phaedrus and Jake. She asked Phaedrus a question about Oxford in the 1970s. Jake listened politely for a moment, then caught up with Mark.

"So, Mark," said Jake. "You say Brigid has learned another ditty?"

"It's the cutest thing," said Mark. "Phaedrus and me – I mean, Phaedrus and I – taught it to her. She gets the notes mostly right, but she sings it her own way most of the time. It's just the first two lines so far, but that's a start."

"Not Puccini?" said Jake.

"Yes! Puccini! We debated whether to go with 'O mio babbino caro' or 'Vissi d'arte.' Phaedrus said I should choose, and so 'O mio babbino caro' was an easy decision. It seemed more appropriate, you know, for a kitten that wasn't yet old enough to know much about art."

Mark and Jake hummed the first two lines together of "O mio babbino caro."

"Have you learned the words?" asked Jake.

"*O mio babbino caro, mi piace, è bello bello,*" sang Mark.

"Very good!" said Jake. "Do you know what the song means?"

"Ha!" said Mark. "Phaedrus translated it for me. It's a silly song, really, to sound so – you know – serious. That's one reason I liked it. It means, 'Oh Papa, Papa, feel sorry for me. He's so handsome and I love him so much. If he doesn't love me back I'll go to the river and throw myself in.' Can't you just imagine a kitten singing that, even though she sings just the tune and not the words?"

McGlennon overheard all this and shot them a sneering look. Mark looked puzzled. Jake ignored it.

"There you have it," said Jake. "The dread of unrequited love, the worst thing that can happen to a human being."

"I never thought of it that way," said Mark. "Maybe it's not so funny after all."

"Why so serious all of a sudden?" asked Jake.

"He really misses you, you know," said Mark. "He tries to hide it, but I can tell. I don't know how to talk to him the way you do. Y'all know so much, and I don't."

"But you're learning, and you're learning fast," said Jake. "Can you imagine having a better teacher than Phaedrus?"

"It's a whole lot better than going to school," said Mark, "except there are no friends around. But that's OK. We've got a cat now. I wish you weren't leaving, though."

"When I get back, you'll practically be a Ph.D.," said Jake. "What about the sheriff's great-nephew," said Jake. "Aren't you and he about the same age?"

"Yeah, but you know. Girls," said Mark.

"I know," said Jake. "I know. But you have to look after Phaedrus and cheer him up as much as you can."

They arrived at the broch. It was a round, ruined wall of stones, eight feet thick in places. Some of the wall was hollow, and remnants of stairs and small chambers could be seen inside the wall. They entered through a section of the wall that had collapsed almost completely. They stepped into a grassy inner courtyard. The acoustics changed dramatically. The sound of the sea below them, crashing on rocks, was diminished. But the wall that partly surrounded them seemed to catch and amplify the sound of the gulls. The wind whistled around the stones.

As Judith described the broch, Jake's mind kept returning to McGlennon's sneer. Jake wondered if Phaedrus had noticed McGlennon's attitude. Jake wondered why he felt vaguely embarrassed, something akin to shame, as though he was a schoolboy secretly being bullied at school, and now his parents or a sibling had found out about it. Since they've noticed, thought Jake, we should talk about it tonight. Besides, he thought, I could use Phaedrus' advice on how to handle it. It's stupid to hide being bullied, thought Jake. I'm not fourteen anymore.

Henry was talking now, introducing Phaedrus rather formally. Clearly Henry had asked Phaedrus to speak.

"I'm told," said Phaedrus, facing the little knot of people and raising his voice slightly to be heard over the wind and gulls, "that Henry's assistant will be here soon with sandwiches and tea. So I'll be brief. But Henry has asked me to say a few words on the subject of the ancient Celts. Why do we think they're so important that we should go to all this trouble? Why is the galactic union helping us?

"Now, we've all been polite and haven't mentioned it, but how many of you have noticed that rotting smell coming up from the beach?"

Everyone nodded.

"That's a seaweed that people call green sea-fingers," said Phaedrus. "It accumulates on beaches. It rots. It stinks. It's an invasive species. It's a native of the Pacific. It has been dragged around the world, snagged on the hulls of ships. It displaces native seaweed species. It smothers mussels and scallops. It fouls fishing boats, fishing nets, and jetties. It first showed up along the Devon coast in 1939. Now it can be found all the way to Argyll. It doesn't belong here.

"But I'm not a biologist. It is history and culture that interest me, so no doubt you've already guessed that I'm setting up a metaphor, and that I'm about to compare green sea-fingers, an invasive species, with something else. People have been living on these islands for thousands of years, all the way back to the Stone Age. We know remarkably little about them until the Bronze age. Then, in the Iron Age – the age of classical Greece and Rome – we know a good bit more. Obviously those people had a culture. All people do. Their culture was a living thing. Their culture evolved as it did because it was compatible with the way they lived, with the way they thought. It was compatible with the way they dreamed, with the way they loved, with the way they died. They were a pastoral people. Their lives depended on their animals. They raised their flocks on these hills. They grew a few crops. They fished in these seas. They were rich enough to produce quite a lot of art in gold, silver, and copper. They were superb weavers of wool. They loved music. Their philosophy is thought to have had much in common with Pythagoreanism. They had many gods – major gods, minor gods, male gods, female gods. They studied the stars. Their women were empowered. Their laws provided for the care of the poor and sick. They probably believed in reincarnation. They had an educated class of trained leaders, the Druids. Many of the Druids could read and write in Latin and Greek, but their own Celtic history and learning was strictly oral, never to be written down. Soon you will know quite a lot about these people, far more than I know, because you're going to meet some of them. For now we know far too little, because the written record that has come down to us from Greek and Roman historians is both scant and prejudiced. We've learned a bit more from archeology. But my intent for the moment is not so much to describe the culture and religion of the Celts. Rather, I want to point out that their culture and religion evolved here, over thousands of years, on this land, from the forests in the headwaters of the Danube to these remote northern islands, where these people were eventually driven by the Romans.

"The imperial Romans, of course, had their own imperial religion, Christianity. I use the word 'imperial' not just to insult the religion of Rome, though I admit that I do that often enough. Rather, my point is that Christianity was well suited to being put to use as an imperial religion. It originated, of course, in the Middle East, among a desert people who were very different from the Celts. Those desert people had one god, a male god, a sky god, invisible. They were a heavily oppressed people, few in numbers, nomadic, always threatened with oblivion. They were fierce in their struggle to survive, and they needed a fierce religion. If the Celts or the Druids ever tried to convert anyone to their religion, history did not record it. On the contrary, the Celts felt honored when they encountered new gods. They respected the new gods and added them to their pantheon. Finding new gods was like finding gold. But the religion of those desert people was a jealous and proselytizing religion. Other gods were immensely threatening to their god and ought to be destroyed. For reasons that are largely mysterious – though historians and theologians have debated it for centuries – Christianity exploded out of the tiny desert region in which it originated. Even Rome fought it at first, then embraced it. This new religion had all the markers of an invasive species and of an imperial religion. You all know the attributes of an invasive species. They are capable of rapid reproduction. Where their seeds fall, they grow fast. They disperse easily. They are flexible and can easily alter to suit new conditions. They can tolerate a wide range of environmental conditions. They are able to live off a wide range of food types. When they invade, they outcompete and destroy native species. They disrupt ecological systems. They cause collapse.

"Our collapse has occurred. Only about seven percent of us remain. Here in Western Europe, and in much of the Americas where Western Europeans migrated, our culture is so shattered, so diminished, that we are forced to rebuild it.

"Like the Romans, we have choices. We've already made a choice, actually. We've decided to rebuild with a native species rather than an invasive species. We will rebuild with the native religion of all those peoples who lived on this land for thousands of years. It suits the wiring of our psyches. Its remnants – Yule, Halloween, fairy tales – still enchant us because it is in our cultural DNA. But that DNA has mostly been lost – partly to time, and partly to deliberate genocide. Your mission is to recover that DNA, to bring it back to us. We will cultivate it and propagate it. We will adjust it as needed. If we are successful, then an old culture – a culture that suits us far better – will live again.

"It's up to you to bring us the seeds, the DNA, that have been lost. That is your mission. I envy you. I count the days until you return. But now I believe our sandwiches have arrived."

Jake looked at Mark. Mark was looking at Phaedrus, admiration in his eyes, as though he had never seen Phaedrus before. Judith stepped forward to shake Phaedrus' hand. Henry looked pensive. Slowly everyone started to file toward the golf cart that had arrived with sandwiches and tea. Jake fell in beside Mark again with the intention of silently waiting, in Phaedrus' Socratic manner, to see what Mark would say. But McGlennon said something to Aderyn in a voice just loud enough to carry:

"I don't know which one of them is his boyfriend," McGlennon said, "the teenager or the old man."

Mark lunged. He had his arm around McGlennon's throat in an instant.

"We're a family, you fucking bastard! We're a family! Every fucking bit as good as yours!"

McGlennon flung Mark sideways. Henry and Phaedrus got to Mark and were holding him back. Mark was in a rage, crying now. Harris grabbed McGlennon by the shoulders and turned him away. Just before Jake's anger had a chance to explode, Henry's arm was on his shoulder, then Aderyn's, gently pulling Jake toward Phaedrus and Mark. Then there was only the ostinato of the waves, the chorus of the gulls, and the continuo of the wind.

CHAPTER 4

The enormous space cruiser was in orbit two lunar distances above earth. As Jake approached it, alone in his gnat, he struggled to judge the size of the space ship, looking out through the transparent dome of the gnat. Then he glimpsed the two gnats that were ahead of him, carrying the other four members of the team. The gnats were tiny specks against the cruiser. The cruiser was as least as long as four football fields. It was cylindrical, with an external skeletal structure. It clearly was made of two independent halves, like an elongated hourglass. It was rotating around its middle, slowly twirling like a baton to create on-board gravity while it was in the free fall of earth orbit. Jake, securely strapped into his couch, quickly figured out how the docking was going to happen. He was afraid that he'd need the barf bag after all. Jake's gnat approached the middle of the hourglass and began rotating until the gnat's rotation matched the rotation of the space ship. Then the gnat slipped into a slot in the exact middle of the cylinder. Then Jake felt as though he was in an elevator. The gnat slowly descended, and as it descended Jake felt gravity returning. The gnat stopped. Its doors opened. Jake unfastened the straps and followed a line of blinking green lights on the floor. The lights led him to a lavishly furnished anteroom. The other members of the team were waiting for him there. They all looked a little seasick, tired, and nervous.

The lights dimmed, and a hologram lit up at the front of the room. The hologram showed a female member of the clearly mammalian species that Phaedrus had called the squirrel people. The hologram, no doubt, had been beamed to earth orbit from somewhere many light years away. Judging from the vastness and splendor of the empty room behind her in the hologram, this person was the equivalent of royalty. The room looked much like a gothic cathedral – immense height, a vaulted ceiling, tall columns, and colored glass. But there were trees – large ones – inside the room. Blooming vines wound up the columns. Jake thought he occasionally saw bright-colored birds flitting from tree to tree. Her fur was white, her eyes were black. Her robes were extravagantly draped. The robes were emerald-colored. She was tall, not exactly lean, and impossibly elegant. The postures of royalty, thought Jake, must surely be universal.

The squirrel queen never mentioned any title as far

as Jake could tell. Her name was sibilant and not pronounceable by a human. Speaking precise English, she welcomed the expedition on board the ambassadorial cruiser and said that the ambassador would not trouble them until they had rested. She congratulated them on being selected for the mission and emphasized the mission's importance to earth. She spoke briefly about the galactic union, of which earth soon would be a part. She made some comments about what a beautiful planet earth is, by all accounts one of the most beautiful planets in the galaxy and a planet that she hoped to visit someday. She wished them success on their mission and promised to speak to them again after the mission's completion. She ended the recording with something like a curtsy.

When the hologram blinked out, the five were left standing in dim light in the anteroom, a formal chamber paneled with dark wood and richly furnished with heavy furniture suitable for a palace. Then five little androids, each about three feet tall, filed silently into the room. The androids wore livery. Four were identically dressed, but the one in front wore a green sash. The android with the sash spoke with a male voice.

"Welcome, friends," he said. "We are at your service. With your permission we will show you to your quarters."

"Mrs. Roberts," said one of the four, "if you would be so kind as to follow me."

"Miss Collins?" said another.

"Mr. Harris?" said another.

"Mr. McGlennon?" said another.

"Mr. Janaway?" said the android with the sash.

Jake got puzzled looks from the others. Jake was as surprised as they were that the junior member of the expedition would get the attention of the android with the sash. No doubt, thought Jake, that's just some nicety of their protocol – honor in humility. After all, the queen had curtsied.

They each followed their android into a plush, curving corridor which seemed to be gradually spiraling downward. One by one the androids peeled off through side doors. Jake was last. They approached a heavy wooden door, which silently slid open. The android stood aside, waiting for Jake to enter. Then the android followed Jake into the room. The room was large, with the same royal decor that they had seen everywhere else on this ship. The room could have been lifted out of a 17th Century German castle – a curtained bed, tables, chairs, and another doorway that Jake was quite sure led to a bathroom. There was nothing alien about it. The bed looked magnificent, and inviting. It was now about midnight in Scotland. Jake was exhausted.

"There is a note for you from the ambassador on the writing table," said the android. "Do you have any questions, Mr. Janaway, or is there anything further that I can do for you at present? I'm sure you must be very tired."

"I don't think I need anything," said Jake. "Oh yes. How would I get a message to the others?"

"You'll find pen and paper on the writing table," said the android. "Pull one of the blue cords and I will retrieve your note and deliver it for you. If you have questions, pull the cord and speak. I never sleep, and I am at your service."

"Thank you," said Jake.

The android dipped in a charming way reminiscent of a bow. Then it turned and glided toward the door, which slid open as the android approached and then closed silently behind it.

Jake realized now that it was a kindness for the ambassador to postpone the formal greeting until they had rested. Everyone was spent – emotionally and physically – and needed to go to the bathroom. Jake took a turn around the room and its adjoining bathroom, intimidated by the poshness, half afraid to touch anything for fear of getting it dirty. Then he sat down by the writing table and opened the note from the ambassador. The note was in a gray envelope. The note paper was the same gray. It was handwritten in blue ink. It was a formal welcome and an invitation to breakfast. It was signed "Bendigeid Vran."

Harris and Judith had said that they'd take two days off to adjust to the space cruiser before classes and physical training would resume. Jake was looking forward to the time off. He felt desperate for some time alone to recharge. But now he'd have to see the whole crew at breakfast and stay on his toes for meeting the ambassador. Judith was a climber. She'd be all over the ambassador. Harris and McGlennon would alternate between a certain quiet reserve and an inappropriate tendency to let their authoritarianism show. Aderyn was kind and likeable, but she was succumbing to McGlennon's moves – she had already succumbed, for all Jake knew. McGlennon had probably already gotten his android to sneak him to her room in the Victorian manner – nocturnal traffic in the hall.

Books, thought Jake. It's going to take a vast library full of books to get me through this trip. Tomorrow after breakfast, Jake thought, I'll ask the android to show me the library, or whatever the system is for reading aboard this ship. There will of course be something for entertainment as well as for information. They're obviously prepared for us, and they know a lot about us. I wouldn't be surprised, thought Jake, if Henry knows the title of every book I ever bought on line, or every book I ever checked out of a library. And now the ambassador would know that, too. They're discreet, but they're extremely thorough. You'd have to be thorough, to reach this level of galactic power. Imagine it, being all alone on an enormous, priceless, long-haul cruiser like this, on a mission to try to save a beautiful but dumb-ass planet down on its luck. And for the thousandth time, what are you, Jake, a nobody, doing here? A nobody so underqualified that they assign me an android with a sash to salve my humiliation. But I'll make nice drawings for them. And I can treat the natives like human beings rather than field specimens or threats to our safety. What a team. No wonder we earthlings blew ourselves up. The ambassador will probably call the whole thing off after he actually meets us. What is this, Jake? Search your feelings. It's shame. That's what it is – shame. Shame for the planet you come from, shame for the state it's gotten itself into, shame for the pathetic crew who are supposed to find a cure for their pathetic planet, and shame because your even being here is some kind of mistake. You're a hayseed tracking mud into a royal palace.

Jake had one book in his backpack, a fantasy novel. You're deranged, Jake, he said to himself. You must be one of the first human beings to ever actually escape from earth, but you need to escape from the escape with fantasy. You should have brought porn novels, loser. Do they even publish those anymore? But where would I hide them? Under the mattress? I'd be embarrassed even for the android to find them. Stop it, Jake. Think about something else, Jake. He kicked off his shoes and stretched out on the bed to read himself to sleep, but after three pages he fell asleep with the book on his chest.

Jake wondered if the android was taking a roundabout route to wherever they were going, just to give Jake a tour of the ship. There seemed to be miles of wide, spiraling, richly paneled corridors with heavy wooden doors, always closed. They were moving upward in the spiral. Occasionally they would pass what appeared to be a small sitting room, with tables, a few chairs, mirrors, and fresh flowers. Fresh flowers! The flowers appeared to be real, and some of them were familiar – roses and carnations. There was never the slightest sign of any electronics, not so much as a thermostat on a wall or a light switch, unlike Jake's room, which did at least have a few buttons for the lighting. How was this ship controlled, anyway? The android was still wearing its sash today. When it had first come into his room a few hours ago to bid him good morning (how did it know he was awake?), it had been fitted with an arm and a small tray that held a glass of orange juice. The juice had tasted real. Now the arm and the tray were gone, and the android floated down the corridor ahead of Jake unencumbered. Occasionally they would pass other androids, some of which were carrying what appeared to be little work satchels. Jake checked his watch. It was almost noon. This morning he had returned to his room after a tense and rather formal breakfast at which Judith had done most of the talking, as expected. An hour after breakfast, just as Jake was about to venture out of his room to explore, the android had brought Jake a hand-written note from the ambassador inviting Jake to join him at noon. Fifteen minutes before noon, the android had come to retrieve Jake.

"Are you magnetically levitated?" asked Jake. Two androids pushing a cart stood aside to let them pass.

"That's right," said the android.

"Are there a lot of you?"

"Quite a few," said the android. "It's a large ship."

"How many models?" asked Jake.

"There are two basic models," said the android. "There are those like me, who take care of interior work. And there is another type – much more hardened, as you might imagine – for exterior maintenance and haz-ardous work."

"Do you have a name?" asked Jake.

"I have only a serial number," said the android. "But it is not uncommon, when we are assigned to personal service, to be given a name."

"Are you assigned to my personal service?"

"I am."

"What would you like to be called?"

"Normally that would be your choice, Sir," said the android.

"I would prefer that you not call me 'Sir,'" said Jake. "It makes me feel old, and – I don't know – imperious is the word, I guess. Would it be possible for you to choose your own name?"

"I don't see why not," said the android. "How should I address you, then? As Jake?"

"That would be fine," said Jake. "Now, how about you pick a name."

The android paused for some seconds. Jake suspected that that the pause was artificial, to produce the effect of thoughtfulness. Surely the android had enormous computing power and enormous stores of information at its disposal, because clearly it was in constant communication with the control systems of the ship.

"How about 'Sam'?" said the android.

"How did you know that?" said Jake.

"How did I know what, Jake?"

"How did you know the name of the dog I had when I was a boy?"

Again Sam paused.

"It's in your files," said Sam.

"I don't mean to seem nosy," said Jake, "but who am I actually speaking with right now? Am I speaking with Sam, an individual android, or am I speaking with some centralized control system that knows pretty much everything there is to know?"

"Some of both," said Sam. "We androids do individuate within our own memory stores – within certain parameters. That individuation is in keeping with the roles and responsibilities we are assigned. But ultimately we are subject to the centralized control of this ship, which itself is subject to control from the ship's base, which is subject to control from … You get the idea. It's hierarchical. But information can be exchanged very fast, except when it's limited by the speed of light."

"All the way up to the queen?" asked Jake.

"I am not permitted to directly address queries or reports above a certain level," said Sam.

"Can you look things up for me, retrieve information for me?" asked Jake.

"Of course."

"Are there restraints on what information I'd be allowed to access?"

"If there are, Jake, I would not be aware of them."

"Well, then. Let's see. What was my final grade for math the first year I went to public school?"

There was no pause this time. "That was a B, Jake, and it was the seventh grade."

"Who was the first girl I ever kissed?"

"That is not in the record, Jake. Though there are

strong suggestions in your school records that you became sexually active around the age of fifteen."

"Who was the first boy I ever kissed?"

"The evaluations in your records suggest that you have never kissed a boy."

"I see," said Jake. "At least I have some secrets."

"If I ask you to forget something, can you do that?"

"Within certain limitations that are beyond my control, and which have to do with your safety and the success of the mission, yes," said Sam. "I am permitted to comply with your wishes except when protocols take precedence. I cannot, however, forget any information that was added to your files before you came on board this ship. There are two categories that you may request – confidential, and forget completely."

"I like the confidential category," said Jake. "We can be friends. Tell me something about yourself that embarrasses you."

"Once I instructed the ship's kitchen," said Sam without pausing, "to add a smeganara worm, which is a delicacy on a planet in the Rigel system, to the breakfast omelette of a military officer from a planet near Fomalhaut. It was payback for the hours I spent scraping his posterior folds for him. You will never mention this, I hope?"

"Keeping your secret will be a point of honor," said Jake.

Jake heard the sound of birds chirping. The corridor had entered a kind of gallery, and they were facing an elaborate decorative screen of a shiny metal. The screen slid open, and Jake followed Sam onto a high catwalk across an enormous cylindrical atrium with an even higher ceiling. It was like a jungle, with green things, blooming things, and birds.

"Wow," said Jake. "This ship is huge. This place is amazing. May I come here on my own?"

"Of course," said Sam, "though you may need my helping finding it at first."

"Is food grown in here?"

"No," said Sam. "Food is grown in an area which is optimized for efficiency. This area is optimized for aesthetics."

"These look like earth species," said Jake. "Are they?"

"They are indeed."

"But I don't understand," said Jake. "How did they get here? Surely this ship doesn't always transport, you know, earthlings."

"The ship," said Sam, "is highly configurable for its mission and its expected passengers. At present the ship is configured in what you could call earth mode, since it's on an earth mission. There are other modes."

"I see," said Jake. "And how did all this get here?"

"They all are descendents of specimens that were gathered on earth long ago," said Sam.

Just then a brightly colored bird, a parrot, flew down from high above and alighted on the rail of the catwalk. The bird studied Jake.

"*Feasgar math!*" said the bird. "*Feasgar math!*"

"*Feasgar math*, Kildydd," said Sam.

"Jake," said Sam, "this is Kildydd, a friend of the ambassador's. I think Kildydd likes you because you look a bit like the ambassador."

"Hello, Kildydd," said Jake.

"*Haló*," said Kildydd.

Another parrot called from below, and Kildydd hopped into the air and glided downward.

"I can't wait to come back and explore this place," said Jake. He could see fountains below, and artificial streams running in wide troughs. He wondered how they managed the shift from 1G acceleration gravity to the twirling of free-fall orbital gravity without spilling the water. Then Jake realized that he had not felt the transition, though they were surely under way now.

"How far are we from earth now?" asked Jake.

"Just under five million miles," said Sam.

"Our rate of acceleration," said Jake, "must of course be the acceleration that produces 1G of gravity. Could you remind me what that is?"

"Nine point eight one meters per second per second," said Sam.

"And our present velocity?" asked Jake.

"A bit above one million kilometers per hour," said Sam.

"Wow," said Jake. "That's fast. But it would be a tiny fraction of what our maximum velocity will be at our halfway point. There's something I can't figure out, though. When we reach the halfway point and start to decelerate, how can we avoid a moment of zero-gravity? I'm sure that whoever designed this ship was too smart to spill any of that water down there."

"At just the right moment," said Sam, "the ship will rotate through a half spin, as though it were orbiting in free fall. That will point our engines toward our destination for the deceleration thrust. When you saw the ship from space, perhaps you noticed that the ship is divided into halves. Each half is supported by an external superstructure. Each half is capable of rotation independently of the other. The gravity maneuvers involve having the entire ship rotate around its middle while the two halves rotate as necessary to maintain the direction of gravity. These two axes of rotation can be controlled to maintain gravity on the same vector. Of course, when the ship is rotating to produce gravitation centrifugally, not all levels of the ship are at precisely 1G gravity, because they are not the same distance from the axis. However, the inhabited parts of the ship, and the parts that are gravity-sensitive, are concentrated at levels that hold gravity between point eight and one point two."

"Brilliant," said Jake. "I think I understood that. The pharmaceutical must be kicking in."

Jake followed Sam along the catwalk. Periodically they passed long flights of stairs leading down to the water level. At times Jake could reach out and touch the branches of treetops. Small birds casually watched them pass. They came to another decorative screen that led to another gallery. A brown rabbit that had tagged after them for a while turned back onto the catwalk.

"The rabbits like to exercise on the stairs," said Sam. "They chase each other up and then down again."

The screen opened, and Jake and Sam entered another paneled corridor.

"We're almost there," said Sam. Now as they continued up the corridor, the lights gradually grew dimmer. The corridor ended at a wide wooden door. The door opened into what appeared to be a small, dark room. Sam led Jake into the room. A kind of handlebar was fixed to the floor.

"I would suggest that you grasp the bar," Sam said. Jake grasped it.

The floor slowly rose. It was an elevator with no sides.

When the elevator stopped, Jake's first reaction was vertigo and panic, but after a second his brain was able to interpret what he was seeing. He felt stable floor under him again. He was in a large round room with no walls and no ceiling. The floor was covered with a soft, black carpet. Over his head was a black sky filled with a galaxy of brilliant stars. The room was extravagantly large and perfectly circular, the full diameter of the ship itself. The ceiling was so transparent that no glass and no barrier against the vastness of space could be perceived. It was as though they were standing on a plush, black-carpeted disk in the middle of the universe. At the center of the room were two large, deeply upholstered chairs. In the starlit darkness beside one of the chairs, a tall figure wearing an ankle-length mantle rose from the chair and stood facing Jake, silhouetted against the stars. It was, of course, the ambassador.

Jake walked toward the caped figure, aware that his

heart was pounding while his body strained to convince itself that he was not in danger.

"Hello, Jake," said the ambassador. "I had almost forgotten how disorienting this room can be at first. Please. Sit. Look up. You'll soon feel grounded again."

Jake sat, still too in awe to even say "thank you." Out of habit and compulsion, he surveyed the stars. It took a few moments, given the perspective and the many fainter stars that he had never seen before, to orient himself against the constellations.

"Where is your home?" asked Jake.

The ambassador pointed toward Ursa Major, which lay about halfway between the horizon and the apex of the ceiling directly over Jake's head.

"I came from there," said the ambassador.

"Ah," said Jake. "Ursa Major. But that's not the direction we're headed, is it?"

"No," said the ambassador. "Our trajectory lies straight above us, toward the nearest jump station."

"The shock and awe just keep coming," said Jake. "But I think I'm already starting to get used to it. I never imagined anything like this. I mean, in our movies, this is not what space ships are like. They're cold-looking and made of metal, like an aircraft carrier. They're cramped. There are blinky lights everywhere. They make a rumbling sound. But then, this is an ambassadorial cruiser, isn't it? Maybe you don't even have military vessels. I hope you don't."

"This is an old ship, and it has been on many different missions, with many different configurations. Right now it is on a mission to earth, and it is configured for the comfort of people from earth. Space travel is never truly comfortable. But creature comforts and plenty of onboard space help make it bearable. As for military vessels, we do have some, but it has been a long time since they were used."

"Does this ship totally fly itself?" asked Jake.

"It does," said the ambassador. "Even in the early stages of space-travel technology – as on earth, for example – the need for automation becomes apparent. The androids, of course, handle all the maintenance. As for blinky lights and controls, there really aren't many other than some display walls that provide information and surveillance images to the passengers as needed. Under almost all normal circumstances, the ship is controlled by talking to it."

"Amazing," said Jake. "Would the ship take orders from me?"

"Under some limited ordinary circumstances and in many hundreds of improbable contingencies, it certainly would take orders from you. Its overriding priorities, of course, are the safety of the passengers and attaining its destinations. The ship will consult its passengers as appropriate. The ship also can initiate autonomous actions as necessary to achieve its priorities. It will explain its actions later. All of its autonomous functions are managed here within the vessel, but of course it is in constant communication with its base, and the exchange of information with its base is constant."

"What about water and consumables for the passengers?" asked Jake. "Is everything supplied and stored, or recycled?"

"Some of both," said the ambassador. "But mostly everything is recycled. Most of the food is grown here on the ship."

"Was that real bacon at breakfast? I was afraid to ask."

"On earth you might have called it cultured bacon," said the ambassador. "It's made in automated labs here on the ship. I don't think your conscience needs to bother you for eating it. And speaking of breakfast, you were very quiet at breakfast, Jake. I know it must be challenging to adjust to all this. If there's anything I can do to help, any questions you might have, just let me know."

"I'm nothing but questions," said Jake. "Questions are eating me alive. As for my being quiet at breakfast – well, Judith. Need I say more? I also should say – though I don't exactly know how to say it – that you're a galactic ambassador. I'm – you know – just Jake, the bottom rung of this expedition. I don't know what the protocols are. I might as well be at Buckingham Palace right now. No, wait. It's even more confusing than that, because Buckingham Palace is on earth, and you can read up on it in books before you go there, if you're ever lucky enough to get invited. But there's no way to prepare yourself for this. Is there still royalty in Britain, by the way?"

"Royalty in Britain are alive and well," said the ambassador. They are very flexible and too feeble to be a problem. I hope you'll soon feel at home here. Now, please ask me another question. And please call me

Bendigeid. Your rank is just the same as mine, Jake, and I'm not that much older than you."

"My rank is the same as yours?"

"Of course," said Bendigeid, "because you were chosen for this mission."

"Why do you look so much like us?" asked Jake.

"Why do you think?" said Bendigeid.

Jake laughed. Bendigeid responded with a slight tilt of the head and a quizzical smile.

"Do you always answer questions with questions?" said Jake.

"Like Phaedrus?" said Bendigeid. "No, not always. But why do you think we look alike?"

"How do you know that about Phaedrus?"

"I believe you too just answered a question with a question," said Bendigeid, laughing. "First question first, though. Why do you think you and I look alike?"

"Because the galactic union has somehow been involved with earth's evolution? You know, borrowed a few genes here and inserted a few genes there?"

"Close enough," said Bendigeid. "My genetics are more like yours than you might think."

"Are we really worth saving?" said Jake. "I mean, you heard us at breakfast, quibbling with each other, tossing little barbs at each other, even in the presence of a galactic ambassador. And look at what we did to our planet."

"You're all competitive," said Bendigeid. "Most species are competitive. Even social species compete for resources. There's no need to be ashamed of that. But, however, fouling the planet and almost blowing it up, that's a bit more serious. It's true that the galactic union takes a dim view of that sort of thing. I've watched your movies, you know. I love your movies. So, your planet is a bit like a child – please don't take that personally – who knocks a vase full of water and flowers off a table. And the grandmother says, 'Now look what you've done! Get back in here and clean that up!' *You* didn't break the planet, though, Jake. It wasn't you, or even your generation, that broke it. But it has fallen to you to clean it up. And my situation, as strange as it may sound to you, is not all that different from yours. It's as though the grandmothers of the galactic union said to me, 'Look at what your genetic kin have done to their planet. Now get in there with them and go clean it up.' And so here I am."

Jake laughed. "You're actually being held partly responsible?" Jake said.

"I am," said Bendigeid, "Not for the calamities, but for the cleaning up. I'm not one of the grandmothers, you know. Far from it. They themselves are not going to spend three years aboard one of these things. I'm here because I have a particular interest in earth and its history. If you're just Jake, then I'm just Bendigeid. And after this is over, the grandmothers want their car back – this space ship, I mean. I'm no one special back where I came from. I'm just a student of humanity with connections to the wrong people, just like you. After we do this job, we can move on to whatever comes next."

"There was a second question," said Jake. "How do you know so much about Phaedrus?"

"The file on Phaedrus goes back for thirty-five years," said Bendigeid. "The grandmothers foresaw what was going to happen on earth. So did Phaedrus. Earth's fate was inevitable after a certain point. The grandmothers can do a lot of monitoring just from small orbiting probes, eavesdropping on earth's communications and relaying it back. But that's not nearly enough intelligence when the stage of inevitable calamity is reached. The protocols involve contacts with a team of smart and well-connected citizens of the delinquent planet. Phaedrus was one of those, obviously. As for you, your record too goes back farther than you might think. I know how strange it must seem – we've been snooping on you. But it all comes down to trusting the grandmothers and their protocols. They're stern, but they're experienced. The prognosis for earth is very, very good."

"Well, that's good to hear," said Jake, "though I don't understand most of this. It's like the sheriff says back home. It's above my pay grade."

Jake lowered his eyes from the stars and noticed, in the dim light, a small gray shape against the black carpet. Green eyes were looking up at him out of the small gray shape. Jake gasped.

"You guessed correctly," said Bendigeid. "Meet Brigid's mother."

A somewhat smaller gray shape came slowly across the carpet and merged into the larger gray shape. Now four eyes were looking up at Jake, one pair of eyes smaller than the other.

"And Brigid's sister," said Bendigeid.

There was a kittenish, musical trill, and suddenly Jake thought that he might not be sleeping alone after all.

— ▪ —

Jake later admitted that he was the one who started it. It was a hand-to-hand combat class, taught and refereed by Harris. McGlennon had taken his shirt off, so Jake did, too, making the point that he felt nothing to be ashamed of, even if Aderyn and Judith whispered comparisons. The pharmaceuticals had given Jake's body an almost magical feeling of quickness, strength, and invincibility. Jake and McGlennon circled, waiting for a vulnerability. McGlennon taunted Jake, as usual, as McGlennon danced away from Jake's quick leg work.

"You're too slow, faggot," said McGlennon. "Watch my eyes, not my crotch."

Jake kicked him sideways in the ass, hard, as a properly timed insult rather than as an appropriately timed offensive move.

McGlennon caught Jake's foot. Jake was off-balance as he jerked his foot free, and McGlennon caught Jake's left arm. McGlennon pulled Jake's arm with the strength of a madman. Jake rolled over McGlennon's shoulder and landed hard, flat on his back at McGlennon's feet. McGlennon stepped on Jake's stomach as he pivoted to stay on his feet. Jake's fall had knocked half the air out of his lungs, and the foot in his stomach finished the job. Jake tried to pull up his knees and roll sideways to draw breath, but all he managed was a pathetic squirm as the pain in his arm and shoulder shot into his brain. He panicked as though he was suffocating but finally managed to suck a little air into his lungs.

An android outfitted for emergency medical response emerged from a side door before Jake had managed to exhale.

"Everybody back," said Harris. "The droid knows how to handle this."

"Please don't move, Mr. Janaway," said the android. It had four arms. One arm checked Jake's vital signs and gave him an injection. Two other android arms scanned Jake's left shoulder all the way down to the fingertips.

"Mr. Janaway, your shoulder is moderately torqued, and your wrist is broken," said the android. "We're taking you to the surgery now." The android gave Jake another injection, and Jake blacked out.

By the time a team of androids appeared with a stretcher, the four-armed medical android had immobilized Jake's wrist with some quick-set foam. The four humans stood back, unneeded, and soon the androids had Jake on the stretcher and were floating down the corridor with him. Sam followed like a loyal dog.

When Jake awoke, he was in his room. The ambassador and Sam were with him.

"Ugh," said Jake. "I remember now." He looked down at the cast on his lower arm.

"Did you do this?" said Jake to the ambassador, nodding toward the cast.

"The androids did it," said Bendigeid, "though I was there to learn what I could from watching them. I have some medical training, but the androids and the surgery robots are much better than I am. How do you feel?"

"Like a fool," said Jake. "Why does he hate me?"

"Andrew has a crush on you, Jake," said Bendigeid. "He barely realizes it himself, but he suffers because his feelings aren't returned."

"Why do you think that?" said Jake.

"Watch, with that idea in mind," said Bendigeid. "You'll see."

"I guess he's not my type," said Jake. "I like my guys sweet and vulnerable, with longer and messier hair."

"Bad boys aren't for everyone," said Bendigeid. "Can I get you anything? Do you need to go to the bathroom? They've been pumping you full of fluids."

Soon Jake was settled in bed again after a trip to the bathroom, propped against a mound of pillows. Sam had brought in two cups of tea and a plate stacked with little sandwiches. Bendigeid sat on one side of a small table that Sam had placed near Jake's bed.

"Dang. Why am I so hungry?" said Jake.

"Sam, do you know why Jake is so hungry?" asked Bendigeid.

"Pharmaceuticals," said Sam. "Jake needs protein after several hours on glucose."

"I was the bad boy this time," said Jake. "For an instant I lost it and fought dirty. Did the pharmaceuticals have anything to do with that?"

"I watched the video," said Bendigeid. "I don't think the pharmaceuticals induced your anger. I think the anger was already there. But your anger is understandable. He taunts you. He wants to dominate you, but you won't let him. You wouldn't engage him in a way he understands. You frustrate him with your coolness, and he can't compete with that. But finally you made the mistake of engaging him in the way he wanted, and your wrist got broken. I'm sure you won't make that mistake again. But the pharmaceuticals may have tricked you into being a little overconfident. That's part of what the training is for, I'm sure – to help you get the measure of yourself. Harris knows what he's doing. But Harris also feels guilty. He thinks he let you two get out of hand."

"I'll speak to Harris," said Jake. "It was all my fault. I guess I owe Andrew an apology. Is he gloating? Or feeling remorse?"

"He crossed the line, too," said Bendigeid. "He meant to hurt you. Harris had a little talk with him and implanted some remorse. But an apology from you would be a good thing. Andrew says you started it, and you seem to be conceding that point. Do you still feel angry?"

"No," said Jake. "I just feel like a fool."

"I expect this will be the end of it," said Bendigeid. "It was your coolness that he wanted to break, not your wrist. And now that he's succeeded in breaking your coolness, he'll probably be nicer to you. He's cracked your armor and got you down to a level he finds less threatening. He's a military type, after all. I'm sure you understand. You needn't hold it against him. But may I offer you some advice, if you want to get along with Andrew?"

"Yes, please," said Jake.

"Andrew will submit to the superiority of your intellect

and the superiority of your coolness, if you will submit to the superiority of his masculinity," said Bendigeid.

"Ouch," said Jake. "Can't we think of a better way to phrase that?"

"Andrew has worked very hard on his masculinity," said Bendigeid. "He felt compelled, in his milieu – which was very different from yours – to purge any taint in his masculinity. That's hard work, you know – perfecting a swagger and being careful where your pinky is when you hold a cup. You're lucky. You never had to do that. Freeze! Don't move. Now look at your pinky on your teacup. It's perfectly masculine, curved inward. You never had to think about it. Your masculine style of androgyny is perfectly natural to you, whereas Andrew had to cultivate his swagger and stand watch over his pinky finger. Andrew is attracted to your androgyny, Jake. He's finding that he likes, in you, what he worked to kill in himself. He could learn from you not to fight it, to embrace the flaws in his masculinity as natural and beautiful."

"How in the world could I teach him such a thing?" asked Jake.

"Just be ever so slightly submissive to his masculinity," said Bendigeid. "Dim your lights. Lower your eyes. Think of Princess Diana. Think of the way she always kept her eyes low and modest, even though she was a princess, even though she probably was the most admired person in the world. You're a prince, Jake, though you don't yet know it. Andrew admires you. Surely you've noticed that he's picked up some words and gestures from you? He's even let his hair grow a little longer."

Jake laughed.

"Not long enough," said Jake. "I like a little curl, enough to flutter when the wind blows. Enough for a bee to get tangled up in."

"And flirt with him," said Bendigeid. "That's what he wants. Acknowledge that his masculinity is powerful and sexy."

"Damn it," said Jake. "That almost makes sense. I refuse to go out with him, though. He's not my type."

"He's not a prince like you," said Bendigeid. "He's only a soldier, and a good one. You don't need to go out with him. Just honor his terms. In return, he'll protect you with his life, because he admires you, and because it's his duty. As soon as the cast comes off, challenge him to a fight. Let him beat you. After he's pinned you, yield. Submit. Let him feel your muscles go slack. Open yourself to him. Make yourself vulnerable. Then note how he'll hold onto you for half a second too long. In that half a second, he'll communicate to you his willingness to fight for the love of you. Let him do that, Jake. Give him what he deserves. Give him what he's earned. Compensate him for what he's promised to you. You can't hold anything back from a man who is willing to risk his life for you. This is one of the things that a prince must learn, Jake. Your role as a prince isn't always so intimate, but in this case it is. Sometimes men fight when what they really want is each other's love."

A chime sounded somewhere in Bendigeid's tunic, indicating an important incoming message. Bendigeid excused himself and stepped into Jake's sitting room to take the message. But Jake was savvy enough now to know that Sam had rung the chime to give Jake a moment of privacy while Jake absorbed the wave of shame and filed it away for processing later. After a minute, Bendigeid returned to his seat on the other side of the little bedside table.

"OK," said Jake. "I'll do it. He'd beat me anyway in a fair fight. How long am I laid up for?"

"Five weeks or so," said Bendigeid. "No fighting for a while, but the medical system will give you a new physical regimen. You'll recover good as new. You'll have more time to concentrate on your language skills. I hear that your language progress is remarkable."

"Who says? Sam? Aderyn?"

"Both," said Bendigeid.

"Well, that's one area, at least, in which I can get the best of Andrew," said Jake. "This medical system on the ship, it can treat most anything?"

"Pretty much," said Bendigeid, "and for multiple species. It even kept watch when the kittens were born."

"Where is little Scena?"

"She's spending a little time with her mother," said Bendigeid. "I'm sure she'll be back soon."

"These sandwiches are good," said Jake. "I was starving. Speaking of starving, most of the time I feel like my brain is starving, too. I know it's the language pharmaceuticals, of course. In a way I wish I could keep taking that stuff forever, make it permanent."

"Much of the neurological change is permanent," said Bendigeid. "You'll probably remember the language you've learned as though you had learned it as a child."

"But the other stuff you gave me – you know, the nighttime stuff. There's nothing permanent about that, is there?"

"No," said Bendigeid. Its effects wear off in a little less than eight hours, before you wake up."

"That's a good thing," said Jake, "because if I woke up in the morning feeling like that, I'd be an even greater danger to myself and others. Even Sam wouldn't be safe from rape if I could shut his cameras off."

"Have you been feeling guilty?" asked Bendigeid. "Some people would not be able to handle the dissonance between the sexual effects of the medication and their belief systems."

"I don't think I feel guilty," said Jake. "Not now, anyway. If I were still sixteen or seventeen, it would freak me out. But I guess I've learned not to be much afraid of my, you know, fantasies, even if I've lived a vanilla life."

"Remember Saint Augustine? He begged God for the grace to 'quench the fires of sensuality' that he felt in his dreams. He was afraid that he would be held morally responsible by God for what he did in his dreams."

"I guess I'm no saint," said Jake. "In fact I look forward to going to sleep now, and if anything I'd beg that God will have the grace to make tonight even more wicked than the night before."

Bendigeid laughed.

"How does that stuff work?" asked Jake.

"For one, it keeps you asleep and pretty much immobilizes the body," said Bendigeid, "for obvious reasons.

It enhances your consciousness while you're asleep, a kind of lucid dreaming. The enhanced consciousness pretty much ensures that you remember most of it in the morning. It all but removes your inhibitions, to a far greater degree than alcohol. And it's a powerful sexual stimulant."

"And it's prescribed only during space travel?" asked Jake. "People would pay big bucks for that on earth. I would myself, if I had any bucks."

"It's occasionally used for therapeutic purposes," said Bendigeid. "But it was developed to make space travel more bearable. It was discovered early on that, if basic physical needs could be satisfied during sleep, then people could be more productive and less distracted during waking hours."

"I guess the only guilt I feel," said Jake, "is that I don't want the others to know. Sam, you keep quiet, OK?"

"Yes, Jake," said Sam.

"They won't know," said Bendigeid.

"Good," said Jake. "At least it proves that my kicking Andrew in the ass wasn't because I'm secretly hot for him, since I'm not really hot for anybody during the daytime. Why are we all so secretive about our sex lives? I don't think I'm a prude, but I still don't want people to know."

"Monkeys seek privacy and seclusion to have sex," said Bendigeid. "Even dogs do, when they can, though dogs aren't quite as particular as we hominids."

"Yet human cultures are different," said Jake. "Some are a lot more prudish than others."

"In human cultures, people always know in general what others are doing, because they're doing the same things themselves. But people still want privacy, no matter how unprudish they may be."

"Do you miss your family?" asked Jake.

"Very much," said Bendigeid.

"What are they like?" asked Jake.

"My wife is a musician," said Bendigeid. "One of my daughters takes after her mother in her musical aptitude. My other daughter is more drawn toward cultural work. She wants to be an ambassador to earth like her father."

"I keep wondering about your rank," said Jake. "You're an ambassador, and you have all this responsibility for executing these complicated protocols on earth. You have this incredible ship at your disposal. And yet you're modest about your rank and say that you're just a regular guy. How can that be?"

"Why don't you ask me that question again after the expedition is over, when we're on our way back to the 21st Century."

"All right," said Jake. "I will."

There was a low chiming sound from somewhere inside Bendigeid's tunic.

"Excuse me for a moment," said Bendigeid. He touched his ear.

"The ship says that some messages have arrived from our home base," said Bendigeid. "That would be our final communication before we jump. I'll have to go in a moment."

"It's incredible," said Jake. "In two days we'll actually

be in 48 B.C., even if we've got six more months of traveling to do. Bendigeid, can we not tell Phaedrus about my little accident? He'd just worry. And besides, by the time he gets the message three weeks from now, I'll be almost healed."

"I agree there's no need to tell him," said Bendigeid. "And besides, it's your choice. When you send your final pre-jump communication back to earth, by all means keep it upbeat. No doubt they'll do the same, when we receive their final transmission tomorrow."

"Good. When we get back to the 21st Century, Sam can show him the video for all I care. We'll be able to laugh about it then. But for now I don't want Phaedrus to worry."

Bendigeid stood to leave the room. He was, as usual, wearing a gray tunic with a high collar, belted at the waist, with dark trousers or leggings. He wore a simple ring, which appeared to be of white gold, on his left hand. His hair was black with touches of premature gray at his temples. His eyes were almost the same gray as his tunic. He was not wearing a mantle now. The mantle seemed to be reserved for more formal occasions. He always wore the mantle on the star deck. Jake couldn't help thinking that Bendigeid looked like a prince, or a king. Often during the past few months, Jake had discreetly studied Bendigeid's posture, so regal and confident, yet so casual. Aderyn often commented on Bendigeid's accent. His English was perfect, but Aderyn said that there were elements of his cadence and diction that she could not place. To an American like Jake, though, Bendigeid just sounded royal. Sometimes during language tutoring Aderyn would imitate Bendigeid for Jake's amusement. Jake was learning to detect the subtle elements in Bendigeid's speech that Aderyn could imitate but not identify. And – funny how those speech-enhancing pharmaceuticals worked – sometimes Jake even heard bits of Bendigeid's speech patterns creeping into his own English. But I'd settle just for that confident posture, thought Jake. I want to understand how he pulls that off.

"Is there anything I can get for you," said Sam, after Bendigeid had gone out. "More tea?"

"No tea," said Jake. "What time is it? That late? I was out longer than I thought. Do you know where my kitten is? And, Sam, would you bring me one of those, you know, pills?"

"Of course," said Sam. "Scena is walking this way and will be here soon. She tarried a bit in the atrium."

"Sam, do you record everything? Do I ever talk in my sleep?"

"Sometimes you talk in your sleep, Jake".

"Can you not record my sleep-talking, Sam, and erase anything you've previously recorded?"

"Done," said Sam.

"And, Sam, I don't know who does the laundry, but my underwear and sheets are nobody's business, either."

"I understand, Jake."

— ◆ —

They all came to the star deck for the jump. It was

rare for the others to come here. Judith and Harris, Aderyn and McGlennon – couples now who spent most of their spare time in their quarters – had come to think of the star deck as Jake's and Bendigeid's private space, a place for the two uncoupled men to just look at the stars and talk about whatever they talked about.

Judith was still sniffling from reading the last pre-jump message from her daughter. Aderyn had been trying to comfort her. Harris and McGlennon stood in a military posture, all steel, watching the black orb above them that they were approaching with terrifying speed. The ship wasn't going to hit the orb, exactly. It was going to pass through a tunnel straight through the moon-sized jump station's axis. Somehow the gravity of the dense alloys of the rapidly rotating jump station, combined with the tuned electromagnetic effects of a helix that wound around the tunnel, combined with the ship's velocity, would create an effect that Bendigeid compared with cracking a whip. Just for an instant at the center of the jump station, an aperture would open leading to 48 B.C., and the ship would pass through it. When the ship emerged on the other side of the jump station, it would be in 48 B.C. at the same point in space, billions of miles from earth.

Jake had managed to stop sniffling and wash and dry his face before he left his room. Telegrams from his parents in Costa Rica were always bland and routine. For security reasons, they weren't allowed to even know where Jake really was. They assumed he was at Phaedrus' place. Jake's last video from Phaedrus and

Mark had shown them in winter clothes walking up to the pasture to proudly show Jake the new mule. Brigid tagged behind, complaining musically, not liking the wet grass. Phaedrus and Mark took turns holding the camera. Phaedrus was doing his best to hide it, but he looked sad and a little weak. He was recovering from the flu. Mark was trying to be funny, but that was harder without Jake there as his foil. The news was all minor. A flu had been going around, but no one had been seriously ill. The sheriff had sent the mule, which had belonged to a family that couldn't afford to feed it and whose barn was in bad shape. Phaedrus' gravity-fed water system had frozen a couple of times during an unusually cold winter, and Mark had to go crack ice from the spring or carry water to the house in buckets from the well. The sheriff had somehow laid his hands on an excellent supply of soybean seed for the spring. Brigid, with some cuddling and encouragement from Mark, sang a new ditty that they both had taught her. Jake would watch the video again after the jump and sniffle some more, but for now the looming black orb was completely distracting. And thanks to the design of the ship and the star deck, their direction of travel always seemed to be straight up.

Bendigeid was wearing his mantle. He spoke occasionally to Sam, who seemed to be relaying information back and forth from the ship's primary intelligence. Brigid's mother, Irnan, sat on her haunches at Bendigeid's feet, ignoring the collision scene developing above their heads. Scena was asleep somewhere.

The other four androids were waiting silently near the lift.

The blackness of the jump station filled more and more of the space deck's dome. Judith shuddered. Aderyn stood behind Judith, hands on Judith's shoulders. Harris and McGlennon laughed, but it was a slightly nervous laugh. Jake realized that he was completely trusting of alien technology. Did he have any choice?

Sam counted down, making no attempt to be theatrical: "Ten, nine, eight, seven, six, five, four, three, two, one."

Everything went black. For a few seconds, it was like passing through the tunnel under the English channel on the way to Paris. Then suddenly the dome was full of stars again.

"Affirmative," said Sam.

"We are now in 48 B.C.," said Bendigeid. "Sam, would you and the androids like to bring in our little luncheon now?"

The androids descended on the lift.

"Funny," said McGlennon. "Nothing feels any different."

"I didn't feel anything happen, either," said Judith. "How do we know we're in 48 B.C.?"

"The ship's observatory," said Bendigeid, "has already measured slight differences in the location of certain stars. It has confirmed that we are in 48 B.C. Not that confirmation is really necessary, because I have never heard of a jump being less than accurate within an acceptable tolerance."

"Amazing," said Jake, thinking of Phaedrus and Mark. They weren't really there anymore, in a sense. They had not been born.

"I mean," Jake continued, "we haven't been born, and yet here we are. How can there not be a paradox in that?"

"Think of it this way," said Bendigeid. "Even at earth's level of technology, small displacements of time because of differences in gravitation and velocity were well known. Einstein predicted those displacements as a matter of theory before the displacements were ever actually measured. If nature permits small displacements, it follows that nature permits large displacements. It's all a matter of technology."

"I'm just a historian," said Judith. "I don't understand all that. But I do understand champagne. I brought champagne."

Her sweater was on a chair, and tucked inside her sweater was a bottle of champagne. Harris, McGlennon, and Aderyn cheered.

"No glasses until the androids get back with lunch," said Judith. "Shall we just pass the bottle? Who knows how to open it?"

Harris took the bottle, popped the cork, and handed the bottle to McGlennon.

"McGlennon first?" said Harris. "He's always the thirstiest."

They all laughed, because they all knew that McGlennon already had been drinking today.

Suddenly Sam appeared on the lift with some luncheon things. Sam shouted in a booming voice that they didn't know he was capable of.

"Stop!" Sam said. "Don't drink that! It's not in the inventory!"

McGlennon's intoxicated reflexes were slow. The bottle was already almost to his mouth. Something flew from one of Sam's arms and struck the bottle hard. The bottle flew, spinning and spewing foam in a spiral. It landed on the carpet and spun, still spewing foam. Irnan fled with a howl and wasn't seen for a while.

"What the fuck?" said McGlennon.

"Sam," said Bendigeid, "Do you have a test kit?"

"It's on the way," said Sam.

Soon an android arrived with some glassware and a small instrument. Right behind the android with the test kit was a gaggle of hardened cleanup androids bristling with gear.

"It's chiefly botulin," said Sam, "with an array of some other faster-acting components."

"Jesus," said McGlennon.

"Judith," said Harris, "where did you get that?"

"A friend gave it to me just before we left," she said. "It was a kind of historian's little joke, to celebrate being in 48 B.C. Or so I thought."

"Just when we have no communication with earth," said Harris. "At least, well, you know what I mean – earth in our time."

"Sam, what does the ship say?" asked Bendigeid.

"The bottle wasn't detected because it was with Judith's personal items," said Sam. "We must, of course, search everyone's personal items. But otherwise there is no evidence of further security risks."

"That was another crude, low-budget attempt to get us," said Harris.

"Boy will Henry be pissed when he hears about it two thousand years from now," said Jake. And he thought, Damn it. Three nights of unwashed underwear for Sam to snoop through looking for bombs.

"Sam," said Harris. "What was that you threw?"

"A potato, sir," said Sam.

CHAPTER 5

They rode down out of earth orbit in the black triangle rather than the gnats. Bendigeid rode with them. Jake had known from the miles of corridors and the two atriums that the cruiser was huge, but he was surprised to learn that it carried a black triangle – no small ship itself – in its belly. They had discussed the plan for landing in great detail. All of them knew the plan thoroughly, along with a dozen contingency plans. It was April, almost a month earlier than intended. It was an unusually large error in the jump station's precision, but Bendigeid had explained that it was within the expected tolerances and was nothing to worry about.

The black triangle descended through the cloud layer, revealing a Julie Andrews landscape of snow-capped mountains and lush Alpine meadows. Wild goats scampered over rocky hillocks, but there were no signs of human settlement here. They descended into the lushest of the meadows. The ship never actually touched the earth. Rather, it hovered silently just above treetop level, though there were no trees here. There was only green meadow and acre after acre of wildflowers. A narrow stair telescoped from the bottom of the black triangle into the meadow. Harris went first, followed by Judith, Jake, Bendigeid, Aderyn, and then McGlennon. All of them carried empty baskets. It had been a year since they had last set foot on the earth. None of them could stop laughing. Bendigeid, too, seemed relieved. They were in the Alps to pick flowers.

Aderyn went twirling into a dense patch of wildflowers.

"*The hills are alive!…*" she sang.

"*With the sound of music,*" responded Jake.

They finished the song together, as a duet. Jake improvised on the harmony. They both knew all the words. They had discovered their mutual love for sappy songs on board the star ship and had sung together often. Aderyn, after all, was Welsh, with the Welsh love of music.

"What a beautiful voice you have, Jake," said Judith. "I never get tired of hearing you and Aderyn sing. Do you know the words to every song there ever was?"

"Only the sappy ones," said Jake. "I had a friend once who made me listen to lots of sappy songs, over and over. I shouldn't use harsh words like 'sappy.' Some of them are pretty good songs, actually. They grew on me."

"Did you sing with her?" asked Judith.

"The friend was a he," said Jake. "And, yes, we sang together."

Judith gave Jake another funny smile. Jake thought she must be theorizing about why Aderyn had chosen to partner with the unambiguously straight McGlennon. Let her theorize. As for McGlennon, he pretended not to hear, apparently having learned some things from his exposure to the grandeur of the universe versus the smallness of human social conventions. McGlennon had stopped needling Jake after the incident with the broken wrist. After the past few months in space, they were even starting to get along, with McGlennon taking credit for the modest improvements in Jake's martial skills.

"Here I am," said Harris, "an officer in the special forces, gathering flowers into a basket like Julie Andrews."

"I'm applying for conscientious objector status," said McGlennon. "Can't the droids do it?"

"Pick flowers and shut up, McGlennon," said Harris. "That's an order."

Jake longed to linger, to wander off and explore the hills in solitude. But soon they were back on the ship with their baskets full. Jake consoled himself with the knowledge that they'd be back on the ground soon enough, though there might not be as much solitude.

Then they began the aerial tour that Judith, as a historian, had been so much looking forward to. Bendigeid kept their altitude low, a few thousand feet above terrain. Bendigeid said that, in the greater scheme of things, it mattered very little who might see them. Their course was an arc to the north and west. It would take them over the headwaters of the Danube, over the Low Countries, then over the Channel to Britain. As they left the Alps behind and glided over what is now Germany, they saw mostly dense forest. But along rivers and in valleys suitable for farming, there were green pastures and small Iron Age villages. The buildings were made of wood. The roofs were thatch. Smoke rose from crude chimneys and outdoor fires. Jake had never seen Judith, usually so dour, so happy.

"Are we filming this?" asked Judith.

"Yes," said Bendigeid. "But of course all our image capture must be done from the ship, according to the protocols."

"I know," said Judith. "No advanced technology on the surface that the people couldn't understand. But it's a shame."

"Jake can make as many sketches as he likes," said Bendigeid.

"I'll keep him busy," said Judith.

"Now, now," said Aderyn. "We'll share him. Jake has turned out to be a gifted linguist. His Greek is better than mine. He remembered a shocking amount of Latin, too, on that long trip. As for Celtic, he'll cram as quickly as any of us after we get down there."

"Jake has an extraordinary memory," said Bendigeid.

"Nah. Just pharmaceuticals," said Jake.

"Don't be so modest," said Aderyn. "I've heard you recite long excerpts from Homer that you learned fifteen years ago."

"Not to mention all those lyrics," said Jake. "I'm going

to miss those pharmaceuticals when they wear off."

"You can take a small packet of pharmaceuticals with you," said Bendigeid, "if you keep it out of sight."

"I'll hide it in my underwear," said Jake. "No one will find it there." Jake glanced at Sam. Sam made no response.

There was a large settlement along the Channel near what is now Brussels. Ships were packed in its harbor. There were buildings strung together in no particular order, with narrow, crooked streets. The Channel was calm and blue. There were boats with crude sails, some of brown linen and others of animal skins. The black triangle glided over the swampy land of southeastern Britain, toward London. There were plank roads through the swamps linking little villages. Some of the buildings were on stilts above the water. They came to the Thames and its vast estuaries. London was by far the largest settlement they had seen. There were many boats on the river. Buildings, some large, pressed up against the river on both sides. Roads led in many directions. They flew over one of these roads toward the northwest. It led through forested hills and shallow valleys of lush pasture. The ship gained altitude as it approached the mountains of Wales.

"It's so apparent from up here," said Judith, "why Wales was always such a refuge whenever there was turmoil in England – which was often. If it were not for mountains and the Irish sea, the British Celts would have been wiped out or assimilated completely, the way they were in Gaul."

"There are theories in linguistics," said Aderyn, "that the Celts in England did assimilate into the Anglo-Saxon invaders. The case for that is based not so much on words that English picked up from Celtic languages, because there aren't a great many Celtic words in English. Rather, the case is based on grammar. Some of the Germanic grammar of the Anglo-Saxons was displaced by grammatical habits that are distinctly Celtic. Still, the Welsh mountains were a barrier. It's always in the mountains that languages and dialects persist the longest. Anyone who wants to study dying languages had better develop her mountaineering skills."

They passed over the island of Anglesey, largely obscured by clouds, then out into the Irish sea. Bendigeid asked the ship to climb, to bring the green terrain of Ireland and northern England back into view. Bendigeid wanted them to have a feel for the geography of the Irish sea, since their plan called for them to find a ship to take them southward by sea to Brittany. They descended for a better view as they passed over the Isle of Man. Soon they saw the Scottish headlands materializing through the clouds, rocky and green, edged with the white of surf against rock. Dusk was an hour away. They had spent the day watching the terrain roll beneath them, as though they were drifting in a fast balloon. At times Bendigeid had even opened a window so that they could feel the air. They had not yet seen the Mediterranean. That would come tomorrow. They would use the last hour of daylight over Scotland to make their presence known to the population of the village they had chosen.

They followed the Scottish coastline. Then the ship began to slowly descend.

They were just inland from the broch. The tower was tall and stately, a living thing, far different from the rocky ruin in which Phaedrus had talked to them about the purpose of their mission. Smoke rose from the broch's chimneys. To the north was the castle, with not a stone fallen and with low wooden structures all around it. To the east, the village backed up against the hill, and on the other side of the hill lay rich pasture. The ship descended to about four times the treetop level, though there were few trees so near the coast, and silently hovered.

They watched as a crowd gathered near the village, half a mile to the east. A dozen people on horseback came from the castle and joined the crowd. A few figures stood near the broch. All eyes were looking upward, pointing and gesturing.

Androids opened hatches on the bottom of the ship and started dropping flowers. The crowd swirled and drew back, then drew closer again as the shower of flowers ended. A horseman rode out, keeping a watchful eye above as he rode. He dismounted from his horse, gathered up some of the fallen flowers, and rode back to the crowd.

Now the black triangle dipped to one side, then to the other side, a gesture of salutation. Underneath the ship, bright beams of light lit up the evening mist. The beams swept back and forth across the green ground, crossing each other like searchlights at a Hollywood premiere.

Then the lights winked out, and the black triangle rose into the clouds.

"Wow," said Harris. "That must have impressed them."

"They'll have something to stay up all night talking about, that's for sure," said Judith.

"I wonder what they're saying," said Aderyn.

"They have to know that we mean no harm," said Jake. "Those were some nice flowers."

"There will be alpine flowers in every house tonight," said Aderyn.

"And in every castle and broch," said Jake.

"They seemed unafraid and receptive," said Bendigeid. "That went well. Now has everyone agreed on where you want to go tonight?"

"Yes," said Harris. "We want to see the lights of Rome at night."

"And we want to watch the sun rise on the Mediterranean," said Aderyn.

"And we think there would be time for a quick spin over Alexandria and Athens," said Judith, "with time to spare to fly over Gibraltar and then be back here tomorrow at dusk."

"So it shall be," said Bendigeid.

◆ ◆

They flew over Gaul on a path toward Rome. All of Gaul was veiled by mist and darkness. Near midnight, as the moon was setting, Bendigeid said that they would soon be flying directly over Rome.

"How low can we fly?" asked Harris.

"As low as you like," said Bendigeid. "Few will see us. We'll be only a shadow against the stars. And those who do see us won't be believed."

"I want to see the coliseum," said McGlennon.

"I'm afraid the coliseum won't be built for another hundred years," said Judith.

"Ouch," said McGlennon. "Pardon my history."

"I'm afraid we won't see much at midnight," said Judith. "That's a shame. But I'm certain that Bendigeid wouldn't want us to be seen in daylight, because that might get into the history books."

All along the surface, the small yellow lights of primitive lighting and outdoor fires appeared and thickened as they neared the center of the city.

"Bendigeid," said Judith, "would it be possible to open some windows?"

"Are you sure?" asked Bendigeid.

"Yes," said Judith. "I'm going to guess that of the five human senses, our noses will provide the best observations tonight."

Cool and humid air poured through the windows.

"Oh my God," said Aderyn.

"Jesus," said McGlennon. "It smells like horse shit in a frying pan, with undertones of garlic and burning trash and a Dumpster rotting behind a grocery store."

"I think I caught a whiff of incense," said Jake.

"And piss," said Harris.

"Shh," said Judith. "Listen."

There was the sound of iron-rimmed wagon wheels,

heavily loaded, rolling over cobblestones. Men shouted. There was the sound of a woman's laughter. There was a sound like wagon filled with pots dumping its load, pots shattering.

"The streets are so congested," said Judith, "that they run the wagons at night, like the freight trains in England."

A high hill, with the windows of many low dwellings brightly lit, came into view. The street sounds subsided. The music of a stringed instrument and a flute drifted up into the sky.

"The rich people live on the hills," said Judith.

There was the sound of a drunken man raising his voice.

"Did you catch the Latin?" Judith asked Aderyn. "It sounded like a curse or an insult."

"I think he said, 'Caius wouldn't know a friend from a climber unless Caesar kissed him on the ass,'" said Aderyn. "They all seem to be too drunk to notice us."

"That's not quite what I heard," said Jake. "It sounded more like, 'Gaius is just a climber who kisses Caesar's ass.' That could be Gaius Asinius Pollio, who was a friend of Caesar's. Pollio helped talk Caesar into crossing the Rubicon."

"How do you know all this?" asked Judith. "You're putting a linguist and a historian to shame."

"Reading, I guess," said Jake. "It was the pharmaceuticals. I couldn't stop reading. It's easy to increase your Latin vocabulary with Sam hanging out in your room. You never have to pick up a dictionary. Just ask Sam."

"What will you read on the way home, I wonder?" asked Aderyn.

"I don't know," said Jake. "Are there pharmaceuticals for writing?"

"Sam?" asked Bendigeid.

"Perhaps something could be concocted," said Sam.

"It's a shame," said Judith. "Stench or not, what wouldn't I give to spend even an hour down there. I begged Bendigeid to let us do that, you know."

"I'm so sorry," said Bendigeid. "I can bend the protocols only so far. With the Romans, there would be too great a risk of straying over the threshold of deniability and getting onto the historical record. When a few provincials see this ship and tell the story, no one will believe it. But with Rome it would be different. Cicero is down there somewhere, you know. They have the equivalent of newspapers."

"I like that you have such a good feel for how far to bend the protocols," said Judith. "Because whoever you report to is certainly going to know where you flew this ship."

"The ship wouldn't fly over Rome in daylight even if I asked it to," said Bendigeid. "The ship knows the protocols even better than I do."

"It's a funny thing," said Jake. "It would seem that the protocols are not exactly black and white, that there is room for judgment. I like that. But I wonder how they turn that into software that a ship can understand."

"I can't really explain it," said Bendigeid. "Machines are not my specialty. But, many times, I have seen these ships act conservatively and then wait for a decision to be returned from base. In every case, I have found that protocol decisions that come from base are more lenient than decisions that the ship can make on its own. There are safeguards built into the protocols."

"And the ship is too smart to knick the top of that obelisk coming up, right?" said Harris.

"Sam?" said Bendigeid.

"We cleared it by just over half a meter," said Sam.

—◆—

The next evening, back in Scotland, they reduced their altitude by half and dropped pieces of silver. The crowd, after understanding what was being dropped, came to gather the silver and stood fearlessly under the ship, looking up. Some of them waved, laughing.

"I think the plan has worked," said Bendigeid. "Now they will be ready to meet you the day after tomorrow."

The ship rose and sped west to cross the North Atlantic. At Jake's request, the ship would crisscross North America during the night, using low light and radar imaging to make a record of the continent's natural state. The information would be used later as part of a plan for environmental rehabilitation. They watched the sun rise over the Grand Canyon, marveled at the grassy beauty of the Great Plains, and looked down almost in disbelief at the endless canopy of the eastern forests. They had lunch hovering over Niagara Falls. The wild beauty of Hudson Bay made Jake long to return there. They even saw some green on the western side of Greenland.

As the ship crossed the North Atlantic heading back toward Scotland, while the others went to take a nap (their euphemism for afternoon sexual activity), Bendigeid asked Jake why he was so pensive.

"I can hardly believe that today I saw North America as nature made it," said Jake. "I'm wondering if we can really make it look like that again. I wonder how long it will take."

"When you say 'we,'" asked Bendigeid, "whom do you mean?"

"I don't know," said Jake. "Those of us who survived, I guess."

"Maybe that's what you meant," said Bendigeid, "but I think you are thinking like a leader. And I think you are making a plan."

"But it would take so much," said Jake.

"Talk to the grandmothers," said Bendigeid. "They are very rich, and they are fond of the earth. The whole galaxy will soon see what we saw today. What do you think they would want you to do? The rehabilitation of fallen worlds and the ironies of religion are some of the most popular entertainments in the galaxy. Everyone knows earth, because cats came from earth. Did I neglect to mention that cats are the most popular pet in the galaxy?"

"But how did cats learn to sing?" asked Jake.

"Ah," said Bendigeid. "That story begins a long, long time ago."

— ◄

At dusk, the black triangle hovered harmlessly over the sea a mile out from the shore beyond the broch and castle. The landing was to be in the morning an hour after sunrise. Everyone had packed and had checked and rechecked their gear. By now, there had been enough time down below for the settlement's leaders to decide that, if the ship intended harm, it already would have acted. The locals would keep watch on the ship all night, of course, with yellow light the color of candlelight glowing from the black triangle's windows. But the watchers would report that there was no aggressive action, just a home-like yellow glow. Morning came, clear and windy.

In meeting after meeting during the past few months, they all had agreed on the plan. There was little that needed to be said now. Once again, Jake dreaded a parting. A year ago, it had been Phaedrus whom he had dreaded to leave. Now it was Bendigeid, whose friendship had kept Jake's chin up on the year-long ride out from earth.

One by one, Bendigeid shook their hands, wished them luck, and handed each of them what they now called the magic pendants. The pendants contained a small piece of E.T. technology, a kind of panic button, tracking device, and emergency communications device. Back at Oxford, a historian of jewelry had mounted the devices on metal chains and made them look like pendants. Worn around their necks and under their clothing, the pendants would be inconspicuous among the jewelry-loving Celts. The pendants were the last resort if something went badly wrong. Still, no gnat would be able to get to them quickly from high orbit, so they would be on their own to look after themselves, with Harris and McGlennon responsible for everyone's safety.

They would go down with no weapons. That would help convince the village and its leaders that they meant no harm. Then, after they were trusted, they would buy knives and swords with their stock of silver. They wore garments that had been designed to imitate what contemporary residents of Marseilles might wear. They wanted to look as though they were earthly travelers, but not extraterrestrials.

The black triangle glided slowly off the sea toward the promontory and hovered over the grass, midway between the castle and the broch. The narrow stairs telescoped down and came to rest on the grass. Bendigeid stood at the top of the stairs and waved to the crowd gathering below. Harris went down first, then Judith, Aderyn, Jake, and McGlennon. A delegation was already on its way to meet them – four men on horses, followed by a small cart pulled by a pony.

The riders drew up and dismounted. All were richly dressed. The garments of two of the men marked them as soldiers and royalty. The other two men wore robes and probably were Druids. None of the men bore weapons. The cart carried an old woman in a long linen gown, also probably a Druid. The youngest of the men helped the old woman climb down from the cart, and the five of them walked somewhat ceremoniously toward the travelers without any sign of fear. As Jake stood waiting for someone to speak, he thought, "They can see that we're neither Druids nor royalty, no matter what we rode in on. But at least they sent Druids and royalty to meet us."

The man whom Jake had marked as the king spoke first. Jake's language circuits, enhanced as they were by the pharmaceuticals and the year of training and practice, could not make sense of it.

Aderyn spoke briefly in 20th Century Gaelic. It was a formal greeting, a suitable thing for a traveler to say to a host. Their five hosts looked at each other and spoke quietly to each other, but clearly they had not understood.

"Jake," said Aderyn, "Try Greek."

"What do I say?" said Jake.

"We planned for this," said Aderyn. "Just ask politely if they speak Greek."

Jake greeted them in Greek as politely as he could manage and asked if they spoke Greek. The eyes of the three Druids lit up. The old woman stepped forward.

"Indeed we do speak Greek," said the old woman. "And we welcome you. Where are you from? Did you come from the stars?"

"No, not from the stars," said Jake. "We came from earth, from earth's future."

The Druid woman translated this for the two non-Druids, whom Jake had marked as a king and his son, while Jake translated for his companions. The old woman spoke again.

"Then you have come to warn us," she said. "You have come to warn us about what will happen. This was prophesied."

Jake waited for a gust of wind off the sea to pass before he spoke. It was as though the wind blew away his doubt. They were going to understand. The old Druid woman exuded serenity and strength.

"Yes," said Jake. "We came to warn you about what is going to happen. We also came to learn from you, because much may be lost."

After the next round of translations, the king spoke, and the Druid woman translated for him.

"Then you are doubly welcome. How many are you?"

"Only we five," said Jake. "Our ship will wait for us far above the earth, as far away as the moon. If you are willing, we would like to remain here for a season or two."

"We have many questions," said the king, "as no doubt do you. Please share our table and refresh yourselves, and we will talk. This is Gwenlliant, our provost."

The old woman made a low bow that must have hurt her back, but she did not flinch.

"This is Lodan, our prelate, and Bergan, his novice."

The older and the younger Druids bowed.

"This is Lairgnen, my son."

The prince nodded.

"And I am Jowan, protector of this desmesne."

Jake introduced everyone, starting with Judith. He

couldn't think of any titles, so he introduced them only by name. All bowed.

"I shall send for horses," said the king, turning to give a signal to a knot of troops who were keeping their distance.

"Thank you," said Jake. "We won't need horses. We have been riding for a long time and would prefer to walk."

"As you wish," said the king.

Jake turned to his companions.

"I think we're to follow them now to breakfast, at the castle, I assume," said Jake.

"Does everything look OK to you?" Harris asked McGlennon.

"They seem friendly enough," said McGlennon.

"Then here we go," said Harris.

Harris gave a pre-arranged signal to Bendigeid, who was waiting at the top of the stairs. Bendigeid gave a wave and a salute. They all waved goodbye. The stairs retracted, the hatch closed, and the ship rose slowly, with its dipping wave before it disappeared into a cloud.

The prince helped the old woman back into her cart. The men led their horses, and they all walked together toward the castle.

Lodan, the older Druid, walked with Jake.

"Only you speak Greek?" Lodan asked.

"Aderyn also speaks Greek," said Jake.

"And the others?"

"Our native language is English, a language that — it's strange to say this — doesn't yet exist. We all have been learning a descendant of your language that survived until our time."

"How long is that?" asked Lodan.

"About two thousand years," said Jake.

"This danger that you have come to warn us about. It already has started, has it not?"

"Yes," said Jake.

"In Gaul?"

"Yes," said Jake.

"The Romans mean to destroy us?"

"Yes," said Jake.

"This has been foreseen," said Lodan.

"Prophesy?"

"Yes, and also no," Lodan said. "The stars have their uses, though no doubt you know more about the stars than I. Yes, it has been prophesied by those who consult the stars. But it also has been foreseen by those who study people here below, and events here below. But this is much in dispute. There are those who say that our future is with Rome, that Roman ways will bring a better life. But there also are those who say that Rome will crush us, and that our people and our way of life will end."

"And how do you see it?" asked Jake.

"I see Rome as a predator that will devour everything in its path," said Lodan.

"I'm afraid that it will get even worse," said Jake.

"Why is that?" asked Lodan.

"Because you have not yet met Rome's new religion," said Jake. "Rome's armies will cut you down. Rome will take your land and your taxes. Rome will sell you wine and oil. But Rome's religion will destroy not only your way of life, but also your memories of it."

Lodan quoted from the prophecy:

"It will burn the forests and make sheep of the people. It will foul the rivers and the sea. It will drive the gods out of the earth and make them into ghosts. It will have only one god – a hard god of hard words and no joy who lives in the sky. It will make wretches of the people and promise them recompense in the sky. The earth will become a corpse before the people discover that there is nothing in the sky but the stars and other earths."

"Yes," said Jake. "That pretty much covers it."

"This has been prophesied from the stars," said Lodan. "But it has not all been foreseen by those who study the ways of Rome. Because, as you say, we have not yet met Rome's religion. I have much to learn from you."

"And I from you," said Jake.

➤ ◆

Everyone was drunk. Jake sat with the elderly Druid woman, Gwenlliant, in the quietest corner of the dining hall. The softness of the hangings on the walls and the fifty or sixty bodies in the room did little to dampen the acoustics of the stone walls and high ceiling. Outside, it was dusk. Wind and rain were blowing in off the sea. A fine fire blazed in the wide fireplace. A serving girl with a pitcher offered Jake and Gwenlliant more ale. They both held out their cups to be refilled.

At a long table on the far side of the room, Aderyn

was leading a word game, though the soldiers at the table seemed to think it was a drinking game. Judith, Harris, and McGlennon were with her. The king had joined in. One of the locals would point to an object, and one of the travelers would try to guess what it was called. Hits and misses seemed to involve someone taking a drink. Jake could see that Aderyn was making progress. Increasingly, they were understanding her questions, and her sentences were getting longer. Aderyn had explained to Jake how the process works. One starts with body parts and familiar objects, then proceeds to pantomimes that describe common verbs. Having gotten a feel for a new verb, one applied methods of exploring the verb's conjugation. Soon a simple conversation was possible. Then one built out from simple conversations to more complex ones. A drinking game was an ideal way to start.

Jake wondered what was bugging the prince, Lairgnen. Lairgnen sat to one side, obviously preoccupied, because he was missing some of the laughter cues. Lodan was talking quietly and seriously with the queen. The queen nodded from time to time. Bergan, the younger Druid, was talking with a bard. The bard was drinking now rather than singing. A very beautiful young woman sat with Bergan and the bard. Like Bergan, she wore the robes of a novice Druid in training. She had sat beside Prince Lairgnen at supper. Jake had watched them, because he found it hard to keep his eyes away from her for too long. It was clear that she and the prince were lovers. But something seemed to be wrong between them this evening, and that probably was why the prince was sulking. She had made eye contact with Jake only once. She had nodded politely, and that was it. There were other young women, and it was clear that they were trying to get Jake's attention. Jake smiled back when it seemed appropriate, but his thoughts were all of the young Druid woman.

"They all like you, you know," said Gwenlliant. "At least a dozen of the young ones, and a few of the older ones, too. There will be many negotiations tonight."

"What?" said Jake. "Why do you think that?"

"You don't see it?" asked Gwenlliant.

"Maybe just those two young women over there by the tapestry," said Jake.

Gwenlliant laughed, a dry old laugh but hearty.

"Your innocence is strange to me," she said. "At first I thought it was just you, because you are such a gentle lad, and kind. But now I see that the strangeness also has something to do with the ways of the place you came from."

"It is a strange place I came from," said Jake. "But why do you say they like me? What am I missing?"

Gwenlliant laughed again.

"First, it is your hands. You wear no rings. Of the five of you, there are only two rings among you. This leads me to guess that your ways are different. But here, they look at your hands and cannot understand why you have no lovers."

"Rings? For lovers?" asked Jake.

"Oh, yes," she said.

Jake looked at Gwenlliant's hands. She wore three rings. All appeared to be of brass.

"You have three rings," said Jake. He stopped, not sure whether the question he was going to ask was polite.

"I see that you do not understand," she said. "The rings on my hands say that I had three lovers whom I wish to remember, that I was never married, that I have no children."

"Your rings say all that?" said Jake. "It must be a complex code, if only three rings can say all that."

"It matters what the rings are made of, and on what hand and what fingers one wears them. There are a least a dozen people in this room who would like to get a leather ring on you, tonight if possible. When you are not looking, they give me hard looks for keeping you occupied."

"Leather?"

"That's how it often begins," she said.

"I'm afraid to ask," said Jake. "But who are the twelve?"

Once again Gwenlliant laughed. It was infectious. Jake laughed with her. They both took a drink of their ale.

"First of all, there is Heledd, the young Druid. She and Prince Lairgnen wear each other's brass rings. Then there is the prince. They had some words about this earlier. Prince Lairgnen is sulking. There are the two young women by the tapestry, as you mentioned. They are from the hill country and are fostered here. Four of the soldiers are drinking themselves into a stupor because they calculate that they don't have a chance with you. There is the bard, Nemed. And there is the queen."

"The queen?" said Jake.

"Don't get your hopes up. She won't. She wears gold. She will have no more children. I'm only telling you who wants you."

Jake counted on his fingers.

"I believe that was ten," he said.

"And there are several others," said Gwenlliant, "who are giving it thought but who wish to stay out of the fray."

"Are you teasing me?" said Jake.

"Yes," said Gwenlliant. "But I am not lying to you. So tell me. Which ones are your favorites?"

Jake laughed. "You mean I can choose more than one?"

"Of course," she said. "Fill both your hands with leather rings. It will soon be Beltane. Many will want your seed and your babies in the spring. You are young. You seem to have some catching up to do. But I warn you. Some will be wanting brass. Those who want brass will be more patient. You need not feel rushed. The truly lucky ones will be those who can get silver on you, or copper."

"Silver?" asked Jake.

"Children," she said, "if the father claims them and the mother agrees."

"And copper?"

"Lodan and Bergan wear each other's copper rings," said said.

Lodan and Bergan were the older and younger druids.

"Lodan and Bergan are lovers?" asked Jake.

Gwenlliant laughed again.

"I am not sure what you mean by that," she said. "No one inquires about such things, with copper. Perhaps this is not understood where you have come from, because Rome also does not understand. Copper does not lie in the fields to enrich the wheat, as may happen with leather or brass. Copper starts slowly, but it lasts as long as silver and gold. There can be no children, as with silver. But copper is not barren. What copper creates is not of flesh, but is instead of mind and spirit. Without copper, we would be a crude people."

"You are right about Rome," said Jake. "Rome changed many things, for men and for women. We almost have lost our understanding of how things used to be."

"Almost?" asked Gwenlliant.

Jake searched for an answer.

"I believe," said Gwenlliant, "that you want to say that where you come from, the authorities interfere in love."

"Yes," said Jake.

"That is Rome," she said. "It is part of why they hate us. They believe we are barbaric. You are loved?"

"Yes," said Jake. "I am loved."

"But there is interference?" she said.

"I suppose there is," said Jake.

"I am sure that you are greatly loved," said Gwenlliant. "I believe that you will have many lovers and many children."

"Maybe someday," said Jake. "I feel too young for children."

"But tell me," said Gwenlliant. "Whom would you choose now? It will be our secret."

"I am from a strange place," said Jake, "where the choices are far fewer. That may take some time."

"Well said," said Gwenlliant.

The bard has just finished a song, accompanying himself on a lyre. The soldiers were laughing at the song and kept glancing at the travelers, so it must have been a hastily written song about the travelers. The drinking game seemed to be well along. The word "stewed" came to Jake, and he wondered what its Gaelic equivalent might be.

Aderyn caught Jake's eyes.

"Jake!" she called. In English, she said, "Put that lousy bard to shame. Sing something!" And then, in the language of their hosts, she called, "Jake! Song! Song! Song!"

The drinking table joined her:

"Song! Song! Song!"

"Only a duet," called Jake.

"Deal!" called Aderyn.

Jake crossed the room to where Aderyn was sitting. She stood to join him.

"The fugue," said Jake. She nodded.

They had practiced it often on the ship. Jake had taught her. It was Bach's little G minor fugue, a four-voice fugue rearranged for two voices. The room grew quiet as a dozen would-be lovers shushed their neighbors.

Jake stated the main theme from the upper range of his tenor. Then Aderyn's clear soprano joined him and restated the same theme, while Jake's voice wove a web of counterpoint underneath her. The room was perfectly silent, as it had not been for the bard, and the sound of their two voices blended and echoed off the stone. It was as though the two of them were weaving a spell together, a new magic. Nothing like it had ever been heard in this time. Even the scale was unknown. And with only two voices, because of the mysterious time shift of counterpoint, it was possible to create harmonies that require three and even four notes to define. When they reached the end of the fugue and ended in unison, an octave apart, no one seemed even to be breathing, drunk as they all were. One by one they came out of their trances. Starting with the soldiers, they started to clap their hands in time with a chant that clearly meant, "More! More! More!"

"You have to do a solo this time," said Aderyn.

Jake was drunk enough.

He sang Jamie's favorite song, Jerome Kern's and Oscar Hammerstein's "All the Things You Are," just as Will Young had sung it in the film "Mrs. Henderson Presents." Jamie used to play it over and over. Jake heard, in his mind, every note of the piano and strings accompaniment. But the others would just have to imagine it. Jake could not bring himself to face the room as he sang. Instead he looked off toward a corner with his eyes half focused, hands clasped behind his back. There was a service door there. As Jake sang "You are the angel glow that lights the star," a face appeared in the doorway. It was a boy, fifteen or sixteen, dressed as a servant, with a majestic shock of dirty blond hair. Something was wrong with his face, though. Not until later was Jake able to think back through it and recognize the flaw. It was a cleft palate. As Jake finished the song, the boy disappeared back into the doorway. After a long silence, there was much clapping and pounding of fists on the table.

The king rose now. He seemed to be saying polite things that signaled that the evening was over and that he was retiring. After these hospitable words and a cheer from the guests, he and the queen left the room. As Jake returned to where Gwenlliant was sitting, several men clapped him on the shoulder. There were many bold looks from the women. Soon he was back in the zone of safety that surrounded Gwenlliant.

"You just broke many hearts," she said. "And most of them have never even spoken with you."

"I believe I have made some enemies," said Jake. "Why does the bard look like he hates me?"

"He is envious and suspicious," said Gwenlliant. "Nemed is a strange one. He was too long in Gaul. He has listened too much to the Romans. He finds Roman ways appealing. You would be wise to watch him. You have a keen eye, young Jake, because Nemed is masking his scheming and his envy well. He is a mediocre bard, but he is an accomplished meddler. He goes from court to court whispering petty conspiracies, seeking allies for his schemes. The prince does not yet see through him. Now at last Nemed has learned something that is not petty. He will try to use it to his advantage. Nemed will try to worm his way into our talks tomorrow. He will persuade the prince to vouch for him. But we will not permit it. We have many things to discuss that are not for Nemed's ears."

"What will happen next?" asked Jake.

"We will send word to Divitiacus," said Gwenlliant. "He is chief vergobret of the Druids. He, and he alone for now, must know what you have told us. No one has more experience with the Romans than Divitiacus."

As Gwenlliant was talking, Jake noticed that McGlennon was leaving the room without Aderyn. McGlennon gave Jake a hand signal that meant "time to go."

"Gwenlliant," said Jake. "I have greatly enjoyed talking with you. You have given me quite an education in this short amount of time."

"You are a fast learner, young Jake," she said. "I will see you tomorrow."

"Do you live here in the castle?"

"No," she said. "I have a cottage on the edge of the woods. It is half an hour's cart ride. I will be home before the moon sets. I stay there only in spring and summer, though. During the winter I move into the broch with Lodan and Bergan. The fires are much better at the broch, and I help Clood with the cooking. We will meet tomorrow at the broch."

"The broch is where I will be staying," said Jake. "McGlennon and I are to be housed there. The others will stay here at the castle."

"Be careful in the moonlight, my dear," said Gwenlliant.

Lodan showed Jake to his room on the third level of the tower, then retired down the stone stairs. As Jake entered the room, a boy, or a teenager small for his size, rose from the fireplace, where he had started a fire. It was the boy with the cleft palate.

"Thank you," said Jake. Jake pointed to himself and repeated, "Jake."

The boy blushed. "Miach," he said, and left the room.

CHAPTER 6

The little harbor beneath the broch was used mostly for fishing boats. It smelled of fish and smoke. It was a gray morning the week before Beltane, the twelfth day after the visitors' arrival.

The wind off the sea was picking up. The fog was thinning, revealing a few whitecaps a mile out to sea. Gulls were finishing the work of making their breakfasts on what had washed up during the night. Two pony carts, empty now and led by traders' sons, made their way back up the steep track toward the village.

A weathered old sailing ship with a high prow, wide gunwales, and a stained sail was at the dock, loaded and almost ready for departure. It would require some good seamanship by the six-man crew to beat south down the coast against the wind, first to Anglesey, then to Gaul, then on to Marseilles with its cargo of medicines.

Bergan was to be the chief passenger, bound for Gaul. Two of King Jowan's soldiers were to accompany him. Bergan's mission was to find the high Druid Divitiacus and give him letters from Lodan and Gwenlliant. The letters were in Greek, encrypted with one of the Druids' many ciphers.

Few knew where Divitiacus was at present, though he allowed some messengers to find him. After Caesar had returned to Rome, Divitiacus had stayed out of sight. Some said that he was still in Gaul, at one of the forest refuges. Others said that he had gone to Britain and was somewhere in the forests north of the Thames. Wherever Divitiacus was, he was thought to be fasting, arguing with the gods, and rethinking everything after his humiliation by the Romans and the death of his beloved brother. Still, no one doubted Divitiacus' loyalty to the Celtic nations. But Divitiacus had made a terrible miscalculation. Caesar had taken advantage of him. Bergan and the soldiers were to pick up Divitiacus' trail at Cenabum and track him to wherever he had gone.

Jake and McGlennon stood aside on the narrow pier to make way for a young woman who was coming back across the gangplank, wiping away tears. She had gone aboard to say goodbye to Bergan. Jake had been paying attention to rings, and he knew that the young woman accounted for the other of Bergan's two rings. The brass ring on Bergan's hand was hers, and the copper ring was Lodan's. Jake and McGlennon both nodded respectfully. She forced a smile and kept walking. As she headed toward the track that led up through the thicket toward the castle and the broch, Jake saw King Jowan, Prince Lairgnen, and Heledd coming downward. Even the king stood aside for the young woman. A parting was a kind of sacrament here, a sadness that all had known and that all honored in others.

As the two royals and Heledd – Prince Lairgnen's brass-ring Druid lover – continued down the path, Jake watched Lodan and Bergan talking quietly on board the ship. They both held on to the mast against the rocking of the ship from the incoming waves and the traffic on the gangplank.

Bergan seemed to never wear caps. His thick shock of bronze-colored hair served the same purpose. Bergan was dressed in thick trousers, a short tunic, and soft boots for sea travel. The hood of Lodan's gray mantle lay over one shoulder, exposing Lodan's white hair, which was cropped to middle length. Lodan did not wear a beard. There was something very Greek-looking about Lodan, something Socratic that was a lot like Phaedrus. Perhaps Lodan had spent time in Greece as a young man. He certainly was fluent in the language. He did not seem to Jake to be a Sophist or a Stoic. In the long discussions that had taken place in the castle and at the broch, Jake would sometimes find himself mesmerized by Lodan's voice. Jake had decided that Lodan probably was a Pythagorean. It was always Lodan who had led the political discussions. Clearly it was Lodan's task to stay abreast of faraway events. The king deferred to Lodan on all these matters and clearly depended on Lodan's counsel. Though Gwenlliant ranked higher, because of her age she seemed to cede many of her duties to Lodan, except for her medical duties.

After greeting Jake and McGlennon, the king went up the gangplank to speak to the captain, to Lodan, and to Bergan.

Prince Lairgnen lingered on the pier with Jake and McGlennon. Lairgnen seemed to be in high spirits this morning. He had taken up the habit of teasing McGlennon. The teasing had grown out of the many hours of teaching Harris and McGlennon the Celtic sword techniques. Lairgnen also seemed to be determined to teach McGlennon a sense of humor. McGlennon was even coming around, because he respected and liked these people – proud people willing to fight for what was theirs. McGlennon's language skills were improving, too.

"Tell me Jake," said Prince Lairgnen. "Heledd and I were wagering on this. Is it true that, where you come from, it is not proper for a man to make compliments on the buttocks of another man? McGlennon here has received many such compliments from my soldiers, but he always appears to be offended."

Jake was able to follow most of the Gaelic now, but Heledd had to translate the word "buttocks" into Greek. McGlennon only partly followed the question, but he understood that he was being teased.

"Most men where we come from," said Jake, "think that comments about the bodies of others are only appropriate when men are commenting on the bodies of women. However, it is permissible to tease friends.

The most important rule is to ask permission before touching."

Prince Lairgnen and Heledd laughed.

"That is the rule here, too," said Lairgnen.

"OK, what was all that about?" asked McGlennon.

"Lots of people think you have attractive buttocks," said Jake.

McGlennon blushed.

"It's these trousers, or whatever they call them. They're too damned tight," McGlennon said.

Jake translated McGlennon's comment for the prince and Heledd, then spoke to McGlennon in English.

"Well, Andrew," said Jake. "Monotheism won't be here for another fifty or hundred years, so you're just going to have to look out for yourself."

"At least I know now why they use so much butter around here," said McGlennon.

"You're learning, Andrew," said Jake. "I'm proud of you."

On board the ship, someone blew a horn. Soon the king came back across the gangplank. Lodan stayed aboard for a few moments longer with Bergan. The two of them were talking softly. Then Lodan too came down the plank, and the plank was pulled on board the ship. Men on board the ship raised poles and used them to push the ship toward deeper water.

The king gestured toward the path. Prince Lairgnen, Heledd, McGlennon and Jake followed the king up the path to the promontory. Lodan stood on the dock and watched the ship move out to sea.

"In only a couple of months," said Lairgnen, "it will be us on board a ship to Gaul."

"Prince Lairgnen was not born a sailor," said the king. "But he is a fine soldier. Jake, Andrew, do you swim well? Do you have your sea legs?"

Jake and Heledd translated for McGlennon as needed. Both Jake and McGlennon replied that they did indeed swim well and that both had some experience sailing, though on bays rather than seas. The king nodded approval. At the top of the slope, two soldiers on horseback were waiting with the king's horse. The king and the soldiers rode off toward the castle.

"Where are the two of you headed next?" Lairgnen asked Jake and McGlennon.

"I'm off to Gwenlliant's cottage," said Jake. "She has made me a new outfit for Beltane, and I'm summoned for a fitting."

"I am sure that the trousers will be nice and tight," said Lairgnen. "I will walk with Heledd to the hospital. Perhaps we will see you at dinner."

Then they saw a boyish figure running toward them from the broch. That, no doubt, was Miach. When Miach ran that fast, it was always because he was carrying an important message. They had assumed that it was a message for Prince Lairgnen, but the message was for Jake.

"Gwenlliant sends word," said Miach, "that she has been called to the hospital. Someone was brought in from the fields last night. It was a horse accident, serious, I believe."

"We'd better hurry, then," said Heledd.

"May we come along?" asked Jake.

"If you can keep up," said Heledd.

The hospital was a long, low structure built of timber and stone. The roof was partly thatch and partly slate. It stood on the north side of the village, not far from the marketplace. Smoke curled from the hospital's four chimneys – fires to keep the patients warm. Many windows were open to vent the smells. Still, the floor was of stone and was swept clean. The patients were on low cots, divided by linen curtains into wards.

They followed Heledd into what was obviously a kind of surgery. Gwenlliant stood over a narrow table on which lay a young man in his mid-teens. He lay quiet, unclothed. Gwenlliant looked up from her work as they entered. There was blood on her sleeves and a smile on her face.

"It's good you're here," Gwenlliant said to Heledd. "We've washed his wounds and done some of the sewing, but we still have need of your keen eyes and fine stitches. The lad has a pretty face. It would be a shame to scar him any more than necessary."

"What happened to him?" asked Lairgnen.

"A troll of a horse was in a troll of a mood. It kicked him and knocked him around some in a stable. There are four broken ribs, leg broken at the shin, and cuts. The horse was iron-shod. The wounds were as dirty as I've ever seen."

Heledd washed her hands in a basin, took some instruments from a shelf, and set to work sewing cuts on the boy's chin and above his eye. Gwenlliant was putting the finishing touches on a plaster cast on the boy's leg. There were bandages around his rib cage.

"I'll leave you now and wish good luck to the lad," said Lairgnen. "Soldiers don't like the sight of blood, and I haven't had my breakfast."

"Jake," said Gwenlliant. "I had promised you breakfast, but this will keep me a while longer. Why don't you and Andrew go start breakfast at the Cabbage and Kipper in the market. I'll join you as soon as I can, if your morning is still free."

"My morning is still free," said Jake, "and I've been hearing Andrew's belly growling. We'll see you there, then."

The two women – one old, with her comeliness gone but still reflected somehow in her bright blue eyes, the other young and in the springtime of her dark-haired beauty – looked up from their work and smiled at them the way all women smile at young men.

"I wonder how they kept that poor guy so quiet," said Andrew as they emerged into the morning sunlight and headed for the bustle of the marketplace.

"It must be opium," said Jake, "or something similar that doesn't have to be imported from so far away. Medicine, remember, and medical supplies and implements, are a big part of what drives the economy here."

"That boy looked pretty beaten up, and they were both sticking needles in him, but he just laid there. And with his dick and balls right there for the world to see. They're not much for modesty here, are they?"

"I'm starting to get used to it," said Jake.

"One thing's for sure," said Andrew. "They're all fucking each other. I can't keep straight who is fucking who. It doesn't seem to make a damn who is old, or who is young, or what kind of fixtures you've got down there, or who else you're fucking. They're all doing each other. So who are you doing?"

Jake laughed.

"Nobody," said Jake. "How about you?"

"You wouldn't tell Aderyn?"

"Never," said Jake. "Point of honor."

"One of the housekeeper girls at the castle. But only a few times," said McGlennon. "With you and me staying at the broch, there haven't been a lot of opportunities. She's more the shy type. I like that."

"You've had other offers?" asked Jake.

"Oh, sure," said McGlennon. "I think so. Sometimes it's hard to tell. But I don't understand how the jealousy thing works around here. They're all fucking each other, but I never see them fight. Nobody much seems to care. I can't get used to that. As for Aderyn, she'd be jealous if she knew. But these women are wild. They'd eat you alive. I guess that's why I went for the shy one."

"Gwenlliant uses a word for 'negotiate' for what lovers do," said Jake, "but I've never heard her use a word for 'quarrel.' I guess that's partly what the rings are about. It brings some public order to who is doing whom. You're probably pretty safe unless somebody is wearing gold. Even silver doesn't seem to matter much. Plenty of them, the men as well as the women but mostly the women, wear two or three silver rings. Evidently it's not a problem if your children have different fathers, or different mothers. As for the brass rings, or the leather rings, don't let them stop you. If it weren't OK to have several lovers, they'd upgrade to gold. I do like that they negotiate, though. Sometimes the negotiations may take a while. I think it's kind of cool, actually, that they work it out before they do stuff rather than getting found out and fighting about it after. My theory is that, when you're sleeping with someone here, you don't own the deed to that person, but you do have a right to know and a right to negotiate."

"I wish I had the balls to negotiate with Aderyn," said McGlennon. "Maybe you could get Gwenlliant to help Aderyn, you know, learn how to negotiate? When in Rome, and all that?"

"You've got that backwards, Andrew," said Jake. "We're not in Rome anymore. The Romans were prudish, at least where women were involved. And Roman men didn't have to negotiate."

"What about the copper?" said McGlennon. "Almost a third of the guys around here have a copper ring, even the soldiers. Come to think of it, especially the soldiers. And they're not sissies, either, if you know what I mean."

"I know what you mean," said Jake. "But it makes a lot of sense – soldiers looking out for each other, lots of fun in the barracks, less fighting over women, less pining for somebody far away, somebody to wash your back, no risk of unwanted children. That seems like a pretty good deal, something the generals would want to encourage."

"It's Heledd you've got your eye on, isn't it?" said McGlennon.

"Yeah," said Jake. "I plead guilty."

"What are you waiting for?" asked McGlennon.

"I don't know," said Jake. "With the prince and all, and all of us friends, I just feel like she should make the first move. I'm guessing the negotiations with Lairgnen are taking a lot of time."

"Lairgnen is not used to competition," said McGlennon. "I could kick his butt for you, if you want me to."

"Thanks for the offer," said Jake. "Let's keep it as a last resort."

"Say, Jake?"

"Yes?"

"I'm sorry about, you know, some of the things I used to say," said McGlennon. "Bendigeid explained a lot of stuff to me, you know, after I broke your arm. Then, when I got here and saw that the soldiers usually have a nice clean fight before they go fuck, I understood what Bendigeid was trying to prepare me for. It all makes a lot of sense. Back home, it was just one of those things that I'd never really thought about before. You know me. I couldn't care less about all that religious stuff. I can't say that it gave me a boner to see that guy naked on the table, but if they think my ass is pretty, then I'll take it as a compliment. But, as for the butter and all that, well, women are self-lubricating. What about you?"

"What about what?"

"You've got lots of guys hitting on you, I'm sure," said McGlennon.

"I'm afraid I may be a one guy kind of guy," said Jake.

"The prince?" said McGlennon. "Even I can see he's hot. He never has hit on me, though, even after I've fought him. Does he hit on you?"

"No," said Jake. "He's all about Heledd."

"But you're not getting any," said McGlennon. "That's just stupid in a place like this. Are you just a prude after all?"

"Maybe so," said Jake. "I'm slow to put out, I guess. Really slow. Slower than a Mormon girl. Clueless."

"Sounds like guilt," said McGlennon. "Oh, I see. Back home. You're a one guy kind of guy."

"No. Nothing like that," said Jake. "I'm a prude, re-member? I wasn't putting out at home. Home is like a monastery. But look at Bergan. Bergan's not a prude. Lodan worships Bergan. Lodan would die for Bergan. Lodan is worried sick because Bergan is going into danger in Gaul. Do you think Bergan would accept that kind of devotion without – you know – putting out? I've heard them sometimes, at night, in the broch. They are very sweet to each other. If there's a God, he's on their side."

"What do they do?" asked McGlennon.

"Who?"

"Lodan and Bergan," said McGlennon.

"Andrew, I don't spy on them. I just heard them a few times," said Jake.

"And?"

"I think it's pretty asymmetrical," said Jake. "I think it's pretty Greek."

"What does that mean?" asked McGlennon.

"It means that Bergan gets to be the pretty one," said Jake. "It's not like two straight teenagers going at it. I don't know. It just sounds sweet. That's all."

McGlennon thought for a moment.

"I think maybe I see," McGlennon said, "but I'd have thought that Lodan would think that that's not fair."

"I'd imagine that Lodan thinks it's more than fair," said Jake. "You're not the best Greek student in the world, are you, Andrew? I could lend you some texts."

"I don't learn very well from books," said McGlennon. "But I think I see what you mean. I'm sure there are plenty of old folks and ugly folks back home – women, too – who never get any who'd be happy to let someone else always be the pretty one instead of getting none at all. I'm sure I'll be all for asymmetry someday when I'm no longer built like a Greek statue."

"Andrew, those mind-enhancing pharmaceuticals are really working for you," said Jake.

"But you know what? That old woman wants you. She really wants you."

"Gwenlliant?"

"Who else?" said McGlennon.

"Why do you think that?" asked Jake.

"You know why," said Andrew. "Would you do it?"

"If she's interested, she's awfully polite about it," said Jake. "Or maybe things just go slower when things are asymmetrical. After all, copper is slow, she told me."

"So it's like you said with Heledd," said McGlennon. "Gwenlliant would have to make the first move."

"Oh, no," said Jake. "Definitely not. I don't think she'd ever do that. I don't know how I know that. I just do. And I think it's that way with copper, too. It would be all wrong somehow if Gwenlliant had to make the first move. The pretty one always has to make the first move. Maybe that's why it's slow. It's not like dogs, or teenagers – just sniff each other out and biologically get it on. It's a totally different thing, a whole different part of nature. You have to get to know each other. You have to be sure of each other. It's a Greek thing. It comes from some other plane. It's more like a sacrament. Listening to Lodan and Bergan, that's what it was like – it was like a benediction. It's something for the oratory, not the barnyard."

"I heard that at a wedding once," said McGlennon. "The priest was talking about Christian marriage."

"Same thing," said Jake. "But these people let everybody have a chance at it."

"Though you're the pretty one, Gwenlliant must have been really hot, in her time," said McGlennon. "Most of the older folks here, they keep it together, if you know what I mean."

"I think she's still beautiful," said Jake. "And she gets more beautiful as I get to know her better. I guess that's part of it being a slow thing – seeing someone as beautiful."

"Just listen to us," said McGlennon. "We've assimilated. I'm starting to dread going home."

"I know what you mean," said Jake. "I guess we'll just have to change some things when we get back. It would be hard to live like that again."

"Even though you're still not getting any?" said McGlennon. "You know what they always say. Change starts from within. Jake, you need to get laid."

— ◀

As the morning grew warmer, the Cabbage and Kipper rolled up its awnings. Several long tables flanked by benches were now in the sun. There was a pot of flowers on each table. Jake and McGlennon chose the table that was farthest from the narrow street. The street was roughly paved with stones. Carts rumbled by. Farm boys were leading their prize sheep to the livestock pens. Many of the passersby smiled and waved at Jake and McGlennon. Everyone knew the travelers now. Still, no one approached them or sought to start a conversation. It was polite to allow two young men to have their breakfasts in peace. And besides, people who'd already had their breakfasts had their day's work to attend to.

The table reeked of spilled ale gone stale, but that was nothing compared with the barnyard smells from the nearby livestock pens, or from the steaming little piles of excrement that the livestock left in the streets. Several times a day, boys with carts and shovels would clear the worst of it, but there was no way to make the streets smell good.

"I must be getting used to the stink," said McGlennon.

"I'm so hungry I could eat one of those lambs. Or her."

He was referring to the serving girl who had emerged from the kitchen and was setting plates of food on a table near the street. She saw them and smiled.

"Would you order for me?" said McGlennon. "I still haven't quite got the hang of it. I don't want to order sheep's innards by mistake."

"How about smoked fish, bread and butter, and some of their sour cabbage?" said Jake.

"That sounds good," said McGlennon. "They don't call it the Cabbage and Kipper for nothing, do they? Is it too early for ale?"

"I don't think it's ever too early for ale here," said Jake. "I think it will be water for me, though. I don't have time for an afternoon nap. I promised to help one of the king's friends set the ridge beam and rafters for a new barn this afternoon. They cut the timbers from a sketch I made, so now I have to prove that it will work. They're not bad at framing with wood, but there are a few tricks for making things stronger that they haven't yet learned."

The serving girl's apron was of linen, impeccably white and clean. Her skirt was wool, a kind of plaid made from black wool interwoven with white wool that had been died deep red. Her blouse was of linen, died pink. There was a flower in her hair. Her hair was a dark blonde, twisted behind her head and held up by a copper clasp. Jake grinned because McGlennon was blushing. One of her breasts had touched McGlennon's shoulder as she leaned over the table to reposition the flower pot.

Her greeting translated roughly to, "What'll it be this morning, my beauties?"

Jake ordered their breakfasts. The girl winked at McGlennon, then returned to the kitchen.

"Did you know," said Jake, "that they use the same word for 'water' as for 'rain'? I just ordered a mug of rain with my breakfast. And do you know what's in their sacred well? Rain."

"What's the word for pee?" asked McGlennon.

"They use a different word for that, though the words for horse pee and human pee are different," said Jake. "They also use the same word for beauty to describe the beauty of young people, whether male or female. But the word for the beauty of older people is a different word, and again it doesn't matter whether they're male or female. But I have to tell you something that you may not like. When I hear them gossiping about my looks, they use the young-people word. For you they use the older-people word."

"That's not fair," said McGlennon. "I'm not that much older than you."

"I don't think it's meant to be offensive at all," said Jake. "I think it means that they see you as manly, but they see me as still a boy. If anything, I'm the one who should take offense."

"You know what's sad, though?" said McGlennon. "The messenger boy, Miach. He'd be such a pretty boy if it weren't for his ... what's the polite word?"

"Cleft palate," said Jake. "Clearly their surgery hasn't reached the point where they can do anything about that. But, yes, it's very sad. He seems to feel something like shame – shame not only for the way he looks, but also for the way his voice sounds."

"He turns bright red when he speaks to you," said McGlennon. "That's how even I was able to see that he worships you."

"I hope his cleft palate doesn't interfere with his finding lovers," said Jake, "He's almost at that age. They probably think a cleft palate is genetic. I don't even know, now that I think about it. Maybe it is."

"I do know that if another horse shits right in front of this place," said McGlennon, "that I'm going to push my panic button. Bendigeid – beam me up! I'm about to have breakfast, for God's sake."

"Do you know for sure what would happen if we ever did push our panic buttons?" asked Jake.

"I think it depends," said McGlennon. "The ship's onboard intelligence would figure out what to do based on a number of factors. Where is the ship in its orbit, and how far away is it? Where did the panic signal come from? Did we all panic at once, or just one of us? What were we thought to be doing at the time? If we all panicked at once in Gaul, when the mother ship knew that we were near garrisons and soldiers, I'm sure the response would be different than if just one of us got lost in the woods. And because I'm not much of a sailor, I keep wondering what would happen if we panicked at sea. That boat that Bergan got on this morning looked pretty sturdy, but even I know enough history to remember that entire fleets of much larger ships have been wrecked by storms in the Irish Sea."

"What time of year was that," asked Jake, "the wreck of the Spanish Armada?"

"I believe it was September," said McGlennon.

"See there?" said Jake. "Your English education is better than you thought."

"Welsh education," said McGlennon. "Welsh!"

"The Atlantic hurricane season starts earlier than that, of course," said Jake, "and we'll be traveling to Gaul in late July or early August."

"I don't think we need to worry about big storms like hurricanes," said McGlennon. "Judith beams up weekly reports to Bendigeid with that attachment she has for her pendant. Bendigeid will know when we'll be sailing. If there are storms in the Atlantic he'd be able to see them from orbit. Who knows what the ship can see from orbit? It probably has very good telescopes. And for all we know, there may be tiny drones that we can't see, watching us right now."

"You're probably right," said Jake. "Bendigeid and the ship are probably looking out for us in more ways than we know. At least I hope so. Speaking of Judith, look who's coming."

As the serving girl arrived with Jake's and McGlennon's breakfasts, Judith and Aderyn were making their way up the street, escorted by Harris. They all kept their eyes low to avoid stepping into some mess or other. When they saw Jake and McGlennon, they waved. Soon they had joined them at the table. Judith and Aderyn ordered peppermint tea, and Harris ordered ale. They had already had breakfast back at the castle.

"Do you want to tell the story, Judith?" said Harris.

"Sure," said Judith. "Last night, one of the serving women told me that she had seen Nemed, the bard, in my room, snooping around."

"Snooping?" said Jake.

"Looking for what? Underwear?" said McGlennon.

"I'm sure it was more nefarious than that," said Judith. "Some things are missing."

"What?" said McGlennon.

"A couple of my notebooks, and a few of the sketches that Jake did for me," said Judith.

"I was already onto him," said Harris. "He's a Roman sympathizer. Either he wants to warn the Romans, or he wants to sell them a story and some evidence to make us look bad."

"Does he know someone saw him?" asked McGlennon.

"No," said Harris. "And let's don't let on. It's better to keep an eye on him and see if he shows his hand."

"But he'll just leave," said McGlennon. "As soon as he can catch a ship, he'll be off to Gaul."

"Directive number six?" asked McGlennon.

"What's that?" said Aderyn.

"Any hostile operative who threatens the success or safety of the mission is to be preemptively offed – discreetly, if possible," said McGlennon.

"Damn," said Jake. "I had no idea that we're that bad-assed."

"I don't think directive six has been triggered yet,"

said Harris. "The bard is not an imminent threat. And besides, it's a better strategy for now to watch him and see what he's up to."

"But can we let him leave?" said McGlennon.

"Probably not," said Harris.

"What if he sneaks away by land, down the inland roads?" asked Jake.

"That's a possibility," said Harris. "But I think he'll wait a while for a ship. There are a lot of ships during the summer – bringing in patients, bringing goods for trading, and such. Some of the ships are scheduled. Lodan would know. And let's don't tell anyone but Lodan. Let's let Lodan handle this and work it out with the king and the prince. Lodan is a one-man MI-5, if you haven't noticed."

"Speaking of the prince," said Judith, "don't you think he may have some sympathies with the Romans, too? It's often the younger people who are dazzled by Roman wealth and the apparent sophistication of the Romans."

"But sometimes it's the other way around," said Aderyn. "Sometimes it's the younger people who advocate the strongest for Celtic independence and for refusing to assimilate."

"That's true, too," said Judith, "and it's what cost Divitiacus his brother."

"I don't think we have anything to fear from the prince," said Harris. "I think the bard just sucks up to him. The bard has got suck-up written all over him. I'll go talk to Lodan this afternoon. Judith, you should come with me to explain what you're missing."

Aderyn laughed as she watched Jake use his hands to tear another hunk of bread out of the loaf.

"This is wheat bread," said Jake, "not the usual barley bread. It's damned good. It tastes all smoky."

"Have some butter," said McGlennon.

"I don't mind if I do," said Jake.

"Speaking of butter," said McGlennon, "since it's just us chickens at the moment and they'll run out of butter around here come Beltane, why is it the prince's duty to go off to the sticks at Beltane? I would think that's the very time he'd want to be here."

"Ah," said Judith. "That's something that I've actually been making notes on during the past few days. Historians have done a lot of theorizing about the matter, but of course the actual evidence that survived into our times was extremely scant. But it boils down to this: The Celts have lived for many generations as pastoral people, with much of the population living in isolation. Most of their wealth is in their cattle, so they have developed sound methods of animal husbandry."

"Funny word, 'husbandry,'" said McGlennon.

"You've got it," said Judith. "They have long understood that the genetic stock for cattle breeding that is available in their isolated little villages is too small for good breeding. That's a big part of what the annual markets and seasonal festivals are all about. People travel partly to trade cattle and mix up their genetic stock."

"Yeah," said McGlennon. "I think I see where this is going."

"Maybe you don't," said Judith. "Inbreeding – or consanguinity, as geneticists call it – has occurred on and off in human history. But in our modern world, at least, the prevalence of consanguinity seems to be more a matter of culture than how isolated people are. Some groups have taboos against relatives marrying relatives, whereas other groups put a high social value on it. So what we want to know about the people here is not so much how isolated they are, but what their taboos are."

"And?" said McGlennon.

"I had a nice talk with Gwenlliant about it," said Judith. "Their ring tradition made it easier to talk about. I asked Gwenlliant whether cousins exchange rings, for example."

"And?" said McGlennon.

"Exchanging any kind of ring with a cousin is strongly taboo. It's probably one of the few sexual arrangements that people would ever be furtive about. They're consistent. Their system of fostering children distributes even the rearing of children far beyond the family. So it makes sense that their mating system would favor the same kind of wide distribution. I get the impression – though this is something I need to better understand – that silver rings are, or at least can be, more about the selection of desirable qualities for one's children than about love. Did you know that it's women who usually make the decisions about cattle breeding? It's assumed that women are better at it. Loving a woman, or even living with her, does not necessarily mean that a man has the privilege of having a child with her. Many women seem to want some variety in the fathers of their children."

"So are you saying," said McGlennon, "that the prince is a stud with good genes providing his services in the backwoods? Or is he just exercising his privileges as a prince?"

"I wasn't saying anything quite that crudely," Judith said. "But I think that in Lairgnen's case it's some of both. The prince is hot. He makes pretty babies. He's in demand. And he's also a prince. But everyone is free to travel at Beltane, women too."

"We need a holiday like that," said McGlennon.

"But it's just a Beltane thing," said Jake. "There are still 364 more days of the year."

"Women save themselves for Beltane," said Judith. "They dream, they plan ahead. I think it must be like our drama around who's taking you to the prom. Plus Beltane is a good time for getting pregnant. Beltane babies are born right at the end of winter, at the Imbolc festival, when the sheep are lactating and giving birth to lambs. So it accords with the cycles of nature."

"So much for romance," said McGlennon. "Long live good breeding."

"Fuck romance," said Judith. "Romance won't be invented for another thousand years. The idea of romance is scarcely even possible – and it's certainly not necessary – outside the Augustinian system of sexual control of both men and women. Romance is just a disguised part of the Christian system that tolerates sex for only one purpose – procreation."

"I like the way they think here," said Aderyn. "Why shouldn't the breeding and rearing of children be carefully considered and distanced from transitory sexual affiliations?"

"That's right," said Judith. "Children aren't at the mercy of adults' fickle sexual choices. The fostering system takes it even further. Children benefit, because they see multiple adults as their parents. All males are needed as providers and protectors, so the less desirable males are loved, too, even if they don't have as much fun at Beltane."

"As a feminist, I think you're right about female choice," said Aderyn. "Women naturally want the best possible genes for their children. And those with the best male genes aren't necessarily the best family men or the best providers."

"People still argue about it, probably for political reasons," said Judith, "but it seems very likely that, where females have more choice, they choose elite males to father their children. Less lucky men may have fewer children, but, as Aderyn said, they're still loved and needed. There's always a reward for commitment from a good provider."

"That reminds me of a famous quote," said Aderyn. "Wasn't it Julia Domna, the wife of Septimius Severus?"

"That's right," said Judith. "That was Britain in the early third century A.D., when Britain was a Roman colony with a Roman governor. Do you remember what she said?"

"I think I do," said Aderyn, "I learned it in a women's studies class, and I've always admired Julia Domna for it. She was speaking of Celtic women. She said, 'We fulfill the demands of nature in a much better way than do you Roman women. For we consort openly with the best men, whereas you let yourselves be debauched in secret by the vilest.'"

"Precisely that," said Judith.

"Openly?" said McGlennon. "Can't we even sneak into the bushes?"

"But seriously," said Aderyn, "what I find remarkable is how little jealousy they seem to feel, in spite of their casual attitudes about sex. Either they control their jealousies really well, or they just don't get very jealous."

"Andrew and I were just talking about that," said Jake. "If I understand Gwenlliant, they negotiate about what they can do instead of arguing about what they weren't supposed to do."

"As I said," said Judith, "the Romantic myth is still a thousand years away. The concept of 'one man one woman' marriage, which is taken as a given in our time, doesn't yet exist outside the Greek and Roman world. And that's just where the *laws* of marriage are involved. As for sexual expression as distinct from marriage, even the Greeks and Romans have no concept of any 'one man one woman' rule. Aderyn, when you're up early at the castle, have you noticed the soldiers all crawling out of bed with each other?"

"I have," said Aderyn. "I'm from a different century, and it gets me a little envious at times."

"Oh, they'd sleep with you if they could," said Judith. "But if they don't get any offers from a woman, then they'll take the next best thing. Even Greek historians found the casual Celtic attitude toward homosexuality remarkable. One of the Greeks wrote that Celtic youths would offer themselves to men and would be offended if they were turned down."

"I can vouch for that," said Harris. "I wouldn't say that they were offended when I turned them down, exactly. It was more like, 'Whatever. You people sure are strange.' I never get drunk enough to try it."

"Send them my way," said Aderyn.

"Or mine," said Judith.

"Send them Jake's way," said McGlennon. "He's still not getting any."

"Still feeling prudish, Jake?" said Judith. "Or just picky? It certainly is nice that you and Andrew have learned to get along, though."

"Jake is like Jacob and Rachel in the book of Genesis," said Aderyn. "You have to work for seven years to get in bed with Jake."

"Wasn't it fourteen years?" asked Judith.

"That's right," said Aderyn. "Rachel's father changed the deal."

"It's its own punishment," said Jake.

"Punishment for whom?" said Judith. "Be careful, Jake. When you're older, it'll be the other way around."

Gwenlliant and Heledd appeared off the street and joined them. The two Druid women had changed out of their hospital clothes and now wore the cream-colored linen robes that were their everyday clothing.

"This looks like a breakfast party," said Gwenlliant. "May we join you?"

"Of course," said Judith. "Good morning to you both."

"You were having a good conversation," said Gwenlliant. "Don't let us interrupt. Let us eavesdrop."

"We were talking about how sexual arrangements in your culture differ so much from our own," said Judith.

"For the better or for the worse?" said Gwenlliant.

"For the better," said Jake.

"Then this should be most interesting," said Gwenlliant.

"I have a question about children, though," said Aderyn. "Many children are fostered. They live with someone other than their parents. Why is that?"

"Is that a question for me?" asked Gwenlliant.

"Yes," said Aderyn.

"It is not that way in your time?" asked Gwenlliant.

"Not at all," said Aderyn. "Children are fostered only if they have lost their parents, or if for some reason their parents can't keep them."

Gwenlliant thought for a moment.

"Sometimes it is hard to say why we do things," said Gwenlliant. "Maybe it is because that is the way things have long been done. But it is strange to think of a world in which children are not fostered. How would these families come to know each other? By what means would they know to send milk if some have not enough and others have more than they need? How would children learn about the world if they always stayed so close to home? We would travel less. We would have fewer friends. We would not know much about who our neighbors are. How could a single family survive cut off from others? Are children the property of their parents? Try telling that to one of our children! But I cannot really answer your question. It's how we are and how we have been as long as anyone, even the Druids, can remember."

"I was fostered," said Heledd. "My father was a Druid. My foster parents were farmers. Had I not been fostered, I never would have learned about the land. Birthing lambs was the start of my education. I was a midwife's helper when I was twelve. I would have no brothers were it not for my foster brothers. They still look out for me."

"Yes. They chide you about who you will choose for your firstborn," said Gwenlliant. "To them, no man is good enough."

"But the prince …" said Aderyn.

"A prince might do," said Heledd.

"He's tall," said Aderyn.

"Not the best lover," said Heledd.

"He has beautiful teeth," said Aderyn.

"He's too quick," said Heledd.

"Is he … ?" asked Aderyn.

"Yes," said Heledd. "So much that it hurts sometimes and it's good that he's quick – even though I rarely let him put his seed where he wants."

"He's not exactly poor," said Aderyn.

"I don't need money," said Heledd.

"You could do worse," said Aderyn.

"He might do," said Heledd.

In the street, the wheel of a cart broke, and the cart fell with a crash. The donkey pulling the cart stopped and looked back over its shoulder. The boy leading the donkey, who was no more than eight years old, looked as though he was going to cry. A basket of eggs, a basket of celery, lots of turnips, and several baskets of spring flowers had fallen into the street.

The passersby and the proprietors of nearby stalls stopped what they were doing. Baskets were refilled, the unbroken eggs were salvaged, the donkey was unhitched, and blocks were placed under the cart's axle. Soon a man appeared, the boy's father or foster father.

"There you have it," said Aderyn.

"Is it not so in your time?" asked Gwenlliant.

"Yes and no," said Judith. "There is an old story, true I believe, about a man who was walking down the street with a bag of coins. The bag broke, and the coins scattered. Passersby stopped to help pick up the coins. Afterward, when the man counted the coins, he had more money than he had started with."

"Then you have not changed in that way," said Gwenlliant.

"I'm not sure," said Judith. "It wouldn't always be that way. It might depend upon where you are. And that's an old story."

"Gwenlliant," said Jake. "We were talking about Miach. Can nothing be done for him?"

"For his palate? No. There have been experiments in the past, efforts made. But the results have rarely been good. It is dangerous. Heledd and I have discussed this. Heledd is our most promising surgeon and can do uncommonly delicate work. But we do not risk it. The condition is rare, which is one reason that we have not taken greater risks in hopes of a cure. Broken bones, the injuries of fishing and farming, the injuries of war – those things are common enough, they are equally disfiguring, and they are not a matter of choice when repair is needed. And there are always the sick to keep us busy. Perhaps someday a way will be found."

After their cups of mint tea, Gwenlliant and Heledd returned to the hospital. The final fitting of Jake's Beltane outfit was rescheduled for the next day. McGlennon was yawning from his intake of ale. The broken cart had been fitted with a new wheel and had gone on its way.

"Where next's for you?" Harris asked Jake.

"To help set a beam and some rafters, then back to the broch," said Jake.

"I'll nap while you do that," said McGlennon.

"Aderyn and Judith and I are off to the broch, then," said Harris, "to tell Lodan about the bard."

"I meant to ask you, Judith," said Jake. "You said that Nemed took some of my drawings. Do you know which ones?"

"There was a sketch of Aderyn and me sitting on a rock near the castle," said Judith. "There was a sketch of Glyn and Andrew practicing with their new swords with Lairgnen yelling at them. And there was a sketch of the black triangle hovering over the broch. Those three, I believe. I'm pissed, because they were some of my favorites."

"Just what the Romans would want to see," said Harris.

Lodan's study, though small and cluttered, was the best and best-lighted room in the broch. Two arched windows tunneled through the thick stone wall of the broch's second level. The windows faced west toward the sea. Heavy rain all morning and all afternoon had kept everyone indoors. But the sky was clearing now, promising a few hours of golden evening light, perfect for going outside and drawing. For most of the rainy afternoon, Jake had sat in a heavy oak chair across from Lodan's heavy oak table. For hours, they had more or less taken turns asking each other questions. Periodically, Clood had sent Miach up from the kitchen with hot mugs of tea and just-made oat cakes sweetened with honey. Miach had just set a plate of oat cakes on the table and turned to leave.

"Why so downcast, Miach?" asked Lodan. "Clood again?"

"Yes, sir," said Miach. "Some of the wood was wet. The oven got too cold. She said I ruined the oat cakes."

"Don't take it too hard, Miach," said Lodan. "The oat cakes are not ruined, and it's not your fault if the woodshed leaks. The sky is clearing. You'll be able to get outside and get away from Clood for a while."

"She wants me to sand the big copper kettle," said Miach. "The stew boiled over this morning and turned the kettle black as iron, she says. The quicker it's cleaned, the easier the job, she says."

"I'll speak to her," said Lodan. "I'll tell her that I have some errands for you."

"Thank you, Sir," said Miach. "A message for King Jowan?"

"Yes," said Lodan. "But the message is not urgent. Before you take the message, perhaps Jake could use some help getting his pencils and paints and parchments down to the big rock. He wants to perch there for a while and draw the ship that put in here yesterday. After you take the message to Jowan, go to Gwenlliant's place. She's coming here for supper, and you're needed to lead her pony. There's no hurry as long as you and Gwenlliant are here by suppertime."

Suddenly Miach didn't look downcast anymore.

"Go tell Clood that I have need of you until suppertime," said Lodan. "Jake will be down shortly."

Miach scurried out and bounded down the stone steps two at a time. Lodan rose and went to a window. He stood, looking out at the sea with his hands clasped behind his back, his hood thrown back. His linen robe was always perfectly clean and perfectly pressed – a job that Clood saw to. He wore a golden torc. The only other adornment was Bergan's copper ring. His white hair and shaggy white eyebrows looked golden in the light angling through the window. Lodan was tall and lean. He must have been very handsome once. Jake wondered why Lodan wore only the one ring. Surely he must have had many lovers. Perhaps it was because Lodan had traveled so much when he was younger. Perhaps he had never been in one place long enough to have old rings and the memories of old lovers to cherish, as Gwenlliant did. Lodan had been in Greece, in Alexandria, and in Rome. He had traveled in Gaul and Britain and over much of Ireland. Until ten years ago when he came to the broch, he had never missed the annual gathering of the Druids at Cenabum, not since becoming a novice at the age of seventeen. Lodan was modest, but Jake and Judith were convinced that Lodan was the Divitiacus of the north. Lodan was deep in thought now. Jake went to the other window, naturally assumed a posture much like Lodan's, and waited for Lodan to speak.

"The mountains of Caledonia are both beautiful and safe," said Lodan. "But the land is rocky and cannot support our people in the tens of thousands. Only Hibernia is large and fertile and safe. I had never thought to move again. Perhaps I won't. If Gwenlliant stays, I will stay. Perhaps Hibernia is for those who are younger. Some, of course, will want to stay in Britain and fight. But Britain and Gaul are the domain of Divitiacus, not me. Divitiacus, I am sure, will reason with those who live in Britain and Gaul. As for those of us in the north, we must prepare the Hibernians for what is to come. What did you call that land?"

"Ireland," said Jake.

"Yes. Ireland. We must smooth the way for the many who will come," said Lodan. "My fear is that the people of Ireland will see such an influx of outsiders as an invasion. Here in Caledonia people will understand. But the people of Ireland are far more insular. They know too little of what has happened in Gaul. You say that the Romans will never project their military power into Ireland. That is a certainty? Somehow it seems unlikely. The distance is not great."

"Unless there is some quirk in the workings of the universe that permits multiple outcomes and alternate histories," said Jake, "then Ireland has nothing to fear from the Roman army. The damage to Ireland will come instead from the Roman religion, from an invasion of priests."

"That sounds almost worse," said Lodan. "But multiple outcomes? Alternate histories?"

"Those were only theories in early versions of earth's science," said Jake. "Those theories have been discarded. Everything that I have learned from our friends from the stars holds that there is only one track of history. Our friends from the stars know much more than we do. They are hundreds or thousands of years ahead of us in what they know."

"It is all very complicated," said Lodan. "Many would not believe it. And yet you yourself have traveled among the stars, and you have met these people. I have seen your ship. It is comforting that they care about us, that they would send us help."

"A great leader who died not long before I was born," said Jake, "said something that my mother quoted often. His name was Martin Luther King. He said, 'The arc of the moral universe is long, but it bends toward justice.' Not until I was out among the stars did I notice that he said 'moral universe,' not 'moral world,' or something more limited. I looked it up. Martin Luther King actually got this idea from someone who lived a hundred years earlier, Theodore Parker. Parker said the same thing a little differently. He said, 'I do not pretend to understand the moral universe; the arc is a long one, my eye reaches but little ways; I cannot calculate the curve and complete the figure by the experience of sight; I can divine it by conscience. And from what I see I am sure it bends towards justice.'

"The important thing is that both of them saw the vastness of the moral universe," said Jake. "They saw that the concern for justice extends beyond our own planet. And they saw the smallness of the human delusions that cause so much suffering and despair here on earth. Even small minds – religious minds, greedy minds, minds that demonize creation though they'd grovel before the creator – look to the sky, thinking that their invisible God is out there, ready to tell them what to do. But small minds cannot see what greater minds see. The world is still a terrible place, Lodan, even in my time. And yet I think that some people do get a glimpse, almost with their eyes, of what Theodore Parker saw only with his conscience. I do believe that the arc of history bends toward justice, Lodan. What you are doing, it is worth doing. It is what bends the arc."

"You give me courage, Jake. I am greatly in need of courage, because these are dark times and growing darker still. But look at the sky! How quickly the air has cleared. One could almost see Ireland from here. I have kept you for too long today, Jake. You should go and make your drawings. We will talk more at supper, and we will hear Gwenlliant's thoughts as well."

The path down to the big rock was slippery from the rain. The mayweed and gorse that lined the path were practically rioting in the spring weather. The big rock was just south of the harbor, on a steep slope a third of the way down from the crest of the promontory. The rock afforded a view of the docks lit obliquely from the seaward side by the lowering sun. An oaken ship out of Marseilles, old and battered but proud, sat rocking in the waves, tied to the dock. The gulls, like the gorse, were rioting, delighted by the change in the weather and the chance to feast before sunset on the leavings of the storm. The waves crashed relentlessly into the rocks below, turned to foam, and then boiled away into the next wave.

Miach had insisted on carrying Jake's sheaf of papers. It was mostly incomplete work that Jake wanted to finish, plus some blank paper for the new drawing of the ship. Miach was diligent lest the wind catch any of the paper and blow it away.

"What did you call this?" Miach asked.

"A portfolio," said Jake.

"What a funny word," said Miach. "What does it mean?"

"It comes from French," said Jake. "French came from Latin. The word has to do with an object for carrying leaves, or sheets, of paper."

"How do you know so many things?" asked Miach.

"Oh, I don't know," said Jake. "Maybe it has to do with liking the sound of words. Before we came here, we had to learn a lot about languages, to be able to communicate with you. But I'm sure that you know plenty of words that I don't know. For example, what is that flower called?"

"The yellow ones?" asked Miach. "*Aiteann*."

"Ah," said Jake. "We call it gorse, a word we got much later from invaders from the north. I like the sound of your word better. Look. The rock is almost dry over here. Let's sit."

"Would you let me see what you are working on?" asked Miach.

"Of course," said Jake, untying the cord that bound the portfolio and removing a sheet.

"That's Heledd!" said Miach.

It was a portrait in profile – Heledd with her hair bound by a ribbon, smiling, long lashes, full lips, straight nose, turned-up collar.

"Let's draw some *aiteann* in her hair," said Jake. With a few strokes of a black and a yellow pencil, it was done. Miach laughed with pleasure.

"Who else have you drawn?" asked Miach. Jake pulled out another sheet.

"Lairgnen!" said Miach.

It was another portrait in profile – hair tousled and thick, a princely nose, a short stubble of beard, a simple torc.

"He looks so stern and beautiful," said Miach. "He is stern with the soldiers, but he is never stern with me. Everyone says that Lairgnen and Heledd are the handsomest around."

"But look," said Jake. "Here's a certain young man named Miach. He's pretty handsome, too, wouldn't you say?"

Jake pulled out a third sheet. It was Miach, drinking water from a dipper. The dipper hid Miach's deformity. The emphasis was on the light and exuberance in Miach's eyes and his unruly hair, always windblown and tangled.

"Ha!" said Miach. "Do I look like that?"

"You do," said Jake. "Don't tell Lairgnen I said so, but you're at least as handsome as he is. Don't tell Heledd and Lairgnen about these drawings, though. It might go to their heads, and they're already haughty enough. Uh-oh. Look. There come Heledd and Aderyn along the path. Quick. You pick some *aiteann* for their hair while I get these drawings out of sight."

"Ho!" called Aderyn as they got within earshot. "Everyone is restless. May we join you for a minute?"

"Of course," said Jake. "Come on down."

Soon the four of them were crowded onto the rock. Jake had closed the portfolio and tied the cord. Aderyn and Heledd each had a sprig of gorse in their hair.

"We've come from the castle," said Aderyn. "We took Judith something for her cough. I helped Heledd at the hospital all morning. I saw a baby born, for the first time!"

Heledd laughed.

"At her age," said Heledd. "For the first time!"

"How did that go?" asked Jake.

"It was easier for her than it was for me, I think," said

Aderyn. "I think it was her sixth. So she was experienced. She's probably already back home, stirring pots."

"I'm trying to convince Aderyn that it's not too late for her," said Heledd. "Don't you think Aderyn would be a good mother?"

"I do," said Jake. "A daughter of Aderyn's probably would be born speaking three languages."

"Miach," said Heledd, "how did you escape from Clood and get time to sit on the rock?"

"I owe Lodan for it," said Miach. "But I have to take a message to King Jowan, and then I have to fetch Gwenlliant to the broch for supper."

"Then poor Clood will have no one to blame if the flatfish is scorched and the moosh won't thicken," said Heledd. "But you mustn't take it hard, Miach. Clood has been too long without a man."

"Where are you from, Miach?" asked Jake.

"From the village," said Miach. "My mother died when I was nine."

"I'm so sorry," said Jake. "And your father?"

"My father is a seaman," said Miach proudly. "Veneti. I have not seen him since before my mother died. He will come back someday. He used to sail all the way to Africa. He brought my mother a bracelet from Hispania. I still have it."

There was the sound of horses' hooves approaching along the path to the north. They all looked up to see Lairgnen accompanied by two soldiers.

"Still others who are restless," said Heledd. "It is the weather, and the moon."

Lairgnen motioned for his soldiers to ride on. Lairgnen dropped the reins of his horse and left the horse to forage in the grass at the top of the cliff.

"I'd better go," said Miach. "No more room on the rock, and I must carry Lodan's message to King Jowan."

They all bade Miach goodbye, and soon Lairgnen was seated on the rock, which was a little more crowded now with Lairgnen's long legs and heavy boots.

"It's a shame about Miach's father," said Heledd. "He probably died when Caesar put down the Veneti. I remember Miach's father. He was a good man. He looked a lot like you, Jake. I think that is why Miach is so drawn to you. It is almost as though his father has returned. Both of you arrived in ships – one off the sea, the other from the sky. That must be very magical for a boy like Miach who has not yet been anywhere."

"What kind of education will Miach be given?" asked Jake.

"You think like a father," said Heledd. "Miach learned to read and write as soon as he came to the broch. Clood has been a good mother to him, in many ways. But she interferes, and Lodan has so little time."

"It's time we discussed it with Lodan," said Lairgnen. "Miach should at least be trained as a scribe, or as a cryptographer. He could do much that Bergan used to do now that Bergan is away more. But Bergan doesn't take much interest in Miach."

"No," said Heledd. "Bergan does not think like a father. Jake, please tell us about your family."

"My parents both were teachers," said Jake.

"Brothers? Sisters?" asked Heledd.

"No," said Jake. "Just me."

"So you got all the attention?" asked Heledd.

"I suppose so," said Jake. "But I was always what we call an underachiever. My parents were much more accomplished than I."

"Ha!" said Aderyn. "That might have been true a few years ago. But I think your self-image may be lagging a bit. How many languages do you speak now, Jake?"

"I don't know," said Jake. "It's getting harder to tell where one language ends and another begins."

"I rest my case," said Aderyn. "Spoken like a linguist. And your talents go far beyond language."

"What are Jake's other talents?" asked Heledd, looking at Aderyn. Jake glanced up to see if Heledd was teasing, but it seemed to be a serious question.

"Jake is giving me a dirty look," said Aderyn. "He doesn't like to be talked about. When Jake blushes, it's time to change the subject."

"Such talk easily gets out of hand," said Lairgnen. "Every man blushes when people want to talk about his talents."

"Even princes?" asked Aderyn.

"Especially princes," said Lairgnen. "What was Jake's word? Underachieving? You should hear my father talk about my talents."

"Your father is proud of you," said Heledd.

"He has never said so," said Lairgnen.

"He will someday," said Heledd. "Where were you

going, Lairgnen? Letting the wind decide, like the rest of us?"

"Yes," said Lairgnen. "The horses were restless, too. And you?"

"We have another house call to make," said Heledd. "Aderyn and I were at the hospital all morning. Then we took some medicine to Judith. I believe she stayed in bed all day. And next we must check on a sick baby. Aderyn has a talent for nursing."

"Is there some illness going around?" asked Jake.

"Not really," said Heledd. "It is just the usual quotient of croups and colics and coughs. But we should go, Aderyn, and check on our colicky baby."

Jake and Lairgnen were silent as they watched the women walk back up the path. Heledd and Aderyn were laughing and pointing out the flowers. When the women were out of sight, Lairgnen laughed.

"Heledd is like a riddle, you know," said Lairgnen. "Just so you know."

"A riddle?" said Jake.

"It goes like this," said Lairgnen:

"You can have me but cannot hold me;
Gain me and quickly lose me.
If treated with care I can be great,
And if betrayed I will break.
What am I?"

"Oh my," said Jake. "That does sound serious. What's the answer?"

"Trust," said Lairgnen.

"I see," said Jake. "But surely you have not lost Heledd's trust?"

"No," said Lairgnen. "We are very careful about trust. But Heledd is a strange one. She demands nothing. Yet she expects much. It keeps a man on his toes."

"Then I suppose that is a good thing," said Jake. "But that's a funny word, *demand*, easy to misunderstand from language to language. You say she does not *demand*, but does she *ask* for what she wants?"

"Oh, yes," said Lairgnen, looking at Jake with a faint smile. "She will ask for what she wants. And I believe that she has something to ask you."

Jake looked out to sea, brushed a finger across his cheek.

"I'm sorry, Lairgnen," said Jake.

"There is no problem, Jake," said Lairgnen. "I trust you, too. Perhaps you misunderstand me. I am only asking you to be kind to her, to keep her trust. When people can talk, things always work out. Heledd and I have talked. But I suppose that I needed to talk with you, too."

"I am not accustomed to this," said Jake, "such honesty and generosity."

"Why not?" asked Lairgnen. "Heledd is hers to give, not mine to share. And Jake, too, is both honest and generous."

"Are you sure?" asked Jake. "We've not known each other for very long."

"I can tell," said Lairgnen. "As can Heledd."

"Thank you," said Jake. "I wish I had known you longer, both of you. We could be such good friends."

"We will do the best we can in the time we have," said Lairgnen.

Jake glanced at Lairgnen and tried to read Lairgnen's eyes in the golden light. Lairgnen's eyes were looking out to sea. His hair fluttered in the wind. There was a sprig of gorse in his hand. Perhaps he'd meant to bring it to Heledd but had seen that she already had some. Jake, too, looked out to sea now, in the direction that Lairgnen was looking. The sounds were just the same as that day on the cliffs with Phaedrus – the music of the wind, the sea, and the gulls. Together the sounds struck a chord. Just for a moment this perfect chord seemed to resonate throughout all time and all space. It was the sound of unbearable longing satisfied, of unbearable pain soothed, of wrongs made right, of patience rewarded, of lost things found again at last.

And thus in unexpected moments, thought Jake, do abstractions – beautiful abstractions but elusive – suddenly take form, like spirit entering a body. Just for a moment, thought Jake, I do believe that I actually saw it, heard it, touched it, felt it. There *is* only one moral universe, and as it bends toward justice it might brush against us. My great shame is that I saw it in a moment of joy that I don't deserve. Others have seen it from the blackness of despair.

CHAPTER 7

Jake's room near the top of the tower was always poorly lit, with only one small window facing the courtyard of the broch's interior. Normally Jake drew and sketched outdoors, in the morning and evening light. But this morning Jake was finishing a drawing for Gwenlliant, and he wanted to give it to her today. The drawing was of her little cottage at the edge of the woods, surrounded by the bluebells of late spring. The cottage walls were a random mixture of stone, clay, and timber. The roof was thatch. A stone chimney emitted a curl of smoke. Jake used his colored pencils to brighten the flowers.

He held the drawing near the window and studied it. It would be the perfect witch's cottage, thought Jake. But one thing is missing: a cat. These people know about cats, but cats are still rare in the north and greatly desired.

Jake drew a black cat into the picture, sitting on the window sill. Why not? He also drew in a broom propped against the door, and a cauldron in the yard with a fire burning under it. It would be interesting to see how Gwenlliant responded to these symbols – everyday objects here but symbols of enchantment in Jake's time.

There was the sound of light steps on the broch's stairs, followed by the noise of a heavy door being opened. Jake went to the door to look into the stairway. It was Miach, with a candle, opening the trap door that led up to the catwalk on the roof.

"What's up, Miach?" called Jake.

"I'm going to the roof," Miach answered, "to look at the fires."

Jake picked up his mantle, because it would be windy on the roof. A wet mist was blowing.

"They've already lit the Beltane fires?" Jake called. "Wait for me."

Jake climbed the ladder onto the catwalk. The catwalk curved around half of the top of the broch, affording a panoramic view. From here one could see far out to sea to the south and west. On the eastern side of the catwalk, there was a view of the village, and beyond the village the pastured hills. On those hills at least a dozen fires were burning, each more than half a mile apart.

"It's beautiful," said Jake. "But do you think this drizzle will stop?"

"It usually does, Sir," said Miach, "by afternoon."

"Will you not call me Jake?"

"Jake. I'm sorry. I forget," said Miach.

"You're going, aren't you, Miach?" asked Jake.

"To the fires? Oh, no, Jake, I don't think so."

"But you're old enough," said Jake. "Old enough to stay out late, I mean."

"Someone has to put out the home fires, and clean out the ashes, and bring new wood," said Miach. "Lodan will bring coals from the Beltane fires, and I must start new fires with the new coals. Clood will be angry if I'm not quick about it. You know how she hates for her oven to get cold."

"Why not start the new fires and then go?" said Jake.

Miach shook his head.

"Clood wouldn't like it. She keeps me twice as busy on Beltane," said Miach. "She complains about all the extra work for her."

"Doesn't she go to bed early?" said Jake. "Wait until she falls asleep, then go."

"I can't," said Miach. "What would I wear? I have no new clothes. Clood scolds me. She says my things won't come clean. She makes me wash my things last, before I throw out the wash water."

"When will Lodan go to Beltane?" asked Jake.

"Oh, he left very early already," said Miach. "He lights the fires."

"You really should go," said Jake. "Leave the house to Clood. Bring her back some barley cake. Some Beltane cake would do her good. You must be a fine dancer, since you are so fast on your legs. Lots of people would like to dance with you. I'll dance with you."

For a shy moment, Miach's eyes met Jake's, then returned to the fires on the hills.

"Everyone knows," said Miach. "This is the Beltane for you and Heledd. When she has led you away, then who would dance with me? You are very kind to me, Jake. I think you are the kindest person I have ever met."

"Gwenlliant will dance with you, too," said Jake.

Miach laughed. There was resignation and longing in his laugh, and his cleft palate gave it a nasal sound. When he laughed he put his hand over his mouth to hide his flaw.

"Gwenlliant is kind, too," said Miach. "But I must stay and make the new home fires. I cannot go."

"Well," said Jake. "If you change your mind, I will dance with you."

Miach smiled, but he avoided Jake's eyes. Out over the sea a brief flash of yellow sunlight broke through an opening in the clouds.

"It is clearing already," said Miach.

— ▸ ◂ —

When Jake arrived at Gwenlliant's cottage, with his drawing rolled up and tied with a strip of kitchen linen that Clood had given him, a boy and girl from the village were decorating Gwenlliant's cart with flowers. Her donkey was in the paddock, and no doubt the pony too would be wearing garlands before evening.

"I've just finished," said Gwenlliant from her chair near the window. "The shoulder should lie a little better now. You have such wide shoulders. What's this? A present?"

"It's a drawing I made for you," said Jake. "Let's unroll it."

She brushed at her eyes as she studied the drawing.

"How do you do this?" she said. "No one here can do such work. It looks as real as life."

"It's a bit of a science, actually," said Jake, "People have had a long time to study art. Many artists over the centuries have carried the science forward. I wish you could see some of what has been done. How I'd love to take you to the Louvre."

"The Louvre?"

"It's a great museum in Gaul, where the Seine is bridged. A beautiful city will be built there, one of the most beautiful cities in the world."

"In Gaul? The Romans do that?"

"I've never really thought about it that way," said Jake. "But, yes. I'd have to say that the descendants of the Romans built it. But the descendants of the Celts also helped. Much of the Celtic spirit remains there, under a Roman veneer."

"I feel sad that I will never see such things," said Gwenlliant. "But at least I have seen you, and you have told me about these things. That is a great gift. This drawing is a great gift. I will cherish this. I know that you cannot stay with us forever. Indeed, I suppose you cannot even stay with us for much longer. Do you know when?"

"A month or two," said Jake. "But much depends on Bergan's news from the south, and when a ship can take us."

"Then let us try not to think of it too much today," said Gwenlliant. "It is Beltane. Here. Let's stand nearer the window and have a better look at this picture. Look at the cat! I have rarely seen a cat. There are cats on Anglesey."

"Would you like to have a cat?" asked Jake.

"No," said Gwenlliant. "I think that would be wrong."

"Wrong?" asked Jake. "Why?"

"I have heard that cats become very attached to old women," said Gwenlliant. "It would be wrong to have a cat, and then to leave it."

"Leave it?" said Jake.

"Jake, you are pretending to forget, I think," she said. "You are young, and I am not. My inner sight tells me that not many more times will I see Beltane fires on these hills. Once or twice more I will see them, perhaps. That is what my inner sight tells me."

"Gwenlliant," Jake said, "you shouldn't …"

"Shush, Jake," she said. "It is the way things are. Some parts of our destinies cannot be changed. I have lived to see much, and I may live to see much more. It is the way things are."

They sat down by the window, and Gwenlliant resumed her stitches. The children were leading the pony into the yard, to decorate it with flowers.

"Gwenlliant," said Jake, "may I ask you a question?"

"Of course you may ask me a question," she said.

"You love children. Why did you never have any?"

She finished tying a knot in the last hem in Jake's tunic before she answered. Her eyes looked far away.

Already there were Beltane flowers in her hair.

"I'm not sure that I know," she said. "Perhaps it was an illness I had when I was a little girl. Or perhaps it was because I really didn't want children. There is an old, old wisdom in a woman's body. Without children, I was free to come and go. I have been many places, you know. Often I have been to Gaul for the summer session. I have been as far as the mountains north of Rome. Once I sailed to Marseilles. They used to say that I was like a man in that way, with a yearning for travel."

"So you don't wish that you had ever had children?"

"Oh, no, never," she said. "There have been many fine young people in my life, and there still are. When your body bears no children, you are free to choose your own children, your own young people. That suited me. It suits many who choose to practice medicine. There are always so many who need looking after."

"What about Heledd," said Jake. "What about Lairgnen. Why do you think they have not had children?"

"I cannot answer for Heledd," said Gwenlliant. "You could ask her. But it could be that she, too, has made choices, that she too listens to the voice within her body."

"As for Lairgnen," said Jake, "I suppose he has children enough, somewhere. Do you believe that it is fair that he should have so many children and that someone else should bring them up?"

"Fair? Fair to bear the child of a prince, and a very beautiful prince at that? I believe I have seen some of his children, and they are fine children. What does any mother, or any parent, want, but beautiful and healthy children? As for the price of bringing them up, what wealth would there be without a king and his kin to protect the people? We Druids see to justice, but it is our kings who see to our wealth and safety. What do the Romans want from us, after all? They want our land, our crops, our livestock, our gold and silver, our wool, our roads. Who stands in the way of the Romans? Nothing but the justice of the Druids and the power of our kings. You are such a serious young man, Jake. On Beltane, you must not be so serious. Here. Let's try this on you."

She stood up from her chair, holding up the tunic to the light from the window. These people are innocent of shame and modesty, thought Jake, and now I am going to have to remove my shirt and possibly my trousers as well. He pulled his shirt over his head and waited for her to hand him the new tunic.

"You are beautiful," she said. "Even Heledd's fine stitching would never be able to follow a form so perfect. But what is that?"

"What do you mean?" asked Jake.

"What is that you are wearing around your neck?" she asked.

"This?" said Jake. "It is what we would use to summon our ship if something went badly wrong. It was made by the same star people who made our ship, but, before we left our era, a jeweler – or I should say a historian of jewelry – disguised it to look old, as though it came from here."

"I see," said Gwenlliant. "Where would this jeweler have gotten the pattern?"

"I'm not sure," said Jake. "I would assume that it was from something that archeologists found."

"By that you mean very old things that were pulled from the earth, old things that did not rot in many years?"

"That's right," said Jake.

"I see," said Gwenlliant. "Jake, I must say that I do not like this thing. I think I have seen something like it before, but even to us it is old. We must ask Lodan. He may know its origin. But it is good that you keep it under your clothes. I think that you should continue to do that, and keep it out of sight. And now, as much as I would like to go on looking at your young and manly beauty, you must try this on. Trousers too. Such long, strong legs you have. Such a delight it is to sew for such a beautiful body."

➤ ◄

Judith, Aderyn, Harris, McGlennon and Jake wound their way up to the fires. They followed a stony path that led to the top of the highest of the hills that over-looked the village. It was a kind of promontory above a promontory. Beneath them to the west lay the village, with the castle and broch beautifully illuminated in the light of evening. Beyond the cliffs lay a quiet sea. In the background, on the southwestern horizon, in the middle of the sea, a golden sun was setting. It was not often now that the five of them were alone together. They paused for a while to look at the scene below them, then walked on.

"We'd better figure this out and get our negotiations done early," said McGlennon, "or all the bushes will be taken."

"Who'd go into the bushes with you, Andrew McGlennon?" said Aderyn.

"I was hoping for Jake, for a quickie," said McGlennon. "And then I was hoping that you'd be next on my dance card."

"Ha!" said Aderyn. "I'm going to hire you out tonight. The first job, I was thinking, will be to a country lass who can teach you how it's done. Someone with years and years of experience, I was thinking. Then, next, to the soldiers who've had their eyes on you. You won't bring much, but if I keep you at it all night, I might be able to make a small donation to the hospital in the morning. As for Jake, I don't think there's enough silver left in these hills to get a quickie with him tonight."

"Aderyn," said Judith, "as long as you're brokering for the disadvantaged, what do you think you might be able to do for me?"

"Just whisper to me what you have in mind," said Aderyn. "Then get a big mug of ale, and I'll take care of the rest."

"Just listen to you," said Harris. "You've all completely lost your morals. How long did that take? A few weeks?"

"Morals?" said Judith. "Ha! Morals were never anything more than an anaphrodisiac for the poor, to get them to work harder. Morals just made people sneaky before, guilty after, and inhibited during. I love these people. They're completely untainted by all that horse shit. The sad thing is, we'll never be like them. The damage is permanent. "

"That's why the Gods gave us ale," said McGlennon. "Seriously, Jake, about that quickie…"

"Seriously, Andrew," said Jake, "you've got the wrong holiday. Get yourself a better costume at Halloween, and ask me again."

"I bet Gwenlliant could make me just the thing," said McGlennon. "Be sure to tell her what you like."

Just then they met Lodan coming down the path.

"Are you leaving already, Lodan?" asked Judith. "So early?"

"It has been a long day," said Lodan. "It's my role to oversee the lighting of the fires. My lungs are filled with ashes and my eyes with smoke. I think I need to clear them with some clean air off the sea."

"Are they behaving?" asked Harris.

"Behaving? I should say not, if I understand your meaning," said Lodan. "If the summer rains are good, this will be the most fertile pasture in all the north."

Lodan pointed to one of the fires.

"You'll find Gwenlliant and the king there," he said. "They've been wondering when you would come. Clood sent baskets of wheat bread and cheese, with some crocks of her special mustard. There's plenty of every-thing left. I hope all of you have a fine evening. I shall ask you to tell me all about it tomorrow, or whenever you recover."

They all said good night, and Lodan continued down the hill.

"Now there's a man," said McGlennon, "in need of some time in the bushes."

"I think he's totally devoted to Bergan," said Judith. "He wears only the one ring. And speaking of clean air off the sea, have you noticed how he just stands there at times, on the signal rock, looking south? He's watching for ships, hoping for news from Bergan."

"It's a little early, though," said Harris, "for Bergan to come back, or even for him to send word."

"Lodan worries," said Jake.

"It's Lodan's job to worry," said Judith. "It's his job to know what's going on in as many places as possible. He feels responsible not only for the people here, but also for all the Celts, in Anglesey as well as Gaul. Lodan is modest, but we mustn't underestimate his rank. We mustn't underestimate Gwenlliant, either. I suspected it even from the archeology, but I'm even more persuaded now. I think the Druids see this place as a kind of backup, as a kind of iron mountain at a safe distance from the turmoil. I think that Lodan and Gwenlliant, and to a lesser degree the king, are something like intelligence analysts and strategists. I think their authority extends far beyond this place. I think it threw them for a loop when Divitiacus went dark. Did you look closely at some of the sea captains, and seamen? There is more to them than meets the eye. Some of them are spies for Lodan. Some of them are messengers. They are worried sick about Gaul, and they know that Britain is next. And then we arrived and made it worse. What I would give to see the message that Bergan was carrying to Divitiacus. If only that was on the historical record."

"Speaking of Gaul, Andrew," said Harris, "don't let the fun and games and bushes distract you from your sword practice. You've not yet encountered a Roman's moves. They're experienced, and they're deadly."

"They're rarely very tall, though," said McGlennon.

"You're forgetting about their mercenaries," said Harris. "You could encounter anyone from anywhere – a Greek, an African, a Persian, or even a Celt from Galatia."

"I hear you," said McGlennon. "And don't let Jake off the hook. Even Jake could learn some defensive moves against a bad swordsman."

"Weren't we talking about the bushes?" said Jake.

"It's a deal," said Harris. "We'll talk about nothing but the bushes until the day after tomorrow, when everyone's over their hangovers. Then we'll double down on our training. Imminent threats I can handle. Roman swords I can handle. But intrigue and espionage are not my department."

➡ ◂

Jake was on his third mug of ale. Judith, Aderyn, Harris and McGlennon had wandered off long ago, whether into the bushes or down the hill to bed Jake didn't know. The king had been fetched back to the castle by a messenger. Gwenlliant sat beside Jake on a log, drinking and laughing. Several men, and not a few young women, had asked Gwenlliant to dance. She had danced often. She always returned from dancing flushed and fanning herself with a little wooden fan that she had brought with her. No one had invited Gwenlliant into the bushes, as far as Jake knew. As for Jake, no one had even invited him to dance. It was as though there was a big sign on his back that said, "Reserved. Hands off."

Sparks from the fires flew high into the night air. Everywhere there was the sound of laughter and singing, though the songs were getting a little bawdier now that the children had been sent home or carried home to bed. A drunken young man was kissing a sheep. There were mock sword fights with glowing brands from the fire. Many were playing a game like spin the bottle, using the wheel of a cart that had been turned on its side.

"Do you suppose those bushes over there are occupied?" Jake asked Gwenlliant.

"Is that a proposition?" she said.

Jake knew that she was teasing.

"It's just that I need to ... you know," said Jake.

"Just make a little noise," said Gwenlliant. "That way you're not likely to wet anyone."

Away from the firelight, the stars were brilliant. There would be no moon until shortly before dawn. Torches were burning at the castle, at the broch, and all around the village. There was a clear line where the sea met the sky – black below, glimmering above. The air was cool, and Jake's new woolen mantle and linen tunic felt warm. He walked into a thicket, whistling softly. He held his hands in front of his face to keep the brush out of his eyes. The fastenings of his new trousers were unfamiliar. He found the string, untied it, found himself inside the unfamiliar underwear, relaxed, sighed, and waited for the stream to start. It would be a long one.

"Jake?" whispered a voice deeper in the bushes.

"Jesus!" exclaimed Jake. He fought to stop the stream and refasten his clothing. It hurt.

"Is that you, Jake?" said the voice. It was less of a whisper this time, and Jake recognized the voice. It was Heledd.

"I'm peeing," said Jake in a stage whisper.

"Oh. I'll wait," said Heledd. "What is Jesus?"

"One of our Gods," said Jake.

Jake went ahead and peed and refastened his clothing.

"Where are you?" he said. "I can't see you."

"I'll come get you," she said. "You're still blind from the fire."

Soon she had Jake's hand. She led him deeper into the bushes and farther from the fire.

"Will you walk with me?" she asked.

"Of course," he said. They emerged into a rocky clearing. She found a path that led around the dark side of the hill. He followed her. She was wearing not her Druid's habit but a linen frock and long stockings. There were flowers in her hair and ribbons at the bodice. Jake wondered if Gwenlliant had made the dress for her or if Heledd had made it herself. She smelled like apple blossoms. Her steps were soft and light, as though her boots were made of doeskin. The sound of laughter was farther away now, and Jake could hear the swish of her linen skirts. He could feel the ring on her hand. Her hand was warm and slightly damp.

"Your hand is cold," she said. "You must have been sitting for too long."

"No one wanted to dance with me," said Jake.

"Ha! Everyone wanted to dance with you. But you frighten them tonight, Jake. You are too pretty. You are too much like a God who fell out of the sky – a strange place for a God, to be sure. To be turned down by you would be a shame never to be lived down. Why do you think I ambushed you when no one was looking?"

"I would never turn you down," said Jake.

"I had hoped that you would not," she said, "though I am just an ordinary woman, and I am not from the sky. But tonight I had to risk it. Time moves on. Soon you must go to Gaul."

"Heledd, I also have to fall back into the sky, you know," said Jake.

"I know," she said. "I know. Would you tell me about it? The place you came from?"

"I don't think you would like it," Jake said. "Your earth is so much more beautiful. There were too many of us. The earth was worn-out fields, forests disappearing, the oceans poisoned, the northern ice melting. Many kinds of animals had nowhere left to live and died out. It was like … it was like a pasture too full of cattle, with no rain, and the grass almost gone. There were cities with millions of people. Some people did well, the few who were rich. But others couldn't get clean water, or enough to eat. We thought we were smart, smart enough to fix the problems that we had caused. But it was too late. Most of the people are dead now. We have to put it all back together, if we can. We have to not make the same mistakes again."

"You will have much work to do when you return," she said.

"Yes," said Jake.

"You wear no rings," she said. "You do not have our way with rings. Many peoples don't. But did you not have someone?"

"No, we don't have your way with rings. And, here in this place, where everyone looks out for everyone, I'm not sure what it means to have someone. If you are asking whether I have a lover, then no. I don't. But I do have those who look out for me."

"Would you tell me?" she asked.

"Of course," said Jake. "I have someone who looks out for me named Phaedrus. It was only because of him that I survived what happened to the earth. And there is another person, Mark, who came to live with us after his family died. We are a kind of family."

"They must love you very much," said Heledd.

"Yes," said Jake.

"And women?" she asked.

"I always seem to disappoint women," said Jake. "Or maybe I just haven't met the right one. I haven't had a girlfriend for a long time. That's our word for it – girlfriend."

"And she would call you a boyfriend?" Heledd asked.

"That's right," said Jake. "But I didn't have a girlfriend. I haven't had a girlfriend for a while."

"Your Phaedrus, is he a kind of copper friend for you, though you don't have our way with rings?" she asked.

"I don't know," said Jake. "In the world I come from, such friendships are abased. We're taught that it's wrong."

"Why?" she asked.

"Maybe another time I will try to explain it," said Jake. "On Beltane it seems wrong to even talk about it. I like your way with rings, though. But it is strange to me, to be holding your hand, and Lairgnen's ring is on your finger."

"It is brass," she said. "We are young. I am young. Lairgnen is young. You are young. It takes time to know the world, to know our own hearts, to know the hearts of others. Surely it is the same in the world you come from?"

"Yes," said Jake. "It is the same. But in my world – and I'm not really sure why – it is thought to be wrong to be with more than one person at a time."

"So many things are thought to be wrong in your world!" she said. "Even with brass? But of course you do not have our way with rings. So is it like gold in your world, even though it isn't? One gold, and then another gold, and then another?"

Jake laughed.

"Yes," he said. "That's kind of the way it is. I can't explain it. But in my world, too, young people are given time to know their hearts."

"You say you disappoint women," she said. "Why is that?"

Jake laughed again.

"Do I have to answer that?" he said.

"Yes," she said. "I am holding your hand, so may I not explore your heart?"

"Often they say that I'm too dreamy," said Jake. "They say that I'm too wrapped up in myself. They say that my head is in the stars. Girls – women – expect more than I seem to be able to deliver."

"They are ready for gold," she said. "And you want brass?"

"Something like that, I suppose," said Jake.

"So then what happens?" she asked.

"They dump me," said Jake.

"Dump you?" she asked.

"You know," said Jake. "They give up on me and find someone else."

"You come from a strange world, Jake. Either that or you come from a world with many good men in it, if it is so easy there to find a man better than you. How could your head not have been in the stars? It is who you are. Look at where you came from, from the sky. But it seems strange to me to be required to leave behind a person whose heart is good, to get to know a different heart. There is always gold, when people are sure. Gold would seem like an iron chain to me, if hearts were not in it."

"Yes," said Jake. "Many people in my world wear gold, though it's really iron."

"Then you understand why Lairgnen and I wear brass?" she said. "All know that we are still exploring our own hearts, and others' hearts."

"Yes," said Jake. "I think I understand."

"Jake," she said, "my heart tells me two things."

"Yes?" he said.

"My heart tells me that I want you, but also that I must lose you."

"I understand," said Jake.

"What shall I do?" she said.

"You're asking me?" said Jake.

"Yes," she said.

Jake did not answer. After a while, she said:

"Jake, you are looking at the stars even now. That is the right place to look. Have you found words there?"

"No," said Jake. "No words."

"I understand," she said. "I believe that is the best answer."

And then suddenly they were in each other's arms. Soon they were on the grass, with their mantles to keep them dry – Jake's mantle on the ground below, Heledd's mantle as a coverlet. Their bodies were pressed together. She kissed him, and they lay that way for a long time, savoring the warmth of each other's body.

"You're trembling," she said.

"I don't know what to do," he said. "Your ways are so different."

"I will show you," she said.

She found all the strings that fastened his clothing, as though they were familiar to her. For a long time, they held each other, flesh against flesh, not speaking, each weighing the bliss of a mere moment against the long emptiness that must follow. At last she took hold of him and guided him into her. The softness of her body yielded to his terrible need. It was like falling into the sky, but much warmer, much more comforting, and just as full of meaning and mystery. His trembling became a shudder. It was as though he lost consciousness for a while, embedded in the very definitions of comfort and ecstasy.

"I'm sorry," he said at last. "I was too quick."

"How long has it been, Jake?" she asked.

"Almost two years," he said.

"You poor, sweet man," she said. "Just lie still for a while, then do it again."

Though some of the Beltane fires were kept burning all night, most of them were embers by the time Jake and Heledd made their way to Heledd's little room on a side street near the hospital. A sliver of a moon was rising. To avoid being seen, they had skulked from thicket to thicket and from street to street, giggling when they were almost seen. Though she lit a candle, Heledd had fallen immediately into her narrow bed, on her mattress of down with her woolen blankets. Jake lingered in the corner to fold and stack his clothes. He took off his pendant and wrapped it in his tunic. Then he blew out the candle and crawled into bed beside Heledd. They slept, because they had made love many times and were exhausted.

They must not have slept long, because it was still dark outside. They were awakened by a loud noise and a flash of light from a corner of the room. Jake's clothing was burning, so brightly that the fire had already spread to the hangings on the wall. The flames had melted a nearby candle, and the flowing wax had spread to a box of candles. The box of candles was now a growing flame. Jake jumped to his feet and grabbed the blanket. He was about to start beating at the fire.

"No, don't try," she said. "The burns would be terrible. We must get out."

Jake realized that he was naked. He handed Heledd her frock and wrapped the blanket around his chest. Heledd led him out of the room, and soon they were in the street. It was shocking how fast the fire had spread. It already was nipping at the thatch. People were rushing into the street and calling for water. Others were rushing in from nearby streets and alleys. In the confusion, as Jake picked up snatches of the shouts, he grasped that there was more than one fire.

"Where?" he called to a woman who ran past him with a pail.

She pointed. Jake could see the glow. He told Heledd that he was going to check. She nodded. Jake ran, his feet bare in the filthy street. No one seemed to notice that he was wrapped in a blanket. After all it was the middle of the night. Jake made his way to the edge of the village on the castle side. A fire in a large dwelling had spread into an adjoining building. The building was surrounded by people shouting and organizing a bucket brigade. From here he could see the castle. The castle was like a disturbed ant hill, with ants carrying torches. There was a fire at the castle, too.

And then suddenly Jake knew what had happened. He had taken off his pendant, and it had set fire to his clothes. But there was little reason to hope that the others had been so lucky.

Then Jake noticed that men were carrying someone from the burning building, using quilts as a makeshift stretcher. Jake sprinted to the stretcher. It was McGlennon, naked but partly covered with a linen sheet. The men carrying the stretcher paused for Jake, but one of them said that they had to get to the hospital, quickly. Jake bent over the stretcher as they walked. He could, but only barely, hear the muffled sounds of Andrew's agony against the tumult from the street. There were terrible black burns, some with blood, on McGlennon's neck, face, and chest. His hair was gone. Jake took his hand.

"Andrew?" he said.

McGlennon's hand returned a squeeze. He painfully took in enough breath for a few words.

"God, it hurts," he said.

"They're taking you to Heledd and Gwenlliant," said Jake. "I'll be there as soon as I can."

Andrew squeezed Jake's hand again. Jake nodded to the men. They made their way onward toward the hospital. People in the streets stood aside for them.

Miach appeared at Jake's side, breathing hard.

"Miach," said Jake, "would you ask that woman over there if she would lend me some of her man's clothes? And then let's help with the water."

A dozen candles lit the still-smoky air inside the curtained-off little room of the hospital. Jake sat beside Andrew's bed, still holding Andrew's hand. The hand of an old woman quietly pulled one of the curtains aside, and a young woman crept into the room. It was Heledd. She knelt in front of Jake's stool, took Jake's free hand, and put her head in his lap. Jake released Andrew's hand and stroked Heledd's hair.

"I am sorry that I could not save your friend," she whispered.

Moments passed before Jake could answer.

"You took away the pain," said Jake. "Nothing more could be done."

"They have come for you," said Heledd.

"Come for me?" said Jake. Then he understood. Jake nodded. He stood. He pulled Heledd up to stand beside him. They held each other.

"Must we say goodbye now?" she asked. Her eyes looked as though she had been crying for hours.

"I don't know what will happen now," said Jake. "But I would never leave you without saying goodbye. We will not say goodbye now."

Heledd nodded, wiped her eyes, and pulled open the curtain. Near the door, Gwenlliant sat on the edge of an empty bed, head bowed as though deep in thought. Jake went to her and stood beside her. He put his hand on Gwenlliant's shoulder. Her shoulder felt so small, so vulnerable, so old, and yet so strong, the shoulder of a woman who had always worked and who always would.

"I am sorry, Jake," said Gwenlliant. "I am sorry."

"Thank you for everything you have done," said Jake.

Gwenlliant nodded. She, too, had been crying.

Lairgnen and Miach suddenly appeared in the doorway, as though they had been running. They stopped and lowered their heads when they saw Jake and Gwenlliant and Heledd.

One by one, Jake embraced each of them, first Gwenlliant, then Miach, then Lairgnen, then Heledd. Then he stepped out into the morning twilight.

An enormous black triangle had appeared in the sky between the castle and the village. It hovered silently. Beams of light burst from the black bottom of the triangle and searched the ground methodically. When a beam fell on Jake, Jake was waving his arms. The beams winked out. The triangle turned, moved toward Jake, and stopped. Then the long stairs began to telescope down.

CHAPTER 8

The stairs came to rest on the grass. Miach followed Jake to the bottom of the stairs. The fires had slowly surrendered to the buckets of water. There had been only four deaths, though there were many minor burns and minor injuries from fighting the fires. Dozens of villagers were now homeless. The dead were McGlennon, Aderyn, Judith, and Harris. Lodan had collapsed from exhaustion while working the fire brigade at the castle and had been carried to the hospital.

Miach looked up at the long flight of stairs. His eyes were stained with soot and tears. Sam was gliding downward on his magnetic field, faster than Jake had ever seen him move before.

"Hello, Jake," said Sam. "Are there medical emergencies?"

"No," said Jake.

Sam bobbed slightly, Sam's way of nodding. Then Sam glided upward again. Miach watched Sam go, a look of wonder mixed with his misery.

"Miach, when Lodan is feeling better, please tell him that I will return or send word as soon as I can. I don't know what will happen now. I must go up and talk."

Miach nodded. Jake hugged him again. Then Jake mounted the stairs and started climbing. The stairs telescoped up behind him, and as soon as Jake was aboard, the black triangle lifted into the clouds.

Bendigeid was waiting for him at the top of the stairs. Bendigeid took Jake's hand, clasped it briefly, and beckoned for Jake to follow him to a kind of sitting room. A transparent port made up one of the walls. Through the port, far below, Jake could see the Irish Sea and the Scottish coast. Sam appeared, bearing wet cloths, dry towels, clean clothes, and a pair of Jake's shoes.

"Thank you, Sam," said Jake.

"You're welcome, Jake," said Sam.

Bendigeid waited quietly by the window, looking out with his hands clasped behind his back, until Jake had washed and changed.

"We brought this treachery with us," said Bendigeid. "Jake, I am so sorry."

Jake nodded.

"Would you like to be alone for a while?" asked Bendigeid.

"No," said Jake. "I need to talk. Who did this, Bendigeid? Was it the jeweler who was to make the pendants look native?"

"They must have gotten to him," said Bendigeid. "Either they duped him, or he conspired with them. How did it happen that you escaped? They all went silent at once, yours too."

"I took it off," said Jake. "I had never taken it off before, but I took it off last night."

"Strange," said Bendigeid. "Why?"

"I didn't want … someone to see it. The elder Druid woman, Gwenlliant, saw it yesterday. I had taken my shirt off, because she had made me new clothes. For some reason, the pendant disturbed her, but she wouldn't say why. I think she wasn't sure. And then, last night, I was with someone, and I didn't want her to see it. She is a Druid, too, the woman I was with, and I thought that she also might find it disturbing. Gwenlliant wanted to ask Lodan about it."

"I see," said Bendigeid. "That saved your life. It probably saved your friend's life as well."

"But now what?" said Jake. "The mission is ruined. I might be able to retrieve some of Judith's notes, if they weren't burned. But everything is lost. Our friends are dead."

"Our friends are dead," said Bendigeid, "but the mission may not be lost."

"What do you mean?" asked Jake.

Bendigeid was silent, to give Jake a moment to think.

"Divitiacus?" said Jake. "All the way to Gaul? By myself?"

"I cannot ask you to do that," said Bendigeid. "It is far too much to ask. But I do think you can do it. And, as

I have said before, I have strong intuitions for a positive outcome of this mission."

"I'm not even sure," said Jake, "what the success of this mission would mean now. I always have thought of that as being in Judith's hands."

"Judith's knowledge of history was a great asset, certainly," said Bendigeid. "But you have learned a great deal from Judith. And from Aderyn, and Glyn, and Andrew."

"If it came to swords, I wouldn't last," said Jake. "Andrew was a natural. You should have seen the two of them. The soldiers at the castle knew better than ever to mess with Glyn or Andrew. As for me, I'm a joke. How could I do it without them all? It's only partly the danger, I think."

"You have been through more than you may yet realize, Jake," said Bendigeid. "You need some time to think about it."

"No," said Jake. "What I said was just a reflex, really. It was automatic. No. I don't need to think about it. I will go back, if you will tell me what I need to do."

"You must think about it," said Bendigeid. "Have you slept? It was Beltane. I saw the Beltane fires."

"Damn it, Bendigeid," said Jake. "Why did this have to happen to them? Even Andrew and I were getting along. I watched him die. And the people down there. I love them. Everything they have is worth keeping. I have to go back."

"Sleep first, Jake," said Bendigeid. "Let Sam take you to the surgery and check you out. You've been through a lot. Will you rest some and sleep on it?"

Jake nodded.

"But I have to go back," he said.

—▶ ◀—

That evening, from the village, the castle and the broch, many eyes saw the black triangle descend through the clouds. Many feet sped toward the broch, its clear destination. The ship stopped and hovered. A crowd had gathered. The stairs telescoped down. When Jake appeared at the top of the stairs, the crowd cheered. Miach ran up the steps to meet him.

—▶ ◀—

Smoke was pouring out of the broch's kitchen into the great room, along with banging noises and a stream of lamentations and imprecations from Clood. Lodan asked Gwenlliant to go see what was the matter.

"Clood, what's all this? Do you need help?" said Gwenlliant.

"Oh, Domna Gwenlliant, I don't mean to disturb your meeting, but everything is all contrary," said Clood. Her linen cap was askew, and she held a stick of wood in her hand.

"The mice were in the flour again," said Clood. "This morning's milk has already clabbered, and I've burned the biscuits fightin' with the mice. They get bolder 'n' bolder."

"We'll find you a cat yet," said Gwenlliant. "What's the matter with the milk?"

"They've sent yesterday's milk again, I know it," said Clood. "My biscuits! The dogs won't even eat 'em."

"The hearth's too hot," said Gwenlliant.

"There was nothing but fir," said Clood. "They used all the good wood for the festival fires. And with all that noise and clamor, and people trampin' all over the pastures, it's no wonder the cows ain't givin', and they've sent me old milk. Festivals! Nothin' but grief and extra work, if you ask me."

Gwenlliant opened the kitchen's back door. The smoke and heat rolled out into the morning air. Miach was stacking wood in the woodshed.

"Is that more fir?" Gwenlliant called out to Miach.

"Yes, Domna," said Miach. "It's all they have."

"Well, be careful with it," said Gwenlliant. "It burns too hot, and we've had enough trouble with fire. When you're done, would you sift the flour for Clood? And if the mice have made holes in the sacks, go get some good ones, the Hibernian ones, that came in with the new cloth last week. And while you're in the village, please see if anybody has good milk."

"Yes, Domna," said Miach.

Gwenlliant returned to the great room. The king has just arrived. The great room, too, was a little stuffy, and Gwenlliant pulled aside a curtain to let fresh air in from the courtyard. Around the table near the fireplace were Lodan, King Jowan, Jake, Heledd, and Melwas, the captain of the king's guard.

"Jowan," said Lodan, "would you repeat for Gwenlliant what you were saying about Nemed the bard?"

"He hasn't been seen," said King Jowan. "He was asking about ships to Anglesey and Gésocribate, but if he found passage south by ship, then he was able to do it in secret. And I believe there are some who are spying for him."

"How does he plan to profit?" asked Heledd.

"By selling what he can learn to the Romans," said King Jowan. "He has the drawings that he stole. That will impress the Romans. Many have seen this flying ship, and the story will be told for a long time. The Romans will not believe it, of course, when rumors reach their ears. They will see it only as foolish lore from the bumpkins of the north, unless the drawings persuade them otherwise, which I doubt. But Celts rising up again to defend themselves from the Romans, that will be believed. A strange new troublemaker in the north seeking to spread insurrection to the south, that will be believed. An outpost of belligerents north of Anglesey, that will be believed. Threats of treachery against Caesar, that will be believed."

"Threats of treachery against Caesar?" asked Heledd.

"Judith told Nemed that Caesar will be dead in four more years, killed by assassins," said Jowan. "She spoke freely with Nemed before we counseled her against it. Some say that he slept with Judith, though I disbelieve it. We do not know what Nemed may know, and we may not yet know all his motivations."

"It is best, then," said Gwenlliant, "to keep Jake away from Nemed and to not create any more rumors to be sold in the south."

"That is my view," said King Jowan.

"Jake," said Gwenlliant, "has the king seen your new pendant? It's a strange looking thing, but I like it better than the old one."

Jake, eyes red and distant, fished into the collar of his tunic and brought out the new pendant that Bendigeid had given him. It was on a soft cord, surprisingly strong and of unknown material. Attached to the cord was a flat oval object, made of a shiny metal. Recessed into its front was a small button.

"Would you tell me again what you call this?" asked King Jowan.

"We called them our panic buttons," said Jake.

Lodan picked up an old book that was lying on the table. He opened the book to a page marked by a ribbon and handed the book to Jake.

"Did the old ones look something like this?" asked Lodan.

A drawing or etching in the book showed an intricate design of runes enclosed in knotted cords.

"Yes, I believe so," said Jake. "It was very much like that."

"Then it is as Gwenlliant suspected," said Lodan. "The design was used only on ornaments for the bodies of the dead. It was a kind of token. It guaranteed the bearer safe passage into the next life. I don't believe it has been used for at least a hundred years."

"I'm relieved, I think," said Jake.

"Yes?" said Lodan.

"I was afraid that it was some kind of evil symbol," said Jake.

"No," said Lodan. "It was not evil. "But it was something not meant to be worn by the living. But those things are destroyed now, and you have a new one that I like better."

"Are you still in danger from your own world?" asked Gwenlliant. "You have discussed this with the one who watches over you from above?"

"We should have suspected the pendants," said Jake, "because they were something we brought with us. But I have nothing else that I brought with me, except for my pencils and paper. This must surely be the end of it. Our enemies were improvising without much time to prepare. They were clever and yet crude. My friend who watches from above – his name is Bendigeid – thinks that there is no more danger, at least none that I brought with me."

"What did you say is your friend's name?" asked Gwenlliant.

"Bendigeid," said Jake.

The three Druids looked at each other.

"I don't understand," said Jake.

"It is a name not unknown to us," said Gwenlliant. "Jake is a name we have never heard, but Bendigeid is a name we have heard of, in Ireland."

"Oh, no," said Jake. "It's not, I hope ..."

"Not at all," said Lodan. "It is a good name. Who knows where names come from? You have brought us new names. In a year, there will be babies named Jake, and Andrew. There will be Glyns, and Judiths, and Aderyns."

"Aderyns are not unknown," said Gwenlliant. "I knew an Aderyn once, on Anglesey. She was from the mountains of western Britain."

"Yes," said Jake. "Aderyn came from there. In our time it is called Wales."

"I find this comforting," said Gwenlliant. "Things that last because they were buried in the earth, it would be better that they should stay there, in the world below. But some things, such as names, endure in the world above, in the light and air. But we have strayed. We have not decided what to do."

"How then," said Lodan, "shall we keep the bard and his spies away from Jake until Jake goes south? It is still weeks too early to start the trip to Gaul. We can start the preparations for the trip. We can find a ship. But Jake would be safer elsewhere for a while. If Nemed surfaces again, then perhaps we can smell out his plan."

"The observatory," said Gwenlliant. "Jake should go to the observatory. It is remote enough but not too far. Cymon would have a thousand questions for Jake about the stars."

"I like that idea," said King Jowan.

"I like that idea, too," said Lodan.

Jake was thinking and did not speak.

"Cymon is testy and stingy," said Heledd. "Jake would not want to stay there long. My foster family's farm lies in the valley beyond the observatory. My foster brother has married and left home. My foster family need summer help, and they need a new shed for the cattle. They also need many things from the village. I had thought to go later this summer, to help. Why not go now?"

They all looked at Jake.

"To a farm?" asked Jake. "Cattle? Sheep? A mule? You say they need a shed?"

"And eggs every morning instead of smoked fish at breakfast," said Heledd.

"I'll go," said Jake. "If everyone thinks that's best."

"Heledd is right about Cymon," said Gwenlliant. "He is bad-tempered. He watches the stars, but he can't see what is in front of his nose. He is as poor a judge of man and beast as I have ever seen, though any woman seems to suit him. Heledd is right. A few days at most at the observatory, and then the work of a farm will be a welcome change."

"Who should go with him?" asked Lodan.

"Melwas will go," said King Jowan. "Give Jake a Druid's habit, and no one will question the armed escort."

"I will go," said Heledd.

Gwenlliant saw that Miach had been lurking just inside the kitchen door.

"Send Miach, too," she said. "I don't think he's ever been farther from the village than the edge of the big woods. We can always find help from a boy or girl in the village for a while. A vacation from Clood's scolding would do him good."

— ◆ —

Even as an old man, when Jake thought back to the happiest moments of his life – and there were many – he could remember few times happier than that midsummer trip from Scotland's coast into the edge of its highlands, across green valleys, then up dark and narrow forest roads into the hills. The tracks were too rough and too steep for the Celts' sturdy carts, so each of them led a pony loaded with cloth, salt, oil, herbs, cured fish for the winter, and even a few luxuries. These were gifts for Heledd's family.

They all were in love. Miach was in love with Jake. Jake was in love with Heledd. Heledd was in love with Jake. And the soldier, Melwas, captain of the king's guard, though he wore a golden ring, was in love with all of them. They all were in love with the ponies, and the ponies returned their love.

Melwas, happy with his golden ring and with the woman who had born his two children, expressed his love through kindness. He insisted on more than his share of the cooking. He seemed to need little sleep. He discreetly kept watch during the short summer nights and napped during their long rests – rests for the ponies, they said – during the day.

Jake and Heledd, though they were always hungry for each other's bodies, were discreet and quick and furtive, to spare the feelings of Melwas and Miach. The sneaking into the undergrowth when Miach was gathering wood and Melwas was attending to the ponies made it that much more delicious. On the second night, Miach had crept a little closer with his blankets, and then a little closer still on the third night, so that by the fourth night Jake awakened to find Miach's head tucked up against him. Miach was a year or more into his adolescence, but the cuddling seemed to be all he really needed, because he had had too little cuddling as a boy. This little intimacy seemed to nourish Miach and to infuse a glow of health and happiness, like a small child who was fed too long on oat water and for whom a wet nurse had finally been found.

Heledd understood Jake's constant preoccupation with the death of his friends. She knew what Jake was thinking when his eyes looked far away. She understood Jake's unspoken guilt at being the one who had survived. She understood that only time, and life, would bring relief.

Sometimes Jake would lie awake with Miach snuggled against one side and Heledd against the other. Heledd seemed to think that this arrangement was perfectly natural. A few times they even made love with Miach sound asleep beside them. Jake wished that it never had to end.

When the time came for parting, Miach would be desolate. It would feel to Miach like the loss of another father. Jake would have to leave Heledd. But leaving Heledd felt different somehow. Prince Lairgnen loved her, and Heledd loved Prince Lairgnen. The two of them would return to their love. Jake was only an interlude for Heledd. Jake was the needy beneficiary of Heledd's sexual mercy, and also of her love. He would miss Heledd, but he did not think that he would feel as though he had harmed her, or used her, or misled her, or abandoned her. She knew. She understood. She had chosen. She was happy with her choice and wanted to savor it before it had to end.

Sometimes the forest was so dark that they would walk for hours with no sign of where the sun was. They had taken a little-used and roundabout track, and they never saw other travelers. Sometimes the forest track followed a stream rushing down from the high hills. Sometimes the fir forest, deeply carpeted and eerily quiet, would give way to a dense deciduous forest of oak. In the oak forests, the undergrowth hid dense populations of furry mammals. Troops of squirrels swept in to watch them and scold them from midway up the tall trees. Deer would watch, then amble off. Birds kept up a constant chorus in the canopy, which echoed in the open naves and vaults below. Sometimes they saw owls.

When it rained, as it often did in the forests, they would hold their mantles close and watch their step, to avoid the frogs that liked to congregate on the track. Most nights, Melwas' fire would burn for most of the night. But if Melwas happened to fall asleep and the fire went out, Jake could hear the life of the forest all around – wings in the dark, the stirrings of the ponies, animal footsteps in the distance, the call of an owl, occasionally the scream of some small thing taken prey in the night. But Jake always felt safe, knowing that Melwas and his sword were nearby.

Jake had never felt so loved, with two adoring people cuddled up beside him. Still, there was the ache of fearing that he had too little to give them, including too little time. Again and again Jake found himself thinking: This is wonderful. I am at peace with my human neediness, and I don't deserve it, rare as peace has been for me. Why do I get what I don't deserve, while others never do? I deserve to live no more than my friends deserved to live. It will be many months before their families will even know. The more I know about how the world is and always has been, the more unfair I know it to be.

Phaedrus is right. God deserves our condemnation when we are happy no less than when we are miserable, because the misery remains, all around us. Phaedrus compared that misery with a vast black tide that washes into our rooms at night. I feel it even here. In the depths of it, far away, I feel Phaedrus' portion of it, almost as though I could reach out and touch him. If only Phaedrus could feel the love that I feel now, so close against me on both sides, shielding me from the black tide. If there is such a thing as magic, then I will send him a portion of this love, back through the tide. Perhaps Gwenlliant would know a spell for that. Perhaps Gwenlliant, too, is no stranger to the black tide of suffering and despair.

———

One evening at dusk, after a steep climb through an evergreen forest, they emerged onto a rocky knob of land that stood above the surrounding forest, affording a view in all directions. A mile away, across a deep valley, stood a stony precipice that was shaped like an anvil set a little cockeyed. The horn of the anvil jutted up into the sky above the treetops that surrounded it.

"There it is," said Heledd. "That is the observatory."

She pointed out a stone dwelling at the lower end of the anvil, at the point where the forest resumed. The dwelling was covered with vines that caused the stone-work to blend in with the forest as though camouflaged. The building was round and tall so that its roof, of mossy slate, was just above the treetops.

"Look at that stonework," said Jake. "It's pure magic. I have to draw it."

"Cymon hates the magic," said Heledd. "He wanted to have all the ivy pulled down. He says it attracts spiders. Lodan and Gwenlliant threatened to cut off his stipend if he touched the ivy."

"If we make it to the stream down there in the valley by midmorning tomorrow," said Melwas, "then we can be at the observatory before dark tomorrow."

"The ponies need a good long rest before the climb up the opposite slope," said Jake. "But I can see some grass for them over there."

"There is very little pasture," said Heledd, "though there is a snug little stable. When supplies are brought in, the ponies always have to be put up overnight."

They unloaded the ponies and let them spend the remainder of the evening foraging. The moon was new. The rain had passed, and the air was cool. Melwas and Miach made a huge fire, and they all cooked. They drank some of their ale. Melwas said that Cymon would see their fire and would know that he would have visi-tors tomorrow. Melwas also said that Cymon would be greatly annoyed if the fire spoiled his darkness, so they let the fire die out soon after supper. That night Jake saw more stars than he had ever seen anywhere on earth. Only Bendigeid's star deck surpassed it. Just after sunset, he could see Venus as a crescent, something that even his good eyes had never been able to see before. As Jake's drowsiness increased and he started to doze, he felt grief that this trip ever had to end. Perhaps it was the chill, or perhaps it was that Miach and Heledd felt the same way, because they slept very close to Jake that night.

The boy who carried Cymon's water and cut his wood was watching for them at the lower end of the anvil. His greeting, such as it was, was sullen. He was underfed. It was said that Cymon beat him regularly.

"At least you've brought something," the boy said. "Cymon says visitors are eating us out of house and home."

"You have other visitors?" asked Melwas.

"Two," said the boy.

"Who?" said Melwas.

"A bard and another lazy one," said the boy. "A sailor, from the looks of him. I thought you'd know – came from the same place as you, I'd figure."

"Out of the cauldron, into the coals," said Melwas, looking at Jake.

"Cauldron, indeed," said the boy. "An empty one, unless you catch your own squirrel. What have you got in those sacks? The bard and the sailor brought nothing. Cymon says it's useless singing for your supper if there's no supper to be had."

"There will be supper aplenty for all tonight," said Heledd.

"Then Cymon will be glad to see you," said the boy. "And the bard Nemed will get a better supper than his bad singing deserves. Did you bring honey? Cheese? Are there apples yet? I'm sick of bony squirrels and bitter acorns. There's been nothing from Gilfaethwy since just after the snow melted."

"We'll see," said Heledd. "Supper will be a surprise. Why don't you go on ahead and tell Cymon that we're headed for a farm on the other side of Gilfaethwy and that we won't be here long."

"Two Druids?" said the boy. "To a *farm?*"

"Family visit," said Heledd.

Heledd stopped as though to check the ponies, and the boy went on. He seemed too hungry to run.

"Poor boy," Heledd said. "There's never enough to eat up here. Cymon has silver from his stipend, but he's stingy with silver, too. Nobody wants to trade with him and wear out their ponies and their boots for bad trade."

"Why would Nemed come here?" asked Melwas.

"To conspire with Cymon," said Heledd. "They both have black hearts. Cymon despises the world for not behaving the way his stars say it should. Few Druids want to divine by the stars anymore. Cymon says nobody listens to him. He says that the world is scourged because people won't be governed by his stars. And Cymon has friends in Gaul, behindhand and hoary Druids like himself. I'm thinking that Nemed has some scheme involving Cymon's silver and Cymon's friends in

Gaul. Nemed gets no silver from King Jowan anymore, nor from Lairgnen either."

"And the sailor?" asked Melwas.

"Probably just some thug that Nemed has hired," said Heledd.

"Should we just move on?" asked Jake. "Druid disguise or not, Nemed knows who I am."

"It's too late," said Melwas. "There they are."

Cymon and Nemed had emerged from a decaying shed. Nemed was carrying something that dangled limp and red in his hand.

"What's that he's carrying?" said Melwas.

"Squirrels," said Heledd. "That's where Cymon keeps his squirrel cages."

—▸ ◂—

Cymon, though he was wrinkled and gray-skinned and almost as skinny as his water-and-wood boy, had gray eyes as sharp as a cat's. That only made sense, thought Jake. One needs good eyes to study the stars. Cymon's ears were a different matter. Cymon seemed to abhor using his ears. He preferred to declaim. Supper had gone on for more than an hour. Almost everything on the table had been brought in on the ponies – cheese, sour cabbage, barley cakes, and dried fruit. Cymon was as stingy with his candles as he was with his food. A single beeswax candle lit the table.

"So then, a star," said Cymon, "which you say is a ball of gas that isn't really burning but is some entirely other force that is much hotter, eventually dies. You say that how it dies depends on how big the star was. And then you say that everything in the universe that isn't – what did you call it?"

"Hydrogen or helium gas," said Jake. "They're the two lightest ..."

"And everything that isn't this invisible gas," Cymon went on, "is formed out of that invisible stuff inside the star – things like stone, or silver, or flesh – and that the star blows up when it dies, and it throws these things out into a vast space between the stars, and some of this stuff then starts to fall in circles around other stars, and sometimes this stuff turns into places like the earth, and somehow living things like birds and fish come alive on those balls of stone and silver and iron, and here we are."

"Something like that," said Jake.

"And you can't see how that is absurd?" said Cymon.

"I can't explain it," said Jake.

"Of course you can't," said Cymon. "But back to this big ship that you claim you flew in on ..."

"We saw it," said Heledd.

"... and that Heledd says others saw, what makes it fly?"

"I don't know," said Jake.

"Of course you don't," said Cymon.

"But we didn't build it," said Jake. "No one from earth built it. The other worlds – they have been there much longer than we have been here – they learned how to build it."

"What kind of weapons does this ship have?" asked Nemed. Nemed had not been asking many questions this evening. Cymon had not given him the space. But while Cymon was taking a break from his declaiming to have more of the cheese and sour cabbage, Nemed took advantage of the opening.

"If the ship has weapons, I've never seen them," said Jake.

"No weapons?" said Nemed. "How does it defend itself?"

"I don't think it needs to defend itself," said Jake.

"If it doesn't need to defend itself, then why is it concerned with Rome?" said Nemed. "Rome has armies, and you say that Rome is a threat, but you say that this ship has no need to defend itself. What about the Celts? Are the Celts not a threat? The Celts have armies too. One moment you say that this ship, or at least the people who built it, are unimaginably powerful. And yet you – they – are threatened by Rome, whose little ships sail only on the water. I cannot understand this fear of Rome. Have you talked with the Romans? Have you been to Rome, as Divitiacus went to Rome, to plead for an alliance? Clearly there is trickery here. I saw your ship, too, but it was only a trick. Only a few days before you came, we had seen a ship offshore, a real ship, almost certainly pirates from the south, or spies. That was truly what brought you here – some intrigue from far to the south past Gibraltar, some plot to set the Celts against the Romans again, to bring the Romans back to Gaul and distract the Roman legions. Is it truly the safety of the Celts that you seek? Then I cannot see why you do not talk with Rome just as you seek to talk with the Celts.

Even you say that Rome will rule for hundreds more years, and that – how did Judith say it? – that Rome's shadow will loom over civilization for two thousand years. So why do you not talk with the Romans?"

"You're not understanding," said Jake.

"Of course I'm not understanding," said Nemed. "You are confused. You have not thought your story through and ordered your lies. Not only do you not talk with the Romans, you also have threatened Julius Caesar."

"No one has threatened Caesar," said Jake. "Why do you think that?"

"Because Judith said that Caesar will be dead in four more years," said Nemed. Nemed scratched hard at his scalp again.

"That is – only a prediction, not a threat," said Jake. "Caesar will be killed by his own friends. We have nothing to do with his death."

"Then who set his friends to do it?" said Nemed. "Who conspired with them?"

"As I said, you are not understanding," said Jake.

"It appears to us that you are not understanding," said Cymon, through a mouthful of cheese and cabbage. "You say that Caesar will die, and you say that this is only a prediction. But how is it that you make this prediction? The stars say no such thing."

"You are asking me to repeat myself," said Jake. "We come from the future. That is how we know what will happen."

"But that you have come from the future is clearly impossible," said Cymon. "So tell us. Where are you really from? Are you from Egypt? Persia? I have not seen this ship of yours. Nemed saw that it was a trick. There are many Druids, as well as Egyptians and Persians, with the skill to cause people to believe that they have seen such a thing. Perhaps Lodan and Gwenlliant conspire with you. They have the skill to conjure and deceive, though they claim to disdain such arts. Let us prove this prediction. If you know so much about the stars, then let us go up to the top of the anvil. Show me what it is in the stars that says that Caesar will die in four more years. Show me this future that you say you have come to warn us about."

"Why are you disguised?" asked Nemed.

"What?" said Jake.

"Why are you wearing the habit of Druid, when you are not a Druid?"

"It's hard to explain," said Jake.

"I'm sure it is," said Cymon.

"Melwas, we're all tired," said Heledd. "Maybe we should get some sleep. We have to be on our way tomorrow."

Cymon and Nemed muttered to each other and shouted after them, but the four travelers excused themselves and worked their way to the door. All during supper, the serving boy and the sailor that Nemed had brought with him had peeked around the doorway from the kitchen. Apparently they were not permitted to sit at the table with the others, and so their suppers were delayed until the others had finished. From the doorway, Heledd gestured toward Jake to indicate that Jake should look back toward the table. The sailor and the serving boy had descended on the table and were eating ravenously from their leavings. Cymon was picking his teeth. Nemed was scratching his scalp. Cymon swung his fist at the water and wood boy and told him to slow down. The water and wood boy snatched a barley cake and cringed away.

"They're all mad," said Heledd.

"I believe they may be," said Jake. "There's something very strange about them, especially their eyes. Though I can't blame them for being skeptical."

"I think that what they say about the mushrooms is true," said Melwas.

"Mushrooms?" said Jake.

"There is a certain mushroom that grows in the fir forests here," said Melwas. "They are said to cause visions, but eventually they also make men mad and wear down their minds, filling them with fear and suspicion. I believe there were mushrooms in the soup they were eating, the soup that they didn't offer to share. There are many other ways to gain visions, for those who seek them. But I suppose that the mushrooms are the only giver of visions that they have here. Their visions are dark ones."

"That is true about the mushrooms," said Heledd. "I believe that Nemed has developed a taste for these mushrooms. Both he and Cymon eat them far too often. Perhaps that is part of why Nemed comes here. This is where he gets his mushrooms. And his lice. Even the poorest of our villagers do not have lice. Cymon lives in filth and is stingy with everything, including water for washing."

—•—

They all slept in a single unused room of Cymon's tower, at the top level. Some of the roof slates were broken. The leak had caused a couple of the roof's supporting beams to start to rot. The wooden shutters on two of the four windows were broken. Birds and squirrels had gotten in and littered the floor. Jake muttered curses as he surveyed the damage with the light of a candle. To Jake it was a sacrilege to neglect such a building. Heledd had taken the candle and gone down to find the water and wood boy, who was in the kitchen now, poking at the fire and gnawing on a hunk of cheese. Heledd demanded a broom so that she could sweep the floor upstairs before they tried to sleep on it. The sweeping raised an irritating dust. They opened the remaining shutters to try to clear the air.

Melwas awakened them before dawn. He had decided during the night that they should leave immediately. The room was lit by starlight through the open windows.

"So abruptly?" asked Heledd. "Shouldn't I at least write a note?"

"If you can write a note quickly, and if you can think of anything to say," said Melwas. "But I doubt that there is anything to say that will put the egg we've broken back into its shell. Maybe just thank Cymon, as though leaving this morning was our plan all along."

Their ponies seemed content in the tiny stable. To

their surprise, the packs that contained grain for the ponies had not been disturbed, except perhaps by mice. Cymon's boy had been stingy with water for the ponies, though. The water bucket was empty.

"At least the ale was well spent," said Melwas. "Nemed is still drunk on it. He does not mean for some of us to leave. He wants Jake in chains to sell to the Romans. The rest of us are in his way."

"If only there was some way to get word to Lodan and Gwenlliant and Jowan that the bard is here," said Heledd.

"They already are being cautious," said Melwas. "But I doubt that they will see the bard again at the coast. I was thinking during the night. The inland road lies not too far to the east of here. Nemed and his thug probably will take that road and get a ship from the firth. With Jake as a prisoner, he'd get much more reward from the Romans than he'd get only from strange drawings and stories of conspiracy in the north."

"Aren't we going east now, toward the same road?" asked Jake.

"That is why we must hurry," said Melwas. "We have ponies. We can stay ahead of them. They'd have wanted our ponies, too, you know."

"Where is Miach?" asked Heledd.

"He has run to let the squirrels out," said Jake.

— ▸ ◂ —

They traveled hard all morning through a warm drizzle. The tree canopy high over their heads constantly dripped on them. The air was too hot to wear his mantle, so Jake just let himself get wet. At times, when they descended into cool dingles through which cold streams ran, he could see steam rising from his clothing. He was sweating hard from the exertion.

The ponies, which had mostly enjoyed the trip up to this point, were getting testy at being pushed so hard. Miach talked sweetly to them, though he gave the ponies little peace. In mid-afternoon, they emerged from the forest into a narrow valley through which a cold, fast-moving stream meandered. Lush grass and bright flowers grew in the dark soil among the rocks. Honeybees hurried from bloom to bloom. Clouds of midges were gathering around the ponies' eyes, and buzzing clegs were trying to land on the ponies' rumps, keeping the ponies' tails busy slapping at pests. The midges seemed to have a particular liking for Jake. He waved his arms around his head to ward them off, but the midges immediately returned. One of the ponies kicked at Miach when Miach tried to prevent the pony from stopping to eat some grass.

"Please, Melwas," said Miach. "They want to rest, and drink, and have some grass. They don't understand."

"They can have their fill of water and a mouthful or two of grass," said Melwas, "but then we have to keep moving. I can almost smell that foul bard and his thug close behind us. It's easy enough to follow a trail left by loaded ponies."

"Could we lose them them if we waded the stream for a while?" said Jake. "The cold water would feel good."

"It would slow us down too much," said Melwas. "But if we're lucky we might find some terrain where we won't leave hoof prints two fingers deep."

"Could we travel for part of the night?" asked Heledd. "It would be less hot."

"Too dangerous," said Melwas. "Either one of us or one of the ponies would break an ankle."

Just then a curlew flew up out of the stream where it had been wading, startling the ponies. One of the ponies tried to rear but stumbled. The pony's pack, tied on too hastily that morning, fell with a crash that sounded like shattering pottery, further frightening the ponies. Now Miach was in tears as he tried to calm the ponies, partly out of empathy for the ponies and partly because he had loaded the pony.

"All right," said Melwas. "We'll stop for a while. But we can't stop for long."

"What's the matter?" Jake asked Heledd. He had noticed the dark look on her face and how she had lowered her eyes.

"It can't be good luck to break crocks of honey and jars of salt," she said.

"Can we salvage it?" asked Jake.

"We can eat the honey and do our best to sweep up the salt," said Heledd.

For half an hour, while the ponies grazed, they squatted over the mess and ate honey with their fingers, slapping at midges. The curlew returned and watched them from the top of an alder tree. Ants soon found the honey, and they formed lines between the wreckage of the honey crocks and their thatched ant mounds.

"Let the ants have the rest of it," said Heledd. "Who would like some cheese?"

They were starting to feel less irritable when Melwas said that it was time to go. They washed their hands and faces in the stream, retrieved the ponies, and rushed on.

They had been moving again for half an hour when Miach dashed off the path, bent double over a patch of saxifrage, and puked. Heledd went to him.

"You ate some of the salt, too, didn't you?" Heledd said.

Miach nodded, wiping his mouth with the back of his hand.

"Do you feel better now?" Heledd asked.

Miach nodded and looked toward the stream.

"Have yourself a good drink from the stream," said Melwas. "Ponies, too. We have to leave the stream soon and cross that ridge up ahead."

The drizzle had stopped, and the sky had cleared except for the northern horizon. They toiled up the ridge in the heat of the afternoon with no shade to be had. Finally they reached the top. Their route lay down a steep and wooded north slope toward another narrow valley.

"We will camp tonight in those woods down there," said Melwas.

"Is the bard really desperate enough to follow us so far?" said Heledd.

"Yes," said Melwas. "We have food. They probably

want our food as much as they want Jake to sell to the Romans."

"At least there will be no more climbing today," said Heledd.

Jake was looking back down the southern slope, the way they had come. A light haze hung over the valley behind them.

"What do you see, Jake?" asked Heledd.

"I'm not sure," said Jake. "Maybe nothing."

"Let's get off this ridge," said Melwas.

Melwas kept them moving until the light began to fade. They had come into dense forest again. They had stopped three times while Miach had fits of retching. Heledd had slipped on a loose rock while descending the ridge and had turned an ankle. She protested that it was nothing serious, but it had slowed them down. For their camp, Melwas chose a ravine well off the track where they'd have some hope of hiding from the moonlight in the dense undergrowth. The air was too stuffy for an evening fire, but Melwas went to gather wood anyway, in case they wanted it during the night. A full moon rose as the sun set. On a ridge a mile to the north, wolves began to call, eager for a night of hunting.

It was then that the bard and his thug set upon them. Afterwards, Jake wondered if the mushrooms had affected the bard's judgment. It made no sense to risk a sword fight with the captain of the king's guard. But perhaps the thug was an overconfident type, or they were hungry, like the wolves. They made their move while Melwas was away getting wood.

Miach had unbundled Jake's sword from the pony's pack where it usually was kept and had laid it beside Jake's bedroll. Heledd had disappeared into the brush to attend to personal matters. Melwas had been away for half an hour, gathering a third load of wood. Miach was exploring one of the packs, pulling out items for supper that didn't require a fire.

The bard and his thug came at Jake first, intending to take Jake from behind. But Miach heard their overconfident dash from cover. Miach picked up a heavy stick of wood and was on them with a furious swiftness. He cracked the bard, who was no swordsman or fighter, on the head with the stick, and the bard went down. But the thug changed course toward Miach. The thug hit Miach in the head with the flat of his sword while Miach was trying to regain his balance, still holding the stick of wood. Miach collapsed with sickening suddenness and did not move. Miach's sacrifice gave Jake time to grab his sword and for his body to release a fierce surge of adrenaline. Jake's next move was so crude and so effective that he marveled at it for the rest of his life. A wave of hatred and anger ran through him beyond anything he had ever felt or ever felt again. As the thug rushed toward him, it was as though Jake's young body – his youth, his strength, his agility, his love, and his hatred – all merged into one murderous intent that concentrated itself into a vicious and awkward swing of his sword, as far out as he could reach and certain to end in a fall. The last two inches of the point of Jake's sword caught the thug in the throat and ripped it open. Blood spurted.

The thug fell with a clatter and a sound from his mouth that was half scream, half gargle. Jake fell, rolled, and lost his grip on his sword.

As Jake raised his head, the bard was running toward the undergrowth. It took only a few seconds for the thug to stop gargling. Heledd already had reached Miach.

"He is alive," she said, "but he is bleeding, and the blow was very hard."

She tore off strips of her linen habit and pressed it against Miach's head to slow the bleeding.

For the rest of his life, Jake remembered all this, in every detail. One of the things he marveled at was why he did not just explode then, as he stood there panting, sword back in his hands, into a supernova of rage. He wondered why he did not at least go hack the body of the dead thug to avenge what they had done to this angelic boy.

"Cold water may help," said Heledd, "if you can find some quick. But I am afraid that if he does not wake up soon, then he will not live."

Melwas appeared then, moving warily out of a thicket. Jake called out to him.

"It's over," Jake said. "One of them is dead, and Nemed has run off. We need cold water for Miach."

"He is hurt?" said Melwas.

"There is hope," said Jake.

Jake reached into the collar of his Druid's habit. His hand came out with his pendant. He pressed the panic button.

It was only five minutes until the gnat appeared

above them, searchlight blazing. The light found them. Melwas had gone to get water, and he came running back. The canopy of the trees was dense. The gnat moved off slightly to the east. Narrow beams of brilliant light emerged from its bottom. The beams cut a circular hole through the canopy. Smoking branches fell, and the gnat descended to the forest floor.

"It does have weapons," said Melwas.

The gnat's door slid open, and its interior lit up.

Melwas and Jake lifted Miach gently and carried him into the gnat while Heledd cradled his head. They placed him on the soft floor. Heledd knelt over him. She stroked his forehead.

"My sweet boy," she said. "My sweet, beloved boy."

"Go with him," said Jake. "Take care of him. You will learn."

She looked up, puzzled for a moment. Then she nodded.

"Where will I find you?" she asked.

"How do we get to your family's farm?" asked Jake.

"Stay on the track to the village," she said. "Then ask in the village where Heledd's family lives."

"We will wait for you there," said Jake. "You'd better go now, quickly."

Heledd nodded, said goodbye with her eyes, and Jake and Melwas stepped out of the gnat. Its door closed. The gnat rose silently through the hole that it had cut in the trees. Jake and Melwas stood looking up into the sky long after the gnat had faded into the blackness of space.

The next morning, as Jake and Melwas searched the

ground, they found the thug's heavy pack hidden in the brush. Clearly the thug had been Nemed's beast of burden. They found two small sacks filled with dried mushrooms. There was little food. There was the bard's lyre. Jake's drawings were there, as well as Judith's notebooks. There was a pair of panties stolen from Judith or Aderyn. There were three of Jake's colored pencils and a pen.

"He was in my room, too," said Jake. "I had not missed these things."

Jake took the lyre and smashed it with a rock.

CHAPTER 9

Jake's great fear was that the gnat would return too soon. As long as they stayed away, Miach must be alive. On the second day after Heledd's and Miach's departure, the track left the forest and came into a narrow valley. Pastures alternated with wheat and barley fields. Melwas and Jake each now led two ponies, but the ponies were obedient (though they seemed to miss Miach) and would generally follow without being led at all, unless they were tempted by a shady patch of grass on a warm afternoon.

A brief and timid thunderstorm sprang up from the south over a forested ridge and soaked the little valley, the first thunderstorm that Jake had seen in Scotland. They waited under an elderly apple tree for the storm to pass. The ponies crunched on fallen apples. The green of the valley was almost surreal. The soil was deep, black, and well watered. Vine-covered fences, sometimes of stone and sometimes of weathered wooden rails, meandered around the edges of the pastures. The cows were fat. The ponies had to be diverted from a lush little field of turnips, rutabagas, and onions.

Always as they walked, Jake compulsively checked the sky. At night, under the open sky, he would fall asleep watching the stars, as he had so often done before. But now he scanned the sky with worry. Jake convinced himself that, if Heledd and Miach were gone for at least a week, then Miach surely would be OK.

On the morning of the fourth day, they reached the village that Heledd had told them to look for. That afternoon, they came to the farm of Heledd's foster parents. The farm was miles from the nearest neighbor. They reached the farm by following a narrow stream that rushed clear and cold through a deep valley. Then the valley widened, and they were in fields and rich pasture again – the fields and pasture of Heledd's family's farm.

They told Heledd's foster parents, Pryderi and Deirdre, that Heledd had sent them to help on the farm. Heledd had been detained by a patient, they said, but she should be along before long. Jake was not surprised that Pryderi and Deirdre wore gold rings. They did not seem to think it was particularly strange that Heledd had sent them help, or that she had been detained. They were solid and cheerful country people, generous with what they had and grateful for what the ponies had brought. Heledd had a young foster sister, Ethlinn, age about eight, who adored the visitors and the ponies from the moment they arrived.

Ethlinn, Jake soon saw, was responsible for all the routine care of the livestock. There were about a dozen sheep, a pair of goats with a single kid, three cows, a bull, and two mules. The bull was used for plowing. The mules were beasts of burden and sometimes pulled a wagon with a double-tree and harnesses. Ethlinn saw quickly that Jake was most fascinated by driving the mules and the wagon, but she also insisted on teaching Jake the proper technique for milking the cows, an important job that Deirdre still oversaw, because Ethlinn was still learning to handle milking and milk. Ethlinn had laughed at Jake when she first saw his milking technique. Even Deirdre had been amused.

"I have often seen a cow kick a man or knock over a bucket," said Deirdre. "But I never saw a cow kick a woman."

Melwas applied his sturdy muscles to helping Pryderi with heavy labor. They cut timbers for a new shed. The thatch for the shed's roof was already dry and waiting in a barn. Jake sketched a plan for the shed.

Pryderi and Deirdre were prosperous farmers, a good choice for fostering a Druid's daughter, though they were shorthanded now that their son had married and they had no more sons at home. Soon they would be receiving a new foster son, a boy of fourteen. With a strong teenager to help with the work, they would be ready for six or eight more cattle. The ponies that had come with Jake and Melwas were roaming free now in an upper pasture white with blooming clover.

The farmhouse was rectangular, in two sections. It was built mostly of stone. One section had a low roof, of thatch. The taller section of the house contained a kitchen and a great room. Its roof was of slate. A low stone chimney stood above a large fireplace. Much of the cooking was done in the fireplace, though in the summer some of the cooking was done in the yard in a copper cauldron supported by an iron tripod, both prized possessions. A little fence – a rough version of a picket fence – surrounded the house to keep the cows out, because the house stood in the middle of pasture. Shrubs and flowers edged the inside of the fence. There even was a stone-lined well, of which Pryderi and Deirdre were very proud and which they treated with great reverence. The well's water was pure and icy cold. Ethlinn showed Jake how to draw water with a rope and a bucket made of wooden staves.

Ethlinn had befriended a warren of wild rabbits. Each day she would take the rabbits turnips from the field, herbs that she pruned from her mother's kitchen garden, green apples, and scraps from the table. Most of the rabbits had names, but the summer rabbit crop was so abundant that she was falling behind in naming the kits. Jake told her the tale of *The Flopsy Bunnies*. Soon there were kits named Flopsy, Benjamin, and Peter.

Jake had brought paper and many colored pencils. For hours, when the chores were done, Ethlinn would sit beside Jake and watch him draw. Often, to please Ethlinn, he would draw rabbits dressed in bright clothing. But it was the cottage, more than anything, that Jake found visually arresting. This place and Phaedrus' place were, in a sense, a world apart. And yet they were the same. It struck Jake just how little had changed in how subsistence farming was done, if you subtracted gasoline and put mules and a wagon in the place of a truck. How well Jake understood now the role of manual labor and the value of healthy children. Jake made detailed drawings of the cottage for Phaedrus. He also drew maps of the farm that showed the pastures, the fields, the streams, the rabbit warren, the well, the sheds, the outhouse, and the paths and tracks that connected everything.

Phaedrus, Jake knew, would ask him to describe how these people expressed their sense of magic. Jake wasn't yet sure how he would answer. Their sense of magic – even their sense of religion, if you wanted to call it that – was never very overt or conspicuous. There were no pious rituals, no such thing as prayer since none of their gods were invisible, and no concept of evil that Jake could discern. Rather, the magical elements were just an everyday part of the landscape, like the rabbit warren, the wild walnut tree, or the spring that the cows drank from. Ethlinn had warned him to be careful not to knock loose stones into the well, or to splash too much with the bucket, or even to talk too loudly around the well, because only the sounds of dripping and trickling and raindrops were pleasing to the well spirit. Everyone knew that trees hated iron and fire, and that when you took a tree it was best to bring its neighbors offerings of water and loam to soothe them and to make sure that there were nuts or acorns nearby to shelter the soul of the departed tree.

On the seventh day, Jake was truly happy. There was simply no way that Bendigeid and the incomprehensibly advanced medical systems on the ship would let Miach die if he had managed to live for seven days. Jake then tried to refine another calculus. When would they return? How long would it take Miach to heal? His skull probably had been fractured, and the concussion to the brain would have been very dangerous. Perhaps Bendigeid, Heledd, and the ship's medical systems were being very cautious, though pharmaceuticals would hasten the healing. After Jake's wrist had been broken, they had nursed him like a new mother cat. Jake figured that three weeks was the minimum time for them to be away. Then they could return any time after that.

Speaking of cats, everyone here had the same problem – mice in their barns, mice in their granaries, mice in their flour sacks and flour barrels. Cats had begun their slow migration northward from the Mediterranean, but the day had not yet come when cats' numbers would explode in the north. For now, cats were prized. Not for a long time would they become so common that it would be hard to give them away.

On the twenty-fourth day, the entire family including Jake and Melwas were in the paddock to greet a healthy new calf that had been born during the night. There was a new human member of the family now, as well. That was Rath, the new foster son. He looked every bit of fourteen, freckle-faced and lanky, ever so slightly sullen, with a changing voice that sometimes cracked when he spoke and embarrassed him.

Jake had not prepared the family in any way for Heledd's return, thinking it best that Heledd herself should explain it. Maybe they wouldn't come on the gnat. Maybe they would just come walking up the narrow little road that led to the village, with the gnat staying discreetly out of sight. But Jake was getting the idea that Bendigeid enjoyed a little drama. If you've got that kind of ride, why not show it off? In fact, Jake wondered if they might not arrive on a gnat at all, but instead in the big black triangle, its stairs extended ceremonially for a grand descent. That would certainly make an impression. Once, on a visit to San Francisco, Jake's parents had taken him to the Golden Gate Bridge for the arrival of an aircraft carrier, the *John C. Stennis*. There was heavy fog over San Francisco Bay. Jake was wondering if they would be able to see the aircraft carrier at all through the fog as it passed under the magnificent bridge. And then suddenly there the ship was. It materialized out of the mist off the Pacific, as silently as a black triangle materializes out of the clouds. Sailors in dress whites were arrayed around the edges of all the decks. They stood perfectly still at attention as the enormous ship glided under the bridge. Jake had been Rath's age then, but he had realized even then how much the military depended on theater, especially in a time of peace, or when war was threatening. Military theater was a form of shock and awe, but without a single weapon fired.

Then the gnat appeared. It came straight down out of a clear sky, decelerating as it descended. Jake pointed. The others seemed more nervously curious than afraid, but then they saw how happy Jake looked. The gnat landed, with a neat but minor last-second course change to avoid a cow patty. The door slid open.

Heledd, too, had a flair for drama. Miach emerged first. Heledd waited inside a good half a minute, to let Miach have the stage. Miach was radiant with happiness, looking completely recovered. He wore a black outfit that looked a bit like something that Bendigeid sometimes wore. Miach must have taken a fancy to the outfit. But, best of all, just as Jake had expected, there was no longer any sign of Miach's deformity. Instead there was a beautiful, happy boy with a dazzling smile and pretty teeth. Miach saw Jake and lowered his eyes, as though he still had not quite learned that he was beautiful when he smiled. Jake stepped forward, and Miach ran to him. Even Melwas was crying now, though Pryderi and Deirdre, and Ethlinn and Rath, weren't quite sure why. Then Heledd appeared in the doorway of the gnat and waved. Then everybody was happy, and everybody was crying except for Rath, who must have wondered what he had gotten himself into. The gnat still sat there, door open.

Heledd pointed to the door. Sam emerged. His levitation mechanism didn't work outside the ship, so he moved on three struts, each with a wide wheel. Sam steered around the cow patties.

"Hello, Jake," said Sam.

"Hello, Sam," said Jake.

Sam extended an arm.

"A message from Bendigeid," Sam said.

"Thank you, Sam," said Jake. "All is well?"

"All is well," said Sam. "Miach loves cats. Perhaps you can find him one?"

Heavy rain was falling on crop and cottage out of a gloomy sky. The empty woodshed was a dry, though a crowded, place to work. Jake, Heledd, Miach and Melwas were washing a cartload of fresh turnips and preparing them for storage in the root cellar. A young goat was nosing through the pile of surplus turnip greens. It was the day before they were to return to the coast, and Melwas finally said what he'd been dreading to say for days:

"We can make it quick, but Cymon has to know about Nemed's treachery. We can stay at the observatory one night and then be on our way again."

Everyone groaned.

"Just look at this healthy soil," said Jake. "There's another earthworm. What a shame to feed all these turnip tops to the cows."

"The chickens will eat them, too," said Heledd. "And the pigs as well. It won't fatten the pigs, but it will make their skin glow. And the chickens will lay eggs with yolks as golden as King Jowan's torc."

"Should we take Cymon some turnips?" asked Jake. "I didn't see any sign of a garden at the observatory."

"There hasn't been a garden at the observatory in years," said Heledd. "Cymon would eat nothing but pig if he could get it, but he always eats his last sow even before midwinter. Then he writes to Lodan to send more pigs. Cymon thinks he's too good and too highborn to eat turnips."

"What about his water and wood boy?" asked Jake. "Some turnips would do the poor boy good."

"We'll take him some turnips," said Melwas. "The ponies won't have much else to carry on the way back."

"I'm sure we can spare some cheese," said Heledd. "I'd send barley and wheat, but there's nobody at the observatory anymore to grind and bake."

"They can make mush and porridge," said Melwas. "Let's take some grain anyway, if Pryderi and Deirdre are willing."

"Crocked strawberries? Honey?" said Miach. "Llud never gets anything like that."

Llud was the water and wood boy.

"Of course," said Heledd. "Llud shall have it. We'll make a feast for Llud, with turnips that Cymon won't eat, we'll rest the ponies and sleep a few hours, and then we'll be on our way."

They left the farm the next day shortly after dawn. The rain had stopped, at least for a while. Low, heavy clouds continued to roll out of the southwest, dragging their gray underbellies across the ridges. Ethlinn cried to see them go, clinging first to Heledd and then to Jake. Heledd promised Ethlinn that she'd return to help put away the fall turnips. Jake gave Ethlinn four of his drawing pencils, the four colors of her choice, and a few sheets of his precious paper. Deirdre, Pryderi, Ethlinn, and even Rath, the new foster son, stood watching them, waving, until they were out of sight.

As they led the ponies along the track beside a rushing stream, Melwas kept looking at the sky.

"This rain hasn't finished," said Melwas. "We won't be dry for long. Even if the rain holds off, the fording is going to be much wetter work than before. What did you call those things that you make to start fires with?"

"Feather sticks," said Jake. "Some people call them fuzz sticks."

"You'd better whittle as many of them as you can," said Melwas. "They're our only hope for sleeping warm and dry."

An hour before dusk, they forded the first swollen stream. Jake cursed at the coldness of the water against his belly. The ponies had to swim, snorting with disapproval. They camped under the cover of an evergreen grove just above the stream. Jake's teeth were chattering as he blew on the feather sticks to start their evening fire. Melwas laughed with pleasure at the efficiency of Jake's fire-making. They had an evening routine. Melwas would strike the tinder, and then Jake would take over with his feather sticks. The first feather sticks were of fir, for a quick start. Then there would be a sequence of hardwood feather sticks of increasing size. Soon the fire would be big enough that even wet wood would begin to sizzle and burn. As soon as there were coals, Heledd was ready with the pots, and savory warm smells would waft out of the fire along with the smoke. As long as the light lasted, Miach and Melwas would keep adding to the wood piles. There would always be three wood piles, sorted by size. Jake would tend the fire while Heledd cooked. Even in the rain, they always had a hot supper.

Cold water dripped from the canopy of the trees. A little roof of hides tied to the tree trunks kept most of the cold water away. They huddled in their little shelter, smoke in their eyes, tummies full of warm food, Miach leaning against Jake on one side and Heledd on the other.

"Will you tell us another story?" Miach asked Jake.

"Tell us a story about one of your womenfolk," said Heledd. "There have been too few of those."

"Let's see," said Jake. "How about Joan of Arc. But how in the world would I explain her?"

"What do you mean?" asked Heledd.

"For example, Joan of Arc dressed as a man and went to war," said Jake. "But in her time no woman did that. They said she was a witch, because as a child she had danced under a fairy tree. It's terrible what they did to her, because she disagreed with the Roman church. First she was a heretic, and then she was a saint."

"What is a heretic?" asked Miach. "And what is a saint?"

"Start explaining," said Heledd. "What is so strange about dressing as a man, or going to war?"

It rained every day. Traveling was so slow and miserable that they started looking forward to arriving at the observatory. Melwas had even suggested remaining at the observatory until the weather changed. Everyone groaned on cue when the observatory was mentioned, then laughed. Being cold and wet was worse than Cymon's company. Besides, they could take refuge at the top of the tower. They could even make excuses for not taking their meals with Cymon.

Around midday of the sixth day, at last they saw the anvil of rock standing above the treetops, and the gray slate roof of the observatory tower. It had been raining since dawn. This time the water and wood boy did not come out to meet them, though they called out to make their presence known. They led the grateful ponies into the dry stable, unloaded the packs, and slogged through pouring rain to the tower.

The door was standing half open. They called out and got no response.

Melwas drew his sword.

"Something is wrong," Melwas said. "All of you wait here."

The heavy door groaned on its rusting hinges as Melwas went inside. Jake, Heledd, and Miach waited silently by the door. Miach held Heledd's hand. At times they could hear Melwas' feet on the wooden stairs, or Melwas opening and closing doors. At last he returned to the doorway, sword sheathed.

"There is no one here," said Melwas. "You can come in out of the rain now."

They all unconsciously avoided the cluttered table, where they had had their strange supper with Cymon and the bard. Cupboard doors were standing open. A sealed crock had been smashed on the floor, and its fragments were scattered. Wooden boxes were on the floor, lids removed, as though someone had plundered through them. They followed Melwas into the kitchen. The room was damp and stank of rotting flesh. The hearth was cold and overflowing with wet, black ashes. Dirty rainwater had flowed down out of the cold chimney onto the stone floor.

"Where do you think they've gone?" asked Jake.

"I fear we will never see Cymon again," said Melwas.

"I too have a bad feeling about Cymon," said Heledd. "As for Llud, he'll have gone to a place where there's something to eat. The rummaging and pilfering look like Llud's work, before he vanished. But shall we look for them outside?"

"Not in this weather," said Melwas. "I'll climb the anvil and have a look in the morning. But no one has been here for days. I don't think we'll find much. Now let's clean this place up and try to get rid of this smell."

"There's no wood," said Jake.

"I saw a little wood in the woodshed," said Miach. "We'll soon have more."

"Miach," said Melwas, "see if you can find some cedar wood – anything that smells good."

They worked like dwarves until dusk. Fires roared and crackled in two fireplaces – both the fireplace in the kitchen and the enormous fireplace in the great room. Floors were swept and the sweepings burned. They scrubbed tables and floors with hot water and the soap they had brought with them. They sang as they worked. The stink was steadily sucked up the chimneys, replaced by the fragrance of rosemary soap and burning cedar. Heledd festooned the mantels with ivy. She had insisted that it was worth going out into the rain to get, and she did it herself, though Miach had volunteered. A pot of cheery greenery and a flower or two was in the center of the big table in the great room. Outside, the rain fell like a tropical squall. The wind whistled around the shutters, which were open just enough to let in some of the gray light. Occasionally there was the rumble of distant thunder.

As dusk approached, Heledd put turnips and onions onto the kitchen hearth to roast. In the great copper pot over the fire, which she had carefully scrubbed, a soup was bubbling, with barley, cabbage, and savory vegetables and herbs.

"What a place!" said Jake. "It feels completely different now, almost homey. I almost think the stones are relieved to be rid of Cymon and his stink."

"Not to mention his foul temper," said Heledd. "But I do feel sorry for Llud. He deserved better. If Llud did Cymon in, nobody would hold it against him."

"Have any theories occurred to you about where they might have gone?" asked Jake.

"None that I want to talk about while it is dark," said Heledd. "Let's be of good cheer this evening. We're warm and dry and safe. Let's build up the fire in the great room and set the table for a feast. What's that sound?"

They all had heard it. It was the high-pitched sound of a dog barking. Then there was the sound of pounding on the great wooden door. Melwas drew his sword.

"Stay near the kitchen," said Melwas. "If there's any kind of trouble, get out by the kitchen door and go to the ponies."

Melwas stole quietly to the great wooden door and stood with one hand on his sword and the other hand on the iron latch.

"Who's there?" Melwas called.

"It's Derbhorgill. Let us in. It's pouring."

Jake didn't know who Derbhorgill might be, but he did see that Miach was suddenly beaming and that Heledd's shoulders had relaxed. Melwas lifted the latch and opened the door. A white fox bounded into the room. It saw Miach, who was kneeling now, and crashed into Miach's arms.

"Fingal!" cried Miach. "Derbhorgill!"

Two figures in wet cloaks came in and paused beside Melwas. Melwas closed the door. The latch clinked. The two figures threw back their dripping hoods and stared around the room in wonder. Clearly this was not the greeting that they had been expecting. Heledd approached one of the two figures, beaming. They embraced. Miach was still rough-housing with the white fox.

"Let me have your cloaks," said Heledd. "Come to the fire."

"I don't understand," said the smaller of the two figures. "Where is Cymon? I never thought to see you here, Heledd, Melwas and Miach. I haven't seen such a fire in this room since I was a little girl."

The two figures went to the fireplace, and Jake

studied them more closely in the firelight. The taller one was bearded and muscular. The other was beardless, but Jake nevertheless had taken her for a youngish man not much older than Jake himself.

"Derbhorgill," said Heledd. "How fit and healthy you look, though you are soaked. I believe some introductions are needed."

"Yes," said Derbhorgill. She gestured toward the tall man.

"This is Leonard," said Derbhorgill. "He has come from from the south and has many stories to tell. We have traveled together from Anglesey, on the inland road."

Leonard bowed. Derbhorgill looked toward Jake.

"Come closer, Jake," said Heledd. "This is Derbhorgill, the greatest seer in either Gaul or Britain. Derbhorgill has foreseen much that you have told us, and it was his words that Gwenlliant respoke to you."

Jake almost tripped over a happy fox and a happy Miach as he made his way from the kitchen door to the fireplace. Heledd had used the pronoun "he," though Derbhorgill had spoken of being a little girl. In the firelight, glowing with an aura of faerie, was a person of elven beauty – red hair, bright green eyes, slightly built but tall and regal, though not as tall as Jake. Jake reached out to shake his hand. Derbhorgill's eyes, like Jake's, were full of wonder in the firelight, as though Derbhorgill, too, felt himself to be in the presence of magic. Their hands met and clasped.

Just then there was a flash of nearby lightning and

a crash of thunder that made the floors of the tower shake. Jake felt Derbhorgill's hand tense and then start to tremble. Derbhorgill's eyes rolled upward, and his knees crumpled. Jake and Heledd both caught him as he fell. They lowered his slender body slowly to the floor. The white fox suddenly was standing over Derbhorgill, licking his face.

"It will soon pass," said Heledd. Derbhorgill's body twitched as Heledd cradled his head and gently stroked his cheek. Derbhorgill's hand was still clasped tightly onto Jake's. They all waited silently, with no sound other than the popping of the fire, the wind against the shutters, and a few soft whimpers from Fingal, the fox. There was another crash of thunder, a little more distant this time.

At last Derbhorgill raised his head and looked at each of the faces arrayed around him.

"Well," said Derbhorgill, sitting up. "That was quite a story. I wish I had been able to stay longer to hear more of it. Jake, you must tell me the rest. But we have so little time. We must start right away. "Where …"

"There now," said Heledd. "There will be time soon for storytelling and talking about the whereabouts of Cymon. Derbhorgill, you are exhausted and half starved. Come, sit at the table, both of you. Supper is almost ready. Sitting on a cold stone floor is no place for stories. Jake, help him stand. Don't worry, little Fingal. He's fine now. Come. All of you. Sit down."

Miach, who knew what fir wood was good for, stoked the fire yet again as Heledd and Melwas brought the soup and roasted vegetables to the table.

"I first saw you years ago," said Derbhorgill to Jake. "You were standing in the open sky, with such stars over your head as I have never seen. There was no earth beneath you. Where is this place?"

"It is not on the earth," said Jake. "It is on the ship that brought me here."

"There was a man with you," said Derbhorgill. "What is his name?"

"His name is Bendigeid," said Jake. "He comes from far away."

"He has told you many stories, many things?" asked Derbhorgill.

"Yes," said Jake. "Many stories and many things."

"I must hear all that, too," said Derbhorgill. "I must hear everything, until you are emptied of stories and as light as a ghost. But I will not ask you to retell tonight stories that the others already have heard. Leonard has been to Rome and has passed through the lands of the Germans. Leonard's stories also must be heard."

"Rome?" said Melwas.

"I was not there long," said Leonard. "It was not safe, much less safe than Greece, or than my homeland in Galatia. I came across the mountains north of Rome and then down into the low country to the sea. I changed ships four times before I arrived at Anglesey. Derbhorgill and I have been traveling since then. There is not much to my stories. Only war and danger and misery."

"What brought you here?" asked Melwas.

"It is a haven that I seek," said Leonard, "a refuge from war and misery and slavery. I have seen enough. I had heard rumors of this place of yours even in Greece and Galatia. My brothers' wives and children were stolen, carried away as slaves to Rome. My brothers died trying to find them. Someday I will have a wife and children. I do not want them to be slaves. I want my wife and children to be as far to the north as possible."

"Lodan and Gwenlliant also must hear Leonard's stories," said Derbhorgill. "It has been years since they have had the report of travelers who have been in Rome. We did not mean to stay here long with Cymon. We can finish our journey together and make a start on the storytelling."

"Derbhorgill," said Heledd, "don't you notice anything different about Miach?"

Derbhorgill studied a smiling Miach in the candlelight and firelight.

"A year older?" said Derbhorgill. "A soft boy down on his upper lip? Happier than before, much happier."

Heledd laughed.

"You always have seen Miach this way, haven't you, Derbhorgill?" said Heledd. "Your eyes do not see the world the way the rest of us do."

"I see Miach giving Fingal cheese under the table," said Derbhorgill. "I see the stars of first love in Miach's eyes. I see things that Miach and I will discuss alone. There is much that is new in your eyes, too, Heledd, since I saw you last. Even if I didn't see you blushing, I would know that you want to discuss these things alone. How strange, though. I came to this tower dreading Cymon's self-deceit and bitterness. I did not expect to find all this happiness instead. Something blinded me. I must discover what that was. But my gift has always been like that. There are shadows that I cannot see into, and it is happening more and more. I hope that I am not losing my gift."

"Even if you lost your gift of far seeing," said Heledd, "you have many others. Even the oldest cannot remember a Druid with a memory as fine as yours. Surely that is not fading?"

"It is not fading," said Derbhorgill. "I am as starved as I ever was for new things to commit to memory. But I don't need the gift of far seeing to see that I am about to have a feast for the memory, if Jake can bear my questions, and if he does not lose his voice from giving the answers."

Derbhorgill's green eyes settled on Jake and seemed to be searching for his soul. Jake cleared his throat.

"I am flattered," said Jake. "I wouldn't want to bore you, but ask and I will tell."

"You blush even more easily than Heledd," said Derbhorgill. "But Heledd can tell you that blushing will not cause me to relent on my questions. It only makes the questions worse, and closer to the mark."

The intensity with which Derbhorgill studied him caused Jake to lower his eyes. Derbhorgill's hands were resting on the table. He wore no rings.

—•—

The rain stopped during the night, and the sun rose the next morning in a golden sky. Jake was awakened by the sound of iron hinges as Heledd opened the shutters on the windows in the top story of the tower where they had slept.

"Listen," she said.

"What?" Jake mumbled. They had gone to sleep late, and he had slept soundly.

"Birds," said Heledd. "I have never hear birds singing here. Is it the sun that makes them sing? Or the news that Cymon is gone?"

"Where are Melwas and Miach?" asked Jake.

"They have gone to climb the anvil and look for signs of Cymon," said Heledd.

"What's that scraping noise downstairs?" asked Jake.

"Derbhorgill and Leonard are emptying the filth out of Cymon's room," said Heledd. "We're burning all his things."

"What if he comes back?" asked Jake.

"He's not coming back," said Heledd. "Look."

She pointed out the window. Jake joined her at the window sill. She was pointing to Melwas and Miach descending the stony path that led up to the anvil. Melwas was carrying something wrapped in a muddy rag.

"That would be Cymon's skull, I am sure," said Heledd. "The wolves will have taken the rest. Let's go out."

Derbhorgill and Melwas were sitting on a moss-covered rock, talking quietly. Miach and Leonard had gone to gather wood.

"Did he fall?" Heledd asked.

"Yes," said Melwas. "Or he was pushed off the path, onto the rocks below. The skull was broken."

"How long ago?" asked Heledd.

"Many days," said Melwas. "This is all that was left."

"The bard? Llud?" said Heledd.

"Llud, more likely," said Melwas. "They often quarreled."

"We will bury his head today," said Derbhorgill. "He was a Druid."

"And that is all I wish to say," said Heledd. "He was a Druid."

"Jake," said Melwas. "We need a few of your fuzz sticks to get that heap of rubbish burning. We can't leave this place until the stink is gone and it's fit to be lived in."

"Derbhorgill," said Heledd. "Will you not stay here? This place should be yours now."

"I must talk with Gwenlliant and Lodan," said Derbhorgill. "I do not yet know what the future holds for me."

"Yet you are an ovate," said Heledd, "and the future is your skill. There are choices, then?"

"There are choices," said Derbhorgill. "Not only mine, but the choices of many people."

— —

On the trek back to the coast, Heledd, Melwas, Miach and Leonard tried to stay as close as possible to Jake and Derbhorgill, to hear what they were saying. Derbhorgill's questions were endless, and as Jake gave answers Derbhorgill would listen carefully:

In this plague in the 14th Century, how many millions died? At least 50 million, said Jake. In the wars of the 20th Century, how many millions died? About 100 million, said Jake. In this final event, as you call it, how many died? About 6 billion, said Jake. Why did they punish this man who said that the earth moved around the sun? It threatened the authority of Rome, said Jake. This recipe for gun powder, you please will not reveal it? I will not, said Jake, though I'm not sure that I even know the recipe. This coal that we often find when mining for copper and silver, there really is that much more of it? They will destroy entire mountains to dig it up, said Jake. It is not just the flapping of a bird's wings that allows it to fly, but also the shape of the wing? That's right, said Jake; I will draw it for you; we could even make a wing out of linen stretched over a wooden frame; it is much like the sail of a ship; you would see how it works when the wind blows across it.

Derbhorgill was an extraordinary camp cook because he had traveled so much, often well supplied, sometimes foraging. For supper on their last evening before arriving at the coast, Derbhorgill made a kind of rustic pilaf of barley, herbs, and wild onions and berries. He roasted the roots of some lilies they had found beside the woods. He roasted the last of their turnips on spits, seasoned with the last of their butter. He had taken honey from a hive of wild bees without getting stung, though Miach, always curious, had gotten a little too close and was stung on the tip of his nose.

Under bright stars in a black sky, they sat around their campfire, bellies full, content. Everyone waited for Derbhorgill's next question.

"When I have learned to write," said Derbhorgill, "what you have told me will fill many pages. But tell me this. Of all the dreadful things that you have told me about the future, when and where would you have wanted to live, if you could choose?"

"They *were* mostly dreadful things that I told you, weren't they?" said Jake. "There must be more good things that could be told. I will think about that. But I've never thought about choosing when and where to live."

"With Robin Hood, perhaps?" asked Derbhorgill. "You seemed to like that time and place, though you say it may be a myth."

"Yes," said Jake. "I might have liked that. I would have loved to help build a cathedral. If only you could see one! I would have loved to explore the earth in the days of the great wind-powered sailing ships. Florence during the Renaissance would have been a beautiful place to live, as long as you were rich. The tribes who lived on the plains of North America, before the Europeans came, must have had good lives, simple lives. I admire the monks of Tibet, though I'm not sure I'd want to live like them for an entire lifetime. Oxford must have been a fine place to be, after the Enlightenment, always so much talking and drinking and reading. I would have loved to be one of the engineers who built the first ships that left the earth and that took men to the moon."

"What kind of life will you return to, Jake?" asked Derbhorgill.

"I often wonder," said Jake.

"Will you have choices?" asked Derbhorgill.

"I hope so," said Jake. "Though I'm afraid that when I chose to come on this trip, I was locking in a certain kind of future for myself."

"What kind of future?" asked Derbhorgill.

"Work," said Jake. "Traveling – though not just to see the sights. I will be expected to put what I've experienced to use and to make what I've learned known to others. Thinking, lots of thinking, including thinking with others – perhaps even arguing with others – about what's best. Learning – trying to fill in the gaps in what I don't know, so that I can think more clearly."

"Will there be time enough for love?" asked Derbhorgill.

"I hope so," said Jake, glancing at Heledd. Her eyes were on the fire. Miach was leaning against her as though he felt cold.

"Will you always remain on the earth? Or will you travel again to the stars?" asked Derbhorgill.

"I don't know," said Jake. "Except for Bendigeid, I have not met the people from the stars, nor seen their worlds."

"You don't think that Bendigeid is preparing you for that?" asked Derbhorgill. "He has to prepare someone to represent earth on their worlds, does he not? Is there anyone else he is preparing?"

Jake laughed.

"There always is a backup," Jake said. "And there are other cultures on earth that never had a history with Rome that needed fixing."

"But only you have gone out into the stars," said Derbhorgill.

"As far as I know," said Jake. "That is the case."

"Did you ever dream of going to the stars," asked Derbhorgill, "before you knew that it was possible?"

"Oh, yes," said Jake. "Many times."

"I have dreamed it, too," said Derbhorgill.

Leonard, who had been coughing, excused himself and went off into the dark for the third time.

"He is sick," said Derbhorgill. "And he is sickest after he eats. I'm afraid he is getting weaker. He needs rest. He has nightmares. He is a brave man, but he is only half the man he was when we left Anglesey."

"Does he ever have trouble breathing?" asked Heledd. "Does he ever have chills as though he is freezing?"

"No," said Derbhorgill. "His troubles are with food. He eats but still slowly wastes. He is strong, but eventually he will be skin and bones if this keeps up."

"We have seen this before," said Heledd, "in travelers from those parts. We have a remedy. The sickness comes from the filth and bad food in Rome. Gwenlliant will be able to cure him."

Leonard quietly reappeared out of the dark and resumed his place by the fire.

"Leonard, tell us about Rome," said Melwas.

"Rome is packed with people living on top of each other, in rotting houses three and four levels deep. Almost all of them are poor. Most are hungry, and many are starving. Gangs of young men roam the streets, killing all those whom they think are enemies. No one tries to stop them. There are not enough soldiers to keep order. In the summer, as when I was there, the few rich flee to the safety of country, and the many poor are left to die in the flies and the heat. Often they die in the streets and are left to rot. Dead babies are thrown out of windows, like trash. Filth, and often blood, run in the gutters. All they talk of is war, war, war, and now civil war. My brothers thought that they would find their wives and children there, steal them back, and take them home. But my brothers died, one of disease, the other murdered. Our mother and our two sisters will never know what became of us, but I will not go home to Galatia. I had heard much of this land called Britain, across a narrow sea from Gaul, that Caesar left unconquered. I could understand much of the speech of those who came from here. So I set out for Britain. The gods led me to Derbhorgill. I was a farmer, but I also learned to fish, and I worked on many ships to travel so far. I like this place. I would like to stay. I will work."

"We have need of men like you," said Heledd.

"Leonard can read," said Derbhorgill.

"Only a little," said Leonard. "For many months I traveled with a Greek. He taught me."

"You will have choices," said Heledd.

<hr>

Lodan was one of the most aloof and serious men that Jake had ever met. But Lodan's delight at seeing Miach was a transformation. Lodan's joy caused him to set aside, at least for a while, his worrying about Bergan's safe return. Lodan insisted on a feast at the broch. It would be a kind of coming-out feast for Miach. Everyone needed to see this miracle. And now, surely Miach would find someone to court him, though everyone knew that's Miach's heart was hopelessly set on Jake. The feast also would be the broch's good-voyage party for Jake. Any day now, Lodan was expecting a trading ship from the south. Depending on wind and weather, Jake's departure for Gaul was probably only days away.

Beltane had been a drunken chaos. But at the broch party, out on the flat between the broch and the sea, first in the dusk and then in the torchlight, the Celts proved that they truly knew how to dance. Jake did his best to make quick sketches of the reels, jigs, and horn-pipes. When the prince arrived, he said that the music could be heard all the way to castle. Everyone wanted to dance with Miach, though Miach required some quick coaching in the steps. Once, when the music slowed to give the dancers a rest, Gwenlliant took Miach's hand, and they did an improvised little *pas de deux*, with Gwenlliant leading. Miach blushed, and his smile was as shy and crooked as always. It would take a long time, Jake realized, for Miach's self-image to catch up with the new reality.

After the *pas de deux*, Gwenlliant took a break to sit with Heledd, Prince Lairgnen and Jake, who were in the torchlight on an improvised bench made from a log. Derbhorgill was dancing with Miach now, with Fingal at their heels – a *pas de trois* for man, fox, and boy, though Derbhorgill had insisted that Miach lead.

"Do you think you would be able to do this surgery yourself?" Gwenlliant asked Heledd.

"I believe I could," said Heledd. "But it is delicate. Worse, the pain would be intense, and the obstruction of the nose and mouth would be almost unbearably frightening. Total anesthesia is the key."

"Did you discuss anesthesia with the ambassador?" asked Gwenlliant.

"I did," said Heledd. "There are possibilities, but we do not have the skill, the apparatus, or the raw materials here to produce it. There may have been chemists in Gaul who might do it, but I feel sure that their work has been disrupted by the war."

"I hear that you have become quite a swordsman," Prince Lairgnen said to Jake.

"It was not skill," said Jake. "Actually it was very clumsy. I hit him, and then I fell down. I did not know that I had such anger and hatred in me."

"I often have heard," said Gwenlliant, "that human beings fight more valiantly for the lives of those they love than for their own lives. It is an instinct in all living things, I think. I have seen it in hens, in sheep, and even in rabbits. Our feelings restrain us when we must kill. But when we kill to protect our loved ones, our empathy vanishes, and we kill with a fury."

"What Gwenlliant says is true," said Lairgnen. "All armies know it to be true."

"My dear Jake," said Gwenlliant. "We should not have brought up that deed and made you feel so glum. This is an evening for celebrating."

"It's not that I regret what I did," said Jake. "I had to do it. But I never thought that I would kill a man, or that I would be glad for having done it."

"You were not trained for killing," said Lairgnen. "Does it weigh on you?"

"No," said Jake. "It doesn't. Especially when I see Miach dancing."

Miach had picked up Fingal now, and the white fox was licking Miach's face.

Heledd put her arms around Jake, and they all sat quiet for a while, watching the reel. Jake sneaked a glance at Lairgnen. If there was jealousy in Lairgnen for Heledd, he hid it well. But fair is fair. Such generosity of spirit deserves its reward. So Jake yawned. Gwenlliant yawned.

"I am exhausted," Gwenlliant said. "It has been a long day, and I have not danced so much in years."

"I will walk you to your cottage," said Jake.

Jake well knew how much the prince wanted to be alone with Heledd. They had been apart for weeks. Jake went to say good night to Miach and promised to get him up early for breakfast at the Cabbage and Kipper.

"Clood will sleep late," said Jake. "Just look how drunk she is. There will be no breakfast in the morning at the broch. After breakfast maybe we can practice our sketching with the view from up the hill. What do you think?"

"I would like that very much," said Miach. Miach understood that Jake was telling him that he would not be cuddling with him at the broch that night. After Heledd and Miach had returned on the gnat, the three of them had resumed their sleeping together, even at the home of Heledd's foster parents. Sleeping arrangements seemed to be of little more concern than who sat beside whom at table, though of course sleeping space was always scarce in these simple homes. Whether people slept together for sex, or for warmth, or for comfort, or for lack of space, it never seemed to matter. Night was not a time to be wasted here, no matter what the nature of the relationship.

Gwenlliant had left her cart at home. A waxing moon lit their path. The starlight was brilliant in the clear air and refused to be outshone by the moon. The sound of music and dancing faded into the distant sound of waves on rocks and the nearby sound of crickets in the grass. It was the sound of life and joy, all too priceless and temporary, against the sound of the eternal sea.

"Such music the crickets make," said Gwenlliant. "Crickets are the bards of the night, our folk say, just as the lark is the bard of the day. When a single cricket gets into your house, it merely croaks. But when there are many cricket voices together, their voices become a song. *Croger guthaigh* is what we call the cricket music. We use the same words for the sound of many children when they are together, which is a sound our people love."

Gwenlliant laughed.

"For the sound that old men and old women make when they are together," she said, "when they all talk at once, we use different words for different animals, words that are not so nice. What would be your words for the cricket music?"

"We might call it a chorus," said Jake. "Our language

kept that word from the Greeks. But I think that my friend Phaedrus would hear not only the chorus of the crickets, but also the accompaniment of the sea pounding the rocks. He'd hear the dogs barking, and he'd hear you laughing. He swears that the stars make tinkling sound like snowflakes, or like tiny silver bells. So maybe 'chorus' is too plain a word for something so complex that involves so many instruments and so many voices."

"Do you have another word, then?" Gwenlliant asked.

Jake thought for a moment.

"The word 'oratorio' might do," said Jake. "We got that word from the Romans. An oratorio might require a hundred voices or more, and a hundred musical instruments. Oratorios are a kind of musical storytelling, and the story usually has a religious meaning."

"*Oratorio*," said Gwenlliant. "I like the sound of it. And that sound that the stars make – I believe that I have heard it, too. What you have told me about your religion I find very hard to follow, but this *oratorio* of the night, that I can understand."

They fell silent and listened, their feet swishing in the grass as they walked.

Jake's heart ached with the knowledge that he must soon leave this place. Jake could have walked until dawn with Gwenlliant, holding her warm hand, listening to the music of nature. But soon they found themselves outside Gwenlliant's witch's cottage at the edge of the woods.

At the cottage door, Jake said, "May I come in, Gwenlliant?"

"Is it what you want?" she said.

"It is what I want," Jake said.

"How the stars favor me," said Gwenlliant. "A summer night. I thought they all had passed."

"They have not all passed," said Jake.

"Come in," she said. "I will leave the door open, so that we can hear the music."

CHAPTER 10

Jake had often been invited to supper at the castle, but this would be the last supper at the castle before the travelers left for Anglesey, if their ship arrived as expected. The four travelers were the guests of honor and sat at the great table on the dais – Jake, Prince Lairgnen, Melwas, and a soldier named Peredur.

"You call this supper," Jake said as Lairgnen refilled their cups with ale. "I'd call it a party. You party well, you know."

Candles were being lit as dusk faded to dark. From the dais, a harpist was accompanying a singer. King Jowan and his queen had left the room an hour ago and gone upstairs, leaving the dining hall to the younger folk. The room was noisy with laughter, the clatter of cups, and stools and benches scraping against the floor.

"That's a new word, *party*," said Heledd. "But I think I

know what you mean. Where did that word come from? You've gotten me all interested in where your words come from. They seem to come from all times and all places."

"It's from Latin, I believe," said Jake. "The original meaning had to do with pieces of things, or dividing things up. I have no idea how it came to mean a group of people drinking and having a good time."

"Suppers are not parties where you come from?" asked Derbhorgill.

"Not usually," said Jake. "But then, we don't live in big houses like you do, with lots of people under one roof. We aren't as *convivial* as you are, at least not in my country. The French are more convivial – that is, the people who live in what is now Gaul. Maybe they've remembered your conviviality for all those centuries. That's a strange thing to forget, isn't it? How to sit down at a big table with other people and talk and eat and drink."

"People still drink ale, surely?" asked Lairgnen.

"That they do," said Jake. "Though now that I think about it, not many have ale with their food."

"That's a pity," said Lairgnen. "From some of what you've told me, people in your time have so little fun that it's a wonder that they even manage to conceive children."

Everyone laughed.

"Somehow they do," said Jake. "I try not to think about how they do it. They make a quick chore of it, I've read. A few minutes and then they roll over and go to sleep."

"Do you hear that, Lairgnen?" said Heledd. "You'd fit in just fine in Jake's time."

"How can I help it?" said Lairgnen. "You get me so — how would you say it, Jake?"

"Hot," said Jake.

"Hot," said Lairgnen. "You get me so hot."

Fingal the white fox, who had been dozing at Derbhorgill's feet, sprang up and ran toward the door.

"It's Miach," said Heledd. "He must have brought a message from Lodan for King Jowan. I hope it's not bad news. Miach! Come join us! Come and be — what was the word, Jake?"

"Convivial," said Jake.

"Come and be convivial with us," she said.

All of them gestured toward Miach to come to the table and join them. Miach blushed as he approached the table, flattered.

"Who is the message for?" asked Lairgnen.

"For Jake, mostly," said Miach. "But it's news for all of you. The *Slippery Seal* put in an hour before dusk. It can take passengers to Anglesey."

"Have some ale, Miach," said Lairgnen. "And join the party. This may be our last party for a while."

Miach knelt, partly because he was not accustomed to standing on the dais, and partly to scratch behind Fingal's ears.

"The ship's captain is at the broch," said Miach. "Lodan would like for Jake and Lairgnen to come and talk."

"Drat," said Jake. "Just when the party was getting started."

"Why don't all of you walk with us," said Lairgnen. "We can have a moving party and then continue the party at the broch."

Miach and Fingal led the way, romping and playing a game with a stick. Heledd and Lairgnen were talking quietly as they walked. Jake and Derbhorgill walked a discreet thirty paces behind Heledd and Lairgnen to give them privacy.

"I'm almost sorry that a ship has been found," said Jake to Derbhorgill. "I don't want the parties to end."

"I had hoped we'd have longer," said Derbhorgill. "There is so much that you still have not told me."

"If you're really that interested," said Jake, "I suppose I could try to talk twice as fast. Would you be able to memorize twice as fast?"

"There is another way," said Derbhorgill.

"There is?" said Jake. "What's that?"

"Mushrooms," said Derbhorgill. "I brought some with me from the observatory."

"Mushrooms?" said Jake.

"Mushrooms would be like talking ten times as fast," said Derbhorgill.

"Cymon's mushrooms?" asked Jake. "Isn't that dangerous? Isn't that what made Cymon mad?"

"Cymon already was mad," said Derbhorgill. "The mushrooms do not change anyone. They only make you more of what you already are. Mushrooms also are much faster than words. With the mushrooms, words are not necessary. It is more like traveling together, seeing the same things."

"Traveling?" asked Jake.

"Of course," said Derbhorgill. "It is like riding a fast horse, but farther and faster."

"How long would it last?" asked Jake.

"Half a day," said Derbhorgill. "Perhaps a little less."

"Are you certain that it would it be safe?" asked Jake.

"I am not sure what you mean," said Derbhorgill. "Is traveling by ship safe?"

"I hope so," said Jake.

"I do not think your time has come," said Derbhorgill. "You will be safe, I am sure."

"When?" said Jake.

"Tomorrow," said Derbhorgill. "Lairgnen and Fingal can watch us, in case either of us tries to follow a gull into the sky or a mackerel into the sea."

"Where? asked Jake.

"Here along the path, and on the big rock," said Derbhorgill. "It is always best to be out of doors."

—▶ ◀—

For a while, Jake thought that nothing was happening. He and Derbhorgill sat quietly on the big rock with Lairgnen. Fingal was asleep, his head in Derbhorgill's lap. Then Jake started to notice that colors were growing brighter, that Lairgnen was glowing with a golden aura, that Fingal's white fur was sparkling, that Derbhorgill, fire in his hair, at one moment looked like a man and at the next moment like a woman. The gulls seemed to be gossiping with one another, and the sea was alive and breathing, with powerful exhalations of white foam.

Derbhorgill smiled knowingly and brushed his flaming, windblown hair out of his eyes. Derbhorgill's arm left a trail of neon-purple light against the neon-blue sky. The mayweed and gorse were colors that Jake had never seen before. Some of the flowers were whispering to each other. A cloud that had been blocking the sun floated inland toward the mountains – a curtain opening on a drama – and the lights came up. Such a set! Such costumes! The sophistication of the drama as its curtain opened for another act, with its perfect staging, filled Jake with awe and suspense. What will happen next? Jake was both actor and audience. The cost of putting on such an elaborate drama was infinite, beyond calculation. All the resources in the entire cosmos were devoted to the drama. A brief overture, a *scherzo*, had subsided into a theme from the cellos and brass that spoke of suspense and of nobility in conflict with treachery. Occasionally the flutes and piccolos flitted in and out with hints of humor. The orchestra and conductor seemed to be concealed. Jake couldn't figure out where.

Then the first wave of ecstasy hit Jake. He was sitting cross-legged on the rock, and the first wave of overwhelming bliss seemed to lift him upward so that he hovered in midair. Then, as the laughing of the gulls and the breathing of the sea slowly faded back into his hearing, the next wave of ecstasy came and seemed to lift him even higher. Each time, the ecstasy felt like the greatest ecstasy possible, and yet the next wave took him higher still. Again and again this happened until Jake found himself gliding downward into darkness on outstretched wings. Except that the darkness was not darkness. There were clever patterns of moving colors, incomprehensibly complex, each detail as full of meaning and feeling as the music. Jake vaguely understood that he had closed his eyes. He tucked in his wings and opened his eyes again. The world was a hundred times brighter than before. Lairgnen and Derbhorgill were still with him, sitting quietly and looking out to sea. A gull descended, slowly flapping its wings and calling out to Jake.

"Come with me," said the gull.

Jake closed his eyes and felt the wind rush into his wings. The wind picked him up and carried him with exhilarating speed. Scenes swirled all around him. There were rain forests filled with a thousand shades of green, brightly colored birds, and luminous flowers of extraordinary colors. There were snowy mountain peaks lit by a golden sun. Rivers rushed through valleys in which fields of tulips grew, their colors ordered in bands like a rainbow. Then Jake was in a cave. The walls glowed, sparkling as though the entire cavern was made of jewels of many colors. Jake realized with alarm that his body was not with him now. It was as though he was only a point of consciousness, infinitely small. The walls of the cave grew dimmer until Jake was surrounded by darkness.

Jake felt fear now. Where is my body? Am I dying? Have I already died? There was a brief wave of panic before Jake caught himself. Even if I am dying, he thought, it is useless to fight it. When death comes, it cannot be resisted. Fighting it would mean only terror. Yielding and accepting it mean peace. How do I know that? Is it because I have died before? The fear subsided the moment Jake decided not to resist. Now Jake was floating passively in a dark, warm stream of peace and resignation. He waited to see what would happen next, where the stream would take him. Then suddenly he was out of the cave. The rushing stream broke through a great opening in a wall of rock, into the light. The water roared out of the cave and fell in a white cataract to the green below, but Jake soared. Now he was flying up from the earth. Bright stars appeared all around him. He was an accelerating point of consciousness in deep space. He was moving many times faster than the speed of light. He was moving upward from the earth so fast that the stars left little trails of light in their wake. He could hear the distant stars making their little tinkling noises like falling snowflakes.

Then Jake stopped moving, as though he had come to rest on a lush planet. He was in a deep forest, where two paths crossed. All four paths trailed off into dense undergrowth. Jake looked in all four directions, not sure which way to go. Before he could become afraid, he saw a small animal trotting toward him on one of the paths. Jake watched the animal approach. Jake squinted in the dim light. It was an ocelot, with bright golden eyes that seem to glow. The ocelot made no sound, but Jake heard it speak.

"Come," said the ocelot. "Follow me. I know where you mean to go."

Now Jake trotted along behind the ocelot. Jake's body was back. It seemed to make little difference whether he had a body or not, useful and intriguing though a body was at times. On and on they went, winding through the forest undergrowth. At last the light grew a little brighter, as though they were approaching the edge of the forest. They trotted into an orchard with green grass and apple trees heavily loaded with pink blossoms. Honeybees buzzed around the blossoms. The ocelot stopped and pointed with its nose.

"What is that?" asked Jake.

"You know what it is," said the ocelot. "Go and look, but don't stay for long."

It was a large house, very old, surrounded by a high brick wall. The wall was covered with ivy and blooming vines. The house was four stories tall with a five-story turret, made of brick and stone. Parts of the house were surrounded by scaffolding, as though the house was being renovated.

"Go ahead," said the ocelot. "Don't stay long!"

The path out of the orchard led to the high brick wall, where it joined another path that went around the wall. The brick work of the wall was ancient. The ivy looked as though it had been growing there for hundreds of years. The wall was much too high to see over. Jake took the path to the right, because he could see something like an arbor at the corner of the wall. When he came to the corner, there was a heavy wooden door through the wall with an iron latch. The door looked as though it had not been opened in a hundred years.

Jake heard music on the other side of the wall. He listened. It was music that he had heard before, music that he knew well. Someone laughed.

"Jamie?" said Jake.

The music suddenly stopped.

"Jamie?" said Jake. "Is that you?"

Jake tried to lift the latch. It was stuck. He picked up a rock and struck the latch. The latch flew open with a spark and a dull clang. Jake pushed on the door, but the door was stuck in the moist soil and barely budged. Jake threw his weight against the door. The door opened no more than an inch.

"Jamie?" said Jake. "Are you there?"

"You mustn't come in now," said a voice on the other side of the door.

"Why not?" said Jake.

"You know why," said the voice.

"But I want to see you, Jamie. I want you to understand," said Jake.

"I know," said Jamie. "You've told me a thousand thousand times, and I do understand. Don't push! You mustn't come any farther."

Jake put his hand into the narrow crack. For a moment, their fingertips touched.

"We have to close the door," said Jamie.

"Will I see you again?" said Jake.

"Of course," said Jamie.

"When?" said Jake.

"You'll know when," said Jamie.

"What is this place?" said Jake.

"You don't recognize it?" said Jamie.

"Somehow it looks familiar," said Jake. "But I can't – "

"It's your place, dummy," said Jamie.

"Mine?"

"Of course," said Jamie. "If you go quickly, you can go into the house, but only for a minute. Don't open the shutters! Don't look out at the garden! Go now. And don't worry."

"Jamie?"

"Yes. Go! What is it?"

"I want you to know that I'm fixing things," said Jake. "I'm doing everything I can to fix everything."

Jamie laughed.

"Then hadn't you better get going?" Jamie said. "You have a lot of work to do if you're going to fix everything. I'll be waiting for you. You'll find me. But I have to close the door now."

The door closed with a heavy scuffing sound. The music started up again on the other side of the wall. Jake started to call out again, but he realized that it would be futile. He followed the path around the corner. The path wound through shady tunnels in the bases of enormous magnolia trees in full bloom. Jake could smell the orange scent of the magnolia blossoms. He came to wide brick steps that led up to the front door. The great door stood halfway open. Jake went in.

It appeared that all the furnishings had been removed for renovation. The finish had been stripped from the wide boards of the oak floor. Scaffolds stood against some of the walls for plaster work. The ceiling in the entrance hall was three stories high. A wide stairway with ornate railings made of oak worked its way up and around galleries on three sides of the hall. Massive double doors on each side of the hall stood open, revealing huge front-facing rooms with high windows. Jake walked straight ahead toward the back of the house, through high double doors of heavy oak. It was the library. The library, like the entrance hall, was three stories high. All the walls were lined with shelves, all the way up to the ceiling. An elaborate system of catwalks and ladders gave access to the shelves, which were empty now. Jake wanted to explore every room, but he knew that he was running out of time. He turned back toward the front door. The ocelot was sitting by the door, waiting for him.

"Follow me," the ocelot said with its mind.

When Jake reached the front steps, the ocelot was no longer an ocelot but was a bright-colored jungle bird. It was climbing into an azure sky on its great wings. Jake followed, without wondering how he did it. They flew on their great wings over the forest toward green hills, rising and gliding and winding around and between the tunnels through the clouds.

"Look," said the bird, turning its head and looking back at Jake over its wing.

Jake looked down. It was Phaedrus' cottage. Smoke was curling up out of the kitchen chimney. There was laundry on the line, chickens in the orchard, and two cows in the pasture. Jake smiled, and they flew on. They flew over an adobe building with a tile roof. It was his parents' house in Costa Rica. All was well. People always wait for those they love.

The air became turbulent as the sky darkened. The clouds were no longer white but were now a deep gray and growing darker. Up ahead in the gloom, fading in and out of view in the turbulent atmosphere, Jake saw an enormous and imposing building with several spires. The architecture was Gothic. The building stood its ground between a wide river and the overgrowth of a jungle behind it that threatened to asphyxiate it.

"What is that place?" Jake asked the bird.

"Don't you recognize it?" said the bird.

"It looks like Westminster," said Jake.

The bird tipped its tail and started to dive downward toward the great Gothic building. Jake could see the clock on the tower now. The time was one minute after midnight. Jake had to shout to be heard over the rushing wind.

"Let's go back now," shouted Jake.

"Don't you want to see more?" said the bird.

"I've seen enough. I'd better go back," said Jake.

Instantly the bird vanished, and Jake fell upward through dense clouds into the sky. The sky went dark and filled with stars. The feeling of falling into the sky felt thrilling and familiar, as though he had done it a million times before. He fell and fell, sometimes steering with his outstretched arms, sometimes losing control and tumbling. Then suddenly Jake was on the rock again with Derbhorgill and Lairgnen. He was lying on his side, as though he had fallen asleep. He sat up, and Derbhorgill looked at him.

At that moment, but only for an instant before the realization evaporated, Jake was certain that he had understood how it all worked – everything in the universe. All of creation was a drama, made of nothing but light and love. The drama was profoundly meaningful, a serious matter of life and death, joy and misery, and yet it also was completely meaningless, nothing more than a play to entertain the actors for an eternity. All the actors knew that it was only a play, but all willingly forgot that to enter into the drama as though it was real, the better to play one's role with conviction and to wring meaning out of the drama.

Every perception was layered. There sits Lairgnen, my friend, skin golden and eyes sparkling in the afternoon light, restless and looking as though he's impatient for supper. And there sits Lairgnen, my *friend*, a single and fascinating example of a pure and perfect concept, something Platonic, something containing the entirety of all the meaning, all the beauty, all the love and joy and comfort eternally contained in *friendship*. And look now at Derbhorgill, how he smiles at me. He – she? – already knows all this, and he knows what I am seeing. He has been here before. He already knows. He holds out his hand to me and asks me with his eyes if I trust him.

"Yes," said Jake, with his mind. "I trust you."

In an instant, as their eyes met, Derbhorgill knew everything that Jake knew or had ever known. Derbhorgill knew every thought, every secret, every feeling – even everything that Jake had forgotten. Jake lowered his eyes. He felt ashamed.

"No," said Derbhorgill with his mind. "No shame. We all are like that. One day we will *all* know *everything* about each other. We will see each other from every possible angle, as though we had lived each other's lives. It will take time – a great deal of time. But we have begun, and we have all the time in the universe."

Jake nodded. Fingal looked at him and winked.

Then Jake felt a peacefulness – a pure, perfect, Platonic *peace* and wellbeing, beyond anything he could have imagined existing. This, thought Jake, is what the universe has given us as compensation for the dark tide of suffering and despair. From time to time, we flail our way out of the dark tide of despair and rest for a moment on a tiny island of peace. We cough the black water from our lungs and inhale the fragrant air of peace. Then the tiny island washes out from under us, and we are flailing again.

Don't go there! Not now! Look away!

Jake looked away from the dark tide, clinging to the *peace*. He slowed his breath, calmed his heart, resolved to remember.

Derbhorgill, Lairgnen, and Fingal were all looking out to sea now. The curtains, Jake knew, were about to close on this act of the drama. The orchestra, with a sequence of chords that made Jake's heart ache, modulated and slowed into an adagio – the *finale* – restating the theme that was becoming one of Jake's favorites – the ostinato of the waves, the chorus of the gulls, and the continuo of the wind. Then, *morendo*, the music was gone. Jake marveled that he was always so confused that he could not always hear the orchestra.

Then there was a feeling like a train rolling to a stop, with that tiny last lurch that cannot be avoided no matter how skillfully the engineer applies the brakes.

Jake was back in the everyday world again.

———

It was their second day at sea. The wind and the waves were always from the wrong direction. The ship fought hard for every mile of progress southward. Jake did not know which was more terrifying, the peaks or the troughs. The terror of the troughs was of foundering, with waves looming above the mast on two sides and the ship at the bottom of a deep canyon between the waves that always seemed ready to swallow the ship. There was generally one tiny moment of equilibrium at the very bottom, just as there was at the top, before the world wheeled sideways again. The terror of the peaks was the fear of rolling over in the wild skid downward to the bottom of the next canyon, the mast at an alarming angle to the waves. Then the terrors repeated.

The captain steered with a frenzy. Jake clung to the rail on the landward side, always with an eye on the rigging to keep from getting hit by something. Jake's eyes stung from the wind and the vomiting. The wetness of his eyes sometimes blurred his glimpses of land. Prince Lairgnen stood near him, also holding the rail. Lairgnen had not puked since yesterday. But Jake leaned over the rail and puked again, struggling not to puke into the wind. An upward surge of splashing seawater caught him in the face and washed it.

The captain heard it first. He cocked his head, trying to identify the source of the banging sound. Jake heard it and wondered if some essential part of the rigging was coming apart. Prince Lairgnen heard it and was watching the captain to see what he would do. The captain pointed to a crate that was lashed to cleats near the front of the ship. Two of the crew approached the crate, laid their hands on it, and listened. Then one of the men retrieved an iron bar and pried the lid loose from the crate. When the crate was opened, a boyish figure rose and stumbled out of it. The figure slipped, fell on the wet deck, and convulsed with a dry heave.

It was Miach.

The captain scowled. Prince Lairgnen laughed so hard that he bent double, holding his sides. Jake tried to laugh, but instead he puked again. Miach never thereafter revealed who had helped seal him into the crate, but Jake suspected a conspiracy – Gwenlliant and Derbhorgill.

———————

When they finally drifted into the little harbor at Anglesey, Jake wanted to kiss the ground. He was dressed as a Druid. On Anglesey, that was a common costume and would attract no attention. Jake, Miach, Prince Lairgnen, Melwas, and Peredur, the other soldier, struck out from the harbor to find an inn. Jake's body told him that he was starving, though he had no appetite. The fishy stink of the harbor had not helped his appetite either. They passed an inn.

"Let's find another," said Jake. "It stinks too much here, too close to the harbor. I want to smell hot wheat bread and strong mint tea. If we're lucky, and if we sleep a little, we might even be ready for some ale by evening."

It was a large harbor and an ancient settlement. The place was a little too big, Jake thought, to be called a village. A wide street led toward a high hill. Jake pointed toward the hill. Hills always attracted him – Lairgnen, too – so they walked that way. Miach insisted on carrying one of Jake's packs, to make himself useful. Jake sighed and let Miach carry it, though Miach looked to be in worse shape than anyone. Jake had never seen such a mess of hair. They had washed their clothes in buckets of seawater several times when the sea was calmer, but Clood would never have allowed them into her kitchen in the condition they were in. After half an hour of walking in a fresh breeze, Jake's malingering vertigo and nausea were clearing. Most of the people in the street paid them little notice, though a few of the younger people tried to make eye contact with Jake, despite his dishevelment. But Jake felt filthy and starved, in no mood for flirtation. Vendors sold little cakes and berry tarts, but Jake persuaded the hungry travelers that it would be best to hold out for a real meal at an inn, after a bath.

They came to an inn. Its sign gave its name as the Rose and Thistle. It was a small inn, but it looked clean. The smells of warm food and stale ale wafted into the street.

"Will this do?" asked Prince Lairgnen.

"We're unlikely to do better," said Jake. "I'm desperate for a bath and a nap. And after that I want a meal that isn't salted fish and barley mush."

The others nodded wearily.

They took the inn's three remaining rooms. The prince had a room of his own. The two soldiers shared a room. Jake and Miach would share a room.

Jake ordered two tubs of hot bath water, though he knew there was no way that such a small inn could provide hot water for five baths at once. Miach followed Jake into the tiny room they were sharing. It looked clean. The bed was narrow. There was one chair and a rough table.

"Just look at us," said Jake. "We're so filthy from puke and deck slime that I'm surprised they let us into this place. What would Clood do if she saw us looking like this?"

"She'd make us wash our clothes in the ocean, and she'd make us sleep in the woodshed," said Miach. "Once I came home from cleaning stables. She made me stand in the yard, and she stood on a stool and poured water over me. Cold water, too."

"What are we going to do about your clothes?" said Jake.

"I have some," said Miach.

Miach showed Jake the little woolen bundle that he'd been carrying, tied up with a strip of leather. Miach untied the cord and set the bundle and its contents on the table. There was a lightweight tunic of linen, and linen trousers. Miach had wrapped the clothing tightly around a shiny object.

"What is that?" Jake asked.

Miach reverently picked up the object and handed it to Jake.

"Bendigeid gave it to me," said Miach.

It was a simple silver pen for writing, and it was not of earthly make.

"It's beautiful," said Jake.

"He was teaching me to write," said Miach. "He let me keep it, but he told me to keep it out of sight."

"You do well to keep it out of sight," said Jake. "If anyone saw it in a place like this, they'd find a way to steal it from you. Bendigeid was teaching you to write? Why didn't you tell me?"

"You were so busy," said Miach. "I didn't want to bother you. You and Heledd and Melwas always had such serious things to talk about."

"Would you show me what you can write?" asked Jake.

Jake opened his own pack and fished out a piece of sketching paper. He gestured for Miach to sit at the table.

Slowly and deliberately, in simple but strangely elegant strokes, Miach wrote the Greek alphabet.

"That's beautiful!" said Jake. "What else did Bendigeid teach you?"

"He taught me the sound that each letter makes," said Miach. "He showed me how the alphabet can be used to write any language."

Miach wrote a four-letter word.

"Let's see," said Jake. "That sounds like 'meow.'"

"That's right," said Miach. "It's cat language."

They laughed.

"That was the first word that Bendigeid showed me," said Miach. "He said that cats don't speak Greek very well, but that Greek letters can be used to write the cat's language."

"I'm so glad," said Jake, "that you got to meet Bendigeid."

"He showed me everything," said Miach. "He showed me pictures that moved, birds that can talk, and cats that can sing. He showed me the stars. He showed me books. You say that the world you came from is a bad place. I thought it was wonderful."

"But that was Bendigeid's world, Miach," said Jake. "I came from a different world."

"Still … ," said Miach.

"You have a taste for adventure, Miach, and for mischief," said Jake. "What are we going to do with you? Lairgnen will find a ship to take you back."

"But …"

"He will not listen to me," said Jake. "Even if …"

"Yes?" prompted Miach.

"Even if I asked him to let you stay," said Jake.

"I won't be any trouble," said Miach. "I can help. I want to see what Gaul is like. I want to …"

"Yes?" prompted Jake.

"I want to be with you," said Miach.

"Miach," Jake began, and then he stopped, looking for words that were kind enough.

"I know what you're going to say," said Miach.

"Tell me, then," said Jake.

"You're going to say that I'm too young. You're going to say that you love me, but that we can't be lovers. You're going to say that it's not my fault, that there's nothing wrong with me, that you come from a broken world. You're going to tell me that you treasure the love I feel for you, that it is a great gift, and that you will remember me always."

"Oh, Miach," said Jake. "You break my heart."

"There is no need for that," said Miach. "I understand. Gwenlliant helped me understand. I think she loves you, too, but I did not dare to ask her."

From the other side of the door, there was the sound of clumsy feet and imprecations. Then there was a knock on the door. The bathtubs had arrived. After more bumbling and more imprecations by the innkeeper and one of his sons, the two tubs were deposited in the little room, and the door was closed again.

Think of it, Jake told himself, as an exercise in innocence. Think of it as a test of your fitness to live in a world in which that which is natural and human is no big deal, with no fuss made about it. Miach already had started to undress. Miach, who still held his hand in front of his mouth when he laughed, showed no more diffidence about undressing in front of Jake than if Jake was Miach's cart pony. Jake had managed to never be naked in front of Miach before, but he undressed with a quiet sigh and tested the water. It was lukewarm, as Jake had expected. Miach was already crouched in his tub.

"Your stowaway hair is like nothing I've ever seen," said Jake. "If I'm going to sleep with you, then we're going to get it clean."

Jake knelt beside Miach's tub and ducked Miach's head in the clean water. Miach came up laughing. Jake began to scrub his hair. When the innkeeper and his son came to retrieve the tubs, the innkeeper scowled at the water that they'd splashed on the floor.

Miach had laid out Jake's clean tunic. Their dirty clothes had been thrown into the tubs to soak and sent to the inn's laundry.

"I'm ready for a nap now," said Jake.

Miach smiled his crooked smile.

They lay down together on the little bed, in their clean clothes. They spooned, with Jake's arms wrapped around Miach's shoulders and Miach's back and bottom pressed firmly but innocently against Jake's long body. Jake pulled Miach close. His body was bony and hard. He was warm. But the radiance of Miach's quiet bliss at being alone this way with Jake was like a hundred years of happy Christmases, or a thousand Lassies come home, or a million cruelties undone. How little it can take, thought Jake, to make the dejected so happy, to roll back for a little while Phaedrus' dark tide of despair. Why would nature make us all this way, to lose our souls in others and to suffer such unendurable need?

—▶ ◀—

Bergan had been watching all the ship traffic into and out of Anglesey. He had found them by suppertime at their inn. Jake and the others were at the board, loading their plates with second helpings, when Bergan stooped through the doorway and into the crowded, smoky dining room.

"I've caught you eating, as usual," said Bergan.

"Bergan!" called Lairgnen. "We had no idea that you were on Anglesey!"

"Yes," said Bergan, "safe, but with nothing good to report. You arrived this morning, then, on the *Slippery Seal*."

"We did," said Lairgnen. "Come, join us."

They had to struggle to hear each other over the clatter of dishes, the thumping of mugs, and the kind of hubbub that only a harbor inn can generate, with its constant flow of news and its many unexpected meetings. Bergan slid onto the bench beside Miach.

"Miach?" he said. "What has happened to you?"

Miach grinned and remembered that there was no need to cover his face with his hand.

"It will take a while to tell the story," said Lairgnen. "And we'd best not tell it here, in spite of the noise. You've some telling to do as well. We can find a quieter place as soon as everyone has made up for days of nothing but puking. Will you join us and eat?"

"I will," said Bergan. "You've smelled out the best eats in town with your good noses. Miach, I can't take my eyes off you. It must be some kind of magic, some kind of miracle, or some kind of..."

Bergan stopped what he was saying and looked at Jake. Jake grinned.

"I see," said Bergan. "Not that I ever doubted anything you told us. How is Lodan? How is everyone? Is it just the five of you?"

"It is just the five of us," said Lairgnen. "And all are well. Lodan is always bleak from worrying about you."

"Are there any messages?"

"No," said Lairgnen. "We did not expect to see you. Were you not able to send word? Where is your guard?"

"We've been on Anglesey only three days," said Bergan. "Cynddylan and Lugaid are at our inn, nearer the harbor. We bribed a filthy little fishing boat from a place near Tintagel to get here. We've bribed a lot of filthy little fishing boats. We've come from Samara in at least a dozen hops, first down the coast of Gaul. A filthy little fishing boat got us across the channel. And then other filthy little fishing boats got us around the peninsula. There are not many ships left in Gaul, you know. It was Caesar's way of teaching the Veneti a lesson."

"What is the news from Gaul?" Lairgnen asked. Then he added in a low voice, "For now, let's keep to regular seafarer gossip, the things people in this room already know, though it will be news to us."

"Gaul is a ruin," said Bergan. "The poor are starving. Villages have been burned, and no rebuilding done. Farms produce less than half of what they use to. Many of the people who worked the farms were taken to Rome and sold as slaves. The roads are campgrounds for maimed soldiers and deserters, many of them just boys. There is no law beyond the garrisons. Orphans scrounge and wander in bands. The orphans are treated like dogs, though dogs are rarely fucked. Except by the Romans. I have seen a hundred people die, and a dozen murdered. I have for the most part been left alone, because of my robe, though a large band of Roman deserters robbed us on the road from Uxello. If you travel, you are prey to violence and scam. Everyone argues. It is tribe against tribe and sometimes brother against brother. The Romans bully anyone whose looks they don't like. They'll run you through if you talk back to them and kill you more slowly if you resist. It was foolish of me to go to Gaul. It is foolish for you to go. We did not know that it was so bad, because news no longer travels as it once did. Harbor towns get their news only from other harbor towns, and sometimes off the rivers. But where there are only roads, news travels more slowly, or not at all. Trade has collapsed. Few are foolish enough to travel. And many who do travel don't survive. We must all return together. It is hopeless."

Prince Lairgnen whispered, "Did you find Divitiacus?"

Bergan looked almost angry.

"Of course we did not find him. It was madness to think that we would find him."

"Come," said Lairgnen. "Let's walk. Our rooms are too small for the six of us, and the walls are thin."

It was past dusk now. Most of the traffic in the streets had died out. They came to the stall of a tart and tea seller, now closed. It smelled better than the other stalls. They sat at a narrow table with benches on each side and talked, keeping their voices low.

"Is there word on where Divitiacus might be?" asked Lairgnen.

"Everyone thinks he is near Cenabum. I believe it may be true. There were Druids at Cenabum, arrogant Druids, rich ones, important ones, who saw me as just a novice and a bumpkin. Each time I tried to talk to them, I was rebuffed."

"Were they not even curious?" asked Lairgnen.

"Why should they be curious?" said Bergan. "Everyone thinks he knows how to deal with the Romans. What do you think they argue about?"

"Did you try to send a message to Divitiacus?" asked Lairgnen.

"The only message I sent to Divitiacus was my request to talk to him," said Bergan. "Lodan was clear. I was to talk only with Divitiacus. That was wise advice. The unity of the Druids is gone, at least in Gaul. Caesar saw to that. Now there are only factions, one snarling at the other. No one challenges Divitiacus' priority, at least as far as I know. But Divitiacus will not win another election. The next election probably will be won by fighting. But all the Druids still compete for Divitiacus' attention. They want his blessing as his successor. They all step on their rivals, or worse. It is impossible to know whom to trust. So I trusted no one. I said nothing. And when we saw the futility, we returned. Even a Druid can no longer travel safely in Gaul. It is good that you brought Melwas and Peredur, but still you must not go. The channel coast swarms with brigands, and the sea coast is thick with pirates and Roman mercenaries, deserters who are desperate to get back to the Mediterranean, or whatever place they consider home. We were fools. We thought that Gaul was still a place where a Druid could go, to carry a message. We lost touch with Gaul, but we were too slow to know it. This is partly my fault. It was my job to know these things. Now I know. We must all go home and make new plans. Gaul is lost. The channel is our only defense now. We must build new ships and raise new armies, in Britain. Divitiacus cannot help us."

"We must sleep on these things," said Lairgnen. "Come to our inn at breakfast. Or move to our inn."

"We will move to your inn," said Bergan. "It would be a comfort to be nearer friends, and more arms, though we are safe on Anglesey. I have been in danger for so long that I look over my shoulder even here. Even Anglesey cannot be safe for long. The Romans have ships, and they will use them. Look at what they did to the Veneti. What need is there to tell Divitiacus that the only safety for the Druids is in remote places? That is all too clear. Divitiacus will know that already. We can resist the Romans and die quickly, or we can join with the Romans and die slowly. Let's go home. Let's start our migration into the highlands. The coasts and Gaul will never be safe again."

➤ ◄

Miach, still asleep, had rolled out of his spooning position during the night and had turned facing Jake. Miach's head was pressed again Jake's chest. The boy is all knees, thought Jake as he quietly slipped out of bed.

The first hint of dawn had come through the tiny inn window. Jake let Miach sleep a little longer while he wrote a note to Lairgnen. Lairgnen would be annoyed that Jake and Miach had gone out without an escort. But even Bergan said that Anglesey is safe. The authority and order of the Druids still overhung the island like the canopy of a forest. Pirates, slave traders, and other ships that steered clear of the law, both Roman and Celtic law, never landed here. Jake chose to dress as a Druid for this mission, though he felt guilty about the deception.

Jake shook Miach's shoulder lightly.

"Let's go for a walk," Jake said, when Miach opened an eye.

"Where are we going?" Miach asked.

"It's a surprise," said Jake.

Jake could have asked for directions, but it was early, and few people were out. Besides, he wanted to explore. A creek cut through the town. Jake figured that the best bet would be to follow the creek upstream toward the hills. They walked toward the hills as the town gradually came awake. Half a mile upstream from town, the creek started to narrow and run more swiftly. As Jake had hoped, a well-used road followed the creek on the creek's left bank. They passed a cart or two headed for town. The drivers waved or nodded greetings, but no one attempted to strike up a conversation.

"Jake," said Miach, "you won't let Bergan send me back, will you?"

"I'm not sure I've got a vote," said Jake.

"Would you vote to send me back, if you did have a vote?" said Miach.

"It's impossible to know what we're headed into," said Jake. "You heard what Bergan said about Gaul. And besides, look how much danger you've already got into, traipsing off on road trips with the likes of me. You saved my life with that stick of wood, but you could have been killed. In fact, you would have died if it weren't for our friend Bendigeid."

"I thought it was wonderful," said Miach. "If it even hurt, I don't remember it. Besides, you've got your panic button, or whatever you call it."

"We could all be dead a dozen times before the panic button could bring help," said Jake. "That ride on the gnat that you enjoyed so much – sure, the gnat's fast, but the ship is as far away as the moon."

"I know," said Miach. "We could see both the earth and the moon from up there. We would sit in that big room – what did you call it?"

"The star deck," said Jake.

"Heledd and I would sit in the star deck with Bendigeid and the cats and watch the earth circling. The first time I saw it, I asked Bendigeid why the earth was going in circles. He said that really the earth wasn't going in circles, that instead the ship was spinning. But it didn't feel like we were spinning."

"Did Bendigeid explain why the ship spins?" asked Jake.

"Yes," said Miach. "But I didn't really understand. I think that might have been because Heledd had such a hard time translating it for me. Heledd and Bendigeid spoke Greek, but, after a while, Bendigeid could understand us. Sam showed me some pictures of the earth, the moon, and the ship. The pictures moved. And then I think I understood it. The room I stayed in, Sam said it was your room."

"My room?"

"Yes," said Miach. "Some of your things were there – your books, your clothes. I liked that. I wanted to read the books, but of course I couldn't. And so…"

"Let me guess," said Jake. "Sam read them to you."

"Yes," said Miach. "Sam couldn't read to me at first. He didn't know our language. But Bendigeid and Heledd would talk for hours sometimes. Sam would listen. Sometimes Sam would ask questions. Before long, Sam knew our language better than Bendigeid. We had so much fun. Sam would show us pictures – movies, he called them. Then he'd ask us to describe the movies. That's how Sam and Bendigeid learned so fast, I think."

"What were the movies like?" ask Jake.

"Some of them were funny. Some were like puzzles. Some of them made Heledd cry. The puzzles got harder. Only Heledd could make sense of them – you know, her training. But they were fun to watch all the same. Except the ones about medicine and surgery – they weren't fun to watch, but Heledd couldn't watch enough of those. Sam and I would go do something else. Sometimes the cats would go with us, even to the atrium. The cats would watch the birds, and Sam and I would feed the rabbits and lizards. There was a big bird, a parrot, that would fly down and sit on my hand. Sam gave me a glove to protect my arm."

"By the time you left," said Jake, "could Sam talk with you and Heledd about pretty much anything, without any Greek?"

"Yes," said Miach. "Sam loved to talk. He was with me almost all the time, especially when Heledd and Bendigeid were busy with their medicine."

"Sam was keeping you out of trouble," said Jake. "You and Heledd have done a great service, though – probably much more than you realize. That was Aderyn's job, you know – to learn your language. I could not do half as good a job as Aderyn. But now Sam has learned it from you and Heledd."

"Jake," said Miach, "you didn't say how you would vote if Bergan and Lairgnen want to send me back."

"If you really want to risk your neck," said Jake, "then I will vote for you to go with us to Gaul. You've a thirst for adventure. It would be wrong to stand in your way."

Miach hugged him, and they walked on in silence for a while. Miach looked thoughtful, so Jake waited to hear what he would say.

"When will you go?" asked Miach.

"To Gaul?" asked Jake.

"No," said Miach. "When will you go home, back to that world you come from that you say is so bad?"

"As soon as we are done in Gaul and have found a way back to Britain," said Jake.

"Do you want to go home?" asked Miach.

"In a way I would like to stay here forever," said

Jake. "In the north, I mean. Not in Gaul."

"Why don't you stay then?" asked Miach.

"You understand, don't you Miach? You've been on the ship. You've gotten to know Bendigeid. You understand, don't you? You understand why I'm here and why I have to go back."

"Yes," said Miach. "I understand. But I'd like for you to stay."

The road widened a little. They passed some cottages and a blacksmith's shop. And then, tucked up against some trees, Jake saw what he was looking for – a taller building beside the stream. It was a mill.

"What is it?" asked Miach.

"It's a water mill," said Jake. "I think the Germans invented them, though I doubt there are many yet, in Britain or even in Gaul. I want to draw it. But I have another reason, if we're very lucky."

A sturdy bridge across the stream connected the mill with the road. They found the miller on the mill's lower level, fussing with tightening a wide belt that connected two enormous pulleys with wooden spokes.

"You're looking for a cat?" said the miller.

"Preferably a kitten," said Jake.

The miller called out to his wife and a mill hand.

"There's a Druid here asking about cats!" he shouted. They all laughed.

"No flour or meal today, then? How much might a cat be worth to you if I give you the sack for free?"

There was more laughter. The wife and the mill hand came closer, to grin and stare.

"I don't know," said Jake. "A few coppers? It depends on the cat."

They all laughed again.

"Aren't they all the same?" said the miller. "I tell you what. I'll give you two coppers each to take them off my hands, as many as you want, if you can catch 'em. They breed almost as fast as the mice."

The wife's frock was dusty from bagging flour.

"I know where there are some that you can catch," she said.

"I was joking about giving you two coppers," said the miller. "A cat will cost you a piece of silver."

Jake nodded. The miller's wife beckoned for them to follow. They climbed up narrow, creaking stairs to the mill's third level. Jake marveled at the mill's wooden works, its gears and its linen sifters. He would have liked to draw here for days. The miller's wife led them to a corner where some crates were stored on a worn wooden floor thick with dust. In one of the crates, which had been lined with rags, was a mother cat and five kittens. The mother cat was skinny but seemed to be holding her own. She was a gray tabby, with two white feet. She was nervous, but she let the miller's wife scratch her head. The kittens looked up and mewed. Four were gray tabbies. One was almost pure white.

"I've never seen such a little one!" said Miach.

The miller's wife laughed.

"Once you've seen the first one, you never stop seeing them," she said. "If you touch them when they're little, they'll never leave you alone. And if you don't touch them when they're little, you'll never catch them. Why do you want a cat? Druids don't spend much time in mills, or in barns, or in kitchen pantries."

"They make good pets," said Jake.

"Pets?" She laughed heartily, showing yellow teeth. "Maybe if you coddle them and give them cream. But who has time for coddling cats, with so many hungry babies to coddle? Take 'em all if you want. They're old enough to wean."

"I wish we could," said Jake. "But we'd better take just one, if you're willing."

"That's a pity," she said. "Pick one, then. And if there are more Druids in town lookin' for cats, send 'em here. We've got cats aplenty, now that we know there are rich Druids who'll pay good silver for 'em."

"You pick," said Jake to Miach.

"Me?"

"Yes," said Jake. "You and Clood can share."

Miach chose the white one, as Jake knew he would. For the rest of Miach's life, Jake knew, Miach would identify with the odd ones, the marked ones, the ones who don't fit in. And that would be a good thing.

CHAPTER 11

In the end, they decided not to make Miach go home. Lairgnen said that it was only fair that Miach should endure, and learn from, the full consequences of what stowing away had gotten him into.

Bergan found a ship, and when Bergan and his two soldiers sailed out of Anglesey on the way home, they carried a kitten, but no Miach.

Jake and Miach had prepared a wooden box for the kitten. Jake had given Bergan a crash course on a kitten's care and feeding. Miach adored the kitten, a shy female. She had slept with Jake and Miach for four nights, in a kind of three-spoon with the kitten against Miach's neck.

Two days after Bergan's departure, Lairgnen found a rickety ship bound for the Mediterranean that was willing to drop them off at Gésocribate, near the western tip of Gaul. Their passage would cost an absurd amount of silver. Honest men, the captain said, had little business on the western coast of Gaul these days. As they boarded the ship, the crew stared and whispered. The captain told the five of them where to stand so that they'd be out of the way of the crew, and the ship sailed out on an afternoon ebb tide, in promising weather.

Jake and the others pressed against the rail, in spite of the frequent splashes, and strained their eyes to hold land in sight for as long as possible. The crew was sullen. None of them sang. As darkness approached, with land out of sight, Jake watched the captain steer. Jake wanted to see if he could deduce any clues about how the captain was navigating without instruments, even a compass. The captain was watching the setting sun, and the sky. The Great Bear, Ursa Major, was twinkling into view in the northern sky. Jake soon saw that the captain was steering to keep the Great Bear in the same part of the sky. They slept packed together on the deck under some dirty sail cloth.

The next morning, the weather was fine, and the captain was in a mood less surly than usual. Jake asked him how they were to find Gésocribate. The captain broke into a kind of song, or ditty, or poem, about forty lines long. It was a kind of recipe involving the setting and rising sun, the Great Bear, the direction of the swell, the time of day, the flight of birds, the type of clouds, and finally the sighting of the island of Ushant. Then, beyond Ushant, the ditty gave a poetic description of landmarks on the coast of what Jake knew as Brittany.

Jake relaxed. The weather was good, and the captain was at ease.

The good weather held. No one got sick. They had brought lots of good bread, good cheese, and even wine from Anglesey. They ate and drank for entertainment. They shared food and wine with the crew, to win their good favor. They sat near the prow when the captain would allow it, enjoying the little ship's skipping over the waves. The spray was bracing and made everyone feel cheerful and alert, even though they all wrapped themselves in their mantles against the wind. Melwas and Peredur amused themselves by teaching Miach some soldierly defensive moves. They had bought Miach a knife on Anglesey, though they deemed him far too skinny to be trusted with a sword. Still, they admired Miach's quickness. They had told Miach again and again that, if there was trouble, run! No one will ever catch you.

A pair of porpoises chased them, soaring and diving. Miach was as happy as the porpoises. He stuck to Jake like a shadow. Sometimes Jake would catch Prince Lairgnen watching the two of them, wondering if they were lovers. Jake was amused. Let Lairgnen think what he will. Miach is a fine cuddler and nothing more. But what was so wonderful about Lairgnen's curiosity was his lack of opinion. Lairgnen's curiosity was merely the natural human curiosity. Even children want to know whom adults are partnered with. All humans wanted to know who was whose lover. Was that not what the rings were about? Gossip did the job, to be sure. But rings added something else. Rings added depth, both outwardly and inwardly – outwardly as a reminder to others, inwardly as a comfort to the heart.

In the world that Jake came from, there was a rule that said that lovers must be sequenced, that there must be a break with an old lover to accommodate a new. But these people were never each other's property. They saw love as a sharing. Love and sex, like wheat from the fields, came from a common fund from nature's increase. All had a claim, and all owed a part of themselves to others. Miach deserved this happiness, and Lairgnen knew it.

On the fourth day, the headlands of Brittany came into view. Seabirds came out to meet them. The captain repeated the terms of the deal, as though it was a warning: They would anchor in the outer harbor. It was not safe to go any closer. Skiffs would row out to them, to scam or to solicit for goods or services. They would hire a skiff to take them in. Once the passengers were unloaded, the ship would head out to sea again on the next ebb tide. Then they would be on their own.

And so it went. It took two little skiffs to get the five of them ashore. As Bergan had warned them, all manner of shady characters haunted the harbor. No one made trouble, at least in the daylight, since three of them were fighting men. But they got many dark stares and hostile looks. Desperate-looking men tried to question them about why their ship was leaving, where it came from, and where it was going. Many of the harbor-watchers, hoping for passage south, were angry that the ship never docked. But it was not the first time that the wretches stranded here had seen a ship anchor in the outer harbor, discreetly do its business off shore, and then slip away.

Their only plan was to get away from the coast and into the forests as quickly as possible. They would make their way toward Cenabum stealthily, even if it meant traveling some at night. They couldn't get too far off course if they just kept due east, guided by the sun during the day and the stars at night. They were almost a week behind the schedule they had hoped for. They would need to waste no time getting to Cenabum if they were to be there for the summer gathering of the Druids. They did not yet have a plan for returning to the north, but they were counting on forming a traveling alliance with some British Druids until they were safely back in Britain.

Prince Lairgnen and the soldiers argued about whether to stay the night in the grime of the harbor town or to make for the fields and woods as quickly as possible. At last Lairgnen made the call. They would stay the night in town, because they knew too little about the terrain and hazards to the east. There was too great a risk of being followed and getting trapped in the open after dark. Lairgnen insisted that they get indoors as quickly as possible, stay out of sight, and get some rest.

The inn they chose was a small one. It was crowded and noisy, with a clientele far rougher than what they had seen on Anglesey. There was a mixture of languages and polyglots. Jake couldn't identify many of the languages, though he could make out some of the polyglots. There seemed to be a brisk business upstairs, where slaves, male and female, were providing sexual services for a few coppers. Two of the women and one of the men approached Jake, offering him a special deal.

"That one probably would have paid you, if you'd bargained," Melwas said to Jake as a male prostitute, who had been particularly persistent, moved on to the next table.

"I'm looking the other way," Melwas said to Peredur, "if you see anyone who interests you. This may be your last chance for a while."

"And piss blood all the way to Cenabum?" said Peredur. "And then hope that some Druid can cure me with an infusion of vinegar and salt water? I don't think so. I'll wank it until we get home."

Alone in a corner was a dark young man with a scar above his eye. He was drinking wine. His worn-out clothing was more or less Mediterranean. He had watched them during their supper. Jake wasn't sure who had caught the man's eye, but Jake was pretty sure that it was Miach who interested him. Miach, with eyes only for Jake, had not noticed. Lairgnen had noticed, though.

"I've seen at least a dozen washed-up soldiers sizing us up," said Lairgnen. "Surely they're not stupid enough to mess with us."

"All travelers have silver," said Melwas, "especially princes and Druids. You do look like a prince, you know. And if you'll pardon me for mentioning it, boys seem to be worth money around here."

"The truth is," Lairgnen said, "that we're all worth money on the slave market, if they could take us. And we'd all be fucked half to death before we could get to Rome."

— ◂

They all slept – or tried to sleep – in the same small room. Lairgnen and the soldiers insisted that Jake and Miach should have the one rough little cot. The innkeeper sent three lumpy straw mattresses for the others to be laid on the floor. The two soldiers slept by the door.

Jake lay awake for hours, wanting to squirm and toss, but he tried not to disturb Miach. Through the thin walls, Jake heard the sounds of the inn and of the street slowing dying down. Except for an occasional drunken voice, or a cry of pain or whimper of protest from one of the prostitutes, the place grew mostly quiet in the hours before morning.

About an hour before sunrise, they all were awakened by a light tapping at the door.

"Who's there?" said Melwas. "What do you want?"

"I want to talk to you," said a man's voice. The voice had an accent that Jake could not place.

"Go away," said Melwas.

"I can get you out of here," said the voice.

"Go away, I said," repeated Melwas.

"But you need my help," said the voice.

"We don't need your help," said Melwas.

"But you do," said the voice. "The road is thick with armed men. They are more than you. They are watching you already."

"And you'd take us right to them," said Melwas.

"Let him in," said Lairgnen. "Let's see what he looks like and what he has to say."

As Melwas pulled the curtain aside, Lairgnen fumbled in the darkness and found a candle stub. He handed the candle to Melwas.

"Here," Lairgnen said. "Tell the man to go light this, then come back."

A minute later a dark-haired young man, dressed in tattered clothes, eased through the door with the lit candle stub. Jake recognized him. It was the same man who had sat in a corner last night with eyes only for Miach. Even now his eyes searched the room for Miach and saw him sitting on the edge of the cot, squinting against the candlelight.

"Talk," said Prince Lairgnen.

"There are bands of many men on the road. They are dangerous and desperate – maimed soldiers, deserters, and outlaws," said the man. "The roads are not safe. I think I know where you are going. You must not go by the road. I know a way."

"Where do you think we are going?" asked Lairgnen.

"To Cenabum. There is a Druid among you."

"Are you a deserter?" asked Lairgnen.

"Yes," said the man.

"Infantry?" said Lairgnen.

"Archer," said the man.

"Where are you from?" asked Lairgnen.

"A place you would not know," said the man. "North of Greece."

"Why don't you go home?" asked Lairgnen.

"I have no money for passage," said the man. "There are no ships. And besides, there is nothing for me where I came from. Why do you think I left?"

"Why do you keep staring at him?" asked Lairgnen.

"He is beautiful," said the man.

The soldiers looked as though they were barely able to hold their tongues to let Prince Lairgnen do the talking. Melwas spoke.

"Let me give him a copper for a bath and a whore and send him on his way," said Melwas.

"If these men are so dangerous," said Lairgnen, "then how do you avoid them?"

The young man hesitated for a moment, stole a glance at Miach, met Jake's eyes for an instant, and scratched at his shoulder. Jake thought the young man must be no older than twenty-two.

"They needed me," he said. "They needed an archer. But I do not want to do their dirty work. They don't trust me. They watch me. They could kill me any time, or sell me to traders. I want to get away from them, but how can I, alone? You look like good folk. You have weapons. I would be safer where you are going. There is a Druid with you. I can help you."

"Where would you lead us?" asked Lairgnen.

"We must leave in the dark," said the man. "They drink too much when they come here. They will sleep too late. We must stay off the road and get into the forest."

"How far is the forest?" asked Lairgnen.

"Miles," said the man. "More than ten. They cut the trees. They are always cutting trees. It will be very dangerous until we get to the forest. But once into the forest, there is forest almost all the way to where you are going. There are tracks known only by a few. You would never get there by road. There are too few of you. Only three of you are fighting men."

"How do you know about these tracks used only by a few?" asked Lairgnen. "Who makes the tracks?"

"The Druids made them," said the man.

"How would you know?" asked Lairgnen.

"I came here with a courier for the Druids," said the man.

"Who?" asked Lairgnen.

"I do not think you would not know him. And besides, he is dead now," said the man.

"What was his mission? How did he die?" asked Lairgnen.

"He was trying to get to Anglesey. He was killed by the people who would kill you. They cut him down, a few miles from here, between here and the forest."

"You sold him out, you mean," said Peredur.

"I tried to save him," said the man. "But there were too many of them."

"How did you escape?" asked Lairgnen.

"I hid, in a pig sty. Pwyll was too proud to hide in a pig sty. He did not believe that they would harm a Druid's courier. I found his body. They tortured him. You do not understand. There is no law here, neither Druid law nor Roman law. War has put an end to all that. Near the garrisons there may be Roman law. In a few places the Druids still keep order. Pwyll was a courier, from Britain. He told me much. But even he did not know how bad it had become here in the west. It was the Veneti who always kept order here, until Caesar crushed the Veneti. Now it is deserters and brigands on the landward side, and pirates and slave traders off the sea."

"I say it's a trap," said Peredur.

"I don't trust him," said Melwas.

"Jake," asked Lairgnen, "what do you think?"

"I think he is telling the truth," said Jake.

"Why do you think that?" asked Lairgnen.

"Because he is in love," said Jake. "He is in love, and he would not see Miach come to harm."

All their eyes turned to Miach. Miach's face was a study in disbelief and wonder, because he had never before had the experience of seeing someone ass over teakettle in love with him.

◢ ◣

The young Macedonian's name was Alexis. His eyes were almost as black as his hair. He was not much taller than Miach, but he was muscular and had none of Miach's leanness. His legs were stout, his biceps bulged through his threadbare tunic, and his shoulders were wide and strong. His boots looked fairly new, but no one dared ask how he had acquired them.

They left the inn while it was still dark. They waited for Alexis to sneak into the stables, where he had hidden his bow in the hayloft. Then they ran, eastward. When daylight came, they slowed to a sustainable double-time. They kept up that pace all day, stopping only for water when they could find it. Mostly they found only stagnant water, and it stank. Often Jake looked back to see if they were being followed. An hour or two after sunrise they passed a convoy of wagons, heading back toward Gésocribate from the shabby nearby farms. The convoys were guarded by ruffians with crude weapons. Alexis led them off the road to avoid the convoys.

"It's amazing that they have anything to sell," said Lairgnen.

"They are not selling anything," said Alexis. "They are paying their protection tax."

They ran on. At midmorning, Alexis steered them off the road and into farmers' fields. When they could, they kept near hedges. Gradually, more trees appeared. When there were groves, they ducked into them. It was cooler in the groves, and the day was growing warm. By mid-afternoon, they were in uninterrupted forest. Still Alexis made them keep up a taxing pace, though they slowed from their double-time. Miach was a born runner and never seemed to need to rest.

They came to a stream. It was fresh and fast-moving, the first good water they had seen all day.

"I must rest," said Lairgnen. "Even if there are a hundred hags and golls behind us with barbed belly-spears, I must rest."

Alexis agreed. Apparently ashamed of how dirty he was, he stripped, washed his ragged tunic in the stream, and bathed. One at a time, they each did the same. While awaiting a turn in the waist-deep pool of water, they dozed on the bank. Jake, who was stretched out on his mantle on the forest floor near Lairgnen, noticed Miach watching Alexis. Miach was sitting on the trunk of a fallen tree. Jake tapped Lairgnen's shoulder and pointed. Lairgnen grinned.

"How long do you think it will take?" whispered Jake.

"About three days would be my guess," Lairgnen replied, "if we live that long."

After Alexis had washed his clothing and put it on wet, he said that he was going into the woods to have a look around.

"I'll go with him," said Peredur. Lairgnen nodded.

Alexis and Peredur returned about an hour later and said that this was as good a place as any to spend the night. In the morning, they would have to get across a gap in the forest, they said, and cross a mile or two of fields.

"It would be best to cross the fields before sunrise," Alexis said, "after the moon has set. By sunrise we should be back under the trees again."

An hour before moonset, with Lairgnen on watch while the others slept, the brigands set upon them in the dark and took them by surprise. The peace of the forest had deceived them. All but Lairgnen were sleeping. The brigands had suddenly appeared out of the undergrowth, running, weapons drawn.

"Run!" shouted Lairgnen. They ran. They scattered. Jake tried to keep an eye on Miach, who had jumped and run like a jackrabbit, but Jake tripped on a fallen limb, stumbled, and lost sight of Miach in the dark. Jake heard sword ringing against sword and the shouting of unknown voices in the dark behind him. All he could think to do was to run away from the voices, toward wherever the brush seemed to be the thickest. Jake realized that he was making too much noise, that his crashing sounds were giving away his location. He slowed, tried to see more clearly in the dappled moonlight, and kept moving. He wanted to call out to Miach, but he knew that would be foolish. Jake stopped and listened. Still he heard the shouting of men, but it was farther away now.

Stop and think, he said to himself. Maybe you've run far enough. Maybe you should just hide now, and wait for the moon to set. There was no longer any sound of fighting. That might not be a good thing. Each time Jake heard a voice, he tried to estimate its distance and location. None of the voices was familiar. And maybe, just maybe, the voices were receding. He looked around for a better hiding place but saw nothing more promising than the clump of low trees in which he now stood. He squatted, and listened.

Before he was even sure that he had heard the sound of someone creeping toward him from behind, a hand was around his throat and threw him down. Jake heard himself emit a shamefully unmanly sound, then a hand was over his mouth. A man nearly twice his weight turned him onto his back and put a knee into his stomach. Jake felt the cold blade of a knife against his throat. The accent was strange, but the words were clear enough – if you make a sound, I will cut your throat.

While one hand held the knife to Jake's throat, the other hand lewdly probed his body, looking for valuables or weapons but also enjoying the feel. Jake lay still, submitting to the indignity and trying to think. The hand found the pendant around Jake's neck.

"What's this then?" said the man. "Silver, maybe? Gold? Fit for a Druid?"

The hand jerked the pendant with its cord over Jake's head. The cord snagged on Jake's ear. The man pulled harder. Jake tried to cry for help. Two hands squeezed his throat, one hand still holding the knife. Jake felt warm blood in his ear where the pendant's cord had cut him. The blood muffled his hearing.

"One of those that likes to wrestle, are you?" the man said. "I'll have to choke you out, to get it into you. I'll bring you back, though, after I'm in you, so you can squirm and clench for me. Nice and young, by the feel of you. Always wanted to finish a man while I'm in him, I have. I bet you're a pretty one. Such a fine way to fuck a pretty one. I wish I could see your face when I'm coming and you're going. Got no light, though. I done it with a goose once, and throttled it when I came. It felt good, it did. Never thought I'd get to do it to a young Druid, though. How do you want it in you? Let's have you belly down, like a dog. And when I say get your ass up, you'd better get it up? Hear me? And if you won't let me in, I know what to do to you."

Working with his knees, the knife, and his hands, the man soon had Jake's wrists tied. Jake was on his stomach, and his trousers were down. The man's stinking breath was in his face as he lay on Jake's back and probed with his cock. A hand tightened around Jake's neck.

"Let me in," he said, "or I'll choke."

Jake fell the man's greasy, stubby penis, probing too low. Rough hands squeezed harder on Jake's throat. Then they squeezed harder still. For many long seconds, Jake could not breathe. Before the moment of panic and desperation that would come just before unconsciousness, Jake lifted his hips, whimpering. Then there was a sound, a kind of swish combined with a thud. The man's body stiffened. His hands loosened their grip on Jake's neck, and he cursed in pain and frustration. Then he was off of Jake and went crashing into the dark.

Jake gasped for air. Soon a dark figure was leaning over him. The dark figure saw that Jake was breathing, saw that his wrists were tied, and even in the moonlight saw that the lower part of Jake's body was exposed. It was Alexis.

"I winged him," said Alexis. "We have to let him get away, much as I want my arrow back. Can you walk? Get your trousers up. Come with me."

The next morning, the track rose above the mist hanging over the forest. Tall rock formations forced the track to meander back and forth across the ridges of the hills. The day was hot, and they were exposed to the sun. The slopes were steep, but at least now they had long views in all directions and could be confident that they were not being followed. Four of the brigands had died for the unwise decision to attack them. The one that Alexis winged had gotten away. They had spent as much time as they dared that morning looking for Jake's panic button, hoping that the attacker had dropped it as he fled. They had followed a trail of blackened blood drops until they lost the trail beside a stream. Then they gave up and moved on.

No one had been badly hurt. Jake's wrists and neck were bruised, and there was a minor cut on one of Jake's hips where he had been forced against a rock in the attempt to rape him. But Alexis' shot in the dark had saved Jake from much worse. Jake felt filthy. Sweating in the sun made him feel even filthier. The terror of being strangled, hands tied and helpless, kept replaying in Jake's mind. He kept tugging at his collar, because it felt tight and hot. Yet he felt a kind of void around his neck, a recurring awareness that something was missing, and he realized that the panic button and its cord had given him a feeling of security. It had been a comforting connection to Bendigeid and the ship somewhere above. Jake tried not to think about what had happened. He tried to focus instead on the loose rocks on the steep track that threatened to throw their feet out from under them. Jake had eaten no breakfast, afraid that another bout of nausea would overtake him. If he had slept, he couldn't remember it. Miach had slept near him but understood that Jake did not want to be touched.

As the sun sank behind them, the clouds swelled and darkened. Soon a heavy downpour swept over them from the west. They saw the rain coming and found shelter under an outcropping of rocks. Melwas pronounced it as good a place as any to spend the night.

Jake stowed one of his packs under the rock ledge and went back out into the pouring rain.

"I need a bath," he told them. They understood. The stink of the man who had tried to rape him still clung to Jake. Jake wanted the stink, and the memory of it, gone.

Jake found a place out of sight of the others where a heavy stream of water poured down from the rocks above. It was a natural shower. He stripped and washed. Then he washed his clothes. He rubbed his body with wet sand. Then he washed again. His Druid's habit had several rips in it now, and the bottom hem was starting to fray. It's time, thought Jake, to change back into tunic and trousers. It was the one change of clothes he had. Though a Druid's habit had served a purpose while traveling in places thrown into disorder by war, it could not possibly be right to wear it to a gathering of Druids.

The rain slowed. Jake stood under a shelter of the rock and rubbed his naked body to dry himself. He sniffed at himself to make sure he smelled clean. He sniffed his hands and his armpits. He smelled different, somehow, than he used to smell, though the scent was now all Jake. He remembered reading an article once about how primitive people who lived without modern soaps and chemicals had superior bacteria on their skin and how it almost certainly made them smell better than moderns.

The Celts loved to bathe in the sea. Back on the Scottish coast, there was a tiny strip of beach north of the little harbor that was reserved for bathing. He had bathed there with Heledd, and he could remember so clearly the scent of her body as they had lain on the sand, in the sun. It was a fertile young woman's scent. There was a hint of fresh grass in it, a hint of fresh-cracked walnuts, and a sharp, clear note of apple blossom that seemed ubiquitous in all healthy humans, male or female. Jake had rolled toward Heledd in the sand, touched a breast with one hand, and with the other felt gently inside her. She had laughed and asked him to be careful about the sand. They made love, and afterwards, as he lay beside her, he felt inside her again, savoring the feel of their wetness mixed together. Her scent had changed now. It contained the scent of just-finished sex, which always reminded Jake of walnut blossoms. As an adolescent it had vaguely embarrassed him to walk beneath a blooming walnut tree, because it made him think of the scents and guilt of masturbation. And yet, when he was alone as an adolescent, he had enjoyed the secret new smells and the changing scent of his maturing body. The dark hair sprouting under his arms, more than any other of the changes in his body, had made him feel like a man. His own newly manly scent was a turn-on. Though Jake was secretive, he didn't bother to feel guilty about it. It was, after all, a private thing that only he knew, though he dreamed of sharing it. Sometimes, when he and Heledd were making love, her face would linger in his armpit. No girl had ever done that before. Heledd's ardor would rise then, and she would soon have an orgasm. It made Jake feel proud that Heledd liked the way he smelled. It provided another way that he could give his body to her, another way to arouse her.

In the world that Jake came from, any intimate scent from a man was socially shameful. But in this much more natural world, there was no ignoring the scent of other men. There was no Celtic man with whom Jake had interacted whom he would not recognize by scent alone. It was thought that only dogs recognized people by their scents. How untrue that was. There was Miach in particular, his cuddling companion, whose scent so recently had lingered on Jake's hands and clothes. Though Miach was past adolescence, there was still a boyishness in his scent. Maybe, thought Jake, that is why I cannot think of anything more than cuddling with him. Miach's scent warns me that he is not old enough for that sort of thing, though Miach certainly sees himself as old enough.

On the other hand, Prince Lairgnen has a strangely floral yet manly scent, always clean – though a bit less so when traveling. But it was never offensive to Jake, and something about Lairgnen's scent inspired Jake to a greater manliness, to aspire to bravery and comradeship and noble deeds. It was as though Lairgnen's scent alone revealed that he was a leader, a man with power. It was an alpha scent.

Jake knew that there was something androgynous in his own looks. He had once considered buzz-cutting his hair to see if it made him look totally masculine. Oh, he was safely on the manly side of the line, but he was androgynous all the same. Jake had even asked Phaedrus once whether Phaedrus would describe him as androgynous. Phaedrus had quoted Camille Paglia and said that all charisma is androgynous. Charisma indeed. Lairgnen's masculinity seemed more charismatic, though there often was a gentleness in his eyes, if he liked you.

Jake heard a merry whistling. He picked up the Druid's habit and held it in front of himself, as though he was getting dressed. It was Alexis.

"I'm so sorry," said Jake. "I guess I hogged the shower."

Alexis thought for a moment to be sure of Jake's meaning.

"No worries," said Alexis. "We all found baths before the rain stopped."

"I just hope," said Jake, "that we can find enough dry places to sleep."

"Yes," said Alexis. "There will be no fire. Lairgnen wants to take no chances tonight."

"I can't handle another night like last night, that's for sure," said Jake. "Alexis, thank you. You saved my life."

"We have a saying where I come from," said Alexis. "You cannot kill a cat before its time. It is not your time. So you were easy to save, and my shot could not go wrong. I could see even in the dark that you were flat on the ground. So I knelt and shot straight. Did he …?"

"No," said Jake. "Almost. But a few more seconds and he would have."

"I am glad that you are still a virgin."

Alexis was smiling. He was shirtless. His build and confidence, his archer's grace, his thick hair, reminded Jake of a Greek statue.

"Why do you think I am a virgin?" asked Jake. "Am I that pathetic?"

"You are not pathetic," said Alexis. "You are beautiful. But Miach says that you are a virgin."

"I see," said Jake. "I thought I had sworn Miach to secrecy."

"And Miach is a virgin too," said Alexis. "I cannot see how this could be so. Do you not like him?"

"Of course I like him," said Jake. "But he is so young, and ..."

"He is at just the right age," said Alexis. "You have seen his body. How could he be too young? If he were an acanthus bloom, he would be open and pert on the stalk, and no bee would be able to resist him. No bee but you, I mean. Yours must be potent philosophy, to be able to sleep with such a boy and not to take what he wants to give you."

"Potent philosophy or not," said Jake, "Miach is a fine bedfellow, though he's a bit on the bony side."

"I have come to ask your permission," said Alexis.

"My permission for what?" said Jake.

"Permission to be the one who looks out for Miach. Permission to sleep with him. But I understand if ..."

"Not at all," said Jake. "If, of course, Miach is willing."

"Miach is willing," said Alexis. Again he smiled like a statue come to life, animated by love and desire and joy.

"Then I am happy for you both," said Jake.

A little later, while Jake stood alone under the clearing sky studying the stars, Miach came to him. Miach put his hands on Jake's hips and laid his head against Jake's chest. Then Miach clasped his hands behind Jake's back and pulled him close. Miach looked up into Jake's eyes. The look was heartbreaking – shyness, tenderness, admiration, regret, sadness, love.

"I love you," Miach said. "Thank you."

Jake was going to tousle Miach's hair, but he put his arms around him instead. After all, Miach did not want to be treated like a boy. They stood that way for a while, Miach's head tucked into Jake's armpit. Jake could feel Miach's penis pressed against him, not for the first time, and as always without any hint of shame. Is it my imagination, thought Jake, that Miach smells like Jamie? Didn't I do this once, with Jamie, when we had been drinking? What is wrong with me that I can not give them what they want? Why do I make them suffer so? By the time I regret my stinginess, it is too late. What am I holding back? It would cost me nothing. And even if I found only a little sexual pleasure in it, I would savor the joy of someone I love. I am a fool. I am an obstruction to the ebullience of life. I am a flower that draws precious water and sunlight but won't pass it on to the bee.

Then Miach, wiping away a tear, went off into the dark to sleep with Alexis.

CHAPTER 12

For two days, they had been following a woodland stream that wound between low hills. Alexis recognized the stream and said that they were now less than ten miles from Cenabum.

"Soon this stream will reach the road to Cenabum," said Alexis. "The road then follows the stream to the river that flows through the city. We have a choice. We can take the road and hope for the best, or we can travel through the hills east of the road."

"How safe is the road?" asked Melwas.

"I cannot say," said Alexis. "The traffic on the roads is constantly changing. But the roads are never entirely safe."

Just then Peredur let out a sharp cry, jumped, and came down stamping the ground.

"What is it?" called Melwas.

"A fucking viper," said Peredur. "It bit my leg."

Peredur had instinctively gone for his sword and cut the viper in half.

"Am I going to die?" said Peredur.

"No," said Alexis. "But it's going to hurt. Where on your leg did it bite you?"

"Just below my knee," said Peredur, "in the back of my leg."

"Let's have a look," said Melwas.

Peredur was already rolling up the leg of his trousers.

"It will soon swell," said Alexis. "Walking will be painful."

"Let's get going," said Peredur, "before it gets worse."

In late afternoon, they came to the road.

"The road would be easier for Peredur," said Alexis.

"How long does the woodland continue?" asked Melwas.

"The road runs through woods almost all the way to Cenabum, I believe," said Alexis.

"Then let's try the road for a while," said Melwas. "I'll go in front. If there's anyone on the road, we might be able to get into the woods before they've seen us."

They had been walking for only half an hour when Melwas silently waved his arms and pointed leftward into the woods. As they all dashed for cover among the trees, Jake's nose told him what was wrong. The wind brought the faint scent of smoke and roasting meat. Peredur was limping badly and was falling behind as they ran. Melwas fell back to cover Peredur. Melwas gestured to Alexis to lead Jake and Miach farther up the hill and into the woods. Melwas and Peredur were about fifty yards behind them when Melwas shouted "Run!" Jake looked back over his shoulder as he ran and saw three men with swords closing in on Melwas and Peredur from the direction of the road. Melwas and Peredur had stopped. They stood back to back, swords raised.

"Move!" said Alexis.

They ran up the hill. But it was as though they had been herded into a trap. Three grinning men, dressed in rags, each holding a rusty sword, emerged out of the brush above them. Jake could hear Melwas' and Peredur's swords ringing against swords down the hill toward the road. Jake fumbled to liberate his sword, which was strapped to his pack.

Two of the men made toward Alexis. The other came toward Jake.

"Get behind me," Jake said to Miach.

Miach complied. Jake knew instinctively, before the man spoke, that the man moving toward him already had sized him up.

"Looks like I've got the easy work," the man said.

The man laughed and stabbed at Jake with his sword from two yards away. Jake stood his ground as Lairgnen had taught him, sword up. Both uphill and down-hill now, swords were ringing. Alexis was holding off two men with his heavy sword. Jake circled, with the unarmed Miach remaining behind him. The man leered and laughed. Jake realized that the man wanted them alive. The man confirmed it.

"Drop it before you hurt yourself with it," the man said. "We don't want no damaged merchandise."

Jake lunged with a cut toward the man's face. The man jumped back. The tip of Jake's sword had missed the man by inches, but there had been no parry. The grin turned vicious. The man kept his distance but thrust his sword toward Jake's belly. Jake realized that they both were buying time.

"Do you know how long it takes to die of a belly wound?" the man said. "Just you try that again."

Jake stole a glance toward Alexis. Alexis was being pressed hard from two sides, but his formidable strength and agility were holding the attackers off. Jake could no longer see Melwas and Peredur, but he still heard the sound of swords clashing down the hill. Miach had managed to pick up a rock as they circled. The rock whistled past Jake's shoulder. It missed the man's head by inches.

"You little pecker," the man said. "You'll pay for that, after I cut a pussy in you."

Now there were screams from up the hill. In two successive blows, Alexis had nearly cut the head off of one of the men and had hacked a leg out from under the other one. Now there was a look of rage on the face of the man across from Jake. The man raised his sword to close in for the kill. Another rock from Miach caught him in the forehead. It was not a big rock, but it slowed the man down and forced him to pause to refocus his eyes. As the man raised his sword again, an arrow from Alexis went through the man's throat. Slowly the man teetered, dropped his sword, and fell. Alexis vanished down the hill. But moments later all was quiet in the direction of the road. Then Jake saw Alexis, Melwas and Peredur coming up the hill. Peredur's snakebitten leg was slowing them only a little.

The man whose leg Alexis had chopped was on the ground moaning, bleeding heavily. Alexis stuck his sword through the man's throat.

"The fools finally got what they deserved," said Melwas. "Let's get out of here. The wind has changed, and I can smell the stink of their camp."

Their track broke out of the woods on top of a hill overlooking Cenabum. From this spot they could look down into a once-beautiful valley and once-beautiful city. The Romans had converted it all to squalor.

Cenabum was now a ruin divided by a river. The river flowed slowly through a wide and stony bed. Smokes rose from everywhere. Piles of rocks marked the places where the bridges had been pulled down by Caesar's troops. If only Judith could see this ruin, thought Jake. And yet this is only a small piece of what Caesar did to Gaul.

On the far side of the river, the survivors had thrown up crude shelters amid the ruins. They still were living mostly in the open. Most of the population had died, or had fled, or had been taken as slaves. The remainder were camping in the rubble.

Jake's nose caught the smell of the ruins – smoke

mixed with a thousand other odors the source of which it was best not to think about. The smell reminded Jake of the revolting stink of Delhi – smog, filth, and bodies burning on the Ganges. He had gone there with his parents when he was a teenager.

"Where is the Roman garrison, I wonder?" said Lairgnen.

"It is a mile upriver," said Alexis, "where the air and water are cleaner."

On the near side of the river was the Druid encampment. Hundreds of tents were laid out in orderly rows. Little curving streets between the tents and pavilions followed the topography of the hills.

"They must have been in session for days already," said Lairgnen. "But we have arrived in time."

"The assizes probably require twice as many days as before," said Melwas. "How could there not be more lawbreaking in times like these?"

Lairgnen and the soldiers studied the scene below, working out a plan.

"Before night," said Lairgnen, "we must find a place to camp by the river, on the Druid side, upstream. But first I think we should go into the city. There must surely be a market there. With luck, we might find new clothes. We look like criminals as we are, brought in for trial at the assizes. We can buy food. We can listen for news and gossip. Tomorrow we can go into the Druid camp to look for Divitiacus. Alexis, you look too Roman. You must have new clothes. You must hide your Roman bow."

"I must?" asked Alexis.

"It is no weapon for this place. Buy a sword, if you can find one."

"I have no money," said Alexis.

"We have money," said Lairgnen.

They waited two hours, hungry and thirsty in the hot sun, for a boat to ferry them across the river. Lairgnen argued with the skinny boatman over the cost of it. The other passengers on the boat were hucksters who had been selling pies and barley cakes to the Druids. The hucksters were returning to the town for more stock. One of them was a young woman who couldn't take her eyes off Jake. She opened her robe and flashed a breast at him when she thought no one else was looking, but Lairgnen saw.

"You still blush like a boy," Lairgnen said. "Yet I know you have seen a breast before. Do you like her?"

"Do you see the sores on her neck?" asked Jake.

"They will all have the Roman diseases here," said Lairgnen.

Some dead things floated past the boat. Jake looked away, but his eyes returned to the sores on the woman's neck.

"Once we have found Divitiacus and given him our message, what will you do?" Lairgnen asked Jake.

"I will find a way to get a message to my ship," said Jake. "Or somehow my ship will find me. And then I must go home. That was where our plan ended, with Divitiacus. But until I can find my ship, I will need to stay with you and travel with you back to Britain."

"Do you want to go home?" asked Lairgnen.

"I want to be done with Gaul," said Jake. "I would be very happy in a place like yours. But I must go home."

"Let us hope that we will soon be out of Gaul," said Lairgnen. "There are too many ways to die here."

As the boat approached the landing on the city side of the river, they saw the Roman place of execution. Eight heavy crosses had been planted in the earth. Carrion birds fed at their leisure. On six of the crosses hung rotting corpses, naked and black.

—◆—

Lairgnen complained that it took too much of their silver, but they all bought new clothes at the market.

"It must have taken a dozen armed men," said Lairgnen, "to get these vendors here from Britain. Nothing could be cheap now in Gaul. But we can't go among the Druids looking like slavers."

Makeshift market stalls lined the sides of a dirty street. People dressed in rags were slouching among the ruins, stirring pots over their smoky fires and baking coarse cakes among the coals. Some of the vendors were selling acorns, a survival food carted in from the forests by the few who had the health and stamina for such work. The universal profession of the children seemed to be begging in the street. Lairgnen spent some silver buying the children pies and cakes. Three more women showed their breasts to Jake. Jake kept close to Lairgnen. Melwas walked in front, Peredur behind. Alexis kept Miach always in sight, and often they walked arm in arm. Dogs, ribs showing like the children's ribs, sniffed among the piles of refuse on the street. They passed booths selling pots, shops that repaired harnesses, a boot seller, a jeweler, and a seller of weapons. Alexis refused a sword, but Lairgnen bought him a long knife. They bought clean blankets, a small pot for storing water, a comb, a piece of soap, candles, a torch, and a sack to carry it all in.

On a side street, reasonably far from the stinks near the river, they found a place selling ale and hot bread. There even was a dry cheese, and some onions. To the travelers, it was a feast.

"Pray they don't run out of this," said Peredur.

"Few can afford it," said Lairgnen. "I hope we've not made too great a show of having money. Even so, on the other side of the river, I'm sure the fare is better. I doubt that the Druids put up with the Roman requisitions, or pay protection money to outlaws. Maybe we can sample the Druids' fare tomorrow."

"Why would they even allow us in, since we are not Druids?" asked Jake.

"I carry letters from Gwenlliant and Lodan," said Lairgnen, patting the leather bag that he always kept close to his body and that also carried their coins. "The letters are addressed to Divitiacus. When we find Divitiacus, we will not be turned away."

They lingered, drinking ale, watching the people, engaging a few of them in conversation, and trying to get news and gossip. Two hours before dark, the ale seller announced that he was closing.

"So early?" said Peredur.

The ale seller laughed.

"Just arrived today, did you?"

All the vendors seemed to be packing up and closing. Clearly it was not a good place to be after dark.

"We'd best find a place to spend the night," said Lairgnen. "We must cross the river again. We don't want to spend the night over here."

By the time they found a boat, made the slow crossing, and climbed out of the rotting rowboat on the Druid side of the river, the sun had set. Jake's bladder was bursting with ale. The others had pissed off the side of the boat. Jake had pretended that he was not in distress. There was a kind of latrine at the ferry landing, with some sickly shrubs as a cover for Jake's modesty. He pissed on the rocks at the edge of the river.

As Jake emerged from the bushes, he saw someone he recognized. It was the bard, headed to the latrine. Jake tried to keep his head turned away as though looking for his companions, but the bard did a double-take. Jake sprinted to where the others were waiting.

"It's the bard," Jake said to Lairgnen. "He's behind those bushes, pissing."

Lairgnen, whose education would have let him pass as a novice Druid if he wore the habit, was a military man at his core. He could think strategically as fast as some minds could generate a pun or a clever comeback.

"Alexis," Lairgnen said. "Don't let that man see you, but get a look at him when he comes out of the bushes.

Jake, stand apart from us. Look the other way. If we can, let's let him think that you didn't recognize him."

The bard emerged from the bushes, tying his trousers. He disappeared into the crowd and the growing darkness.

"Follow him," said Lairgnen to Alexis. "Don't let him see you. See where he goes. Find out what he is up to. Then find us."

Alexis nodded. He and Miach looked longingly at each other for a moment, and then Alexis sprang away into the crowd.

— ▶ ◀ —

"Trouble has found us," said Lairgnen. "But at least we're drunk and well fed. Where will we camp?"

"I need a bath," said Jake. "I can't put on these new clothes without a bath. Would there be a place close to the river that is both clean and quiet?"

"That depends on how far you want to walk," said Lairgnen.

"I can walk a long way as long as my bladder is empty and my stomach is full," said Jake.

They walked upstream, along a ruined quay, and then on a muddy path. They stopped in a dense thicket when they could no longer hear the hubbub of the camp. Peredur lit a torch. Miach went looking for wood. Soon Jake and Lairgnen were standing on the riverbank in the starlight, testing the water for a swim and a bath.

Lairgnen stripped, waded into the water, then flipped and dived when the water was chest deep. He surfaced, laughing. Jake could see his head and shoulders glistening in the starlight.

Jake too jumped into the river. The water was cold. It smelled clean. They were upstream from all the foulness below. Jake realized how rarely he been alone with Lairgnen. That was King Jowan's rule – no prince was to be abroad, anywhere, ever, without at least one soldier at his side. Partly it was for protection, but partly it was a show of status. The soldiers normally would enforce this rule even if Lairgnen was lax or tried to evade it, as he sometimes did.

"Why no guard?" asked Jake, treading water against the slow current.

"They're drunk," said Lairgnen. "I told them to go to sleep early, and they didn't argue."

"But ..." said Jake.

"You'll look out for me, won't you?" said Lairgnen.

"You're a bit of a handful," said Jake.

"How would you know?" said Lairgnen.

Jake laughed.

"You're drunk, too," said Jake.

"It's so easy to make you blush," said Lairgnen. "I can almost see you glowing in the dark. Heledd says that you glow in the dark when you blush."

"Lairgnen," said Jake. "Why are you not jealous? In the world I came from, you'd never be my friend. You'd beat me up."

"Heledd is a woman," said Lairgnen. "She chooses as she pleases. There will be no gold ring on Heledd's hand – at least, not until she is almost as old as Gwenlliant.

And besides, if I were jealous, how would that be fair? I don't wear gold, either. Heledd and I have always known each other. Women have an eye for men from far away. Men wander. Women choose. Women choose not just for themselves, but also for their children-to-be."

"Men from far away aren't much help with the children," said Jake.

"There are always men close to home to help with the children," said Lairgnen. "The tribe raises children. Everyone raises children. All hoe. All harrow. Heledd may have many children. Women want variety in their children. All women want beautiful children."

"It must be working," said Jake. "Your people are beautiful."

"And your mother chose your father well," said Lairgnen. "Your father was a handsome man?"

"He was," said Jake. "Many people fell in love with him."

"You have siblings, then?" said Lairgnen.

"No," said Jake. "My father and mother wear gold, and I am their only child. I was thinking of something like copper, though we don't have copper."

"Then this man, your father's friend, helped bring you up, fostered you?" said Lairgnen.

"I never thought of it that way," said Jake, "It was a long time ago that my father broke his heart. They haven't even seen each other in many years."

"Why did your father break his heart?" asked Lairgnen.

"My father did not return his love in the way he

wanted," said Jake. "And I think the end was not kind."

"Were they not friends?" asked Lairgnen. "Is not friendship enough?"

"I can't explain it exactly," said Jake. "They were friends, and they did love each other. It's one of the things that is different about the world I come from. It's good that you don't understand it. I'm still trying to understand it. There are strict rules in my world about such things."

"Ah," said Lairgnen. "The Romans have such rules. So you did not break this rule in the world you came from?"

"No," said Jake. "I never broke the rule."

"You sound sad," said Lairgnen. "You did not break the rule, but perhaps you, too, broke someone's heart the way your father did? Or someone broke yours?"

"Yes," said Jake. "One of those."

"Which one?" asked Lairgnen.

"I broke someone's heart," said Jake.

"Then, when you go home, unbreak his heart," said Lairgnen.

"I'm afraid it's too late for that," said Jake.

"Why?" asked Lairgnen. "Does he no longer love you?"

"Not that," said Jake. "He is dead now."

"I see," said Lairgnen. "I am sorry. What was his name?"

"His name was Jamie," said Jake.

"How do you honor the dead in the world you come from?" asked Lairgnen.

"I haven't thought about it," said Jake. "By remembering them, I suppose."

"Are there other ways?" asked Lairgnen.

"Not that I can think of now," said Jake.

"Here we have many ways," said Lairgnen. "Often, to remember them, we do the things they loved to do, as though they still were with us. And we say their name."

A clammy, dripping fog spread over the river bottom during the night. For the third time, Jake awoke shivering. He heard Miach sneeze. Then he heard the sound of Miach's soft footsteps slowly feeling their way closer in the dark. Miach slipped in beside him, into their usual spooning position. Miach was shivering too. Jake pulled him close, and soon their shivering stopped. They slept until dawn.

There had been no sign of Alexis. He had stayed out all night. Peredur was building a fire, whispering curses at the damp wood. From somewhere nearby in the morning twilight, Jake heard Lairgnen laugh.

"Blow it with your knucker breath," said Lairgnen. "Did you not have onions for supper?"

"I already burned off my knucker breath," said Peredur, "trying to keep my poor pecker warm last night."

Jake and Miach stayed cuddled together until at last the promising popping sounds of the fire drew them. Melwas and Lairgnen were warming barley cakes.

"I think Nemed is gone by now," said Peredur.

"Or mooching off the Romans," said Melwas. "But

he'll stay out of sight. He'll be thinking that we'll bring charges against him at the assizes. He meant to take Jake to sell to the Romans and kill the rest of us. He deserves the garrote."

"He has no thug with him now," said Peredur. "Nemed is a coward. What can he do without a thug?"

"He can spread lies," said Lairgnen. "He can concoct some new deceit and try to get to Divitiacus before we do."

"Why should Divitiacus believe him?" said Melwas. "Nemed has no evidence. His dead hireling, the one that Jake dispatched, was carrying the things that Nemed stole."

"All the same," said Lairgnen, "we'd best get busy finding Divitiacus."

They put on their new clothes, hid their new water pot, and made their way back down river to the Druid encampment.

The smell of warm food mingled with the stink from the river. Most of the congregants were lingering near the breakfast fires. Others were starting to gather for the assizes.

Everywhere there were arguments. Some members of the three major tribes were even wearing little strips of colored linen as a mark of their tribe, and of their politics. The arguments all reduced to one of two positions: Rome is our future, or Rome is our death.

At the lower end of the long hill was a kind of platform made of timbers and rough-sawn boards. At the corners of the platform, the yellow flags of the assizes hung limp on their masts for lack of a breeze. Up the hill from the platform were small shelters with open sides, benches, and rough chairs. The seating was slowly filling as the congregants trickled in from the breakfast fires. Down on the platform, furnished in a way that made it obviously a court, the first case of the morning was getting under way. Prisoners, some in shackles, were queued beneath the platform. A panel of solemn Druids were seated at a long table.

"That's a murder case," said Lairgnen.

Melwas pointed to an empty bench.

"Let's sit," said Melwas. "We'll attract less attention."

"Capital cases come last," said Lairgnen, "so they are nearing the end of the assizes. Tomorrow the arguments will move from quarreling around the cooking fires to bitter harangues from the platform."

"When will Divitiacus speak?" asked Jake.

"Tomorrow or the next day," said Lairgnen. "Divitiacus will speak first, to open the assembly. But I must get these letters to him before all the talking begins."

Lairgnen studied the people standing around the platform. Then he motioned for Melwas and Peredur to follow him.

"Jake," said Lairgnen, "you and Miach stay here. You are safe here. We will return soon."

Jake watched as Lairgnen, erect and princely, a soldier on each side, walked down the slope. Lairgnen spoke with a Druid at the bottom of the platform. The Druid shook his head. After speaking to several other Druids and getting the same response, Lairgnen and the soldiers came back up the hill.

"It is useless," said Lairgnen. "The official story is that Divitiacus is not here, that no one knows where he is, but that he will be here tomorrow. We could ask a dozen of them, but they all will say the same thing. Divitiacus is not ready to be seen."

"What next?" said Melwas.

"Unless you want to watch that poor fellow on the platform wail and tear his shirt when his sentence is pronounced," said Lairgnen, "we'd might as well go drink."

—➤ ◀—

Just before the ale seller gave the last call, Alexis appeared out of nowhere, proving yet again his expertise in the art of stealth.

"Nemed went to the garrison," said Alexis. "He's bringing soldiers. They'll be here soon."

"Romans?" said Lairgnen. He felt for his sword, as his military mind calculated their next move. "His treachery is much worse than I thought. We should all have followed him, and killed him."

"Why is he bringing Romans?" said Jake. He was on his third cup of ale, and his thinking was slow.

"They are looking for you," said Lairgnen. "They are looking for all of us, for fomenting rebellion against Rome."

"Shit," said Jake.

"Shit indeed," said Lairgnen. "We must get back across the river. The Romans will be more circumspect on the Druid side."

"We can't use the boats," said Melwas.

"No," said Lairgnen. "We'll have to wade, or swim. But we have to get out of sight. There are not many who fit our description, on either side of the river."

They made their way to the river through the ruins of Cenabum. They stopped to do surveillance in the shelter of a stone ruin at the edge of the river, upstream from the ferries. The ruin had once been a tall building. Two walls and a corner still stood. One of the walls had left a kind of stairstep pattern when it fell. Lairgnen climbed these steps to scout the river and look for the best crossing. Soon he clambered down again, muttering imprecations as rocks broke loose under his feet.

"Farther upstream," he said, "almost as far as I can see, I believe there is an island. There are some trees on it. Let's try that place."

After fouling their boots and trousers again crossing a muddy flat, they stood facing the island. The river was rocky and shallow. Beyond the shallows a channel of fast-flowing water rushed past the island.

"Do we have a choice?" said Lairgnen. "We have to get across before dark. Who has the rope?"

"I do," said Jake.

"We may need it," said Lairgnen.

They waded in, walking diagonally, to keep as far upstream as they could get. Gradually the water deepened. Jake tested each footstep carefully, expecting a dropoff at any point. Already Lairgnen, who was ahead of them, was in water almost to his shoulders. Jake could see that Miach was getting increasingly fearful.

"Do you swim, Miach?" asked Alexis.

Miach shook his head.

"I've never been in a river," said Miach.

Alexis looked at Jake. Jake threw Alexis the rope. Lairgnen was in deep water now.

"Swim!" Lairgnen called back to them.

The swim was not a challenge to Jake or to any of the others. But Miach was standing in chest-deep water, rowing with his arms to keep his footing. Alexis secured the rope around Miach's chest.

"Just stay afloat," Alexis told him. "Keep your head up."

Lairgnen, Jake, and the two soldiers reached the bank of the island in only a few minutes. Jake got there first, because he didn't have a sword to drag with him. Even powerful strokes like Lairgnen's would not have been able to drag a sword for long. They stood dripping on the bank to watch Alexis' and Miach's progress. Miach was nervously treading water, dragged along by the rope and Alexis' muscles. Miach began to grin when he saw that they were nearly ashore and that he was not in danger. Alexis and Miach were laughing when they climbed out of the water.

"Soon we will learn to swim," said Alexis.

"I would like that," said Miach.

They explored the island. There were signs of old campfires, but there were no signs of recent occupation. There was a primitive slip for a boat on the opposite side of the island on the downstream side.

"We should stay here tonight," said Lairgnen. "Let's find a spot in the trees on the upstream side. It's going to get cold soon with our wet clothes. We can't have a fire."

There was dense cover on the upper end of the island, in the undergrowth beneath the trees. But the ground was wet and would make for miserable sleeping. In the growing darkness, they searched for dry places on mounds of rock hidden in the undergrowth.

"Find a rock, and it's yours," said Lairgnen.

Alexis found a good one – a fairly flat rock not much bigger than a table top. It was covered with moss.

"They'll be warm," said Lairgnen, laughing, as he and Jake pushed deeper into the undergrowth.

"And there's ours," said Lairgnen, pointing to a spot almost as good as the spot Alexis had found.

"Ours?" said Jake.

"We can continue our talk," said Lairgnen. "The talk we started last night before the river got so cold."

Jake nodded.

— ◄

"The Romans would arrest us, wouldn't they?" asked Jake as they sat on their rock in the dark. "Nemed will tell them all sorts of things, including lies."

"Yes," said Lairgnen.

"Then what?" said Jake.

"There would be no trial. I think they would put us on their crosses. I think they would put us at the top of the hill, before the conclave is over, as examples to the Druids. Six crosses would send a strong message. They're itching for that, you know – a way to send a message to the Druids. As for Alexis, they'd figure out quick enough that he is a deserter."

"But *you* haven't done anything," said Jake. "Crucified? Should we just get back into the forest? Find a way to Britain?"

"And let my father down? And Gwenlliant and Lodan? How could I face them? But you – what do you want to do?"

"We have to find Divitiacus," said Jake. "I can't let everyone down, either."

They sat there for a while. The sounds of the river were muffled by the undergrowth. All around them, frogs and insects sang in the darkness. It was the natural oratorio of the creatures of summer, sung at the zenith of their brief lives, calling out to each other in the treacherous night.

"Jake?" said Lairgnen.

"Yes," said Jake.

"Would you let me hold you? I'm cold. You're cold."

"I would like that," said Jake.

Lairgnen moved closer and put his arms around Jake. Lairgnen's body was warm and hard. Jake closed his eyes.

"What are you thinking?" asked Lairgnen.

"I'm thinking that you make me feel safe, even from the Romans," said Jake. "I'm thinking that it's like a dream."

"A good dream?" said Lairgnen.

"Yes," said Jake.

"But you have never … ?" said Lairgnen.

"No," said Jake.

"Is that why you are trembling?" asked Lairgnen.

"Yes," said Jake. "I don't know what to do."

"You don't have to do anything," said Lairgnen. "I know what to do."

Jake nodded, his head against Lairgnen's chest.

Lairgnen kissed him. Jake let himself be kissed. It was a soft kiss, and a long one. Jake felt the stubble on Lairgnen's face, felt the strength of Lairgnen's jaw, the hardness of Lairgnen's body, the power of Lairgnen's arms, the maleness of everything about Lairgnen. Lairgnen's hands explored Jake's body, hardness against hardness, maleness against maleness. All this was new and strange to Jake, but now it made more sense: There really is no Jake. There is only nature, only bodies. Nature will do as nature will do. Life will have its way. We are an ember riding the updraft, lucid as long as the warmth lasts, then falling as ash.

Jake's body began to respond with a spreading fire. His ember grew brighter, rose faster. He rose mindlessly, glowing, burning, shielded by protecting arms. Jake's body knew what to do, because life knows what to do and will always have its way. Lairgnen's arms eased Jake's body down onto the rock. To Jake it felt like the most natural thing in the world, something that had been done millions of times. When Lairgnen's body, warm through his wet clothes, settled onto Jake, it was a comfort. Jake felt not only a timeless need for Lairgnen's body, but also the timeless need to offer his body, to give to Lairgnen's need. Jake felt Lairgnen's hands under his clothes. Jake let him explore. When Lairgnen's hands said that he wished for Jake's body to move for further exploration, Jake moved. Everywhere Lairgnen's hands touched him, the fire grew hotter. The hands withdrew for a moment, and when they came back, Lairgnen was naked. The scent of Lairgnen was like a drug that fed the fire. Lairgnen lifted Jake's tunic and kissed his chest. He moved lower, exploring the yielding firmness of Jake's abdomen. Lairgnen untied the string of Jake's trousers. When Lairgnen spoke, it was a whisper.

"Would you let me?" Lairgnen asked.

"Yes," said Jake.

They did it face to face. It did not hurt. Lairgnen entered him slowly. Jake held Lairgnen close and savored the knowledge that this was Lairgnen, a friend he knew and loved. Jake had been here many times before in dreams. But in the dreams, the lover was never anyone he recognized, never had a name. But this was not a dream. This man's name was Lairgnen. Lairgnen cried out, and Jake felt Lairgnen's body convulse. The throbbing seemed to go on and on. Then Lairgnen lay still, breathing hard.

"I'm sorry," said Lairgnen. "I was too quick."

"Just stay where you are for a while," said Jake. "Then do it again."

"Next time," said Lairgnen, "we will do it for your friend. Say his name."

"Yes," said Jake. "His name was Jamie."

CHAPTER 13

Morning in the river basin was wet, foggy, cold, and miserable. In the weak light of dawn, with their teeth chattering and no fire, they huddled to decide what to do.

"Garrisons are lazy," said Alexis. "They won't be back until they've slept off last night's wine and choked down their morning gruel."

"We can be out of sight in the woods by the time the fog lifts," said Melwas. "If we split into two groups, we'll draw less attention. The Romans are looking for a gaggle of five people."

"It's up to you, Alexis," said Lairgnen. "While we've been fools, eating and drinking in plain view of the whole town, fewer eyes have seen you. You must find Divitiacus and give him the message."

"My paper is all damp," said Jake, exploring his wet pack. "Write carefully, or it will tear."

"I'm terrible at Greek," said Lairgnen.

"Then I will write for you," said Jake.

Lairgnen dictated a note. Jake translated Lairgnen's message into Greek. Jake wrote with the damp paper pressed against a rock. The note said:

"I am Lairgnen, son of Jowan. I carry a message from my father and from Lodan and Gwenlliant the Druids. Their message contains a warning against great danger that must be heard by you and the council. Also with me is a traveler from afar whose news you must hear. We are pursued by the Romans and must remain in hiding. You can trust this messenger, Alexis, to bring you to us in secret. Or we will come to you if we are not seen by the Romans."

"He won't come," said Melwas.

"Perhaps he won't," said Lairgnen. "But he will send for us."

"Where will I find you?" asked Alexis.

"Look for us two miles back into the forest, along the stream," said Lairgnen. "There is a rocky hill above a sycamore grove."

"I will find you," said Alexis.

— ◆ —

They beat their way through thickets and briar-filled ravines to make a wide arc, several crooked miles, to stay safely clear of the Druid camp and Roman patrols. It was mid-afternoon by the time they reached the sycamore grove.

"Why didn't we think of food?" said Jake.

"We were spoiled by the ale seller," said Lairgnen. "It was becoming a habit. My father would beat me for being such a fool, if I weren't too old to be beaten."

"At least we're dry now," said Jake. "But look at the rips in my new clothes, and the mud. If Divitiacus sees me now, he'll think I'm a criminal and hand me over to the Romans."

"The moment Divitiacus hears your Greek," said Lairgnen, "we will all be safe."

"Greek or not, I don't know how to get him to believe us," said Jake. "If only Judith were here. She would know what to say. She would know things about Rome that would convince Divitiacus."

"You have said that Caesar will be killed?" said Lairgnen.

"Yes," said Jake. "That I certainly remember. Four years from now, he will be killed at the Senate, by many assassins, with knives."

"There is justice in that," said Lairgnen. "And so in four years, regardless, Divitiacus will believe you. But perhaps you have a proof for which Divitiacus would not have to wait so long? The Romans are bored. They would hunt us down for sport and crucify us for entertainment, a Roman harvest."

"I will think," said Jake.

—▶ ◀—

At dusk, as they huddled in the gloom, fireless and hungry, they heard horses. Lairgnen closed his eyes and listened.

"Three horses," said Lairgnen.

"That is no Roman patrol then," said Melwas.

"They are speaking Greek," said Jake.

They left their cover in the undergrowth and hailed the horsemen. Three fine horses turned toward them in the shadows and drew up bearing three men. One was Alexis. A bow was attached to his saddle. One was a Celtic soldier, large and heavily armed. The third was a Druid, a man of middle age, tall, tired-looking, and bearing a sword. Lairgnen stepped forward and looked up toward the mounted Druid.

"Welcome, Divitiacus," said Lairgnen.

"So here are the rebels the Romans are seeking," said Divitiacus, dismounting from his horse. "Greetings, Prince Lairgnen, and to your companions. I understand you bear letters for me."

"I do," said Lairgnen.

Divitiacus' guard struck steel against flint, and soon a torch was burning. Divitiacus read.

"You are Jake, then," Divitiacus said, looking up from the letters.

"I am Jake."

"Let us find a place to sit," said Divitiacus. "A story as strange as yours will no doubt be some time in the telling. You all must be hungry. Your friend has brought you food and ale. Please, eat. And while you eat and talk, I will listen."

Jake spoke. Divitiacus listened, occasionally asking a question. At times Jake's Greek would falter, and Divitiacus would prompt him with the word he wanted.

Even when the word Jake wanted was not obvious, Divitiacus' intuition was almost always right and supplied the right word. The torch burned down. Another was lit.

"So your purpose was twofold," said Divitiacus. "One purpose was to warn us of what is to come. The second is to carry back knowledge that will help your people, knowledge that the Romans, and this new religion that has not yet been born, will destroy."

"Yes," said Jake.

Divitiacus sat for a while, eyes intense in the light of the burning torch. The bread, cheese, and onions were gone, but there was still a little ale. Jake took a swallow of ale and realized that he had no idea whether Divitiacus believed him.

"There are many parts of your story that please me," said Divitiacus. "The Druids at least are missed and remembered, though they are gone. The world goes on, and does not end. There are other people among the stars, as we have hoped and believed. And yet you also have shamed me, because I tied my hopes to Rome, and I was wrong. But that mistake I already have corrected. Rome would arrest me, too, now, if they did not fear another uprising while their armies are elsewhere. Your warnings for the future sound true, because the putting down of the Celtic nations already is happening. Each day, more lose the will to fight and instead favor throwing in with the Romans.

"I am sorry that you friends are dead, Jake, and that their deaths have so injured the second part of your mission. Many among the Druids would want to take the place of your dead friends and return with you, but you say that is not possible. As for us, our hope as you say lies in what many already are doing or are planning to do – leaving for Britain, building strongholds in remote places, teaching our children well, and preparing for the violence of this new religion that you say will so entangle itself with the cruelties of Rome.

"In many ways, Jake, your story is not strange to me, because the events that you foretell already are unfolding. It is what my inner sight already has been telling me, though I am stained by my failure to see through Rome's deceptions. You ask for my help. There is little I can do. Soon younger men will have what little of my power remains. My day will soon be over. You said this yourself out of your knowledge of the future, though you are quick to add that you do not predict my death. Caesar, you say, will write about me. And you say that my old friend Cicero will refer to me as in the past, four years from now. Perhaps I will die, or perhaps I will go into hiding.

"Regardless, I do believe you, Jake. But it is not I who needs convincing. Rather, it is that kettle of Druids who even now are arguing, forming factions, weaving intrigues, and recruiting for conspiracies. They must hear you."

"Hear me?" said Jake.

"You must speak to them."

"Speak to them?" said Jake. "How?"

"At the council tomorrow," said Divitiacus. "Roman

patrols or not, I have enough men to get you there safely, and, afterward, to see you safely to the channel. Those who believe you will no doubt go with you, all the way back to Britain. The more of them you can convince, and the more of them you can turn from the Romans, and the more of them you can get to follow you to Britain – even to the north of Britain – then the better it will be for the Druids."

"But what would I say?" asked Jake.

"You have the night to think about it," said Divitiacus. "I will introduce you. I will tell them that Lodan and King Jowan believe you, that they met your companions from the future, that they saw your ship, that they saw this young man, Miach, cured of a harelip. But afterwards you must leave Gaul. You must get to the channel by the quickest route. Find a ship to Britain. Keep to the west of the Thames, as far west as possible. There is a Roman presence all along the Thames. If you see this bard again, someone must kill him. I wish I could go with you, but I must stay in Gaul a little longer. I have a few more tasks here."

"Thank you," said Lairgnen, "for coming to us and for believing Jake's story."

"Jake's story has freed me from a paralysis of doubt," said Divitiacus. "I have met this young man Jake many times before, in many dreams. Waking and sleeping, the story he tells is the same."

——— ◆ ———

Unlike the assizes, which were sparsely attended,

today the main event began. The hillside was dense with Druids. The morning fog had lifted. The news had traveled quickly yesterday that Divitiacus had arrived and soon would speak, though few had seen him. The platform was ringed with Celtic soldiers, swords unsheathed. The assembly buzzed with gossip about the reason for such security. Did Divitiacus fear assassination? Was one of the tribes threatening overt rebellion if the votes did not go its way? Were the Roman patrols trying to stir up trouble?

An elderly Druid led the long and formal invocation. Another elderly Druid led the recitation of the oath. Then a much younger Druid came to the front of the platform to read the agenda, which was a long one.

Then the assembly fell quiet as the platform began to clear. It now was time for the chief vergobret of the tribes to speak. The assembly was so still that birds could be heard chirping from the branches of the trees that ringed the hillside. Divitiacus materialized out of a cluster of soldiers at the back of the platform and walked up the steps. He took his place at the podium. For a moment he surveyed the assembly. Then he began.

"Once again, we meet among the ruins of Cenabum. Once again, we meet as a divided people. Once again, the future of the tribes is a matter of great conflict. We teeter, quarreling, on a rotting bridge over a deep chasm, and we do not know when the bridge will fall or whether we can safely cross. Look around you at the ruins. It has been four years since Caesar laid waste to this city. Are we rebuilding? We are not. Why? It is because we cannot resolve our discord. We cannot agree on a path forward. It is because we are so impoverished from war, and so burdened with Roman taxes, that we could not afford to rebuild Cenabum even if we had the will to do it and could agree on how to go about it.

"Much of the burden of this shame rests with me. I thought we could trust to the honor of the Romans. I thought we could forge agreements with the Romans that would avoid war and protect our lands from the marauding Germans. I thought we could find a way to restore peace among the tribes and to resolve the grievances of our young men who wanted war.

"I was wrong. Every hungry child in the ruins of Cenabum, every fallen stone, every field left unplanted, every cousin or sister or neighbor sold into slavery in Rome, reminds me of how wrong I was. Every day, by the light of reason, and every night, by the light of the stars, I try to see into our future. All I see are turmoil, hard choices, and flight. Indeed, I fear that this could be our last Great Council at Cenabum, and that we must hereafter take refuge in Britain. This will be a great loss not only to ourselves, but also to the people of Gaul. They will be left to the Romans.

"Do the Romans withdraw the garrisons as they promised? They do not. Instead they harass us. They put the bodies of our people on their crosses, for small crimes or for no crimes at all, as a tool of their terror and a reminder of what they call Roman justice. And all the while, the Roman traders and tax collectors pour in. Will these Romans expect to live under Druid law? Will they allow the tribes to do so? They will not. Already the Roman law is starting to devour us. Already they watch us, wary of rebellion, itching to challenge the Druids, to goad us into resistance so that they can crush us."

Divitiacus paused. The assembly was quiet. Then Divitiacus turned and looked toward the back of the platform. He motioned for a young man to step forward. The young man was Jake. With his eyes kept low, Jake stepped forward to stand beside Divitiacus. Prince Lairgnen and his two soldiers followed and stood a few steps behind Jake, weapons sheathed.

"So I ask you, what hope is there in these dark times other than flight? I have little hope to offer. Last night I heard a story that is very nearly beyond believing. Even so, I believe it, because it rings true in all its details. The story was told to me by this young man. He came bearing letters from King Jowan of North Britain, as well as Gwenlliant and Lodan, Druids well known to all of you. Their letters say that they know much of this man's story to be true. I misjudged the Romans. But today, on my last day as your chief vergobret, I dare not risk misjudging this young man. I would have you hear his story and judge for yourselves. His name is Jake. He will tell you where he is from."

Divitiacus put his hand on Jake's shoulder to request that Jake step forward. Divitiacus stepped back, leaving Jake to address the assembly. Divitiacus had urged Jake to be brief and to be direct.

Jake cleared his throat and took a breath to raise his voice. Jake was not accustomed to raising his voice.

"My name is Jake Janaway, and I have come from the future."

"Speak up!" shouted a voice from the back. A little wave of tittering swept across the front rows.

"If you've come from the future, no wonder you're so young!" someone shouted. There was a gale of laughter.

"I suppose you are right," said Jake. "I am in fact so young that I have not yet been born. I will not be born for another two thousand years. But we are not alone here on the earth. Out among the stars there are many people. Sometimes they visit this earth. They know things that we do not yet know, and they have things that we do not yet have. They brought me here. I was sent here to bring to you a warning about what is going to happen. I was sent here to learn from you, because you have knowledge that is at risk of being lost."

"Ask me anything!" someone shouted. Jake waited for the laughter to subside.

"Rome has only just begun its campaign to subdue the Celtic nations," said Jake. "Gaul is lost. Even the language of the Celts in Gaul will be lost in a few generations. Britain will be next. As for the Romans, they will become even more dangerous. In a few more years, a new religion will be born in one of Rome's farthest provinces. That religion will become the imperial religion of Rome. That religion will see the knowledge of the Druids as a deadly threat. Rome and its religion will change this part of the world in ways that you cannot yet imagine. In the end, in a few hundred years, Rome will fall, and new empires will rise in Rome's place.

Everything that was worst about Rome will continue for centuries more. Those new empires will cover the earth. They will perpetuate the worst of Rome and will fall for the same reasons that Rome fell. But they will have grown so large, and the people will have become so many, that their fall will take the earth with them. I come from an earth that has fallen. My earth is like the ruins of Cenabum, except that it is the entire world."

"Helvetii horse shit!" someone shouted. "Why do you insult us with this? Divitiacus is mad! Pull the brat down! Let us have the debates!"

Suddenly the assembly broke into a roar. An onion hit Jake in the chest. Another just missed his crotch. The entire assembly began to shout, some at each other, some at the platform. As Divitiacus stepped forward to try to restore order, there was a loud disturbance near the top of the hill, and those who had been standing there started to run and scatter. A Roman patrol, at least a dozen men on horseback, broke out of the trees. The Celtic soldiers who had been ringed around the platform rushed to regroup at the front in a defensive formation. Lairgnen and his two soldiers leapt to Jake's side to form a defensive triangle around Jake. Lairgnen's eyes quickly scanned toward the river, looking for an out.

The assembly scattered now in all directions as the Roman patrol rode their horses down the slope straight into the crowd and toward the platform. The Roman horses easily jumped the stumps and benches. The patrol reached the front of the platform. Swords began to ring. Lairgnen and the soldiers were easing Jake toward the back of the platform. But then Lairgnen saw another Roman patrol – another dozen men on horse-back – emerge from the river. Two, then three, of the Roman soldiers had made it onto the platform. Celtic swords sped in to challenge them. Clearly it was Jake that the Romans wanted first, but they also wanted Divitiacus. Celtic soldiers formed a circle around Jake and Divitiacus. Within the circle, Lairgnen and his two soldiers held their triangle around Jake. Two of the Romans broke through the circle and sent a Celtic soldier flying from the platform with a slicing blow to the shoulder. A Roman turned to challenge Lairgnen.

All of a sudden and seemingly out of nowhere, six shining spheres, each the size of a melon, appeared over the platform. As the spheres bobbed and spun, narrow beams of brilliant light flew in many directions. The sound of scorching and burning crackled above the sound of shouts and curses. Roman swords turned red hot and were flung from Roman hands. Hot swords landed on the platform and lay there smoking, kindling the planks into flame.

The spheres gathered in a circle just above Jake's head, rotating warily and buzzing like hornets. The Celtic soldiers regrouped in a defensive circle around Jake and Divitiacus. The Roman soldiers, swordless or holding daggers, began to back away. The Celtic soldiers still had their swords, so it had been obvious to everyone whose side the unearthly spheres were on.

Jake looked up toward the spheres.

"Thank you, Sam," said Jake.

"You're welcome, Jake," said one of the spheres.

Then there came a great outcry from the assembly. They had fled to escape the horses and had crept back in to watch the brief battle. Many hands were pointing upward. Then all heads looked up.

Directly above, an enormous black triangle was silently descending. The assembly went quiet to watch. No one fled. Scarcely anyone even moved. The shadow of the triangle fell over the platform and the assembly. At twice the level of the treetops, the triangle stopped and hovered. Its stairs telescoped down and came to rest at the foot of the front side of the platform. Bendigeid appeared at the top of the stairs and started to descend.

He was dressed as a Druid.

━ ━

Divitiacus was first to greet Bendigeid at the bottom of the stairs. They embraced, as though they were old friends. Then Bendigeid reached out to Jake.

"Hello, Jake," said Bendigeid. "I'd have come sooner, but, protocols, you know."

"I know," said Jake. "Even though I was about to doubt you and to wonder what was wrong with that nosy Sam and his telescope."

"Sam doesn't miss much," said Bendigeid.

"I know," said Jake. "We'll do some erasing after I get him alone."

Bendigeid turned back to Divitiacus.

"I apologize for this intrusion," said Bendigeid. "Perhaps they would like to hear an explanation?"

"Let Jake stand with you," said Divitiacus. "They owe Jake an apology."

Bendigeid nodded. Divitiacus gestured for Bendigeid and Jake to step onto the platform. The assembly went quiet, and again nothing could be heard but the chirping of the birds. Romans swords were still smoking. Lairgnen and the others found a seat on a bench in front of the platform. The stairs had withdrawn upward, but the black triangle still hovered. Roman horses grazed where the grass was less trampled, as though this was an ordinary day for a Roman patrol. The Roman soldiers stood, ignored and feckless, on the fringes to watch. Divitiacus' eyes were closed. He was deep in thought.

Bendigeid spoke in the Gaelic that he had learned from Heledd and Miach.

"Grandmothers and Grandfathers," said Bendigeid. "Our people have waited two thousand years for this reunion. To speak to you today is the greatest honor of my lifetime. I speak not only for myself, but also for those who have come before me, down through the ages, all the way back to you yourselves, for you are indeed our grandmothers and grandfathers. I am here today to make an offer.

"Nature is strange, as all the learnèd know. And so I know even before I make this offer that many of you will accept it.

"Those of you who choose to remain on earth, and your children, and your children's children, will find refuge – though far from a perfect refuge – in the hills and remote places of Britain and Ireland. But time, and the suffocating pressure of Rome and its descendants, will obscure much of the memory of who you – who we – are today. The loss will be enormous, because I believe that, were it not for Rome and Rome's descendants, and were it not for Roman crimes against the Celts that will drive our ways into obscurity, the world of the future would be a much better place than it actually comes to be. But, at last, after two thousand years, in my time and Jake's, it is now time for Rome and its descendants – and Rome's way of thinking – to be flung into obscurity and forgotten. The great wheel turns, and now older gods, and older ways, will return to this land and to the people.

"Soon Jake and I must leave. But, a year from now, this ship, or one like it, will return to this very spot. It will carry two thousand of you, and the seed of many more of you, to a new home in the stars. For some who choose to go, and for their descendants, it will be a permanent home. That world in the stars is a world much like this one, where you will be able to live much as you live now. For others who go to that world, that home in the stars will be a temporary home, a refuge, a haven, an asylum from the violence on earth, for two thousand years. Then, in Jake's time, those who choose to do so will return to earth. They will restore to earth much of what has been lost. This part of my story – the part about a refuge for the Druids in the stars – Jake himself did not know, because not until this moment could I tell him."

Bendigeid looked at Jake. Jake mouthed the word "Protocols." Bendigeid continued.

"I hope you will apologize to Jake. He is modest and often fears failure, though he rarely fails. A few moments ago, I am sure that he not only felt defeated, but that he also felt the approach of death. But I have known from the beginning that he would succeed, and it was hard indeed not to be able to tell him so.

"I know that you have many questions. Your questions deserve answers. I can remain here for a few hours, and I will try to answer your questions. After that, Jake, and those who came here with him, will return to the north of Britain. They will be relieved to know that they won't have to walk, or travel on leaking ships on the ocean, to make their way home. I will stand aside now and leave to Divitiacus how he would like to order this discussion."

The assembly exploded into a hubbub. Many hands clapped Jake on the back. Bendigeid and Divitiacus spoke quietly. At the foot of the platform, Lairgnen looked thoughtful. Miach looked starstruck. Alexis looked very preoccupied. The Roman soldiers, looking up warily at the black triangle, found their horses and went away.

Jake jumped down from the platform and spoke near Lairgnen's ear to be heard above the noise.

"Can we take Alexis? There is nothing for him here," said Jake.

"Alexis would be most welcome in my father's guard," said Lairgnen.

"Excellent," said Jake. "Could you tell him before he dies of a broken heart?"

Bendigeid came down from the platform to speak to Jake.

"You should go over to the city to celebrate with some ale," Bendigeid said. "There are still a few who will not believe us. You need not hear what they will say. There is no need to fear the Romans, even if they return in force. Sam will go with you."

"Won't that be a spectacle at the ale tent," said Jake. "Sam, would you like to come along and pour some ale?"

"I'm afraid that I didn't bring the correct arm for pouring ale," said Sam.

There was no waiting for a boat this time. The gaping crowd standing at the river staring at the triangle parted to let them pass. There was wheat bread, freshly baked. They ordered ale.

"I wonder what will become of the bard," said Jake.

"The Druids will find him," said Lairgnen. "There will be justice."

"What is on your mind, Lairgnen?" asked Jake. "Is something troubling you?"

"I was wondering," said Lairgnen, "about these two thousand people. Must they all be Druids? Your friend did not say."

"Why are you wondering?" asked Jake.

"Heledd is a Druid, but I am not," said Lairgnen.

"Yes," said Jake. "We will ask Bendigeid. If you want to be with Heledd, then I feel sure he would not turn you down."

"He is an understanding person, this Bendigeid?" asked Lairgnen.

"Oh, yes," said Jake.

"Where are you going?" asked Lairgnen.

"I'll be back soon," said Jake. "This tunic is ruined, and I have to pee, and I want to see the jeweler. That is, if you could lend me ..."

"Of course," said Lairgnen.

CHAPTER 14

Bendigeid and King Jowan declared a feast and invited the entire village. The king's steward declared that a feast could not be done on such short notice. Bendigeid assured them that it would not be a problem. Decorations at the castle started immediately, and all the tents, tables and chairs in the village that weren't too heavy to move were brought by wagon to the grassy fields overlooking the seas to the west of the castle. Wood was stacked for the fires. Musicians rehearsed. Everyone practiced their dance steps.

The morning of the feast, when anxiety about whether there would be anything to eat reached its peak, the gnats started shuttling back and forth with provisions from the big ship in high orbit. Crowds gathered to watch. The king's cooks, Clood, and innkeepers from the village officiated at the unloading, while androids did all the carrying. Ale was sampled. Containers were opened and tasted. Recipes and ingredients were inquired about. The rumor that the food would be superb, and plentiful, spread quickly. Near the castle, a dais was built for the guests of honor, with a podium for speakers. The dais had its back to the sea, with the castle to one side. The weather was perfect. The yellow wildflowers of late summer dotted the slope. Everyone was careful not to tread on the flowers.

As the sun descended toward the sea and began to turn yellow, the torches were lit. Everyone had gathered facing the dais. The guests of honor took their seats.

The black triangle had been parked far out on the horizon above the sea, well beyond looming distance. Now it approached in the twilight and stopped high above the castle. A wide array of lights on its underbelly winked on and started moving. The lights soon gave shape to an enormous holographic movie screen, in brilliant color, in the air beneath the triangle. The crowd gasped. An image of Judith appeared. Music swelled. Judith was smiling and talking with Gwenlliant. It was a tribute to Judith. Then there was Aderyn, laughing and playing word games with a group of people sitting around a table and drinking ale. Then there were Harris and McGlennon, drilling with the soldiers and laughing at Jake's ineptness with a sword. Not until then did Jake realize that they had been followed by tiny drones more often than he knew. In retrospect, he did not find it surprising.

Bendigeid called for a minute of silence for the dead.

There was only the sound of the sea and a few crying babies. Then Jake rose and said their names.

The musicians struck up a reel, and the dancing and feasting began. An android on the musicians' side of the dais watched the musicians and listened with its android ears. Vast processing power on board the black triangle listened, too. That processing power generated the sound of other compatible instruments, added its own flourishes, and amplified it all. Nothing like it had ever been heard before. Everyone danced. It was impossible not to dance. There were time-outs for ale, but few seemed serious about eating until they needed a rest from dancing. No one worried that the food would run out before they got to the tables.

"There'll be more babies conceived tonight than at Beltane," Gwenlliant said to Jake, "nor will you and Lairgnen have to do all the work."

Then she caught herself and turned red. It took a second for Jake to catch her meaning.

"Truly?" said Jake.

"Can you forgive me?" said Gwenlliant. "That was not my news to give. I am so sorry. I thought she had told you. She said she would."

"You are forgiven," said Jake. "But I will deal with you later."

Jake went to Heledd, who was sitting between Lodan and Bergan on the other side of the table.

"Would you walk with me?" Jake asked her.

She blushed and rose. Jake led her toward the path above the sea. It was dark now. The sound of the waves crashing below mingled with the music of a reel from the castle.

"Might you have something to tell me?" Jake asked.

"I have a thousand things to tell you," she said. "I have been waiting for a moment when I could be alone with you. You have been so busy. And Lairgnen has been so needy."

"Aren't you still keeping me waiting?" said Jake.

"We are going to have a child," she said.

Jake stopped, took her hand, and pulled her close. He laughed.

"And I am the last to know," he said.

"Not quite the last," said Heledd. "Are you happy, Jake? I want you to be happy, but I know you have to go. Our child will never see its father. It breaks my heart for him or her to never know you."

As he held her, the music modulated from a reel to something much slower. The modulation must have taken vast amounts of processing power. If Sam is spying again, thought Jake, I will break one of his arms. Jake recognized the music. It was from "West Side Story," music by Leonard Bernstein and lyrics by Stephen Sondheim – "Somewhere."

"Do you regret that you chose me?" asked Jake.

"Never," she said. "I will never regret it. I knew that you would have to go. But this way I will keep a part of you. I will have our child. That is much to have. All of us here will have this child."

"When the ship comes back, in a year, will you go, Heledd?"

"Yes," she said. "I believe I will. Lairgnen wants to go, and he wants me to go."

"Good," said Jake.

"He will treat your child as his own," she said.

"I know," said Jake. "That will be a great comfort to me."

"Yes," she said.

"I have something for you," said Jake. He reached into a pocket and withdrew a silver ring.

"Will you wear this?" he asked.

"You knew?" she said.

"Somehow, I did," said Jake. "I must be learning your ways."

He put the ring on her finger. For a while they stood there in each other's arms.

"And I have something for you," she said.

Heledd, too, had a silver ring in her pocket.

"I came prepared," she said. "I knew that I must tell you tonight."

She slipped the ring on his finger.

"This is your first ring, a great honor for me, Jake Janaway," she said. "May you have many rings and many children, and may you always be happy."

Jake at last released the sobs that he had been trying to hold back for so long.

"I don't want to leave you," he said. "I don't want to leave any of you."

She held him.

"Jake?" she said.

"Yes?"

"There are others who love you."

"I know," Jake said.

"You also must see them this night."

Jake nodded, wiping his eyes on the sleeve of his tunic.

"I have something else for you," he said.

He reached into the collar of his tunic and removed a silver torc that he had been wearing, unseen since he bought it from the jeweler at Cenabum.

"This is for our child," he said. "Let it be an heirloom, for our child and for our grandchildren. And when you give it to our child, please say that it is an eternal reminder of their father's love."

"I will do that," said Heledd.

They were in Lairgnen's chamber on the seaward side of the castle. The shutters were open, revealing the sea and a sky full of stars, but also admitting a cool night breeze. A fire had been lit in the fireplace. They stood by the fire.

"I have no experience at this," said Jake. "I no more know what to say than I knew how to make love to you. Please tell me. What do I say?"

"While you give thought to that, I could begin," said Lairgnen. "Jake, would you wear this ring?"

Lairgnen held out a brass ring.

"I would be honored to wear your ring," said Jake. "And I shall never forget the moment that I earned it. You were my first. And I have a ring for you."

They put the rings on each other's fingers.

"No one ever forgets the first time," said Lairgnen. "It was something very rare and wonderful that you gave me. I shall feel proud of it until the day I die: 'I was Jake's first.' I will tell your child that, if you like."

"Please do. Lairgnen, will you look after my child? Our child?"

"I will," said Lairgnen, "as though the three of us had conceived it together. Perhaps we did."

"And Heledd," said Jake. "You will look after Heledd?"

"I will," said Lairgnen. "Perhaps someday she and I will wear each other's gold."

"Will you and she go to the Ursa Major haven?"

"If Heledd is willing," said Lairgnen, "we will go. I am my father's second son. We have a saying that the lives of second sons are made for adventure. Heledd will go because she wants to learn, though I don't know how she will bear not being able to return here to apply what she learns."

"Heledd will be loved and needed wherever she is," said Jake.

"I will miss you, Jake," said Lairgnen. "The time with you was short, and we wasted too much of it."

"We did," said Jake. "That is my chief regret, that we had only the once. Or the twice, depending on how you count."

Lairgnen laughed.

"I was so afraid that I hurt you, or that I let you down. I am a terrible lover, I'm afraid, Jake. Heledd reminds me of that often."

"We have a little time to try to do better," said Jake.

The musicians had stopped playing, but many people still lingered in the night air, laughing and drinking. Derbhorgill waved to him from one of the tables. Jake went to him, and they embraced, knowing that it probably was goodbye. They didn't speak. They didn't need to.

The black triangle still hovered over the castle. Sam was moving from table to table, serving ale.

"Sam," said Jake. "Do you know where Bendigeid is?"

"I do, Jake," said Sam. "He has gone up. But I am certain that he has not yet gone to bed."

"Would you ask him if he would mind a few visitors?"

"Of course, Jake," said Sam. "Bendigeid says that he'd be pleased to receive visitors."

"Good," said Jake. Then, turning to Gwenlliant, Heledd, and Lairgnen, he said, "There is someone I want you to meet."

The stairs telescoped down into the grass.

"So many steps!" said Gwenlliant.

"Just sit here," said Jake, "and we all will ride up."

A small seat appeared out of a panel for Gwenlliant, and they all rose as the stairs telescoped back into the belly of the ship. Bendigeid was waiting for them at the top.

"You know how much I worry about time paradoxes," Jake said to Bendigeid. "But I believe that there is something that you have been concealing from me. And I would like for Heledd and Lairgnen to meet their grandson. Our grandson."

"Paradoxes must wait until the right moment in time," said Bendigeid. "That is the protocol. And that moment has come."

"Will you show us?" asked Jake.

Bendigeid reached into the collar of his tunic and lifted out a silver torc so that it lay visible on his tunic. Heledd gasped and reached for her torc. It was the same torc, though her torc did not have an ancient patina.

"Are you … ?" said Heledd.

"I am," said Bendigeid. "I am the eighty-third generation of the eldest children of Heledd, Jake, and Lairgnen. Perhaps you have no idea how revered you are among your descendants at our home in Ursa Major, or how privileged I am to wear this torc."

"Hence," said Jake, "the strongest possible intuition for the success of this mission."

"Now you know," said Bendigeid.

"Not only is there the paradox of knowing the past because you're seen the future," said Jake, "but we also have two copies of the same torc, and nature doesn't seem to care. I'm never going to fret about paradoxes again."

"Nature can be very forgiving," said Bendigeid.

"Then I forgive nature," said Jake.

"Come," said Bendigeid. "Please stay the night here. There is plenty of room. I would not want to waste a single moment of the time we have left."

They talked for hours in a little sitting room with a

large window. The window looked down on the sea, the broch, and the castle. When Sam returned up the stairs, stinking from spilled ale, Jake gave him strict instructions to turn off all recording devices. This history records little more about the evening on the black triangle, but it is recorded that Jake and Gwenlliant exchanged brass rings.

Yesterday's feast had been luckily timed, because a steady rain fell all the next day. As the black triangle hovered, obscured at times in the low clouds, the broch was packed with people for the formal goodbyes. Gwenlliant, blushing when her new brass ring was noticed, officiated. Lodan and King Jowan spoke appropriate words. Jake was brief, and many tears were wiped on many sleeves. Bendigeid was solemn and thoughtful. Lairgnen and Heledd stayed close to each other for mutual comfort. Derbhorgill stood alone near a window. Clood, a nosy white kitten tagging behind her, gave Jake and Bendigeid a basket of scones for the road. Lodan kept nervously and discreetly returning to a window to look for Miach and Alexis, but no one had seen them since the night before.

"I was not thoughtful last night," Jake said to Lodan. "I was going to talk with Miach, but when I looked for him he had already gone."

"And I thought he was with you," said Lodan. "I'm sure his heart is breaking. Poor young Miach has had to compress years of learning about love into two months of joy and turmoil. Such a parting is no doubt more than he is ready to bear."

"Please tell him," said Jake, "that I will never forget him. Please give him this for me."

It was a ring made of mother of pearl, set in copper, on a silver chain. Surely so much good cuddling, Jake had decided, deserved a ring.

"It will be his greatest treasure," said Lodan.

At last, as everyone stood heedlessly in the pouring rain, Jake and Bendigeid waved farewell from the stairs of the black triangle. Then the stairs telescoped up. The ship slowly rose into the clouds and was gone. They all stood silently in the rain, hoping that the clouds might part for another look. But there was only more rain.

CHAPTER 15

On the second day out from earth, Jake, Bendigeid, and the cats were on the star deck. Jake was sketching scenes from memory. Bendigeid was reading. The cats were asleep. Sam approached.

"Yes, Sam?" said Bendigeid.

"Systems aboard the triangle awoke out of standby to report unusual activity on board," said Sam.

"Unusual activity?" said Bendigeid. Jake looked up from his sketch.

"Yes," said Sam. "It would appear that there are stow-aways, sir."

"Do you have a visual?" asked Bendigeid.

The space in front of Sam lit up with a hologram. It was Alexis and Miach, skulking through a semi-dark corridor.

"I should have guessed," said Jake. "I wasn't thinking. Just look at them. They look scared."

"Sam," said Bendigeid, "turn on the lights, send a droid with food and water, and say that we'll be there soon."

"Now what?" asked Jake.

"Sam, what does the ship say?" asked Bendigeid.

"The ship's decision is to stay on course while a message is sent to base," said Sam.

"Is anything like this on the contingency list, Sam?" asked Bendigeid.

"There are several stowaway contingencies," said Sam. "They are based on degrees of risk and hostility. A contingency has been invoked for low risk to the ship, to the passengers, and to the mission. A protocol ruling from base will be required."

"Am I granted any override options?" asked Bendigeid.

"No, sir," said Sam. "It is strictly a matter of a protocol ruling resolvable only at base."

"Jake, you should go to them," said Bendigeid. "Sam will lead you to the triangle's berth."

"I'm not sure what I should say," said Jake.

"Welcome them and show them to their cabin," said Bendigeid, "and invite them here to the star deck when they are ready."

"We'll have to send them back, won't we?" said Jake.

"I have never heard of anything like this before," said Bendigeid. "But there must be some flexibility in the protocols, else we already would be turning around."

The kitten was awake now.

"Want to tag along, Miss Puss?" said Jake. "You've got some new guys to pet you."

—▸ ◂—

"Where did you get the champagne, Sam?" Jake asked.

"The ship made it, Jake," said Sam, "like pretty much everything else."

"The bottle, too?" asked Jake. "Or is that left over from, you know …"

"The ship also made the bottle," said Sam. "The bottle you have in mind actually was ejected into space, for security."

"Along with the potato?" said Jake.

"Along with the potato," said Sam.

"Throw a potato at me if I drink too much," said Jake. "But we're halfway home now, and I'm going to drink."

Jake, Bendigeid, Miach and Alexis were on the star deck. The dark sphere of the jump station was rushing toward them. Then, as before when they were traveling in the opposite direction, everything went dark for a moment, and suddenly they were surrounded by stars again. They were now back in the modern era. Sam handed the champagne bottle to Jake, and Jake did the honors of popping the cork. The cats fled. Then, off to their right, visible from its exterior lights and its silhouette against the stars, they saw another massive ship identical to their own, twirling in a stationary holding position. Their own ship was approaching it for a rendezvous.

"What is that ship?" Bendigeid asked Sam. "I was not expecting this."

"The ship has hailed us," said Sam, "It reports that it has come from earth, carrying passengers into exile."

"Passengers? Exile?" said Bendigeid. "What is that about?"

"Sir, the passengers consist of twenty-three people who have been convicted of conspiracy against this mission and of a bombing and murder back on earth. From their confessions, it also was known that they conspired to cause further violence against this mission. Their ship requested an immediate report on our status and safety and asked whether we need assistance. That report already has been transmitted, and we are receiving their response. One moment."

"They caught them," said Jake.

"Exile, then," said Bendigeid.

"This doesn't seem like a good moment for champagne," said Jake. Alexis was looking longingly at the bottle and at the glasses that Sam was holding.

"Let us drink to justice," said Bendigeid.

"To justice, then," said Jake.

"Sir," said Sam, "The ship sends its condolences for the loss of the four members of the mission. It congratulates us on the mission's success and for fortitude in the face of such loss and adversity. It requests that we rendezvous and that you and Jake board her. The passengers' sentence requires that they hear, in person, your reports on the consequences of their conspiracy."

"Who are those people?" asked Jake. "What were they trying to accomplish?"

"I am informed," said Sam, "that their motive was the preservation of the dominance of the Christian religion."

"Oh, no," said Jake. "I'd rather be beaten. Where are they being sent to? Off-planet exile is a new concept to me."

"It is an earth-like planet," said Sam. "It is a quarantine planet. The protocols relate to the permanent and humane isolation of contagious threats."

"That sounds like an awful place," said Jake. "It sounds like a prison planet. Why go to so much trouble? Why not just put them in prison on earth?"

"I do not have all the data," said Sam. "I will send inquiries. But it is clear that future risks to earth were at a significant level, that their religion is in the highest categories of malignancy and fragility, that these twenty-three people were well-connected and troublingly powerful, and that strong pleas were made that their lives be spared. I understand that trials are continuing on earth and that more convictions are possible."

"Rome," said Jake. "Rome just won't give up."

Alexis now had six months of training in English under his belt, with pharmaceutical assistance, and he had understood most of this exchange. Nevertheless, he gave Jake a puzzled look on hearing the word "Rome."

"We have months to try to explain some history," said Jake.

A few minutes later, Sam reported that data had started pouring in from earth – messages for all, including from the families of Judith, Aderyn, Harris and McGlennon, who still did not have the news of their deaths and would not receive the news for several more weeks, when the ship's transmissions arrived at earth. Instead, the ship was bearing the bodies home.

"How long until rendezvous?" Jake asked.

"About an hour," said Sam.

"May I?" Jake asked Bendigeid.

"Of course," said Bendigeid.

Jake excused himself and went to his room to read his messages.

——— ———

When Jake and Bendigeid emerged from their gnat on board the other ship, they were greeted by a squirrel person. Jake suppressed a gasp, because she was both strange and beautiful. She was tall, matronly, and elegantly dressed in old-fashioned velvets and a bonnet. She was like a Beatrix Potter painting come to life. Her smile was toothy and charming. Her eyes were black. She held her hands clasped in front of her, long fingers intertwined.

"Welcome, my frienthz," she said. "It ith mohtht kind of you to come, for I am thure that thith ith a mohtht irkthome duty. I am called Marananna."

Bendigeid greeted her similarly formally and introduced Jake. Jake, dazzled by her loveliness and aching to draw her, nodded and tried to imitate her slight bow. She gestured toward the corridor. A white handkerchief, or some sort of lace, hung from the cuff of her blouse.

"If you will follow me, our pathengers have been athembled. They are a dithagreeable lot, and theveral of them had to be compelled."

Soon Jake and Bendigeid stood at the front of a long room with walls upholstered in dark green velvet. The twenty-three prisoners were seated on benches facing the front of the room. A few of them were dressed in dark suits and ties. Two wore clerical collars. Others were more casually dressed. Three of them appeared to be quite young, probably in their twenties. They're a dowdy and conservative lot, thought Jake.

"If you will ekthcuthe me," said Marananna, "I will return when you have finithed. Kindly pull the cord by the door."

"Who are you? What is this about?" shouted one of the younger ones who was seated near the back.

"I am an emissary from the galactic union," said Bendigeid, "and this young man was intended to be a victim of your conspiracy. He survived. This occasion may not be pleasant for any of us, so I will be as brief as possible. I will discharge the duties that I have been given, and then we will go on our way."

The room's lights dimmed. A hologram showed Judith, Aderyn, Harris and McGlennon smiling and laughing on the star deck. Harris was opening a bottle of champagne. Harris handed the bottle to McGlennon. As McGlennon started to drink, the potato that Sam had launched knocked the bottle from McGlennon's hand, and the bottle went flying.

"This attempt on their lives was averted," said Bendigeid, "by our ship's intelligence."

Now a hologram showed a Celtic village, seen from high above. Fires broke out almost simultaneously on rooftops. By the light of flaming thatch, people could be seen scurrying and organizing to fight the fires. Now the hologram flickered, then showed the bodies of the victims, blackened holes burned in their chests. Some of the prisoners looked away. Others straightened their backs and masked their faces with defiance. One of the men in suits and clerical collar, who was sitting in the front row, spoke.

"You seek to shame us with this?" he said. "It is nothing – nothing – compared with what you did to earth."

"We are not here to argue with you," said Bendigeid. "But I will say that neither I nor this young man had anything to do with what has happened on earth. Rather, our task is to restore to earth the most benign and supportable culture possible."

"Something other than the church?" said the man.

"Yes," said Bendigeid.

"Why barbarians?" said the man. "If it was necessary to regress to paganism, then why not Greece?"

"Are we done?" said a voice from the back. "Clearly we're about to be subjected to yet another humanist lecture."

"See?" said another voice, the voice of an older man. His eyes had a wild look of barely controlled panic. "See? I told you. I still can't remember dying, though. Why can't I remember dying? This is hell. This is a black void where prayers cannot be heard, this ..."

"Come, Oliver," said a woman's voice. "We will go now. You must sleep. We are here with you. Let's get you to your room."

"Are we done?" the voice from the back repeated.

"Yes," said Bendigeid. "You may go." Bendigeid pulled the cord by the door.

"May I stay for a moment?" asked the man in the clerical collar. "I suspect that I will never have another chance to ask my questions."

"For a moment, certainly," said Bendigeid.

Twenty-two of the passengers filed out. Most avoided eye contact with Jake and Bendigeid. A few gave them dark looks. The man who thought he was in hell was sobbing. Jake and Bendigeid were then alone with the man in the clerical collar.

"May I ask your name?" said Bendigeid.

"Winston," the man said. "My name is Winston."

"You had a question?" said Bendigeid.

"Why barbarians? Why not Greece? Why does your revolution so completely break the thread of civilization?"

Jake studied Winston's face. The man had kind eyes. It was hard to imagine that he was capable of the crimes that he had been convicted of.

"There are many threads of civilization," said Bendigeid.

The man spoke now in Greek.

"*Inferiors revolt in order that they may be equal, and equals that they may be superior. Such is the state of mind which creates revolutions,*" Winston said.

"Aristotle," said Jake.

"You know Aristotle?" Winston said, "And Greek?"

"Do you believe that it was only about power?" asked Jake.

"Of course I believe that it was only about power, and a permanent reordering of power," said Winston. "Do you believe otherwise?"

"Have you spent much time in America?" asked Jake.

"I have never been to America," said Winston. "I never felt a need. If you are American, I apologize."

"If there has ever been a thread of Greek thinking in America," said Jake, "it would be hard to detect it. Sure, our Founding Fathers, as we call them, had classical educations. There are some Athenian ideas and rhetoric in our founding documents. But the American people are decidedly un-Greek in their temperaments and in the wiring of their minds. I would ask you a question. Think of Augustine of Hippo, surely the most successful theologian who ever lived. Did he think like a Greek?"

"No," said Winston. "I would say that he did not. At least, he did not think like an Athenian. He thought like a Roman. I see your point."

"Then when was this thread in our civilization broken?" asked Jake. "The Latin language seemed to suit Augustine, but somehow I have to think that even the Greek language itself would have refused to contain Augustine's kind of thinking."

"Yes, yes," said Winston. "I see your point, though you belittle Augustine and would try the patience of a linguist."

"Augustine was such a successful theologian," said Jake, "because he was able to take an alien way of thinking from the Middle East and reframe it in a way that corresponded with the minds of Europeans, whose cultures were not at all like the cultures of the Middle East. And though I would say that Augustine was essential to that project, it required several more centuries to complete the Romanization and to break the other threads."

"You are a very sharp and opinionated young man," said Winston. "Oxford, like the rest of us?"

"No," said Jake. "The University of Virginia."

Winston laughed, but it was a laugh of irony, not of derision.

"As I said, I see your point," said Winston. "If you are claiming that a more barbarian way of thinking is more compatible with the American mind, then I concede. Well done."

"I have met these barbarians," said Jake, "and I lived with them for a while. I doubt that I can convince you that they are not barbarians. I found them very natural. I miss them and their naturalness. They live here on the earth. They don't obsess over other-worldly doctrine. Nothing requires them to submit their lives to something invisible that I suppose you would call spirit. Spirit can be very dangerous, you know. The catalog of spirit's crimes is long and very black. The deeds that spirit led you to do are the very cause of your being sent into exile."

"Young man," said Winston. "Do you believe in revelation? Do you believe only in what you can see? Is there room in your world for faith?"

"Of course I believe in things that we can't see," said Jake. "Mathematics is invisible. Everything that we might call Platonic is invisible. And yet it seems to me that it can do no harm to approach things that are invisible with some reason and common sense and to not allow ourselves to become possessed by something malignant only because we give it the noble-sounding name of 'spirit.' But what is revelation?"

"I sense a challenge in your question," said Winston. "And it is an old challenge. If God once revealed important truths to man, then why did the revelation stop? How do we choose between one claim to revelation over another? How do we decide between the still, small voice inside us and the authority of texts and tradition and miracles? I often have wondered about these things, and I have no answer other than faith. But faith, I feel sure, is not a matter about which you and I are likely to agree."

"Probably not," said Jake.

"Young man," said Winston. "Are you a Druid?"

Jake laughed.

"No," Jake said. "I'm just Jake, a slacker who graduated a semester late at the University of Virginia – architect, underachiever, and sinner. I'm a pizza-loving suburban boy who fell in with the wrong people."

"If often works that way, doesn't it?" said Winston. "One falls in with the wrong people."

"Did you fall in with the wrong people?" asked Jake.

"If you had asked me that question six months ago," said Winston, "I would have said that I was making a very hard choice, a choice that was necessary to preserve everything that I had tried to live for. But for these past six months, I have been traveling out among the stars, on a ship of a sort that I never would have believed even existed. I am with people from another planet – delightful people, really, beautiful people – who have never heard of our revelation and who very clearly have no use for it. And now I am tormented by the likelihood that what I formerly saw as the most important thing that ever happened, at least on our little planet, was in fact a rather small and doubtful thing in the context of a universe that is so large and complicated. Clearly ours is a universe – God's universe, I still believe – that contains far more than I knew. How foolish was I, not to at least have imagined that it might be so? And now here I am, shamed by an underachieving, pizza-loving American, and by the consequences of my own deeds. Perhaps Oliver is right. After all, I have left the earth far behind, and I will never see the earth again. Perhaps we all have died and don't remember it. Perhaps this is our hell. Perhaps my dark fears already have been realized. Perhaps it won't get any worse than this. But perhaps there remains another chance for grace. Who knows? Now I see how little I knew. As for faith, I believe my faith has almost forsaken me. My faith was too small a thing for a universe so vast."

"I don't believe that you are dead, Winston," said Jake. "Do you believe in grace?"

"I don't know," said Winston. "I want to go on believing in grace. But I feel as though I no longer have the tools for grappling with the universe as I now know it to be. Faced with this universe, my doctrine and my faith have fallen apart. Whereas you, with your disdain of doctrine and your distrust of faith, seem to handle such a vast universe just fine. But I dare not ask for grace. Not anymore. I am far too great a wretch to plead for grace. Do you believe in grace?"

"Yes," said Jake. "I think I do."

Tears appeared now in Winston's eyes.

"Will you forgive me?" said Winston. "We would have killed you."

"Yes," said Jake. "I will forgive you. You seem to me like a good man."

"This grace," said Winston. "Where might one find it, with no doctrine and no faith?"

"That is far too big a question for the likes of me," said Jake.

"But you said you believe in grace," said Winston. "You must have some idea. How? Where?"

"Try the star deck," said Jake. "Think of all the things that we locate in the Platonic world – mathematics, music, logic, beauty, Kant's world of *a priori* moral cognitions. That's the first place I would look, I think. And I think that might work anywhere in the universe."

"Thank you," said Winston. "You are a remarkable young man. And to think that we tried to kill you."

"You, too, have been wronged," said Jake. "I will try to never forget that. As for grace, it sucks that grace – if you'll pardon my college-boy talk – that grace isn't visible, that you never know when or whether grace will appear. Because if grace were a commodity that could be weighed and transported, then we'd want every ship in the galaxy to be ferrying it to earth right now."

"If you can send word someday," said Winston, "on how earth is faring, if it is permitted, will you?"

"I will," said Jake.

The gnat carrying Jake and Bendigeid back to their own ship moved silently through the void. They watched as the ship carrying the exiles ceased its twirling and accelerated toward the jump station. Soon it disappeared into the jump station as though it had fallen into a black hole.

"It's funny," said Jake. "Earth is rid of them, but haven't we also seeded some other planet with their religion?"

"I wonder if it matters," said Bendigeid. "I believe you were quite right in what you said about Augustine of Hippo. Wherever they're going, unless someone like Augustine of Hippo comes along to translate their religion into a form that makes sense to the objects of their proselytization, they're unlikely to be very successful. And besides, that translation would make their religion into an entirely different proposition, no doubt with faults and virtues and consequences very different from Augustinian doctrine on earth."

"I see now," said Jake, "after talking with Winston, why my culture so urgently required a change of religion. It wasn't just about what the Roman religion has done, and was still doing, on earth. It also was that such rigid doctrine was too brittle to adapt to the new reality – a galactic union, extraterrestrials, and all that. Whereas the Celts and Druids never lost a wink of sleep over extraterrestrials. If anything, the Druids repeated the same mistake they made at first with Rome – they embraced and didn't fear a larger and more complicated world."

"Yes," said Bendigeid. "There were those who argued half a century ago that Christianity and its institutions could not survive the Twentieth Century. Yet even at Oxford there was a resurgence of Christianity, in particular after World War I, to meet the existential needs of people after such a war. But, after a few decades, Europe began to change quickly. In America it was a different story."

"Bendigeid," said Jake. "Is religion universal? Does it exist in some form everywhere in the universe?"

"It is always so unsatisfying to give a statistical answer to such questions," said Bendigeid. "But, as with many things, it is a bell curve. It varies with species. Earth's history would place earth near the peak of the bell curve – earth's humans are highly religious. Religion in some form is very prevalent among the known civilizations in the galaxy, but on the edges of the bell curve there are a smaller number of cultures that are relatively areligious. One thing we have learned from following particular cultures through long periods of their history is that the level of religiosity tends to persist at more or less the same level, regardless of how a particular culture evolves or devolves over time, and regardless of its level of empirical knowledge and technology."

"As though it is wired into the species?" asked Jake.

"That is a likely cause," said Bendigeid. "There may be other factors with a smaller influence."

"What would you say about Druidism, then?" asked Jake. "In the two thousand years that the Druids have been cloistered off-world, how have they changed?"

"In many ways, we have changed along with earth," said Bendigeid. "In every era, there have been covert agents who spent time on earth and returned with reports. They returned not only with reports, actually, but also with books and documents. In the so-called modern era of earth, it was a simple matter to monitor earth's broadcast media. And as always there were agents whose task it was to infiltrate and return surveillance from earth's highest levels of power. It was necessary that we should evolve with earth and learn from earth. Else we would have returned as aliens of the same species."

"That must have been interesting," said Jake, "comparing what the masses on earth were told versus what you knew the elites actually were thinking and doing."

"We made a study of it, of course," said Bendigeid. "Following and analyzing events on earth was an important part of what you might call the Druidic curriculum. And yes. The gulf between the ordinary people and elites always was very disturbing and usually very dangerous. What was most disturbing, particularly to our young people, was not to be able to get messages to earth, to warn earth about what it was about to step into. At times there even were conspiracies to do that and to send teams to warn earth and attempt reform. One or two attempts over the centuries almost succeeded in getting conspirators to earth."

"That must have been maddening," said Jake, "seeing earth constantly fucking up and not being able to do anything about it. And yet at times earth must have been boring."

"I doubt that it ever was boring," said Bendigeid. "It always was known that some of us would return. Some abhorred the idea of returning to earth. Others relished it. The rehabilitation of earth became a kind of specialization. But even those who have no desire to return to earth are very interested in the outcomes. They follow the story with great interest."

"The rehabilitation of earth is your specialization?" asked Jake.

"Oh, yes," said Bendigeid.

"Then you have been in communication with Henry, or at least Henry's cadre of sleepers, for a long time."

"Yes," said Bendigeid.

"How long?" asked Jake.

"Multiple protocols were triggered during World War II, before I was born. I'm speaking now of the galactic union's protocols, not the consensus among the Druids, though the two were in accord. We Druids consider ourselves very smart on matters having to do with earth, but our insights are nothing compared with those of the galactic union. So it was the galactic union's protocols that were triggered. As a metaphor, think of a panel of warning lights that all began to flash almost at once.

Protocol triggers related to politics, technology, the ability to act outside the atmosphere, population, the environment, and – to use one of your favorite words – even the potential for existential crisis as religions cracked under such strain – all those crossed danger thresholds almost simultaneously. It was in 1946 that earth was put into an accelerated program of intervention. But, even accelerated, such a program requires decades of preparation."

"Was Phaedrus a part of this cadre of sleepers?" asked Jake.

"Oh, yes," said Bendigeid. "He was recruited at Oxford in 1974. I have read his file. All of us assigned to the rehabilitation of earth have read the file of Phaedrus Bartholomew, as well as his books. I hope to meet Phaedrus, soon perhaps."

"Did he ..." Jake paused, looking for the right words.

"Yes?" prompted Bendigeid.

"Did Phaedrus crack somehow, if you know what I mean? He became a hermit. I think there is a great deal that he has never told me."

"I would not say that Phaedrus cracked," said Bendigeid. "Rather, I would say that he was ahead of his time and that he was too stubborn to adapt. In many ways, the British universities after World War II led the world. But think of Alan Turing. Little changed in the twenty years between Turing's experiences and Phaedrus' experiences. Turing cracked. But Phaedrus never did. I believe that Phaedrus did what he thought was necessary to save himself from a world that did not know how to contain him and that he did not know how to adapt to – at least with any integrity, or any support."

"So he withdrew," said Jake. "Celibacy, monkhood, isolation."

"Yes," said Bendigeid. "But Phaedrus remained productive. Henry gave Phaedrus very little peace, even though Phaedrus was in near isolation."

"Of all the things that I hold against the Christian religion," said Jake, "or the Roman religion, as Phaedrus calls it – I hate it for that more than anything. It has never allowed Phaedrus, or anyone like him, to be happy, no matter how hard they have worked to save people from themselves or how much good they have done. The list is a long one, I am sure – Phaedrus, Turing, and backward through the ages, saints and heretics. Some of their names are remembered. But I imagine that mostly they have been forgotten. So many lives – ruined and forgotten. Bendigeid, do all species have our human need for one another? You know – love, sex, animal warmth?"

"Not really," said Bendigeid. "For lack of a more universal term, it is a mammalian kind of thing. What did you call them? The squirrel people? I think that is why they have a particular affinity for earth and earthlings. Humans and the squirrel people share that mammalian need. The social systems are similar."

"Did the squirrel people ever have a period of their history in which they had to be prudes?"

"No," said Bendigeid. "I don't believe so. As far as I know they never had any experience with monotheism. They never endured as much exploitation and social stratification as earth people. Their societies are almost always matriarchies. Males are not physically stronger or larger. They express and satisfy their mammalian instincts with a wider range of physical intimacies, well beyond sexual coupling. Pheromonal cueing is much more conscious among them than it is among humans."

"Cuddling," said Jake.

"Cuddling," said Bendigeid.

"And yet, even among humans, pheromonal cueing is partly cultural, isn't it?" asked Jake.

"Why do you ask?" said Bendigeid.

"Because, among the Celts, I was much more conscious of it. I soon realized that, if you liked a person, you also liked the way that person smelled. It would be easy to recognize someone in the dark, by their smell. That felt strange at first, but I got used to it. When I thought about it and tried to understand it, the first thing I realized was that it was always sexual, always. Pheromones are sexual, after all. At first, my response had a lot of shame in it, I think. Maybe not exactly shame, but something that felt creepy. It was a feeling a little like whatever it is in us that suppresses incest. It was like being very consciously reminded that your own sister is a very sexual being, or even your mother, even though you're not going to do anything with her because something about her pheromones, though you recognize them as sexual, tells you not to. Always there was this sexual potential – with everyone, really – and increasingly it was conscious. After a while I stopped resisting it. It stopped being creepy. I started liking it. Even with the men, when I knew we weren't going to do any-thing, the potential was always there. Eventually I could almost predict who would be attracted to whom, and who was doing it with whom, because I could somehow smell their compatibility, smell their mutual attraction. I began to see that their ring system is a kind of exten-sion of a consciousness they all have. It's a visible token of what everybody already knows. And they knew all about me long before I knew they knew. They knew per-fectly well who I was or wasn't going to have sex with, long before I did. They were always right, every time."

"I'm glad," said Bendigeid, "that you were compen-sated for the deprivation of the long trip out."

"I was," said Jake. "It was honest sex, wickedly honest sex, with few of the complications. I think that sex was a large part of their happiness, you know, just as it's a large part of our misery now, in our so-called modern era. I will miss that. I wonder if sexual happiness will return on its own, if the soap companies and cosmetic compa-nies have gone out of business, and if we ever succeed in finally putting a stake through the heart of Augustinian doctrine. But I think that would be an important step – human beings actually smelling each other again and knowing what it means. I don't have any data, but I feel pretty sure that those nasty perfumes and puritanism go hand in hand. Strong perfumes must have been an important item in the missionary's toolbox."

"Perhaps you will write a paper on that subject," said Bendigeid. "Had you never given thought to it before, though? I mark you as a person with a high sexual IQ.

Your grievances were never as great as Phaedrus' grievances, and yet you, too, were sexually out of place. You, too, came to realize that the world didn't have to be that way, that you were being cheated in ways that you had not yet been able to identify."

"As long as I am over-disclosing," said Jake, "at least I did one thing that lessens my own crimes against others in some small way. I left some of my work clothing, unwashed, in my room for Phaedrus to find, for him to remember me by. You are right. I did it instinctively, though in a deniable way. I didn't really understand what I was doing, the way I understand it now. But I already knew that, when we grieve for the loss of someone, we also grieve for the loss of that person's scent. I don't know why I did that, exactly. I wasn't sure whether it would be a cruelty or a kindness. I hope it was a kindness."

"I assure you that it was kindness," said Bendigeid, "especially if Phaedrus knew that you did it consciously and intended it as a kindness, a compensation for something that you were unprepared to give him."

"Do you think he understood that?" asked Jake.

"Um, how smart is Phaedrus?" asked Bendigeid.

"Pretty smart," said Jake.

"I suspect that is your answer," said Bendigeid.

"I wish our noses were a hundred times more sensitive," said Jake, "like animals. We miss a vast world of pleasure. Though perhaps if we eliminate the violent soaps and aggressive perfumes, and if we pay attention, we can recover much. And that Miach! Every time he's near me I just want to cuddle him. I'm afraid I'll be in trouble when he's older and no longer smells like a boy. Lairgnen gave me one of his tunics. I'm not telling what Heledd gave me. One more question, Bendigeid, as long as we're on this subject. I could never quite figure out Derbhorgill."

"Derbhorgill is not really unusual," said Bendigeid. "Derbhorgill was born into the body of a woman but feels himself to be a man."

"That's what I thought," said Jake. "But why no rings, I wonder."

"Derbhorgill was a great seer," said Bendigeid. "I believe it was because Derbhorgill's lover was …

"On another plane?" said Jake.

"That's one way to say it," said Bendigeid.

"How do you know that?" asked Jake.

"I cannot yet answer that," said Bendigeid.

"Oh, no!" said Jake. "I thought we were done with protocol!"

"I'm afraid that we – you – are not done with protocol," said Bendigeid. "In fact I now have many volumes of protocol for you to read."

Jake groaned.

As the gnat approached the center of their twirling ship for docking, another ship suddenly emerged out of the jump station, its exterior lights flashing red and blue against the blackness and the stars.

"Who is that?" said Jake. "Were we expecting that?"

The gnat spoke with Sam's voice.

"We are being hailed by a transport from base," said Sam.

"Did it come from our time line?" asked Bendigeid.

"Yes," said Sam. "The transport is carrying eighty passengers on their way to earth. We are to take them on board for the remainder of their journey."

"Druids, then?" asked Bendigeid. "This is the first contingent?"

"That is correct," said Sam. "And, sir, your wife and daughters are on board."

As the gnat started sliding into its berth, Bendigeid strained against the restraining belts to look back at the newly arrived ship.

"Wow," said Jake. "The eighty-fourth generation of my grandchildren."

"And now you can get started on spoiling them," said Bendigeid.

—◆—

Jake, Miach, Alexis and Sam were on the star deck nervously waiting for the guests to arrive and for the party to begin. The ship was still twirling to produce gravity. The stars rotating around and around the windows of the star deck caused Alexis to complain of a touch of vertigo. The other ship was five miles off, also rotating, though its passengers had been transferred. And beyond that was the black disk of the jump station.

"Sam, why are we holding?" asked Jake. "Earth awaits us."

"We are waiting for orders from base, Jake," said Sam.

"Why's that?" asked Jake.

"We are waiting for a decision from base on whether

Alexis and Miach are to stay on board and go on to earth with us, or whether they will be required to return. If they are required to return, they will board the waiting ship and go back through the jump station."

"I see," said Jake.

Alexis put his hand on Miach's shoulder, but neither of them spoke.

Bendigeid entered, formally dressed in a black tunic and black leggings. His silver torc, Jake's heirloom, seemed to catch the starlight and glimmer as he crossed the room. On his arm was his wife. They were a perfect matched set. She wore a black gown, the hem of which brushed the floor. Clearly their daughters were twins. They appeared to be about sixteen years old. The daughters wore gray. The twins followed, a step behind their mother, warily watching the spinning of the stars. Bendigeid introduced them.

"At last we meet, Jake," said Grian, Bendigeid's wife. "It was so wonderful to have history come alive, in my husband's letters. When I was my daughters' age, and as the year of returning approached, I used to dream of applying for the returning, and meeting you. And now here we are. As for my daughters, they can hardly believe that their grandfather is so young and handsome."

"Mama, please," the girls said in unison, blushing.

Jake had expected the eighty passengers to resemble the council at Cenabum – mostly older Druids, somber, serious, skeptical, aloof in their gray robes. But, instead, a stream of young people were now entering the star deck. They were brightly dressed in smartly cut tunics.

They were urbane and animated, like a troupe of actors or dancers emerging from a stage door in London or New York. They cast their eyes curiously toward Jake, but they began to align themselves in an arc around the circular floor of the star deck, for the receiving line.

Bendigeid laughed at Jake's distraction.

"Not whom you were expecting?" asked Bendigeid.

"I hope that … I hope that they're not…" Jake stammered.

"You hope that they're not all your grandchildren?" said Bendigeid.

"Yes," said Jake. "Is that terrible?" Jake was blushing.

"Only two of them are your grandchildren, I believe," said Bendigeid. "No doubt those two will let you know when you meet them."

"And they are Druids?" asked Jake. "They seem so young to be Druids."

"Almost all of them are still in training," said Bendigeid. "And this is part of their training, something they have prepared for. They each are committed to three-year stays on earth, with options to renew or to stay permanently, if they wish. As you know, it is always younger people who are most eager for adventure, who have the least to bind them where they are."

"Where …" Jake lost his train of thought again as his eyes roved down the line of attractive young faces. They were laughing and talking among themselves, eyes occasionally darting toward Jake.

Then the last Druid materialized out of the darkness near the lift and walked haltingly toward the far end of the receiving line. She was tall, thin, perfectly erect, and wore a black Druid's habit. She appeared to be at least 85 years old.

"You were asking where they will be stationed?" Bendigeid supplied. "I believe their stations and duties will be determined after arrival on earth, after some touring and some discussions with Henry's team. Now, would you like to meet them?"

Grian laughed her charming laugh.

"Jake," she said, "I regret that it was not possible to give you any notice of so many new passengers. I'm sure that you were expecting a rather quiet six months of returning to earth, with only my husband's dry wit, and two friends who are in love with each other, to entertain you."

"And the cats," said Jake. "And Sam, of course. Sam has the driest wit in the universe."

Jake, followed by Miach and Alexis, walked slowly along the circle as the young Druids introduced themselves one by one. Luckily they each wore name tags. All discreetly noted the silver ring on Jake's left hand and the two brass rings on his right. None of the young Druids wore silver rings, but many wore copper. Other than the elderly Druid who stood silently at the end of the line, the oldest of them appeared to be no more than four or five years older than Jake, in their early thirties. The youngest was a young woman of perhaps sixteen, with the unusual name of Rebecca. Her hands were ringless.

"Hello, Grandfather," said Rebecca.

"Hello, Rebecca," said Jake. He gave Rebecca a hug. "It's going to take some time for me to get used to being called 'Grandfather.' Why don't you just call me Jake?"

"Jake, then," she said. "All my family send you their best wishes."

"Thank you," said Jake. "We will talk more soon. I will want to hear how you got your name."

At last Jake came to the end of the receiving line. The name tag said "Ceridwen."

"Hello, Grandfather," the old woman said.

Jake laughed with joy and surprise and reached out to embrace her. She wore six brass rings.

"I know what you are thinking," she said. "You are wondering why someone of my age would undertake such a journey. But it was an easy decision. It is, I suppose, the last adventure of my life. I never imagined that it would be my privilege to meet you, Grandfather. And yet here I am, still fit to dance a little at a ring feast. Why not have one more adventure? All those whom I loved most are dead. And someone must serve as a mascot for these young ones. Forgive me. I do not speak your English as fluently as they. I never expected to need it."

"Your English is perfect," said Jake. "I hope we will have a chance to dance soon."

Ceridwen laughed.

"We've six months on this vessel," she said, "and just look at all these young people, so full of life and joy. There will be many dances on this star deck before we get to earth, though I pray it stops spinning soon."

"I believe it will stop spinning soon," said Jake.

"I have something for you," said Ceridwen. She held out an object rolled up in linen. Jake unwrapped it. It was a book, very old, in Greek. Jake thumbed through its pages.

"Gwenlliant's memoir!" said Jake.

"Indeed it is," said Ceridwen. "There's quite a lot in it about you."

"But this is wonderful," said Jake. "So Gwenlliant went to the havens, then, with Heledd and Lairgnen."

"She did," said Ceridwen. "There's quite a lot about Heledd and Lairgnen, too. I do believe that Gwenlliant wrote it for you. She wanted you to have it someday."

Jake wiped away a tear and hugged Ceridwen again. She smelled like spring, like lilacs.

"I have something else for you," she said. Ceridwen gestured toward the lift. Sam had just arrived on the star deck pushing a library cart. As Sam and the cart got closer, Jake saw that the cart bore about sixteen heavy volumes.

"And what is this?" asked Jake.

"This," said Ceridwen, "we call Derbhorgill's Encyclopedia. In the first fourteen volumes, Derbhorgill recorded all the Druids' knowledge that was known to her. The other two volumes contain what you told her – a future history."

Jake picked up the first volume and opened it. It was a mixture of Greek and Celtic written in the Greek alphabet.

"I don't know what to say," said Jake. "This changes everything. But I am not surprised that Derbhorgill went to the havens. Everyone here has read this?"

"Of course," said Ceridwen. "It is a major part of the curriculum."

Jake glanced toward Bendigeid, but he was engaged in a conversation with some of the young Druids.

Only once before had Jake been on the star deck when the ship executed the maneuver that took it smoothly from the centrifugal gravity of stationary twirling to the gravity of acceleration. With no notice that Jake was aware of, the ship made one final twirl and then dived into the blackness toward earth. The stars stopped rotating, and the dome of the star deck was now over-hung with bright, fixed stars. A cheer went up from the Druids, young and old. Anticipating the question, Sam glided toward Jake.

"Alexis and Miach will remain on board," said Sam. "We are on our way to earth."

Alexis and Miach were standing with Bendigeid and Grian. Jake walked to their side of the star deck and gave all four of them a hug. Miach looked outrageously happy. Jake tousled his hair.

"Bendigeid," said Jake. "Will the surprises not end? You couldn't talk with me about Derbhorgill's Encyclopedia until now. Is that right?"

"I'm sorry, Jake," said Bendigeid. "I'm sure you understand."

"I understand about the protocol," said Jake. "But I'm not sure what this means."

"I know what you are thinking," said Bendigeid. "We have six months on the way home to talk about it and for you to think it through."

"Another holy book is scary enough," said Jake. "But I am very sure that I don't want to be in it."

"I can understand that," said Bendigeid. "There are many perspectives from which to see this, though, and of course you have not yet read the books."

"I'm not sure that I can live without some peace and quiet," said Jake, "without some obscurity."

"I know that," said Bendigeid.

"So does everyone else, I suppose," said Jake. "And I'll be one of the last on this side of the galaxy to read about my unobscure need for peace and quiet and obscurity."

"There is a galactic perspective, Jake," said Bendigeid. "Remember what you said to Derbhorgill."

"It's only a drama, and we all have our role," said Jake.

"*Act well your part, there all the honor lies,*" said Bendigeid.

Jake looked up at the stars. Then he sighed, smoothed his tunic, and smiled toward the long line of Druids. He'd have to postpone his thinking until later.

A line of androids filed into the room bearing trays of party food as well as wine and ale.

Suddenly all the Druids began to chant in their excellently accented English, looking toward Jake:

"Song! Song! Song!"

"What do they mean?" Jake asked Bendigeid.

"You were not aware," said Bendigeid, "that when you first arrived at King Jowan's castle, everything was monitored by drones for a few days, for security. A drone made a holographic recording of your singing that night. They all have seen that recording."

"Oh, dear," said Jake.

"I'm afraid so," said Bendigeid.

"What was the song? I had drunk a lot..."

"It was 'All the Things You Are,'" said Bendigeid. "You sang it completely *a capella*. But if you would be so kind as to indulge their request, Sam can supply the piano and strings."

Jake held out his cup to Sam for one more bit of ale before he sang. As he sang, he did not see the cats sitting behind him, listening attentively, learning a very complicated new song with modulations so tricky that even Bach would have had to work all day at composing them. But Jake, having listened to the song a million million times, knew each note perfectly. Jamie always had said that it was their song.

CHAPTER 16

Dear Phaedrus,

The video of Mark and Brigid was hilarious. It was so good to see you, and all the hay, the apples, and the sheriff's beloved beans from last fall. No doubt you are still planting now, and by the time I arrive there will be another harvest. I can't wait to meet the new mule. It's good to know that Henry is good for something. She is a beauty. Twelve new chickens! How you prosper. I am a bit jealous that so much progress has been made without me and that so many incredible meals have been had at which Mark – how tall he is! – has eaten my share.

Unless I spend the entire six months of this journey back to earth writing a memoir, I could not possibly give you an account of everything that has happened. Just be assured that I am well, that the mission was successful far beyond our expectations, and that we will have many, many things to talk about when I get home. There will be long winter nights when we can catch up on everything. And somehow I suspect that there are days-long mule trips in our future, with much travel time to be whiled away, if Henry's infernal helicopters have run out of gas and worn out their rotors, as I expect they have. In time, I will tell all, and I probably will become a boor in the telling, because it was wonderful.

I must chide you, however. You are so like an onion that resists the peeling, layer by modest layer. I have met people who have told me things that you never got around to telling me. So you must tell me. If you are to hear my stories, then I must hear yours. Fair is fair. You did tell me about the squirrel people. I actually met them, briefly.

Every day, I have thought of you and missed you. I have been to the place that you were born for, Phaedrus. I have been to a place where you would have been happy. Everything about you, and everything about them, fit so perfectly. At first I felt overwhelmed, confused, and more than a little culture shocked. But when I didn't know what to do, or didn't know what to say, I would always think, "What would Phaedrus make of this?" And then I would be off the hook. Your advice – I mean of course your advice as I imagined that you would give it – never steered me wrong. I realize that this is no accident. I realize that you have studied and thought for years, and that you have connected many dots in a historical picture that was incomplete. I can tell you that you connected the dots brilliantly. I only regret that it was me – naive, undeserving Jake – who had the experience of seeing it all come to life, and actually living there among them for a while, and not you. Now I have six months to prepare myself to return to an earth that I am sure is pretty much the same sorry way I left it. My greatest comfort is knowing that you are there, with Mark and our little farm.

There is something that I must tell you now, and not keep you waiting for. That is that you were right about the most important thing of all: They do live and love in a single moral universe. It was so natural to them that I can't grasp why it is so obscure, on our earth. The power of their single moral universe won over even Andrew, who insulted us so heartlessly that last day in Scotland.

But the sad thing, Phaedrus, is that the great virtue of the Celts also proved to be their fatal weakness. They believed that their single moral universe was large enough to contain almost anything, including new gods and new empires. That also was the terrible mistake that Divitiacus made, in trying to find a way for Rome and the Celts to live peacefully together. But Divitiacus, I can tell you (for I have met him), lived to understand his mistake and to work to amend it.

I am reminded of one of the books you lent me, a book on moral philosophy. The author raised the question of whether we are obliged to tolerate the intolerant. He concluded that we have no such obligation, when intolerance would stand in the way of equal justice for others. The Celts understood tolerance, and that was a noble thing. But too many of the Celts lacked this principle of intolerance for intolerance. And so at last I have come to understand your issues with Rome and its religion. I understand at last why those who would try to reinstate such a religion must be banished to some remote corner of the galaxy and quarantined there. It is a matter of justice. It is a matter of understanding the danger of intolerance unchecked.

How brilliant that a philosopher was able to articulate this principle, seemingly as an abstraction unrelated to the practical problems of our poor planet. But how sad, for humanity, that it is a principle that was not understood – or at least not put into a book – until you and Henry were at Oxford in the 1970s. I now realize that you almost certainly knew this author, because he too was at Oxford. How easily I can imagine you sitting in a pub with him hammering it out. You understood this problem fifty years before some of the rest of us even thought about it.

Sometimes I feel a kind of flailing trepidation and unworthiness, a kind of fecklessness and ineptness, compared with those who are so much smarter than I am. So much has come to me that I don't deserve. All this is because of you, Phaedrus. Remember that first morning? Remember when you and Joanie appeared out of the woods and saved me from that storm? That was the moment at which my life changed completely, as though the earth had suddenly moved from one galaxy to another, or from one universe to another, and my constellations were all new. I owe everything to you.

I have met some of those being sent into exile from earth. This still weighs on me. I need to discuss it with you when I see you. I felt sorry for them, Phaedrus. They were wrong about so many things, and yet, about some things, they were right. Somehow we must find a way not to repeat their mistakes.

I am pleased to hear that Mark is learning to cook, but I must beg you not to eat too much of his cooking, because I need the both of you hale and hearty and well nourished for what comes next, and for all the work that we have to do now. I count the days until I am back in my little room upstairs, under a familiar sky, eating your cooking again, and being nearer to the glow of your love, which I feel even here, 378 billion miles from home and closer every second.

Jake

—▸ ◂—

Mark, an inch taller in his sock feet, padded softly and slowly up to Jake's bedroom door. Brigid was cradled in Mark's arms, sprawled limply on her back, belly up, tail twitching mischievously.

"OK," Mark whispered to Brigid. "Go."

Brigid sang the little song that Mark had been teaching her for the past two weeks: "Good Morning to You, Good Morning to You."

Mark stifled a giggle, listening to hear what Jake's response would be.

The door flew open with its usual squeak, and Jake

was standing there with his hand on the doorknob, fully awake, dressed in a tunic.

"Dang," said Mark. "I've got to have one of those outfits. Have you got a spare one? I'll sit in your lap a couple of times if you'll give me one."

"It wouldn't fit you," said Jake. "Not anymore, anyway. You'll all shoulders and feet."

Jake reached out to scratch Brigid's head.

"Good morning to you, too, Miss Puss," said Jake.

"Those britches really flatter the crotch," said Mark. "Turn around. Let me see how your …"

Jake turned around.

"Nice," said Mark. "Perfect proportions between your hips and shoulders. If I was a little gayer, I'd definitely do you if you wore that outfit for me."

"Watch your mouth," said Jake. "You're too young for that kind of talk."

"I'm old enough to date," said Mark. "Not that I've ever had the chance. There's nobody around here but mules, guys, and more guys. And they're already taken."

"Speaking of," said Jake, "are Alexis and Miach up?"

"They were up hours ago," said Mark. "They've done half of my chores and all of yours, too. But you changed the subject."

"I did?" said Jake.

"We were talking about dating," said Mark.

"And?" said Jake.

"Rebecca," said Mark. "Have you heard if she's going to be there?"

"As a matter of fact, I had a Telegram," said Jake.

"And?" said Mark.

"You'd best be a gentleman if you want me to introduce you," said Jake.

"Really? Hot dang! A date at last!" said Mark.

"What makes you think she'd want to go out with you?" asked Jake.

"Surely you have some influence with her," said Mark.

"We'll see," said Jake. "But you've got a long walk ahead of you first. You need to burn off some of that excess energy before I let you onto the same campus with any granddaughter of mine."

"That's so weird," said Mark. "I still can't get used to that. I hope she doesn't look too much like you. Does she wear tunics? Maybe something a little fuller than yours in the chest, and a little less full – you know – there?"

Mark pointed. Jake slapped Mark's hand away, which caused Brigid to jump down with a clipped meow of protest when she hit the floor.

"Rebecca does wear tunics," said Jake. "They always wear tunics when they're training. And she's got a kick that would topple you from the shoulders like a dropped cat."

"What is it Phaedrus says? 'Harrumph.' And, speaking of Phaedrus, we all had breakfast early, but he saved you some biscuits and beans. He says it's time to load up the mules, because the day's a-wastin'.'"

"Tell him I'll be right down," said Jake.

Jake had made the bed neatly and put everything in his room in order. He picked up his packs, gave the little bedroom a last look, and went downstairs.

The kitchen was in perfect order. Everything had been put away for the winter, out of sight in pantry and cabinets. On the table was a portion of biscuits and beans, neatly wrapped in a precious piece of the remaining waxed paper. Mark was bustling out the back door now with his bags. Brigid was tagging along behind him, looking anxious.

"Where's Phaedrus?" asked Jake.

"He's in the yard," said Mark.

Out in the yard stood some of their most prized possessions – their three mules. Their two cows and all the chickens had been herded and carted off to their winter homes – a two-day job for Mark. Alexis, clearly experienced, was doing an expert job of loading up the mules. Miach was handing him objects to load from a pile of luggage and supplies that were piled on an old blanket in the grass. Phaedrus was by the well, drawing water and filling jugs. Jake went to the well. Phaedrus reflexively handed him the water dipper.

"I already put away the coffee things," said Phaedrus. "So I hope water will do you. Up late? Still sketching?"

"I was up until three," said Jake. "Couldn't sleep. There are a lot of maps to study. Thanks for saving me some grub. Any word from Henry?"

"Yes," said Phaedrus. "We have our final orders, so to speak, before we're incommunicado in the bush. No surprises, though. What do you think? Can you get us there?"

"It won't be a problem," said Jake. "The maps are fairly recent, and the trails were mostly well used. It will be a good trek, about a third stream beds and about a third ridges. When we're above the trees, what stars we will see!"

"You left out a third," said Phaedrus.

"Straight up and down," said Jake.

"Well," said Phaedrus. "At least we have the mules."

"You know what, though?" said Jake. "Mountains or not, I don't miss Henry's helicopters. Now that I think about it, I've wanted to do an Appalachian mule trek like this for a long time."

"You're young," said Phaedrus.

"Don't worry," said Jake. "Mamie is as strong as an ox. She can carry you up the slopes when you need a break."

"Then where will Brigid ride?" asked Phaedrus.

"She can tag along behind Mark," said Jake.

"And mewl with every step," said Phaedrus. "Until Mark picks her up and carries her."

"Your practice runs must have been good comedy," said Jake. "I'm sorry I missed that. Speaking of Mark, his vocabulary has doubled. I cut him off this morning just before he said the word 'derrière.'"

"He's a very smart young man," said Phaedrus. "Miach, too. As for Alexis, his Greek and Latin are better than mine. It's extraordinary that they let them come with you. I've never heard of an exception to the protocols."

"Do you have any idea why they made the exception?" asked Jake.

"I can only speculate," said Phaedrus. "But I think they had a purpose in mind."

"Yes?" prompted Jake.

"Consider," said Phaedrus. "We still have our satellites and a lot of our electronic gear. But there are bound to be failures and outages. It's going to be years – decades – before we recover some of our old competencies. It really started sinking in to me this morning, while we were packing the mules, that we're going to be in this Iron Age for a long time. Nobody knows how long. You're an important person now, Jake. You're modest, and you try to minimize it, and I understand your worries, but you are. I had no idea how important you are when you left over two years ago, but they knew all along. Look at the dangers you've faced. Your four companions were killed. And though they say they've cleaned out the conspiracy, who knows what grudges remain? So let me put it this way. It's very comforting to know that over there stands an experienced mercenary from the once magnificent Roman army, a man who would die for you."

"Phaedrus, are you still worrying?" asked Jake.

"Jake, I never stop worrying. You know that," said Phaedrus. "It's what I do. I worry. But I'm so happy to have you home. All my life, this is what I really wanted, though I scarcely could have imagined actually ever having it. This is where I belong – with this odd little troupe of once-unwanted people. I have meaningful work to do, puzzles to be solved, plots and plans to be hatched, and always plenty to worry about. I am the most contented man in the universe. I even have you – though you were never unwanted like the rest of us, and all the rules say that I don't deserve you."

"Ha!" said Jake. "Those were the old rules. I like the

new rules better. All those arguments that you had with God, all those times you threatened to kill him – maybe you finally scared him. And what's this about unwanted people? I wanted all of you the first time I saw you."

"One thing's for sure," said Phaedrus. "We're motley, but between us we've got a lot of bases covered. The sports metaphor isn't mine, by the way. That's what the sheriff said this morning. He was so grieved to see us go. He wanted to deputize Alexis on the spot. Sooner or later the sheriff is going to run out of ammunition. Whereas Alexis knows how to make his own arrows."

"We make a fine little mule train, that's for sure," said Jake. "As the sheriff says, we've got a lot of bases covered – cook, mule driver, guard, a water and wood boy, and a navigator. Funny how things work, isn't it?"

"The cook has one more chore for you, Mr. Navigator," said Phaedrus. "Since a certain water and wood boy wanted to let you sleep and did your chores for you this morning, he deserves a little payback. Here. Carry some water."

Jake reached out to bump Phaedrus' fist – a new gesture that Mark had taught Phaedrus.

They each wore copper rings.

Jake carried the water jugs to the mules. The jugs were the last items for Alexis to load.

"Are we ready?" said Phaedrus, looking toward the beloved old house.

"Here we go into our Iron Age jump station," said Jake.

They started walking. Brigid hopped on to Mamie's neck. With the morning sun on their backs and the green grass of autumn under their feet, they wound through the orchard and into the woods.

ACKNOWLEDGEMENTS

I am very grateful to the friends who read and advised me on early drafts of this novel: Elissa Schroeder, Ken Ilgunas, Michael Hylton, and Dean Smith.

FURTHER READING

The books listed here were particularly important to the author in writing the Ursa Major novels.

The Celtic World. Edited by Miranda Green. Routledge, 1995. 864 pages.

The Ancient Celts. Barry Cunliffe. Oxford University Press, 1997. 324 pages.

The Fall of Rome and the End of Civilization. Bryan Ward-Perkins. Oxford University Press. 240 pages.

From Sin to Shame: The Christian Transformation of Sexual Morality in Late Antiquity. Harvard University Press, 2013. 306 pages.

A Theory of Justice. John Rawls. Harvard University Press, 1999. 538 pages.

Cycles of Time: An Extraordinary New View of the Universe. Roger Penrose. The Bodley Head, 2010. 288 pages.

Animals in Celtic Life and Myth. Miranda Green. Routledge, 1992. 284 pages.

The Greeks and Greek Love. James Davidson. Random House, 2007. 780 pages.

Greek Homosexuality. K.J. Dover. Harvard University Press, 1989. 246 pages.

Ancient Greece From Prehistoric to Hellenistic Times. Thomas R. Martin. Yale University Press, 2013. 328 pages.

Ancient Rome From Romulus to Justinian. Thomas R. Martin. Yale University Press, 2012. 238 pages.

Basic Writings of Saint Augustine. Edited by Whitney J. Oates. Random House, 1948. 888 pages.

Racial Prejudice in Imperial Rome. A.N. Sherwin-White. Cambridge University Press, 1970. 108 pages.

The Gallic War. Julius Caesar. Harvard University Press, 2006. 630 pages.

Collapse: How Societies Choose to Fail or Succeed. Jared Diamond. Penguin, 2011. 590 pages.

Inequality: What Can Be Done? Anthony B. Atkinson. Harvard University Press, 2015. 384 pages.

The Brehon Laws. Laurence Ginnell. Forgotten Books, 2012. 250 pages.

The Theory of the Four Movements. Charles Fourier. Cambridge University Press. 2008. 328 pages.

The Road to Reality: A Complete Guide to the Laws of the Universe. Roger Penrose. Knopf, 2005. 1136 pages.

Not Gay: Sex Between Straight White Men. Jane Ward. New York University Press, 2015. 240 pages.

The Meaning of Human Existence. Edward O. Wilson. Liveright, 2014. 208 pages.

The Day Care Ritual Abuse Moral Panic. Mary de Young. McFarland, 2004. 304 pages.

The History and Practice of Ancient Astronomy. James Evans. Oxford University Press, 1998. 496 pages.

Sex and Marriage in Ancient Ireland. Patrick C. Power. Dufour, 1997. 96 pages.

The Gods of the Celts. Miranda Green. Sutton, 2004. 252 pages.

Fians, Fairies and Picts. David MacRitchie. (Historical reprint)

A History of Pagan Europe. Prudence Jones. Routledge, 1997. 288 pages.

The Oxford Handbook of Late Antiquity. Scott Fitzgerald Johnson. Oxford University Press, 2012. 1,296 pages.

Mind and Cosmos: Why the Materialist Neo-Darwinian Conception of Nature Is Almost Certainly False. Thomas Nagel. Oxford University Press, 2012. 144 pages.

Conspiracy Theory in America. Lance deHaven-Smith. University of Texas Press, 2014. 272 pages.

Why I Am Not a Christian. Bertrand Russel. Simon and Schuster, 1957. 268 pages.

The Sociology of Religion. Max Weber. Beacon Press, 1922. 304 pages.

Sacred Knowledge: Psychedelics and Religious Experience. William A. Richards. Columbia University Press, 2015.

The Táin, from the Irish Epic Táin Bó Cuailnge. Translated by Thomas Kinsella. Oxford University Press, 1969. 282 pages.

Celts: Art and Identity. Edited by Julia Farley and Fraser Hunter for the British Museum. 304 pages.